BEYOND EROS

The Love Secret: Book One

CHRIS NEO

Beyond Eros
The Love Secret, Book 1

CCNG Ltd
T/A CCNG PUBLISHINGS
Unit 3 Gateway Mews, Ringway, Bounds Green
London, N11 2UT, UK

ISBN: 978-1-7396302-0-1 (paperback)
ISBN: 978-1-7396302-1-8 (ebook)

www.ccngpublishings.com
Author: www.chris-neo.com

All correspondence to: enquiries@ccngpublishings.com

The Love Secret series is fiction based on multiple true-love stories, derived from the clinical experience of the author interweaved with a fictionalised adventure. Names, characters, places, events, locales, businesses, and incidents are either the product of the author's imagination or used in a fictitious manner.

Cover artwork by Art Nedko, www.artnedko.eu
Cover design by www.bookcoverzone.com

Dedication

To the two gorgeous girls who encouraged me to persevere and not only finish but also publish, my granddaughter, Zoe, and Lablin, and to all those pure hearts around the globe who know how to love.

Note to Reader

This is a work of fiction based on multiple true love stories encountered by the author during clinical hypno-psycho-analysis practise and others from the author's imagination.

As a love adventure, I hope this story entertains readers of all genders and ages, incorporating an abundance of love, action, humour and drama, as well as offering therapeutic benefit.

Though I adore literary writing, I do not write in high literary style, but rather with emotion-filled dialogue. Every sentence is part of the story and moves the plot forward. When I read a book, I am impatient. I do not want to read ten pages if only two sentences move the story forward. So my dear reader, be prepared for a fast-moving tale.

Are those clues of the love secret true, or a combination of reality and fiction? You must decide for yourself. Does this powerful love secret exist? Is it possible?

Only the pure of heart will discover it. It will require hard work, intelligence, and imagination, but most of all… faith… to break love's secret code. I cannot guarantee if you will be one of those making a discovery. I will respond with guidance to those who subscribe to my readers list.

I hope you enjoy the Love Secret series. I will be with you all the way!

Subscribe to the email list and discussion groups:
www.chris-neo.com/subscribe
www.facebook.com/ChrisNeo1010
Twitter: @ChrisNeo1010

BONUS!

As a special gift for you,
download your FREE copy of the novella
Assassin's Love.

Two never-fail assassins! Target and client in the same couple. The devil has drawn his double knives. There will be death! But there will also be love. Who can survive when Eros has drawn his bow and pointed his love arrows?

Claim your free copy at this website:
http://bookhip.com/GZKHQLJ

1 Beginning World

Greece, Former British Colony

The soccer ball rolled straight toward Aris's bare feet, over the fallen barbwire fence that marked the edge of the estate's property. He looked down past his faded blue t-shirt and navy shorts, past the holes where olive skin showed through, and watched his toes press down to stop its rolling.

"Get the ball, Gina," shouted a petite blonde wearing a neat pink dress.

A younger girl with dark eyes raced towards him. He couldn't look away, fixated on her smile. She bent down to retrieve the ball.

"I like your name," Aris said, "and your dimples. I'd like to kiss them."

Unimpressed, Gina cast a mean gaze up at him, then stomped her foot. "It's our ball, you peasant!"

Aris pressed his foot harder into the ball while the cluster of neighbourhood boys behind him burst into laughter.

"Move your dirty foot or I will call my father."

Two older boys, brothers from the estate, started towards him. Still enraptured, Aris reached down and ruffled Gina's short black hair. "I will marry you when we grow up!"

Gina stood to her full height and spit on Aris, the saliva landing on his chest. Then she hissed like an angry cat.

Aris burst into carefree laughter and kicked the ball back to the blonde. Gina took a step backwards, still eyeing him in distaste, then returned to the game.

The little blonde girl cooed, "The handsome boy is looking at you."

The other two boys, teenagers, now towered above Aris at the fence line in clothes that would have cost his family two months' food. The younger one stared him down. "Step away from our land."

With almond-shaped eyes half shut, Aris stepped a mere six inches back from the collapsed barbed wire.

"Move away," the elder boy said.

The cluster of children who had come with Aris stepped all the way to the road—all except for the youngest, Nikos, who stood to the right of Aris.

* ◊ *

Half smiling, Aris clenched his fists at his sides. "Not stepping on your land."

Perhaps embarrassed, the older boy glanced back at the girls while his younger sibling moved himself directly in front of Nikos and shoved hard with both hands. "Go away!"

Frightened, Nikos was forced to step back, but Aris picked up a bamboo stick from the ground and shifted in front of little Nikos.

"Do not move," he said. "This is public land." His right fist clenched hard on the bamboo, and he wrapped his left hand around it. All eyes turned his way.

The elder teen shook his head. "You are frightening the girls. Go before I hit you."

Undeterred, Aris stood his ground.

Red faced, the other boy repeated, "You are scaring the girls. Go away!"

"We threatened no one," Aris said. "You are the ones frightening the girls, bullying little Nick just to show off. Try pushing me."

From the short distance, Aris saw the blonde girl poke Gina. "Did you see that? Not only he is cute, he's brave! Not even scared of the bigger boys!"

"He's a peasant," Gina scoffed. "Doesn't even have shoes to wear."

"But he's the best looking," countered the blonde. "Probably clever as well."

Gina remained indifferent. "Then you have him. He's rude. Said he wanted to kiss my dimples and marry me."

The blonde giggled and grabbed the elbow of one of the teenaged boys, pulling them all along back to the yard to resume play.

◆

Aris turned to leave. The other neighbourhood boys went their own way, while he walked through the open fence in front of his aunt's chicken sheds and a pigeon shed that separated his house from his grandparents' yard. Seven cats circled the outdoor table where his grandfather and grandmother were having their afternoon coffee. A tray between them held thick slices of home-baked bread, olives and halloumi cheese.

His grandfather, a tall old man wearing traditional Vraka instead of trousers, a grandpa shirt collar and shrunken waistcoat, had a thick white moustache. He motioned for Aris to sit beside him.

His grandmother, a plump woman with breasts hanging to her belly, cut a slice of bread for him. "What's bothering you, Aris?"

He looked down at the cats to avoid eye contact, then spontaneously asked, "How can I make this new girl love me?"

A chicken squawked behind them, flapping its wings fruitlessly, trying to escape the advancing rooster.

"All the girls come looking for you, Aris." Grandmother placed the bread in front of him. "Why this particular one?"

"This girl is special," Aris whispered, then picked up the slice of bread. "Sweet dimples on her cheeks."

She offered Aris a slice of cheese and smiled gently. "Oh, one of the visiting girls at the corner house by the bakery. She is from a rich family."

Aris shrugged. "Yes."

Both grandparents smiled and shook their heads.

3

Aris wolfed down the cheese. "You are a woman. Tell me, how can I make this girl love me?"

Grandfather smirked and set down his coffee cup, then plucked an olive from the plate. "There is a secret, Aris, of how to make someone fall in love with you."

"What do you mean? What is it to fall in love?"

Grandfather spit out the olive pip. "Falling in love is the thing many have died for. Others went crazy. Many wars began… for the love of a woman… even though no one can explain what it is!" Two cats brushed up against Grandfather's leg. He gave them a hard shove. "Shoo!"

Aris waved a hand at his grandfather. "There you go again with your philosophies."

This time it was Grandmother who reached for her cup of coffee. "It's just how a woman and a man become close, my boy." She took a sip. "So close they always want to be together. To get married. Or at least they think so."

Grandfather ran his tongue across his thick moustache. "Until the honey runs out!"

Excited, Aris jumped to his feet. "I want to be with this girl forever! What is the secret? How can I make her fall in love with me?"

His grandparents exchanged amused sighs.

"Tell me the secret!" Aris challenged impatiently. "How do I make her love me?"

Grandfather guffawed. "Aris, many have walked the high society steps, found riches and fame, but few—very few—ever found true love and happiness!" Then his voice softened. "*True love* is what you should be looking for, not riches."

Turning her small Greek coffee cup upside down on the saucer, Grandmother sighed. "You are so handsome, my boy. You do not need any love secret. All the girls already chase you."

Aris gritted his teeth. "Tell me the love secret!"

She moaned. "Very few people know that secret. It could just be a myth."

"Why keep it a secret?" Aris now asked innocently. "Don't people want to be friends, and have love?"

"Because, my boy," Grandmother patted his head, "this secret, when in the hands of the wrong person, can start a war. You heard your grandfather… hundreds of thousands, millions have died for love, or hatred for that matter."

Aris sucked in his cheeks. "I'm talking about love, not hate."

A pair of young pigeons returned to the pigeon shed, their flapping momentarily drawing Aris's sight.

With gnarled fingers, Grandfather twisted the edges of his moustache. "Love and hate are the opposite sides of the same coin. Love and religion have both killed millions of people. And they will continue to do so in the future."

Exasperated, Aris punched the air. "I'm not a soldier. I'm not a priest. Just tell me the secret."

Granny simply shook her head. "We don't know it ourselves. All I know is that it is supposed to be passed down from generation to generation. If it even exists."

Aris pondered this, his mind spinning. "Then tell me who knows this secret."

Grandfather leaned back in his chair, licking first his thumb then his pointer finger. Aris could barely stand the wait while the man twisted the ends of his moustache. "I only ever heard of one person who is said to know the love secret."

"Who is it?" Aris hopped up. "Where?"

Grandmother shook her head emphatically, exchanging a punishing look with her husband.

"Tell me!" Aris demanded, now nudging his grandfather's shoulder.

After a few hesitant seconds the old man said, "Rosy."

Aris crinkled his brows. "Old Rosy? Her house is empty. She left."

"No," Grandfather said. "Rosy just moved houses. She's now in her permanent home."

Crazy and impatient, Aris smacked the table. "Where does she live then?" He looked from one face to the other, seeing his grandmother's wild gaze.

"Rosy lives behind the old St. Katharine's church," Grandfather said.

Aris sprang away, not hearing Grandmother call, "Stop. Don't..."

Like thunder, his feet pounded the road to the old church.

2 Rosy Guards the Secret

Skidding to a stop at the rear of St. Katherine's, the older smaller community church, Aris gasped for air. Orange orchards stood to the rear and to either side of a cemetery.

His head drooped. Aris kicked a stone with his bare feet. *"Diavole! Diavole and tris Diavole!"* He cursed the devil three more times before anger was replaced by disappointment.

"Why are you blaspheming, young Aris?"

Aris spun around. An old, lean priest stood in a grey cassock by the rear door of the church.

Without thinking, Aris scratched his genitals.

The priest shook his head. "First you call the devil, now you scratch your balls. What is wrong with you, boy?"

Indifferent, Aris replied, "Because that is what all men do when they see a priest, or something bad will happen to them! And I am a man!"

"What are you doing here?" the priest cajoled with a smile. "Why were you swearing?"

Aris's right foot scratched the soft dust. "Sorry, Father! I was looking for Rosy. Grandfather said she lived behind the church. He lied to me! Again."

"Your grandpa did not lie to you." The priest pointed deep into the cemetery. "Rosy does live here."

Suddenly re-energised, Aris turned his gaze. "Where is her house?"

"You will find Rosy's home at the top right-hand corner. The last grave."

Anger boiled as Aris squeezed his lips. "What good is that to me?" he whined. "If Rosy is in the grave, it means she's dead!"

Nodding, the old priest smiled.

This only agitated Aris further. He thrust his arms into the air and simultaneously kicked the ground. "You old people never take us serious! You make stupid jokes. You laugh at us kids!"

Aris turned towards the road. His head drooped as he began a turtle-slow walk.

"If you're looking for love," the priest soothed, "look no further than your own heart. If your heart is full of love, it will win you love from everyone. You do not need a love secret."

Aris stopped in his tracks, eyes wide, then raced back. He stared brazenly at the priest. "How did you know that I was looking for the love secret?"

The priest again smiled in silence.

Aris was triumphant. "Grandfather wasn't joking then! It is true! There is such a secret of love!" His gaze pierced the priest, reading the truth.

A horse trotted past, momentarily drawing the cleric's gaze.

"Answer me!" Aris prodded. "Do not lie!"

Cornered but hesitant, the old priest sighed. "As you can see, Aris, the secret—if there is such a thing—is well guarded by Rosy."

"We'll see about that! I will find the love secret!"

"Watch out, child. A woman's love, as well as love for a woman, can be very sweet, but it can also be dangerous… and usually painful! One may love, but the other may not love back equally. Maybe not at all. Watch out who you want to love!"

"One minute you preach to us to love, now you tell me love is painful and dangerous." Aris raised his voice. "Grandmother said love has killed thousands and millions. Sometimes you old people are full of sh… *sugar.*"

The old priest caressed Aris's hair. "It seems we have upset you today."

Aris fumed.

The priest pulled his hand back tentatively. "Now that you put it like that, you may be right, Aris. Sometimes we do not make sense, but love is complicated! It is not always black and white. You have a fast, clever mind. Be patient. It will all make sense when you grow up."

A line of determination drew across Aris's face. "Now I know there is a love secret. I will find it! Rosy cannot be the only one!"

"You will need to be very clever. Many died searching for it. Many killed, and were killed, without ever finding the thousand-years-old love secret."

Aris cocked his head. "Who was Rosy closest to?"

The priest thought for only a second. "Her granddaughter."

"Then it is obvious, Rosy would have revealed the secret to her granddaughter. I will find this girl, and she will tell me."

The old priest combed a hand through his beard. "That indeed is a clever thought."

The boy smiled triumphantly.

"But you may have a little problem… You see, Rosy's granddaughter lives abroad, thousands of miles away."

"I knew her! The skinny legs girl. She's older than me." Aris was more determined than ever. "I will find her!"

The priest only laughed.

"Rosy told me she came from the village in northern Greece. I will go there."

"Which village, Aris?"

"Just the village."

"There are thousands of villages in Greece, child! Are you going to visit them all?"

The two stared at each other.

Unexpectedly, Aris shook his head. "I am not telling you. Love secrets are not for priests!"

Then the boy waved goodbye and scurried home.

When Aris was out of view, the priest laughed to himself. "Little soul, he absorbs everything he hears. That's why he is such a fast learner. But which Greek village? Does he even know?"

Aris rounded the bend towards home with his hands in his trouser pockets. His grandparents were still sitting at the outside table.

"Did you find Rosy?" Grandfather laughed sarcastically.

Aris paused then declared, "Yes, I did!"

Grandmother snickered. "What is the secret then?"

Still bitter, he smiled enigmatically. "I promised Rosy not to tell anyone! Remember, it is a very dangerous secret! Especially for old people."

"You must respect, you must love… but you must also have good manners!" Grandmother cautioned him.

Then Aris turned slowly and continued to his own front door.

"Are you going to get your girl then?" Grandfather called.

Without stopping, Aris stretched out his right arm, thumb up. "I always get the girl!"

Grandfather raised his voice still further. "Now that you have the secret, how many girls are you going to love?"

The door of Aris's family's house stood open. "I love the whole world! I just love the girls more! I will love all the girls."

The old man chuckled. "Why do you love the girls more, Aris?"

"Stop it!" Grandmother poked her husband's shoulder.

With conviction Aris said, "Because girls make better friends. Boys are dead weights. If there is danger, boys run away while girls stand up, fight and support you—like I fight and support my friends!"

His grandparents sat stunned.

"Girls are also beautiful!" Aris added. "And all boys are ugly and dirty, except me and my father!" Then he walked inside, leaving the grandparents shaking their heads.

"He may be right," Grandmother said. "That's why he is always surrounded by girls!"

"Aris lives in his own world. He's smart, a fast learner. He's fearless. He dares when elder boys do not. He drives for solutions, always willing. He is a doer who gets things done." Picking up his water glass, Grandfather rinsed his mouth.

"Handsome, too," Grandmother added.

"Yes, but Aris is an idealist—a dreamer! Which girl is going to match him? If he does not change, one day he will be badly hurt… over love and women."

"He's only a boy," Grandmother consoled. "He will soon realise, like everyone else, that love is not as simple as it sounds!"

Grandfather set the glass back down. "I'm not so sure."

3 Love and Family Above All

Thursday was a religious holiday. After the church liturgy ended, a two-wheeled horse-drawn wagon headed out of town. Aris saw his father Theo's strong arms clasp the reins, veins bulging, his wavy hair tousled in the breeze. The buttons of the man's short-sleeved khaki shirt were open and revealed powerful muscles above a sunburned face.

Hiding out of sight and dodging amid the houses, Aris, the third child, trailed the wagon until he could covertly jump on the back. He clawed his way forwards, until he sat just behind his father. A smile escaped Aris's face, for the achievement of not being noticed.

But when Theo raised his bottom to one side and shot a loud fart, Aris jumped up and punched his father's back. "Not again!"

"What are you doing here?" Theo chuckled. "Why are you not at school?"

"It is a saint's day. No school today."

"You should be playing with other children."

Aris climbed up onto the bench beside his father. "You always say, 'Love and family above all.' I'm here to help my family, to help my father earn money for my family." Levelling his rear on the wood's edge, Aris added, "Besides, friends are dead weight. They bore me. Girls are better, but they're not allowed to go out far. Their parents chase me away." He then asked, "What job are we doing today, Father?"

"We will take clay from the fields outside town behind the lake and bring it to the pottery maker."

Aris sat silently for a few minutes, pondering. "Father, do you know the love secret? How to make a girl love you?"

"There's no such thing," Theo answered. "It is old people's talk."

"I know there is such a love secret. Grandfather told me about it, and the old priest at St. Katherine's church knew why I was looking for Rosy. He's God's man; he could not lie to me!"

"You have much to learn, my boy." Theo merely smiled.

With conviction, Aris continued. "Grandmother claimed that love is always pain and troubles. I don't understand her."

"She is a wise woman," Theo told his son. "You should listen to her!"

Aris raised his eyebrows. "You don't fool me. Grandfather and the priest told me it's true. Grandmother didn't deny it. Old Rosy knew the secret… but she's dead!"

At an intersection, Theo rose to his feet, holding the horse until it was clear to cross over. "Your grandfather claims to know many things. But your grandmother is the one who knows better. You're too young to understand."

"That's what you all say," Aris scoffed. "Too young for this, too young for that. You don't understand young men! We have brains and feelings, you know!"

⸺ ❖ ⸺

Later that afternoon, Theo and Aris returned on the empty wagon. Scattered clouds glided across the sky, shading the setting sun. Theo turned their horse onto the main road. Houses stood to the left and right, but the town was deserted.

Aris listened as his father gestured and muttered to himself. "No people, no bicycles, no cars. Even the windows are closed and shuttered."

Mini dust tornados formed from the strong wind, breaking the tranquil atmosphere. A few cats and stray dogs were the only other living souls visible.

In the distance, Aris could hear the roaring of army lorries. Mesmerised by the unusual sights and sounds, Aris stood in the wagon looking back and forth between the sky and the deserted asphalt road.

His father kept driving the wagon, bent forward, deep in his ramblings. As if suddenly awakened from trance, he pulled the reins, bringing the horse to a halt.

Aris stared up at him and watched as his father scanned the surroundings, then stretched out an arm with bent middle finger. The sky was an unusual grey.

Nervously, Theo ground his teeth. "No sun. What time is it?"

Bang, bang, bang!

Aris startled at the sound of a metal bucket being thrown around by a mini tornado. It thudded against the concrete wall of the house to their left. Then the wind faded, only to be replaced by a strong gust that lifted the dust into a cloud.

Bang, bang, bang!

A wooden shutter on the house to the right slammed back and forth until a lady's arm reached out and secured it from the inside.

Dead silence returned. Aris stared hard at his father's grinding jaws. The screaming cry of a large ginger cat from a rooftop sent shivers up Aris's spine.

Understanding dawned on Aris. He yanked his father's shirt. "Papa! It's a curfew! The English soldiers will take us to prison. They'll beat us up if they catch us out! They may even shoot us. Quick, hide behind the houses. We can unmount the horse and secretly walk home, house by house."

Jaw still clenched, Theo picked up the long horsewhip from his side and flicked it over the horse's head. "Hold tight on the rails."

The old horse began to trot. Theo's repeated urging and air whipping sent the animal into a fast canter across the long-stretched asphalt ahead. At the crossroad, Theo reined in the horse for a quick right turn.

Aris looked to the left then shouted, "Papa! Soldiers!" A parked khaki green lorry was full of army soldiers at the junction before the small plaza.

The horse knew the way and turned into the front yard of the fourth house to the right. It stopped just metres before the closed front door of the upside-down L-shaped house. Through the glass panels, Aris saw silhouettes of his mother and siblings.

His father leaped off the wagon to undo the long reins and chains to untether the horse. "Go inside!" he commanded.

4 Defending The Family

Aris jumped down and stood by the front door, but turned to watch his father. The door opened behind him and his mother, holding a baby, stepped out. His elder brother and sister also came to see what was causing all the fuss.

"I said, go inside!" Theo roared as an army Jeep screeched to a halt in front of them, sending a fearful, agonising quake through Aris's chest.

The driver had three stripes on his shirt, and sat beside a two-star English army officer. Four strong Epikouriki—something between civilian and military police, all selected from the Turkish Cypriot Muslim minority community of the island—jumped off the open back. The sergeant was a hulking man and moved to the front of his team.

Red-faced, Aris's shaking arm pointed. "Papa! Police!"

Like a pack of raging wolves, the four Epikouriki, sprinted towards Theo with batons raised. Aris backed up against his mother and could feel her body tremble. Brother and sister began to cry, sending the baby into a frightened wail.

Theo continued to undo the horse chains, his teeth still grinding, paying no attention to the attacking policemen. "Take the children inside and shut the door."

Mother just managed to grab Aris's rear trouser strap, pulling him with her. "C-c-come inside, Aris."

Aris resisted. Eyes wide, fury filled his face. His breath came fast. He could feel his nostrils enlarging with every puff of breath.

His older brother grabbed with one hand on Aris and the other on their mother, pulling them into the door frame while their sister hurried inside.

Aris stood his ground and willed his father to action.

The four Epikouriki policemen reached the wagon. Full of rage, they hit Theo with their batons. Soon blood flowed down Theo's forehead. Undeterred, immune to the pain, Theo carried on with the horse's chains. "One minute. Let me free the horse!"

Two of the police tried to pull Theo away, but without success. Aris's father stretched his strong legs to grip the ground, his hands remaining on the wagon chains.

Frustrated, the police clapped Theo's head and body repeatedly. Aris shrank back, squinting when he saw his father's eyelids tighten against the pain.

The two-star officer merely looked on, his gaze fixed on Theo. When the four police together were unable to draw Theo away from the horse, he stepped out of the Jeep.

The struggle had drawn the attention of other nearby soldiers, and a small group strolled within view, led by a young one-star officer.

Watching helpless from the doorstep, the children's cries split the early sunset.

"Aris, come inside!" his mother wailed and yanked at his trouser strap again.

Now fuming like a raging bull, Aris wrenched with his whole body to get away. In a snap, the trouser strap broke and with the sudden resistance gone, he crashed forward, smacking his nose against the concrete.

Meanwhile the sergeant ran his baton around Theo's throat, then pulled from behind in a choking grip. "Clap his thighs," the sergeant ordered one of the other policemen.

Theo's strong arms grabbed for the baton at his throat, forcing it away so he could catch a breath. "I was out in the fields. Did not hear the sirens," he choked out. "Let me free the horse, then take me!"

Simultaneous baton hits from two of the other three policemen struck Theo's thighs and back. The force knocked Theo to his knees.

The sergeant kneeled behind him and yanked hard on the baton at Theo's throat, his own white face now turning red.

Aris could no longer stand the sight. He averted his eyes, only to see his mother's tear-stained face. Tuning out his siblings' cries, he spun his head the other way where he saw neighbours peeking out from slightly opened doors and windows.

Rising back to his feet, Aris wiped the blood from his nose and screamed, *"Bastardi!"* then thrust himself forward like a wild animal, repeatedly punching the sergeant's belly. "Let my father go!"

But his punches had no effect, so he fumbled around behind the man and jumped on the sergeant's back, mimicking the stranglehold still held on his father. Aris wrapped his hands tightly around the other's neck and rocked back and forth.

In desperation, now raging like a dog, Aris bit the sergeant's right ear so hard a wedge came off between his teeth. Aris's mouth filled with blood.

The sergeant railed against his tiny attacker. Releasing his baton strangle on Theo, he climbed to his feet with Aris still on his back. With one hand he touched what remained of his ear and brought the hand into view to stare at his own blood. Then in a rage he shook Aris to the ground.

Aris made a show of his bloodied teeth, then spat more of the sergeant's blood in the dirt.

The sergeant whipped his baton at Aris, who threw himself backwards, narrowly escaping the blow.

Frustrated and wild, the man made a grab for Aris. Simultaneously, the other three Epikouriki seized Theo as he rose to his feet.

In a series of sharp lunges, Aris ran to the opposite side of the horse. The sergeant continued to lash out with his baton, so Aris crossed under the horse's belly, coming to stand beside his father who was now being handcuffed.

One of the other policemen made a grab for Aris, so he squatted to avoid the man's hand and beat a fast retreat back under the horse's belly.

But the sergeant's baton was waiting. He landed a direct hit on Aris's buttocks.

Blocked on two sides by police, Aris rubbed his blistering behind, then bolted between the horse's front legs, scrambling to get out of reach.

He heard the whoosh of air as another soldier's baton went flying past his head, only just missing. *"Bastardi! Bastardi!"* he screamed.

Swerving around the house, Aris jumped onto the wooden ladder which stood on the left side of the house. Climbing as fast as his legs would carry him, he ascended the ladder.

When he had nearly reached the top, Aris felt the ladder move under him, pulling away from the house. He glanced down to see the sergeant yanking the contraption, hoping to shake Aris off.

Aris climbed faster. In a nervous, fearful laugh he repeated, *"Bastardi, bastardi!"*

The two-star army officer and his driver looked on as if in amusement.

When his feet were horizontal with the top of the clay roof, Aris jumped, leaving the sergeant even more frustrated holding an empty ladder. Chuckles rose from the two-star English officer and his driver below.

Aris paused long enough to see two of the other three policemen march his father to the back of the open Jeep before showing his middle finger to the sergeant now climbing after him. Turning his rear, Aris shook his backside and hooted nervously.

Uncontrolled laughter rose from the officers and soldiers witnessing this David and Goliath spectacle.

Undeterred, the sergeant continued his climb while Aris's mother and siblings choked back panicked tears.

Aris stood tall, his legs stretched and arms crossed, head held high and proud. *"Molon lave!"* he shouted, the ancient Greek equivalent of "come and get me" uttered by King Leonidas to the Persians at the battle of Thermopylae.

Humiliated, with his ear still bleeding, the sergeant was slowed by carrying the baton in his right hand as he grasped for the next rung.

Momentarily swimming in a loss for what to do, Aris scanned escape possibilities. He would be cornered on the rooftop. Then he spied something greenish grey and grasped it with both hands.

Reappearing over the edge of the ladder, three feet above the sergeant, Aris raised the rock high above his head. "You are the devil. I am the anti-devil!"

"*Eiiii!*" the sergeant screamed.

"No, Aris! No!" Aris's mother yelled.

The boy took in the gaze of the two-star officer, his smile frozen in place. With a deep breath and his teeth showing like an angry wolf, Aris lobbed the rock like a missile aimed for its target.

Before the sergeant could even close his mouth, the rock crashed into his head, exploding into dust, its clay coating the man's face and clothes.

Realising the blow would not be fatal, the officers, soldiers and other Epikouriki below exhibited relief. But Aris was most pleased to see a proud, silent smile on his father's face as family and neighbours looked on.

Now more frustrated and determined, the raging sergeant resumed his ascent.

Surprised by the relentless chase, Aris scanned the rooftop again. In fearful urgency he rolled up the left leg of his short trousers, holding the material in his right hand while quickly pulling out his penis with the other.

He paused only long enough for the sergeant's mouth to pop open in surprise, then Aris took aim and began to urinate.

A roar of laughter came from below as Aris's urine mixed with the clay dust, becoming a wet grey mud that coated even the blood pouring from the sergeant's ear.

Now frantic, the sergeant sped his climb.

Out of options, Aris tried to push the ladder straight back away from the roofline, but the weight of the sergeant was too heavy. In near panic, he took a step sideways when the man stretched out an arm to grab for him. And then the idea came to him. In a fox move, he knelt to the right of the ladder and pushed it sideways, towards the street.

The ladder barely budged, but with his face now red, Aris gave a desperate push accompanied by a hard cry. "*Aaaah!*"

The ladder slid a fraction. The sergeant raised his baton arm, preparing to swing. In that moment, Aris's face stiffened. With a final deep breath that pumped up his chest, he exhaled and pushed with all his might.

The baton slammed into the pinkie toe of Aris's foot. A cry of excruciating pain, "*Ow!*" was followed by an even harder push against the now precarious ladder.

Relentless, Aris leaned his body weight forward, agonising fright on his face. His bare feet dug into the edge of the clay rooftop and after a second heave he narrowly pulled his left foot back in time to avoid another swat of the sergeant's baton.

Gaining irreversible momentum, the ladder shifted to an angle. A third baton hit landed on Aris's foot, sending the boy into a painful frenzy.

Spectating officers, soldiers and neighbours seemed to be enjoying the entertainment, but Aris was now desperate. He stepped back to bullrush the sliding ladder from the side, letting out a triumphant, "*Ahhhhhhh!*"

"Stop, Aris!" shouted his father from the back of the Jeep.

Aris pulled the worst of the weight from his lunge, and quickly sought out Theo's gaze. That silent smile had turned serious. But the damage was already done. Unable to hold against the slide of the ladder, Aris could do nothing but free his hands.

The ladder was on its way down, carrying the sergeant with it.

Still perched on the corner of the roof, Aris watched slack-jawed at the helpless man's plight.

The officer's and soldiers' expressions morphed as they took in the sideways trajectory—a steaming pile, four feet deep. Theo's face filled with regret and anxiety.

It was as if time slowed. The ladder's descent toward the manure pile stretched out like the last day of school before vacation. Then it happened. The sergeant splattered into the dung heap, covered head to toe.

When the man reached a hand to clear the manure from his face and eyes, onlookers breathed a sigh of relief, then fell into instantaneous laughter at the spectacle before them, like watching a dirty ghost climbing to his feet.

Triumphant, Aris began a hula-hoop style belly dance on the rooftop. Only his clumsy breath gave hint to the fear he held inside.

One of the Epikouriki fetched a nearby water hose and showered the sergeant, rinsing clay muck and blood along with the offending manure.

Aris noticed the English officer turn away from the others in an effort to hide his laughter.

A few moments later, with the manure cleaned from face and body, the sergeant's rage returned. He reached deftly to his holster and removed his weapon. Raising his right arm, he pointed the pistol at Aris, still triumphantly dancing on the rooftop.

"Hey, Sergeant!" shouted Theo from the back of the Jeep, hoping for a distraction. The move invited a hard baton hit on his thigh from the policeman seated beside him, forcing Theo back to the bench seat.

Alerted by the noise, the English officer returned his gaze to the action. Instantly composing himself, he called sharp and loud, "Sergeant! Put your gun down!"

Finally catching sight of what was taking place below, Aris stopped mid-dance. Realising the danger, he glanced towards his mother and siblings watching, then his father and the neighbours. On instinct, he fell flat against the rooftop.

The sergeant, gun still pointing at Aris, turned to face the officer who now approached stiffly.

Lifting his head, Aris watched as the red-faced Englishman pulled out his own handgun and pointed it at the sergeant's head. "I said, put your gun down. He is only defending his father. If you shoot an unarmed child, the local guerrilla fighters, in revenge, will no longer attack only soldiers."

The sergeant held steady, weapon unwavering.

After a short pause the officer continued, "They will start killing English children in revenge. You will spark a massacre."

The beleaguered sergeant stared numbly at the officer.

"If you shoot, you will make the boy a martyr, a hero for the guerrilla fighters. Lower your weapon."

Sensing the man's hesitance, Aris rose to his feet even as the sergeant's pistol arm began to lower. He stretched his arms wide and yelled, "*Bastardi*, shoot me if you can! I will become a hero!"

Reluctantly, the sergeant returned his gun to its holster.

The officer followed suit and called to four of the soldiers, "Get in the car!" They piled into the back of the vehicle around Theo and the driver sped away.

Sensing his victory, Aris jumped down from the roof, onto an empty upside-down oil barrel, then to higher ground, level with the horse manure. He reached for the long bamboo stick with a vee at the top which lifted the washing line. Now racing with the stick in hand, Aris chased behind the Jeep and managed to land a hit on the sergeant's head before the car gained distance.

Above the engine's whine, Aris could hear his father shout, "Go back! Look after the family. Remember, *family and love above all!*"

Reluctantly Aris slowed to a walk, before stopping altogether. "Okay, Papa. Family and love above all!"

5 To Hate or Not to Hate

The young officer and a few of his soldiers remained near the house. Aris started wrestling to untether the horse from the wagon, but moved quickly to shield his mother and siblings when he saw them approach.

"Follow me," the officer commanded the four soldiers with him.

Aris's mother clutched him tighter.

Approaching with a smile, the officer attempted to soothe her. "It's okay, Mama. We will free the horse from the wagon." He turned to two of the soldiers. "Unchain the horse, then lead it to its feed."

Unable to understand English, Aris's mother just stared at the officer while Aris fixed his gaze on the man suspiciously.

The officer made hand gestures and mimicked chewing. "Do you have food, bread?" His words were soft.

Frightened, the mother replied in Greek, "I only have bread, and olives."

Aris jumped in front of his mother, shielding her. With a skinny arm he pointed at the soldiers and declared in English, "Go! Go away! Bread mine!"

A neighbour from the window across the street shouted other English words for the officer who paused a few seconds then called out to the other two soldiers by the wagon, "You two, go bring a tin of food, some bread, marmalade and biscuits!"

One of the first soldiers led the family horse to its trough. The others returned quickly with provisions and handed them to the officer, who in turn offered them to Aris's mother.

Puzzled, Aris pulled his hands back even while his mother gratefully accepted the biscuits and marmalade with a smile.

Seemingly happy now, the young officer and the soldiers retreated.

Puzzled, Aris watched them until they were out of sight. "I don't like the English soldiers, Mama. They hit us with their batons. Those Scottish red berets are the worst, but these ones seem to be better. I am confused. They helped us with the horse. The leader did not beat us, and gave us food. I hate them... yet I do not hate them." After a moment he added, "But I do hate the Turkish military policemen."

Aris's mother smoothed his hair. "Do you hate the Turkish horseshoe man? Do you hate his granddaughter?"

Aris did not hesitate. "I love my friend and her grandfather, the old Turkish horseshoe man. He's a good man. They love me, too."

"You see. You don't hate anyone."

Even more confused, Aris stared up into her eyes. "I don't really hate the Turkish Epikouriki, but they beat up my father. I want to kill them. What's wrong with me?"

"Nothing is wrong with you, my son. You are just upset now. The police were doing their job. You are blessed. It is good you cannot hate. *That's why you have no fear in you.* Those who hate, only bring pain to themselves. Your heart will always be happy. You will always have a smile in your heart, and on your face!"

"Who can I hate then?"

"No one! It is a sin to hate. Hate brings pain, but love brings happiness!"

"That's not what Grandmother said!" Aris blurted.

----- ❖ -----

All night long, Aris waited for his father, pacing by the front door. The morning sun found the child asleep on the front doorstep.

His mother reached down and caressed his head. "Aris... Aris, wake up. Get ready to go to school."

In his classroom, Aris sat in the middle chair at the last desk on the right with two classmates, head down on his crossed arms.

The pudgy teacher made his way along the first corridor of desks, then silently approached Aris from behind. "Aris! What is the name of the Cyprus Archbishop who was killed by the Turks?"

Aris lazily lifted his head and mumbled, "Kyprianou."

The teacher's lips tightened. He resumed his stroll among the desks while Aris's head fell back on his folded arms. Halfway up the corridor, the man stopped abruptly. "Aris, what is the sum of eleven times eighty-nine?"

Head still down, Aris replied, "Nine hundred and seventy-nine."

The teacher's movements belied his age. Failing to catch Aris unprepared, he wrenched Aris's right ear, causing the child's head to lift. A second harder pull forced Aris to his feet, head bent to ease the pain.

"Look at you, sleeping in class. Long hair, patched clothes, rotten shoes..."

Aris noticed his classmates, some watching tensely, others snickering. "Fancy clothes and expensive shoes do not give you brains, sir. Jesus had patchy clothes and no shoes."

The teacher gave another twist to Aris's ear, causing the boy to squeak and lift onto his toes. Through gritted teeth he seethed, "You think you know all the answers?"

Aris ducked away. "I know the answers because you are a good teacher, sir! You taught us the quick formula for the number eleven last week."

Bested, the teacher gave Aris a shove back to his desk. "Keep your head up. No one sleeps in my class."

⋯ ❖ ⋯

Sunday morning at dawn, three days after his arrest, Theo returned home in his torn and bloodied shirt. Aris and the rest of the family gathered around him and danced with joy.

"Prepare me a sweet coffee," Theo asked his wife.

Mother hesitated. "We do not have sugar. We ran out of money for shopping, and Manousios, the grocer, stopped the credit."

Exchanging a stiff glance with her, Theo moved to change into a clean shirt. "I will go see the grocer!"

Aris followed fast, glued to his father's side, until they reached the small and only local grocery.

Without discussion, Theo called, "Half a kilo of sugar!"

Manousios, a fat man of medium height, filled a brown paper bag and offered it to Theo.

"I was held by the police for three days, no work," Theo explained. "Write it down on the account!"

Wild anger flared in Manousios's eyes. He yanked back the bag from Theo's hands.

Instinctively, Theo squeezed. Manousios jerked harder, and the force ripped the bag, spilling sugar all over the floor.

Aris stared at his father and the ruthless grocer.

Manousios kept on ripping the bag and shouting, "Told your wife already... no more credit!"

Tight lipped, Theo dropped the rest of the bag, then wiped the sugar off his hands. Without a further word, he turned and walked out of the grocery. Aris paused by the door to shoot a stunned look at Manousios, then trailed after his father.

Returning home, Theo took a deep breath. "Forget the coffee. I will go to work."

"It is Sunday," his wife reminded. "No one works on Sundays."

"Have to. I will be the only wagon. Maybe I will find a fare, or something."

"I need money, at least for sugar and beans."

"I did not work for three days. The pottery man did not pay me. I gave you all I had!"

Aris could hear the bitter disappointment in his father's voice from where he stood between them, watching like a tennis game, left then right.

His mother's eyes brimmed with tears. "We have no money for beans. We only have bread and olives. I can't kill the breeding rabbits, nor the h-hens!" Her voice cracked at this last bit.

In a mixture of sympathy and anger Aris shouted, "Mother is right!"

Theo turned out his empty pockets, shouting back, "I do not have a single *grosi*. That's why I am going to work on a Sunday. Hoping I can earn a few shillings."

Aris turned his pleading gaze to his mother. "Father is right, too!"

The floodgates burst with tears as emotions flared, both sides arguing their case like two barking dogs.

Instinctively, Aris jumped to slap one parent's face then the other. "Stop fighting! I will bring you meat for the family!"

"Don't you dare steal," Mother scolded. "We are not thieves!" Then she went silent, head drooping.

"Did you hear what Mother said?" Father stared hard into Aris's eyes. "We are not thieves!"

Aris clenched his jaw, full of confidence. He stepped over to the bed and grabbed the strap of his khaki cloth schoolbag. Notebooks fell to the mattress as he emptied it then threaded the strap across his shoulders.

"Remember the church." Aris's eyes beamed as he made his way to the door. "God provides for the wild birds. Will he not provide for us, his children?"

6 Meat for the Family

"Where are you running to, Aris?" called Nikos, the kid he'd rescued at the rich boys' ballgame.

Aris slowed to look back. "Going to get meat for my family."

"We're coming with you," said a girl next to Nikos.

Shrugging his shoulders, Aris waved his right arm to have them join, and kept the slower pace.

Along their way, they passed Father Dimitris, a beloved old priest, tall with long white hair. Children playing in the street paused their game to kiss his right hand.

Aris and his friends stopped in front of Father Dimitris. When the other children stepped away, the priest offered his hand to Aris.

The boy hesitated.

Sweetly, Father Dimitris asked, "Don't you love me anymore?"

Aris was caught in a moment of indecision. "I do. But your hand is dirty with saliva now."

The priest chuckled, then spit on the upper part of his right hand, wiped it on his long grey robe, then extended it towards Aris again.

Moving sharply, Aris lifted the priest's left hand and gave it a quick peck before heading off again.

"Always finding a solution, young Aris," Father Dimitris chortled. "Clever and good hearted. You will succeed for sure!"

A couple hundred metres beyond the outskirts of town, they reached a non-paved stretch of road. "Stop!" Nikos tugged on Aris's arm. "Snake!" He pointed ahead, his hand now trembling.

Some two metres beyond, an enormous black snake was crossing the soft dirt road.

"Don't be scared," Aris soothed. "The snake is going to find food, just like we are. But it can't eat us. We're too big for that."

Nikos tore out of there so fast his heels hit his buttocks, while Aris and the girl continued their slow walk, allowing the snake to cross out of the way.

"But I'm scared to go back on my own!" Nikos's voice wavered behind them.

Aris signalled the boy to join them. "The snake's gone. Come on, or go home by yourself."

Nikos had to sprint to catch up. After a mile and a half they reached a small patch of densely planted slim pine trees.

Aris handed his bag to the other boy. "I'll climb to the nests at the top and throw down the baby sparrows. You bite their necks and put them in the bag. Don't miss any!"

"How is he going to climb to the top?" Nikos asked the girl as they watched Aris scramble with hands and feet just to get to the lowest branch.

"Aris climbs trees faster than he walks," the girl admired.

At the first nest, just a metre from the top, Aris wrapped one arm around the trunk and stretched out with the other. The tiny bird in his hand had just a few feathers. Gently kissing it on the top of its nude head, Aris whispered, "Sorry, baby sparrow! I do love you. But my family needs meat. Your mother will make you again! Soon you will come back, and you will grow long feathers and learn to fly." Aris looked down to his friends below and called, "Here's the first one," before lobbing the baby sparrow.

Afraid to catch the bird, Nikos hesitated.

"Kill it quickly, so it doesn't suffer!" Aris shouted.

Nikos and the girl each took a step backwards, still not daring to touch the tiny bird.

In a huff, Aris shimmied down the tree trunk. He picked up the baby sparrow, popped its head in his mouth, and bit down hard, cracking its neck. He dropped the body in the bag, turning to Nikos and the girl. "You're cruel! You let the baby sparrow suffer. Next time, kill it quick so it doesn't suffer!"

The boy and the girl stood speechless, staring at Aris.

— ◇ —

From the top of the next tree, Aris spied two nests. Reaching into the first, he came up empty handed, but the next netted two baby sparrows. He bit down on the neck of each and pushed them into the bag he'd finally decided to loop over his own head and arm while Nikos and the girl watched in disgust from the ground.

Aris fixed his sight on the top of the next tree to his right. Clutching the centre trunk, he swung back and forth, gaining momentum each time.

Horrified Nikos yelled, "You're going to fall!"

"He is not." The girl smiled proudly. "You'll see."

At the end of the third swing, Aris made the leap, catching the top of the other pine tree with both hands and scrabbling to find support for his feet.

"You're crazy!" Nikos jumped in admiration.

"I told you," the girl hooted.

Picking more baby sparrows from the nests, Aris continued his routine, bagging them and swinging to the next treetop until his bag was three-quarters full. At the next nest, Aris stopped with his arm muscles tensed, his face filled with horrifying fright.

— ◇ —

Aris's eyes grew wide. He could tell it was no baby sparrow he'd snared this time. He knew what to do, but that didn't make it any less terrifying. Slowly he pulled that tensed right hand out of the sparrow nest. His veins were bulging from the pressure. A bit at a time, a large snake head appeared in his grasp. The snake's mouth was open, staring at Aris.

"*Aaah!*" The scream ripped from Aris's throat. He could feel a trail of warmth running down his left leg. Instantly his face soaked with sweat, beads running from his forehead into his eyes, blurring his vision.

Frozen in a catatonic state, Aris just stared into the eyes of the snake, his right hand turning hard as a rock and draining of colour.

"Wahoo! Aris is holding a snake!" Nikos admired.

"Good meat!" the girl shouted, unsuspecting of her hero's terror.

Instinctively, Aris flung the snake in the opposite direction and simultaneously somersaulted backwards in a free fall.

"No!" Nikos screamed.

Horrified, the girl watched as Aris tumbled and bumped from branch to branch. "Aris!"

Suddenly their frightful yelling stopped. They watched as Aris clung to a middle branch, securing himself, now bathed in sweat with a huge stain on the front of his pants.

Aris shook his head to clear his vision, one hand rubbing his eyes. He looked up just in time to see the snake, in a slow downward slide, headed straight for him. In leaps of fright, he jumped down from branch to branch. Nikos and the girl let out their own agonising screams.

Finally Aris stood on the second branch from the bottom and paused. With another quick glimpse upwards, he witnessed the snake slithering down the tree trunk towards him.

Bypassing the bottom branch, Aris jumped and rolled before rising fast on his feet.

"Did you slip?" the girl asked.

Aris glared up into the tree, but didn't pause. "Run! A big snake is chasing me."

This time all their heels hit their buttocks, running for a good mile before slowing to a walk.

Still catching his breath, Nikos gasped, "I thought you weren't afraid of snakes, Aris."

Aris glanced over his shoulder to make sure that snake wasn't still after him. "Now I am!"

7 MEAT ON THE TABLE

Aris emptied his bag on the kitchen table in front of his mother—a good three dozen dead baby sparrows. "Here's your meat. You can cook it with eggs from our hens."

Mother looked in amazement at his offering. "Oh, now you're going to tell me how to cook!"

Like a master of the house, Aris commanded, "Just cook, woman!"

"Watch your language, young man!" Then she softened. "But thank you. I thought you didn't like killing baby sparrows."

Aris brushed it off. "The teacher told us when birds lose their babies, their mothers make more eggs. Then the babies come back again in a few weeks."

That Sunday inside the new church, Aris and some other boys waited outside the altar door to be given the cross and two disks on sticks to carry.

Father Dimitris came out smiling, followed by his intended replacement. Father Andrew was short with a messy black beard. In his mid-30s, his dark complexion and crooked nose made him look mean. The younger man handed over the cross and two discs to his own three sons who were waiting nearby.

Aris pointed to the cross. "Today is my turn to carry the cross, and Andy and Marios's turn to carry the discs. This is an injustice!"

The new priest shook his head. "From now on, only my sons will carry the cross and the discs. They know better how to do it."

With sealed lips, Father Dimitris observed. Aris's eyes blazed, fixed on the new priest. The boy put his right hand in his pocket and scratched his crotch.

Father Andrew pulled Aris's ear. "What did you just do?"

Indifferent, Aris pushed away the priest's hand, while lowering his head to free himself. "Nothing! What did I do?"

Red-faced, Father Andrew glared at Father Dimitris, then back to Aris. "You scratched your balls. Even worse, you did it inside the church!"

"My pants are tight." Aris made eye contact before continuing. "Besides, you do it all the time inside the church. We see you put your hand through your cassock pocket. Everybody knows."

Father Dimitris raised his eyebrows, visibly trying to hide his displeasure.

"I will not tolerate such rude, disrespectful behaviour in my church!" Father Andrew spluttered.

Aris shook his head. "This is not your church. It is our church. Since you arrived, half the people stopped coming."

The new priest poked Aris's chest. "Get out before I hit you. I will speak to your father and your schoolteacher."

Calmly, Aris removed his hands from his pockets. "We all respect and love Father Dimitris. But you are a bad person. There is good and bad. Nothing in between. You are a mean, bad priest." Aris turned and lifted Father Dimitris's right hand, kissing it reverently. "I apologise, Father. But you taught us to always tell the truth, with love in our heart. I'm leaving. This is no longer a loving church." Then he marched out, followed closely by all the other boys except for the three sons of the new priest.

"These boys have no respect," Father Andrew fumed behind them at Father Dimitris. "Is this what you taught? I'll show them how to pay respect."

The older priest only sighed. "Respect is not a privilege. We all need to *earn* it."

"That boy is blasphemous, rude. He has no manners. And you just stood there, saying nothing!"

Father Dimitris nodded. "Aris is a good and intelligent boy. He has the courage to fight injustice, irrespective of where it comes from. In his mind, everything is black and white. Good or bad. Nothing in between. In his mind, he was only standing up to your injustice."

"He's just an ill-mannered, undisciplined boy who needs to be whipped and taught a lesson!"

Father Dimitris donned the green stole over his cassock. "Aris is a leader. Today you lost him, and the rest of the boys followed. Unless he returns, the others will not come."

"That's not my fault!" the new priest shouted.

Father Dimitris simply turned his back to return through the side altar door. "Until Aris realises that injustice is an everyday part of life, he's the one who will suffer most."

8 Varo

Fourteen-year-old Varo Chase readied for the martial arts competition. With long legs and a well-proportioned upper body, her shapely physique already gave her the looks of a near full-grown stunner. Her long brown hair was pinned back in a tight bun. Her mind was whirring, fiercely determined to win the next fight.

Her grandfather, with a head full of pure white hair, sat next to her in his electric wheelchair. "You must remove the emotion," he coached. "Feel only the fight. Block everything else from your mind." With a quick glimpse around the arena, he added, "Every move has its own emotion. Combine that with your intelligence. Let them become one, subconsciously guiding your moves, your actions and reactions."

They both looked up as Victor, Varo's trainer, arrived. Well-groomed and handsome, he stood statue straight, with a soft birthmark between his left eyebrow and sideburn. "Your granddaughter is quite the fighter. She can take on masters much older than her."

A proud smile bloomed on her grandfather's face. "Varo could not have had a better teacher."

Just then Varo was summoned to her next fight. Her competitor, a tall strong boy, was a couple of years older, but in no time she had him splayed flat on his back, her right foot stretched just a hair's distance from his throat.

Triumphantly she returned to where the men were seated. "Soon I'll take on anyone. I won't stop until I find and punish the ones who killed my p—"

A sudden swiping kick from Victor sent Varo into the air before landing on her rump. "You turned your back on an opponent! The fight isn't over until your enemy is handicapped, unable to attack, incapable of hurting you, or too far away," he cautioned. "People don't play fair. It takes only one kick to incapacitate you."

9 Epi

Twelve-year-old Epi's family was gathered to celebrate at her house. A mix of Jewish and Irish flanked the dining table, along with fifteen-year-old Uri and his pureblood Jewish family members.

Epi's cheeks were round and rosy as she declared, "Uri, one day, I will marry you!" She pressed her hands together in her lap and continued, "I promise you this now. You better remember… you are my husband!"

The older party goers burst into laughter, but Uri rose and went to her side. He was tall for his age, with a narrow forehead and dark, curly hair. "But of course!" he said with a fluorish of one hand. Then he dropped to one knee in front of her and looked up beseechingly into her eyes. "I will come on my white horse, wearing my kingly crown, and ride away with you, my princess!"

Epi's easy laughter rang with joy. "You are funny, you know!"

Uri sucked in his cheeks in a false clown's smile. "Am I funny?"

With a poised point finger she tapped the table in front of her. "Whether it's by horse, car, bus, aeroplane or bicycle, you will come to marry me."

Another appreciative round of laughter had the adults patting each other on the backs and smiling.

Only one among them did not seem amused. In a stern voice, Epi's grandfather said, "Uri, my dearest Epi never makes false claims. Remember that, young man!"

10 Leoni

Leoni was fourteen when she was called to the headmaster's office. She saw her light blonde hair reflected in the glass as she peered through the door to see her father already seated inside.

"Your daughter used to be the top student in her class… indeed in the whole school," she could hear the headmaster saying. Leoni took a step away from the door so the man would not notice her eavesdropping. He continued, "That was before she started congregating with the troublemakers. Now Leoni has the worst marks of her academic life."

Her father listened with sealed lips.

"Her teachers and I am aware that she knows the correct answers for her exams, yet all term she has consistently scored poorly. Such a change usually indicates trouble at home."

Her father's head drooped. She had to lean in to the door frame to hear him mumble, "Don't know why. I moved out. Her mother wrongly blames Leoni for our separation—just because she looks more like me. I will talk to my daughter."

When he pushed back from the desk to stand, Leoni quickly shuffled to a chair closest to the hallway, pretending she had been waiting ambivalently.

Her father offered to help with her heavy bookbag, and Leoni silently followed him to the parking lot.

Once they had escaped academic ears, he said, "My love, I am so proud of you. You are the most intelligent in our family. Please do not destroy your future over the mess I created with your mum. You promised me you would do your best in school."

Leoni couldn't help the venom that spewed from her lips. "Oh yeah? And you promised you would never leave me. But you did!"

Out of the corner of her eye, she spotted the headmaster staring at them through his office window. She took three steps to the side, positioning herself so her father's back would block the man's view.

With anguish in his voice, Leoni's father said, "I didn't leave you, darling. I left your mother. We were hurting you every day with our stupid arguments. It became intolerable. Something had to give. So I left. But I never left you. I'm always here for you."

Leoni's chest puffed up. "Well, she blames me. Everything is my fault. So I intend to do everything that she hates. If she doesn't like a boy, I will make him my boyfriend. If she wants me to be the best in class, I will bring home the worst grades!"

Her father shifted his weight from one foot to the other, causing the headmaster to pop back into Leoni's view. "And you," she continued to vent. "You're not any better. You only want me to get top grades so you can brag about how I take after your intelligence."

She watched as his head drooped for a second time inside of ten minutes.

Leoni turned as if to head to the passenger's side of his car, but then spun on him once more "Why are you even here? You don't love me. These days you're only interested in your *girl*friend!" She emphasised the final word in such a way that he couldn't miss the barbs of what she felt about him dating someone half his age.

With all that still hanging in the air, she made a dramatic exit, stomping back to the school, her father left in shock, standing in silence next to his vehicle while the headmaster shook his head and retreated from the office window.

11 THE ORDINARY WORLD

Mid-morning, Aris walked through the corridor of his open-space office. A long-standing employee commented to the new girl, "Look at the boss. He's the oldest, but the most stylish dresser. Never brash."

"Seriously?" The new girl rolled her eyes. "Shirts with long white collars went out of style a hundred years ago."

"Mr. Aris does not follow fashion trends. He makes his own."

"I don't get the whole *mister* thing if you're going to use his first name. But at least he doesn't wear boring ties."

"His suits look better than Armani. And the title is a sign of respect for his age and status, while still showing friendship."

The new girl ran her tongue across her lips. "Maybe I could come to appreciate a mature man after all."

"Put those thoughts out of your mind. The last girl who flirted with him got fired."

The two watched as their co-worker, a hulking black man in his mid-twenties, four inches taller than Aris, struck a boxer's pose, blocking the boss's way.

Aris cracked a smile and gave him a playful push on the shoulder. "Watch it. I can still kick your backside!"

Feet glued to the floor, the other man crossed his bulging arms and stood his ground.

Aris reached into his pocket and pulled out a fifty-dollar bill. He raised it high above his own head. "Kick this and it's yours."

The girls saw Aris's sons, Peter and Gerry, step out of their offices to witness the game.

In a flash, the black man flexed a bulging thigh, but his kick maxed out at Aris's waist.

"Now it's my turn," Aris goaded. "Hold a ten-dollar bill at my head height. If I kick it, I win."

The other man snorted, "I'd like to see that," and complied with the boss's request.

Aris pulled up his loose trouser legs a bit, stretching out for a test at shin height.

"Never gonna happen, old man," Aris's son Peter razzed from a distance.

Aris smiled to himself and stretched his leg a second time to waist height on the hulk standing before him. Then without a moment's more pause, he extended that leg again in a flash of a kick that ruffled the ten-dollar bill.

Triumphantly, Aris grabbed the money and waved it around, graciously acknowledging applause from his employees. But afterwards he gave a conciliatory pat on the black man's shoulder, then handed the money back. The two embraced amid a chorus of "oohs" and "aahs" from the female employees.

A shorter female employee challenged, "Boss, I can do it!"

Aris took out the fifty-dollar bill again and suspended it at his shoulder height.

In her fitted trousers, the girl climbed atop her office desk and took a swipe at the cash, now just a short reach.

Aris pulled the money back with a flourish. "Kick it—without hitting me—and it's yours." Then he bit down on a corner of the note, shaking it between his teeth.

"Always a fox!" The girl climbed down and made as if to go straight back to her work.

Aris returned the bill to his pocket. "Remember… *you have to earn it.*" Then he set off down the corridor again, greeting employees left and right.

A well-shaped Latina in her early thirties clutched files tightly to her bosom, and stepped into the hall ahead of Aris, snaking her rear back and forth.

"Walk straight!" the boss called.

In response, the Latina started swinging her rear even more emphatically and traipsed down a side corridor.

Aris then passed a well-dressed man who just shook his head and laughed. Without looking back, Aris raised a middle finger in salute. "Morning, Asssstronaut!"

The other man instantly returned the gesture. "Morning to you too, Asssstronaut boss!"

Aris heard a newer male employee whisper to a colleague, "I see the old boss really is nasty."

"Oh, you ain't seen nothing," the other man said joyfully. "You'll only get your ass kicked if you earn it."

A long-time female employee who was heading the other way up the corridor slowed, facing Aris. He gave her a wide grin without stopping. "You're smiling today, Denise. You must've had some action last night!"

Denise held her head high and kept walking. "More than others who are *fasting*."

"Fasting cleanses the system!" Aris mused.

"What a waste!"

At the end of the corridor Aris reached his two sons' offices. He motioned them into Peter's room and they all took a seat.

"Dad, you can't say things like that to employees," Peter cautioned. "They can file for sexual harassment. One complaint and it'll cost us!"

"Relax, boys. They joke back! We're friends. The whole office is watching. Where is the abuse?" Aris's secretary entered the room. "Epi, the million-dollar smile," he beamed. "I only come to the office just to see you smile!"

"Tea, no milk, with cinnamon and cloves!" She set a cup in front of Aris and turned to leave.

"You know me better than my wife!"

"Well," Epi smiled sweetly. "Now I'm a wife too. I told Uri we'd be married back when I was just twelve years old. He said he'd come for me on a white horse."

"That boy doesn't deserve you," Aris snickered.

Once Epi left the office, Peter asked, "When are you going to stop callings us *boys*, old man?"

"Yeah, Dad," the younger Gerry chimed in.

Aris laughed and stood to follow Epi. "As soon as you stop calling me old man!"

◇

Aris pulled into the driveway in front of his family home and carried a small boxed package inside. At fifty-four years old, he'd kept fit with his hair well-groomed and those same almond-shaped black eyes still mesmerising.

His wife Gina's hair was cut to shoulder length and she was the picture-perfect housewife, looking more like a late-twenties' stunner. "Nobody asked me if I wanted to marry. I was only eighteen years old." She banged a knife on the kitchen counter.

"I asked you," Aris chuckled. "Your father asked you, too. You replied yes to us both."

She stamped her foot. "I was afraid. All I wanted was to leave that prison of a boarding school. I didn't know I'd become your slave."

Aris set the box down and leaned with his elbows atop the counter. "You're lost in your lies. You used me to escape boarding school."

She pointed an angry finger at him. "You can't stop me from going out!"

"I never forced you to do anything in your whole life. That's not my style. I simply wanted a wife who would be with me." Aris stepped to the fridge to avoid looking at her. "You are free to do as you please."

Gina pulled his arm from behind. "You're telling me I'm free to go fuck about then? Remember this!"

Aris lowered his voice. "I'm telling you that you are free to do as you please. But—like everyone else—you will be responsible for your actions… and the consequences."

A vein bulged at her throat. "Now you're threatening me."

He closed the fridge without taking anything out. "I choose to be with my family. You choose your supposed friends and sisters, all whores. Oh, I'm sorry…" he amended. "Flirts."

Gina tossed her hair back. "Nothing wrong with a little flirting. Life needs some excitement, as long as it doesn't hurt the family."

"There's no such thing as just flirting. You may soon find yourself without a family at all." Aris turned to head towards the staircase.

Chasing behind him she yelled, "You don't scare me with your threats! Once a peasant, always a peasant. I can't help it if men admire me."

Aris didn't turn back. "Advice is not a threat. But you should wake up before it's too late. We have grown children to think about."

"Threats and stinginess—features of a true peasant."

This caused him to pause. "Stingy? Just last month the credit card statement showed four new pairs of shoes, each over five hundred dollars. Am I being stingy?"

"I come from an aristocratic family. I have expensive tastes."

"You have more than a hundred pairs of shoes. But only two feet."

At that, Gina grabbed her handbag and headed to the front door.

"You should stop lying to yourself. Your family was never rich, and neither were they part of the aristocracy. They never even owned their own home."

"I shit on you," she cursed at him. "I can't stand your presence in the air I breathe! I shit on you!"

After she closed the front door behind her, Aris returned to the kitchen and snagged a bottle of juice from the fridge while loosening his tie lazily with the other hand. When he'd consumed half of the bottle's contents, Gina stormed back into the kitchen.

"My vitamin D is low," she announced sharply. "I need sun. I've decided I'm going away for Christmas."

"Now the puzzle is complete." Aris laughed to himself.

Gina's eyebrows knit together. "What nonsense are you talking about?"

"That explains why you asked the boys to take Liza with them on their holiday travels."

Gina shrugged. "Why not? You'll be working like usual, and I'd just be bored."

Amused, Aris continued to watch her in silence.

Finally she got to the point. "I'm going to stay with my sisters."

Aris's arm shot up like an orchestra conductor ready to begin a symphony. "Yes! The best company. Married sisters who like to have affairs with other people's husbands!"

Gina slapped the counter in front of him. "Stop bad mouthing my sisters."

"That's what you told the solicitor when you tried to lure his attention. It's true!"

She waved her arm defiantly. "My sisters have stupid boring husbands who don't pay attention to them. Why shouldn't they enjoy themselves? You're old-fashioned! Today's world is about enjoying life."

Aris took a gulp of juice and swished it in his mouth before responding. "So you just decided to go?"

"I don't need your permission. I have rights, you know!"

He chuckled. "You'll be the first divorced woman whose husband wasn't having an affair."

In her signature move, Gina stamped her right foot hard on the floor and pointed a finger into his chest. "Stop threatening me. This is nonstop psychological abuse! I'm not stupid."

Aris choked down the last of his juice and chucked the bottle before turning to leave.

"Come back," Gina yelled. "Or are you a coward?"

At that, Aris swerved back to the kitchen counter and grabbed the small parcel, handing it to his wife.

"What's this?" she asked. "I'm not your delivery boy!"

"It's a present," he answered. "Open it before you unleash your poison."

With manicured fingers she pried open the box. "A mobile phone? You just want to spy on me. Or you'll keep calling me, giving me jobs to do for your properties. I'm not your servant." She threw the phone down on the counter.

"You're unbelievable." He repackaged the device delicately.

"I'm not going to end up like you—a workaholic." She glared at him coolly. "You have no friends. A man without many friends is a zero."

"I don't buy friends like you do." His retort visibly cut her. "And I don't cry when someone cuts me off. I'm selective about who I choose to be my friends."

"My sister was right. No one's good enough for you! You're a double zero. You don't know how to enjoy anything."

As had become his usual escape, Aris headed for the stairs. "Even if I was a zero man, you still wouldn't be worthy of me. Leave the box on the counter, and I'll return it."

"Why d-do you always have to p-put me down?" Her voice cracked. "Now you're telling me I'm not worthy of your gift!"

"Your crocodile tears can't hurt me anymore. Cry as much as you want!"

Instantly like a closed faucet, Gina stopped crying. "You think you're so perfect. You don't smoke, you don't drink… you don't even have coffee. Worst of all, you think you know it all."

The front door opened to reveal Liza, their teenage daughter. The girl's long wavy hair perfectly set off her Mediterranean complexion.

"No arguing in front of our daughter," Aris muttered under his breath.

But Gina was relentless. "Why won't you stand and discuss it like a real man?"

Liza pretended to ignore them both and headed to the stairs.

Silently Aris motioned for the girl to follow him up.

"Coward!" Gina shouted, clearly exasperated. "Your father is a coward," she repeated.

Liza hurried behind him and took hold of his right hand. Aris gently pulled her up under his arm so they could climb the remaining stairs together.

"Fine, you just run away too, Liza. If no one wants to talk with me, I'm going out." Gina grabbed her bag and slammed the front door behind her.

Aris kissed the top of his daughter's head. "My gorgeous, let me change clothes and then I'll make dinner… unless you prefer we go out."

"I've got a lot of homework, Dad. No time to go out."

"What would you like then?"

"Maybe some cheese ravioli?"

"Oh, that will be very hard work!" Aris laughed.

"Yeah, just take them out of the freezer and put them in boiling water. I feel your pain."

12 Father-Daughter Bond

Aris filled the tea kettle with water. "Remember, Liza. There are three things you need to succeed in life—preparation, courage, and follow-through."

"Ugh." Liza threw her empty design book on the countertop. "You're not helping. I thought you used to design for women's fashion."

"Not by choice. Circumstances forced me." He brushed a lock of hair out of her face. "You're not trying hard enough. Let your mind be free."

"I'm running out of time. Give me an idea!"

He picked up her book and started flipping pages. "What are you trying to design?"

"Anything!"

The two of them leaned over the counter as he opened to a blank page and handed her a pencil. "What are your goals? Write them down here. Who are you designing for? What age? Where are they going to wear the clothing? And what's their budget?"

The seventeen-year-old banged her knee against the side of the counter. "I need something new… something original."

Aris merely pointed to the drawing pad. "Write down those answers. Then come back to me."

"I don't need to write an essay, Dad. None of those things will tell me anything about shape and style, or originality!"

Aris squeezed his lips tight and tapped the blank page again. "Write!"

In anger she gripped the pencil. "You're so stubborn sometimes. This won't help me."

"Add one more question… who will the judges be?"

"That's easy. A famous actress and some designers."

"Okay," he praised. "So you need something youngish then. These actresses like to dress like teenagers!"

Liza exhaled a loud, "Phew!"

Aris began to pace while she took notes. "You need something original, not seen before. But remember, it can be something previously seen, but in a new format or with a new shape."

Her pencil skimmed gracefully across the pad for several minutes. When she finished, she looked up at her father and handed the book to him. "Done."

Aris began reading. "Your target customers are actresses, especially young ones. What do they need?"

Liza threw her hands in the air. "Oh my god, Dad! I told you. They need high fashion!"

Aris handed back the book then stepped around the counter to pour tea for them both. "No! They want something to garner attention! Something shocking to draw the cameras."

Liza added this to her notes, nearly shaking in exasperation. "Each of us has to model our own design."

Aris's mouth twitched. "Ouch! That complicates things. You'll need different versions of your design then. Some that are less risqué."

She scribbled another line on her list.

Aris settled the teacups in front of them, then leaned with his elbow on the countertop, plopping his chin into his palm. "Now you know what you need… but not what you want. Keep writing. What are your customers looking for?"

Liza threw down the pencil. "This is just analysis. When do we get to the design?"

"Read your notes again and again," Aris calmed. "By morning you'll have the ideas."

"Morning?" Liza's eyes brimmed with tears. "I don't have that much time. This design has to be ready in three days. I'll have to withdraw from the competition."

"That's not being fair to yourself, darling. Where is your don't-give-up spirit?" Aris handed her a tissue.

She wiped her eyes. "Just stop philosophising and tell me you don't have any ideas either."

"If I were in your position, I would not give up."

Anger flared in his daughter's eyes. Liza grabbed the drawing book and lobbed it in front of him. "Prove it. Give me an idea."

Aris sighed deeply and picked up the pencil, pointing to each line of notes as he read aloud, "Shocking, original, old in new versions, or old in a new format. Different levels of revealing. Young actresses." This last made him laugh and he jotted down, "Empty heads, seeking attention."

"Dad," Liza bellowed. "You're being a chauvinist!"

He merely smiled. "Remember, whatever you do, make it fun. Have a laugh and enjoy it, my dear." He stared at the page another moment then asked, "Okay, what are you designing—a dress, a skirt, trousers, a coat, suits? Is it day or evening wear? Or perhaps for the disco?"

Liza wiped her eyes again and dropped the used tissue next to her teacup. "It has to be a skirt and top, or trousers and a top. No evening gowns."

Aris made additional notes and began a rough sketch of trousers with a high waist. "What if we went opposite to the current trend, which for a few years has been those ugly low-waist trousers? A high waist would be something different."

"That's not original, Dad!"

"Then let's make it original. And shocking! Reveal some sexuality. What if we cut out a strip along the side to show skin? It would be both shocking and original."

Liza stared hard at his sketch. "Maybe, but their underwear would show."

"Perhaps that's part of the added shock." Aris shaded in a portion of the slit area. "Or we could design special knickers to be worn with the outfit that had higher sides?"

Liza sucked in her breath. "That would make people think she wasn't wearing any underwear."

"Right!" Aris beamed. "That will be the shocking part. And it was your idea! So now we have two versions—one that shows part of the knickers, and one that shows only skin."

Liza pushed her father out of the way and stole the pencil, clearly invested in the concept. "What about the blouse?"

Her hand flew across the page as Aris spoke. "The two should match. Same revelations on top. Maybe a V insert from tits to shoulders with a closed neckline."

"Dad!" Liza fumed.

"Sorry, what am I supposed to call them these days? Then your two versions could be either nude bust, or with a lace inset. Or maybe the V is upside down and begins above the tits…" He caught her glare again. "… I mean breasts… and goes down."

This time Aris saw a glimpse of a hopeful smile on his daughter's face. "You're crazy, Dad. But I like that!"

Aris smiled. "An image just came to mind. What's the most attractive part of a woman's anatomy?"

Liza rolled her eyes.

"Her bum!" Aris answered himself.

"This generation has extra-large Brazilian bumps, Dad."

Undeterred, Aris launched into his idea. "Large, small, extra-large, extra small, still the rump is the number one attraction. In fact, the more defined, the better for our purposes." He scribbled a new trouser sketch, this time from the rear view. "What if we placed the V in the centre on the back?"

Liza burst out laughing. "Wearing that without underwear would be a real shocker! Too daring."

Aris drew another version. "Daring is a good word. This design could also be worn with or without the knickers showing. Still revealing, and drawing attention, still shocking, just not as daring. What do you think?"

Liza's gaze fixed on the page, frozen, until she looked up with a hint of a smile. "Actresses do love attention. It would definitely get them noticed." Joy now danced in her eyes.

"Who do young girls copy these days?"

"I get what you mean, Dad. The young ones will definitely be brave enough to risk wearing this. But ordinary girls aren't going to go without underwear. It's not hygienic."

"My clever girl. We'll have to design new fashion knickers as well."

"You're a genius, Dad." Liza kissed him on the cheek.

"I did nothing. We started from your answers, and you developed it."

"I'm not a child anymore. Remember, you taught me never to steal someone else's ideas."

Aris gave her a high five, even more proud than before.

"The design has to have a name." Liza flicked the pencil back and forth while she was thinking. "What shall we call it?"

"Liza's Design!"

"No, a name of its own."

"Okay. How about the Anafi design?"

"Why? Does that have some significance?"

"It's the name of a small island, east of Santorini in Greece. Tiny, but with high hills—lots of V shapes."

"Brilliant!" Liza clapped her hands. "A nature theme. The judges will love it! An unknown name that's still easy to remember!"

"Now you have to get down to work making samples. You can use my cutting table in the garage. I still have pattern-making tools, rulers, scissors, and pattern paper. We have a sewing machine and plenty of fabric."

"What materials should I use for the final version?"

Aris pinched one cheek then bit his lower lip. "Maybe denim for daywear, and something black for the disco. Especially if it comes with gold, silver or red lace. You'll have to search."

"You make it sound so simple, Dad."

"It is. Remember, getting started is half the job done."

"What about lace? We don't have any on hand."

"Just improvise." Then Aris lit on an idea. "You can steal some of your mum's fancy knickers. She won't even notice. Great selection of colours."

Liza headed straight for the stairs.

"But steal from the dresser drawer," Aris called after her. "Not from the dirty laundry basket!"

13 First Reactions

The next afternoon when Aris arrived home, Liza burst into the kitchen modelling the modest version of the Anafi prototypes.

"Oh my god!" Gina shouted. "I hope you don't think you're going out looking like that."

Aris gave his daughter a hug and motioned for her to spin around so he could take in all the design details.

Gina took two steps back. "And you… staring at our little girl like she was some prostitute selling herself on the corner!"

"Our Liza designed this." He beamed. "It is original."

"Her ass is showing!"

Aris just smiled. "Don't be put off, Liza. Your project called for something to draw attention… and you've certainly snagged your mum's. First test successful!"

"This isn't even the shocking version. Let me change." Liza headed out at top speed.

Gina's eyes were wild. "Do you see what your daughter is doing?"

In no time, Liza was back sporting the immodest version, turning and twirling as if she'd trained as a runway model.

"You look like a stripper," Gina spat.

Aris turned on his wife in a flash. "The only stripper I see in this house is you who hardly covers any of your anatomy." He pointed to Gina's current outfit, a fitted Lycra miniskirt with matching top, fully exposing her belly and thighs.

Still adamant, Gina pointed up and down at Liza's prototype. "This is shocking. No way are you going anywhere with your ass and boobs hanging out like that!"

"It's for a competition," Aris insisted. "Liza is going to win with this brilliant design."

Liza looked less confident than her father.

Gina tapped her stiletto impatiently. "No decent father would allow his daughter to wear this!"

Aris remained cool-headed. "On the contrary. I'm proud of Liza's intelligent design!"

Slowly circling Liza, Gina's expression changed. "So… what you're saying is, it would be okay if I wore this… clothing… out and about."

Aris shrugged. "I don't see why not. You wear much more revealing clothes all the time."

Liza frowned. "This is not for wearing to church, Mum!"

"I don't go to church." Gina continued circling, now with a look of conviction. "But an hour from now I'm attending a charity cocktail party. And I'm going to wear this." She pointed with a flourish at the Anafi trousers and blouse.

In a look of disbelief, Liza stared back and forth from her mother to her father.

"Consider it your second test," Gina cackled. "If it really draws attention and the other girls like it, I'll report back."

"I can't listen to any more of this." Liza headed for her room. "I'm going to change clothes."

Aris laughed out loud at Gina. "A charity event? More like your whore girlfriends staging something which no decent woman should attend. Which makes it the perfect event to test Liza's design!"

Gina stamped her foot. "My friends are not whores. So you'll allow a teenage girl to wear such pants, but not me. Well, I've got news for you. You can't tell me what to wear and what not to wear. I have rights, you know."

Liza returned, holding the more revealing versions of the blouse and trousers.

Grabbing the set, Gina headed for the stairs. "What's good for the goose is good for the gander. I'm wearing it to the party… and you can't stop me!"

Aris chuckled. "I have no intention of stopping you from making a fool of yourself!"

Liza touched her father's jacket sleeve. "Dad, that's a prototype and the seams aren't very tightly stitched. And um… Mum's a size bigger than me…"

Aris's smile increased. "The best trousers for her event!"

"Dad, that's naughty."

Aris jerked his shoulder towards the sewing machine setup. "We have the patterns and all the adjustments marked. Let's get going on your finished product."

Gina descended joyfully, wearing the Anafi set. "This looks way better on me. More womanly curves to fill it out."

Aris looked on in silence.

"Mum… the stitches." Liza pointed at the pants legs, already loosening under Gina's larger size.

"Yes, great feature!" Gina grinned. "Your wide stitching reveals leg all the way down, like little straps. Very clever, my girl!" Unconcerned she grabbed her handbag and headed out.

Aris offered up a high-five to his daughter. "Whatever humiliation she suffers, she brought it on herself."

"But didn't you see the flaw in the design, Dad? If a girl is between sizes, or wider at the hips, the trousers are going to stretch the V line."

"Indeed, so we can add one or two small straps to prevent that from happening—like some bikinis have side straps."

"Another version? That's more work! But… the judges will love it!" Liza beamed.

"Young lady, we have a lot of work to do. Let's order in pizza because we're going to be working past midnight."

＊ ◇ ＊

When Aris returned home the next evening he found Liza waiting with a rectangular blue box. She silently handed it over.

He examined it, turning the item from side to side.

"Open it, Dad!"

"It's not my birthday."

Liza smiled humbly. "This is something money cannot buy."

Opening the lid, Aris's expression morphed to one of complete pride. He lifted a gold medal swinging from its sparkly gold ribbon, followed by an ornate certificate. He read aloud: "Best Young Design—Liza Theo, for the Anafi design!"

He draped the medal over her neck and gathered her into an embrace. "Bravo! I'm so very proud of you, my girl!"

"The Anafi set is going to appear on the front page of a national magazine. But it's your design, Dad. This should be your award!"

A stern voice from behind said, "Just because he helped you by doing his messy stitches, there's no way you should let him take the credit for your artistic designs." Gina broke into the hug and wrapped her bejewelled arms around Liza. "This is entirely yours. You are gifted because you take after my talent."

"But I look like Dad, not you, Mum."

"When you grow up, you'll see that talent has nothing to do with good loo—"

"For a change, your mum is right," Aris interrupted. "This is entirely yours. I only assisted."

Gina shook her head and air-kissed their daughter's forehead. "If I weren't here, he would have claimed credit for your ideas. Don't let him cheat you!"

14 Princess of Business

Varo Chase, now thirty-three, sat looking across the boardroom table. At just under six feet, with an athletic body and chic designer suits—not to mention a multibillion-dollar business empire that spanned tech to hospitals to military aviation and supermarkets—she captivated not only the team members who worked for her but also most of her business rivals… especially the men.

"Gentlemen, you have exhausted my generosity and my patience. Either sign now, or you will force us to pull your credit. You'll be filing in bankruptcy court by the morning. I'm trying to give you a lifeline here. Take it!"

After a short pause, the white-haired gentleman and his son began to whisper.

Varo's top legal advisor sighed. He gathered the documents in front of him and stood. "Miss Chase, this man," he pointed to the elder, "is the cause of their company's destruction. We cannot extend any more assistance. He won't listen. End it now."

She held up her right hand, palm open, to stall the lawyer's departure, then addressed the others. "I will allow you and your son to walk away with a face-saving deal."

The son rose and circled the table, blustering, "Show some respect. My father is a good man, and a good businessman."

Varo stood as well, a mere foot away from him. Looking deeply into the other's eyes, her tone remained compassionate. "It is out of that respect for your father that I am offering you this deal which will allow you to keep your house, and cash in your pockets, which I almost never do."

"You're a fraud!" the son shouted. "You're taking pleasure in burning our business."

"Unfortunately, your father is the one who burned your business. He's not what you knew him to be. You should've taken over before he destroyed your company. Now it's too late."

In a split-second, the son's fist clenched and he raised his arm with a vengeful thrust toward Varo's face.

The screech of chairs pushing back from the table was accompanied by a guttural, "Nooo," emanating from the old man.

But in that same short span of time, the dozen or so men and three women around the table now stared in shock at the son, splayed flat on his back against the conference table. His right arm hung loose, broken at the shoulder, with Varo's strong hand at his throat, ready to squeeze.

"It seems your father's errors have taught you nothing. No one attacks me and gets away with it."

She glanced up to her head of security and personal trainer, Victor, who stood across the room with hands clasped lightly behind his back. He gave a slight nod of amusement.

"You're lucky I only broke your arm," Varo said. "Next time I'll take pleasure in breaking every limb… and more." She turned her gaze on the old man. "You, and your arrogant son's behaviour… You've just cost yourselves everything."

The rival's legal adviser passed a note to the older gentleman and whispered, "Please. Take the deal."

Varo waved a dismissive finger at them all. "This meeting is over. Get out."

The son winced and gingerly moved to pry himself off the conference table, cradling his useless arm.

The other team's lawyer cleared his throat. "One minute," then his tone softened. "Please, Miss Chase."

Varo squinted at him, calculating what might come next. With a slight nod, she gave permission for him to continue.

"Miss Chase is right," the attorney lectured the old man. "What you did was fraudulent and foolish. The two of you will not only be in the streets, without a cent, but you'll both be headed to jail!"

Team members from both sides went silent, wondering what would happen next. Then the son padded his way back around the table to stand beside his father.

The rival lawyer screamed at the older man, "Think of your wife. Do you really want to be homeless at your age?" Then he turned on the son. "Your father committed fraud. Take the damn deal!"

The old man heaved a deep sigh. His son let loose of the now useless arm and grasped his father's shoulder. "What are they saying? What fraud?"

The legal adviser pleaded, "Miss Chase is not obliged to help you. You need to take this deal. Sign now!"

"They both deserve to go to jail," Varo's adviser protested. He turned to her. "You are too good to them. Let them reap what was sowed."

"He's still a good man. We all make mistakes." The latter words seemed pointed like an arrow directly at the son. "He did what he thought was best at the time. Give him the contracts to sign."

The old man's chest puffed out.

"He's been like an uncle to me, ever since my parents were brutally killed," Varo concluded, and motioned to her head legal adviser to pass the forms back across the table.

Once the older gentleman scrawled his signature on the last page, the document returned to Varo who added her name. Her only expression was grim determination.

Both teams began collecting their belongings and heading to the door. From a distance, Varo could hear the son ask their attorney, "What fraud?"

"The less you know the better," the lawyer mumbled. "Miss Chase did you both a great favour today. Let's go!"

— ◆ —

Conference adjourned, Varo stood alone in the hall looking through a glass wall into one of the meeting rooms. The presenter appeared animated and had obviously captivated her staff. Then as if on cue, the well-dressed gentleman looked up and fixed his sights right on her. A charming smile filled his face.

Her team around the table followed his sightline and, upon seeing the boss, turned to face her through the glass.

She tugged at the hem of her tailored jacket and made her way inside. The head of procurement, Mr. Whiteman stood and said, "Miss Chase, I'd like to introduce Mr. Aris Theo from Secure Services, the insurance company I mentioned. His proposals will save our organisations a few million on insurance premiums."

Her gaze fixated on Aris's eyes. The two exchanged handshakes. Feeling his firm grip, she commented, "Imagine… Ares, the Ancient Greek god of war… selling insurance!"

He returned a polite smile and released her hand.

Varo did not move her gaze. "So, am I to understand you are more intelligent than the whole of our insurance and procurement department?"

"Not at all, Miss Chase." Aris's voice was reassuring. "To their credit, it was your team who instigated this search. The results were based on total teamwork."

"Call me Varo." She licked her lips unconsciously. "A rare quality in a man to not claim all the credit. So, you're not just another handsome Greek."

"Merely passionate about my job."

"Passion is a missing ingredient these days. We will meet again, Mr. Aris."

Her face was beaming as she sauntered out of the room. Aris and the rest of her team could not help but follow Varo's feline stroll down the hallway.

◆◇◆

"Great woman, Miss Chase!" Mr. Whiteman sighed in appreciation.

"She's a stunner," Aris conceded. "Her beauty is enough to make a man choke."

Mr. Whiteman waved his finger like a dog shakes its tail. "Not just that. She's fearless, yet compassionate. She sponsors several charities, including her favourite, the police orphans."

Mr. Whiteman's assistant bragged, "She inherited a small company and turned it into a global empire. Now even the President comes to her for advice!"

"It seems you have the perfect boss," Aris mused.

15 Making Her Move

"Epi, hold my calls for the next two hours," Aris instructed his secretary. "I'm headed to the presentation."

Epi smiled to acknowledge her boss on his way to the conference room opposite their offices.

Ten minutes later, a tall, dark-haired woman stood by Epi's desk. "I'm here to see Aris Theo, please. I'm Varo Chase, a soon to be new client."

Epi pointed across the hall. "He's in a meeting and won't be free for a couple of hours. Was he expecting you?"

The stranger swivelled her neck to peek into the conference room. "What kind of man is he?"

Without hesitation, Epi answered, "The real deal!"

The lady named Varo's eyebrows raised.

"Intelligent, warm hearted, fearless. And handsome, of course," Epi sighed.

A hint of a smile crept onto the other woman's face.

Epi had seen that look before on female clients, so she added, "He has *strong family values*. Definitely a one-woman man."

The other lady's gaze drifted back to Epi now showing a warm smile. "No man is a one-woman man!"

Epi gave a proud nod. "Mr. Aris is."

"Mister Aris, eh? That would indeed be a *rare prize*!"

Epi watched as the other woman now rotated to steal a peep of the interior of her boss's office where family photos were proudly displayed. As if drawn magnetically, Varo's feet carried her through the office door and to a section of wall where several past magazine articles were featured. Epi followed dutifully.

"Who are these catwalk girls?"

Epi smiled sweetly. "Just models. They're wearing Mr. Aris's designs."

"The insurance man is a fashion designer?" Varo scoffed.

"Used to be. With that collection, Mr. Aris swept the awards in Dusseldorf, Germany, beating 2500 major fashion houses from around the world."

Varo took her time and scanned other items on the wall. "Any more hidden talents?" Epi remained silent while Varo stepped to a different area of photos. "Is that him on this boat?"

"Yes, indeed." Epi admired the photo of her boss sailing a catamaran.

"Imagine… a sea captain as well! Who's the girl next to him on the boat?"

"Mr. Aris's granddaughter. His treasure!"

Varo nodded appreciatively. "I would love to have a child with such beauty."

"Mr. Aris is happily married, I'm afraid."

Varo brushed a hand through the air as if swatting away the idea. "Who cares about the branch when you can have the tree trunk?"

Epi's patience began to wear thin. "As I told you, he is a one-woman man."

"Yes, you already said as much." The stranger fingered a row of trophies on a shelf. "What about these?"

"Backgammon wins." Epi motioned for Varo to follow her out to the reception area.

Not taking a hint, the other woman exclaimed, "Backgammon? My passion!" Then she took in two engraved plaques bearing slogans…

Preparation —No fear— Follow-through
and
You Have to Earn It!

Walking closer to examine them, Varo asked, "Who wrote these slogans?"

Epi sighed and obliged. "Mr. Aris, of course." Then she placed a gentle hand on the woman's shoulder to turn them both out of the office. "You really must go now, Miss Chase. I will have Mr. Aris call you when——"

"Of course, dear," Varo interrupted. From her leather bag she pulled out a cream linen envelope. "May I leave this with you? It's an invitation to a charity ball. Please make sure *Mister* Aris receives it."

"Perhaps you can come back after lunch. I can fit you in for a few minutes," Epi offered politely.

"Thank you, but I have other arrangements. Just verify ASAP if he can make it."

Epi placed the envelope on the edge of her desk and breathed a sigh of relief when Varo turned to leave. But before the tall lady finished making her escape, Epi noticed the meeting attendees gawking out at them—specifically, ogling Varo Chase.

The chain reaction was instant. Mr. Aris, who had previously been immersed in his presentation, took notice of his audience's wandering attention and looked out to the hall to gain understanding. Staring straight at him was the woman who seemed to be eyeing up his "tree trunk." Varo raised a hand and waved goodbye, smiling all the way down the corridor.

16 Meeting the Competition

Halfway dressed in a black evening gown, Gina's hands flew through the air. "How many times do I have to tell you I don't want to go? You are doing this on purpose to stop me from going out with my friends!"

Aris finished buttoning his shirt and moved to the mirror to fix his black bowtie. "You shouldn't even associate with those girls."

Gina stamped her foot. "You can't tell me who to be friends with."

"Hurry up. We don't want to be late."

She crossed her hands over her chest. "I'm not coming!"

"I'm trying to win this woman's business." Aris's voice remained calm. "She could become our biggest customer. She's looking forward to meeting you."

Hesitant, Gina resumed dressing. "You're lying! Why would she want to meet me?"

Donning his evening jacket, Aris ignored the question.

"Probably because you're sleeping with her," Gina blurted, "and you want to cover it up. I'm not stupid, you know."

"That's an idea! I will keep that in mind." He checked himself in the mirror then turned to his wife. "You look very pretty tonight."

Gina tossed her hair back. "Now you notice. I'm pretty every day. Everyone admires me."

"It's different to be admired than to provoke someone's attention."

"You're just jealous, you out of fashion, old peasant head. I'm always bored at your clients' meetings. This is the last and final time. Never again!" She raised a can of hairspray and coated her locks liberally.

Instantly Aris felt his throat restrict. He coughed just to get air.

Gina's eyes grew devilish behind a subtle smile as she watched him struggle to the bathroom faucet and try to drink from the tap.

Still coughing, Aris washed his face repeatedly and sputtered, "You know I'm… I'm allergic to… to makeup and sprays."

"Oops! I totally forgot." Gina batted her fake eyelashes at him. "You have an allergic reaction. Now we cannot go."

Clutching a wet washcloth to his face, Aris stumbled down the stairs to grab the whiskey. He took a drink straight from the bottle, then gargled with a second shot of Kentucky's finest.

When Aris regained his composure, he made his way slowly back up the steps. After a squirt of nasal spray in both nostrils, he relished a few deep breaths before turning to face his wife. "I am okay. Hurry up. We are still going." Aris yanked open his top dresser drawer and began rummaging around.

Gina grunted and kicked the bathroom cabinet with her dainty high heel. Spraying lots of perfume on her neck and both wrists, she once again faced Aris defiantly.

With a tug, Aris secured the face mask to protect himself. "Come on," he said, motioning to the staircase. "You can sit in the backseat on the opposite side of the car."

◆ ◇ ◆

Aris pulled up outside the entrance to Varo's luxury mansion and got out. He was right on time to pick her up for the drive to the charity event across town.

Varo stepped outside to greet him, glorious in a white fitted evening gown. "Who's that in the backseat?" She peered inside the vehicle.

"My wife, Gina." He smiled subtly.

Instantly Varo's right hand landed a punch to Aris's stomach. He bent forward in an effort to hide the pain.

"The invitation was for *one*."

Mastering half a smile, Aris held open the passenger door. "She's looking forward to meeting you."

"Then I'll sit in the back with your wife."

The two women politely greeted each other, but faced forward while Aris drove away.

Still looking straight ahead, Varo's eyes met Gina's reflected in the rear-view mirror. "Aris tells me you wanted to meet me. Here I am!"

Gina kicked the back of Aris's seat. "Yes, he told me the same thing. You must be a very important client. He failed to say how stunning you are… or how *young*."

Varo matched the condescending tone. "No more stunning than you, dear. What is your secret?"

⸺ ◆ ⸺

Inside the venue Varo summoned an assistant. "Can you do me a favour? The lady over there wearing black is shy and doesn't know any other girls here. Would you show her around, make her feel comfortable? Her name is Gina."

The assistant seemed happy to oblige. "It would be my pleasure."

Approaching Aris from behind, Gina asked, "Enjoying yourself, Mr. Theo?" Then she led him around the room.

"I'm impressed. You have half the government here, even the Vice President."

She fixed him with a charming gaze. "You're the one who is impressive. You turn women's and men's heads alike, Aris."

"Thank you for inviting me." He made a show of reaching into his jacket for something. "Do I need to protect my pockets?"

"No," she demurred. "Tonight is not a fundraising event. That will follow later!"

Threading her left arm through Aris's right, she paraded him around the room, taking special pleasure in Gina's evil glares. Varo also noted Victor, her head of security, discreetly keeping watch from across the room.

"I admit, I want you all to myself," she beamed. "But you do not seem to be acquainted with anyone here. Come, let me introduce you to a few good business prospects."

Aris chuckled. "I don't think the Defence Secretary or the Attorney General will be looking to buy insurance."

When they made their way through the crowd, the Vice President made a special point to lean in close to Varo. "Be on time tomorrow. Don't keep the President waiting this time."

Varo's voice practically tinkled. "A woman's prerogative!"

Heading for the garden exit, she whispered in Aris's ear, "Don't be so impressed. They're just people like you and me. Of course, such friendships always come at a cost."

— ◊ —

She guided Aris through a side door into the deserted garden grounds. "Let's get some fresh air." She noticed Victor discreetly reposition himself, never losing sight of her.

Out of view from the main hall, she tugged on Aris's arm, bringing them face to face. "Since the moment I saw you in my office, I haven't been able to stop thinking about you. I confess this has never happened before. I usually stay away from married men."

Breaking eye contact, Aris remained silent and began leading them on a slow walk through the gardens.

"I'm just bursting to confess my stormy feelings for you."

He took a few more slow steps then paused.

Varo leaned her head on his shoulder, but Aris straightened and wiggled away.

"Tell me about you, please!" she begged.

Aris chose his words carefully. "I am a very simple man. A family-man. Nothing special."

"You're special to me." She paused then added, "And from what I understand, very special to a lot of other women… including your little secretary."

Aris's smile now appeared effortless. "Epi is a sweet girl. Loyal, and in love with the same boy since the age of twelve. They just got married."

Varo was undeterred. "Any other special women in your life?"

Aris now seemed amused. "Three, actually."

Varo took a small step back. "Three women?"

"Yes, my granddaughter, my daughter Liza, and my lovely wife of thirty-five years."

"You mustn't lie to me. I see no connection between you and this woman you call your *wife*."

Aris's smile faded and once again he looked straight ahead.

Varo pulled him to face her, her hands now holding his. Varo reached for her *elixir*, her prize. "Married or not, I was never attracted to a man like I'm attracted to you. My mind is clouded. My body is burning. My soul is demonised… for you!"

The only thing that betrayed Aris's stoicism was the dry swallowing of his Adam's apple.

"Somehow, you've smashed my defences, Aris. I don't know what's happening to me."

Aris's tightly drawn lips now matched the rest of his face.

"Your aura makes me feel emotions beyond my experience, beyond my understanding." Exasperated, Varo declared, "Your silence is torturing me. Say something!"

Aris sighed deeply. "Perhaps drink is leading your tongue and your emotions. A good night's sleep will correct it all."

Varo stood mesmerised like a schoolgirl. "That's just not so!" In a subconscious move, she leaned forward, reaching for a kiss. Out of the corner of her eye she saw Victor shake his head from behind a nearby bush.

Aris suddenly pulled back, refusing her advance. "Miss Varo, a gorgeous girl like you could have any handsome young man at her feet. I'm already past my expiration date! Besides, I'm in love with my wife."

Unrepentant, she volleyed, "Another first. You're the first man ever to refuse me! Yet you called me gorgeous. You're not a good liar, Aris Theo."

"Gorgeous you are, intelligent and successful. You will soon find your prince, I'm sure."

"It is true then!" Varo proclaimed. Aris raised an eyebrow in question. "Your secretary said you were '*a rare, one-woman man*'."

"Yes, I am a family man."

"A family man, sure." Varo nodded. "But in love with your wife? Most definitely not. And she's not in love with you either."

Aris's eyes went wide. Varo thought she could detect his certain surprise that she had so quickly caught the gist of his loveless marriage.

"You are a prize of a man and I'm not embarrassed to admit that I can't maintain self-control. Have I made a big fool of myself? What magic did you apply on me?"

Aris came to her rescue. "You are not a fool. Just temporarily influenced by alcohol. Nothing to be embarrassed about."

"What if I'm not?"

"Let's go back in. I'm sure your many famous guests will be missing you." Turning, he offered his left arm.

Bitter, Varo accepted and they made their way back inside. "And that's the first time I've failed to get a kiss from a man."

A few steps into the crowd, Aris politely turned. "If you will excuse me, I have an early day tomorrow. Will you be all right for a ride back home?"

Varo replied coolly, "My guardian Victor will drive me."

Immediately, Aris bowed goodbye, then turned and moved towards his wife Gina who had attached herself to a cluster of famous people.

"Aris!" Varo called, causing him to pause and look back. She raised a glass to him as if in a toast. "Juice. I never drink alcohol."

Nodding, Aris continued his mission. Reaching Gina he whispered, "Let's go."

"Go?" She balked. "There are important people here to meet."

"I'm tired. Something affected my stomach."

"Nonsense," she whispered back. "I saw you taking your so-called client on a garden stroll. Most probably she refused you, and now you're embarrassed. It serves you right."

"Stop imagining things." He gently pulled her arm. "Let's go!"

"Once a peasant, always a peasant." Her soft words had barbs. "You're simply incapable of mixing with an aristocratic crowd."

"Don't make a scene. Please."

"You leave. I don't want to. I have rights, you know."

Holding her upper arm, he led her away with a false smile.

Gina's teeth were gritted. "I hate you! First you force me to come. Now you force me to go."

Varo's gaze witnessed the argument. With a deep sigh, she nodded and smiled softly to herself.

⸺ ◇ ⸺

The Chief of Police moved to stand beside Varo. "It seems one of your guests has already taken his leave."

She sighed. "He's a tough one. A rare man of principles. He just refused me!"

The Chief's brows raised. "Aris Theo? His wife is a beautiful woman."

She chuckled softly. "A one-woman man, he claims, with ethical values. The bastard."

"I thought you never mess with married men."

Her head swung from side to side. "Not until now. I just can't seem to stop myself."

"It's not easy for a dream girl to be rejected."

Varo brushed his compliment aside. "I've been rejected before, but that was after they bedded me."

The Chief nearly spit out his drink. "Never!"

"Just when I thought the last two were getting serious, they stopped returning my calls."

"That must hurt!" he sympathised.

"This one hurts more."

"My angel," he went into mentor mode, "you can have any man you want."

"But Aris Theo is the only man I want. Handsome, positive, well mannered, respectful, intelligent, no gold digger… and apparently with high ethics."

"Only your father justified those descriptions." The Chief's face went serious. "God rest his soul."

She took a sip of juice to regain control. Despite decades, her parents' death was still raw in her memory. "But I judge Aris to be an altruist, sacrificing his personal pleasure for wellbeing of others."

"Don't embarrass yourself," the Chief cautioned. "You hardly know the man."

"In my heart, I've known him for years. I will have him."

She felt the gentle tug on her arm as the Chief's tone turned even more serious. "Never underestimate the power of a man's love for his wife."

Varo didn't hesitate. "Aris is not in love with her."

The Chief's head flew back from laughter. "Why else would Mr. Insurance Man reject someone like you? Wake up!"

She smiled bitterly. "It's all a pretence. The wife doesn't love him either. Apparently, Aris just does not want to break up his family."

The Chief shook a finger at her. "Watch out! If he's really a family man, he will reject you again and again. You should keep to your principle that served you well over the years. Stay away from married men."

Varo took another slow sip of juice. "You're so right. That's exactly what I will do. Aris is history."

Apparently convinced for the moment, he announced, "The Vice President has been chasing for a few moments with you."

A smile threaded its way across Varo's face and she looped her arm through his. "Well, let's not disappoint the man!"

* ◇ *

Back in the car, Gina was furious. "So your client was looking forward to meeting me, huh? You are such a liar. You're sleeping with her and trying to throw dust in my eyes."

Aris pulled the car away from the drive. "You did great, Gina. A silent flowerpot!"

She punched the dashboard. "I saw how she paraded you around, then took you to the garden, out of view. What did you two do out there?"

Unamused, Aris focused on his driving.

Gina kicked the floor. "Don't get flattered, you fool. She's just a whore after your money."

"So clever." He laughed sarcastically. "You do realise she could buy me a million times over… with her small change!"

This time Gina slapped the dashboard. "You're a blind old fool. I'm sleeping in the other bedroom tonight. And don't you dare disturb me!"

"Someone has a short memory. It's been years since you slept in my bed, and since I *disturbed* you."

17 Tensing the Relation Rope

Gina dressed up, ready for an outing.

"It's Sunday and the boys are coming," Aris called. "Can you not at least wait until after they leave?"

Without pause she applied a garish lipstick in the hall mirror. "It's a charity function. You should appreciate that after the one you just dragged me to for your… *client.* Anyway, the girls organised this a long time ago. I simply cannot let them down."

Their daughter Liza bit into an apple with a vengeance. "Even on Sundays you two don't stop. It's becoming unbearable in this madhouse."

By the time Gina got halfway to the front door, it opened to reveal Peter, their eldest, age thirty-three, and Gerry, now thirty, along with their wives and children.

Gina's expression morphed. Light tears glistened on her gloomy face. "Your father hit me!" She pointed behind her to Aris.

Peter and Gerry exchanged a look.

Aris's bitter chuckle broke the silence. "Your mother blocked my way to the bedroom, wanting to argue. So I lifted her up and dropped her on the bed."

More tears flowed from Gina. "That is domestic violence. It's physical abuse."

Peter shook his head regretfully.

"Mum, stop trying to manipulate us," Gerry said.

"He's brainwashed you against me! You don't believe anything I say."

"Please stop arguing in front of the children," Aris prodded. "That's why they rarely visit us."

Peter nodded to Gerry, then motioned to Liza. "I didn't come here to listen to your arguments. Let's go to a restaurant, sis."

Liza jumped up and ran to them.

"Wait, guys." Aris's disappointment was obvious.

"Dad, we will not get involved in your arguments. To us, you are both equal."

Leaving, the boys and their families shut the door behind them.

Bitterness rumbled inside Aris's voice. "Excellent! You made the children go away again!"

Tears instantly gone, Gina seemed pleased. "You! Not me."

"You are such a manipulator. You wanted to upset them, to make them leave, so they wouldn't see you going out. You are pushing your luck."

"Threats. Threats. You're an abusive male chauvinist. I have human rights, you know."

"You knew the boys were coming around, yet you didn't offer to cook."

"I'm not your slave, nor your mother, nor your aunty! You can cook by yourself, or there is always delivery."

Frustrated, Aris walked out the front door. He traipsed down the driveway, greeting neighbours who were working in their front garden. Another elderly couple sat in a swing on their veranda.

He grabbed for the water hose, squeezing the trigger on a bed of various coloured flowers. Absent-minded, the powerful stream forced petals away from stems, littering the bed like so many colourful tears in the soil.

— ◇ —

A fancy convertible bearing three girls in their mid-forties pulled up. The driver remained in the car, but the other two got out and headed for the front door. They were provocatively dressed in short, tight skirts, fat flaps visible beneath belly shirts.

Aris shouted to them, "The three devils. Leave Gina alone! She's a married woman." The noise drew the neighbours' attention and he instantly regretted it.

The women sauntered over, swinging their hips. "We're married too, old man. You're just jealous because we aren't here for you!"

He pondered the situation for a brief moment, patience draining from his mental reserve. In a fit of madness he turned the hose on the women, sending them racing back to their car screaming.

Delighted, the older neighbours' faces lit up.

Out of the front door, he spied his wife, walking with difficulty in a form-fitting miniskirt. "Ariiiis!" she screamed at the top of her lungs. "Stop harassing my friends. I'll call the police!"

When Gina was halfway to the convertible, Aris sprayed her too.

"That's abuse. I have witnesses now!"

The neighbours started to cheer. "Long overdue. Well done, Aris!"

Undeterred though soaked, Gina jumped in the front passenger seat. In unison the women raised their middle fingers at Aris and sped off.

Turning to the neighbours, Aris gave a theatrical bow.

"About damn time!" the older lady shouted.

— ◇ —

At a reserved corner table in their favourite restaurant, Gina led the conversation. "I am restricted. I'm being held back from my development and abused by my husband." She didn't even feel guilty for lying to Aris about where she and her friends were going.

"I never would've expected that from Aris," Mary, one of the girlfriends exclaimed.

Gina pouted. "If dinner isn't ready, he complains and puts me down. But why should I have dinner ready? The kids learned to cook pizza and French fries in the oven. He can do the same."

"You're absolutely right," another girlfriend chimed in. "You shouldn't have to put up with it."

But the final girlfriend Jenny's eyebrows knit together like an old woman's sweater. "You girls have no idea what it really means to be restricted by an incapable husband. If you were better friends, you'd tell Gina the truth."

The other two looked like they had been called to the principal's office.

Jenny turned her gaze on Gina. "Even your best friends aren't allowed to call you before noon, because you never get out of bed before mid-day. You run what you call a 'self-service' house. As soon as you wake up, you go out with friends."

"Aris is abusive," Gina moaned. "He shouts at me."

Mary looked down at her stocky thighs. "You're lucky Aris only shouts at you. A lesser man might have beaten you up."

"He's stingy with his money. He even does the supermarket shopping."

Jenny laughed out loud. "Someone has to buy the groceries since you won't do it, Gina!"

All the girls, even Gina herself, burst into laughter.

"As for stingy," Jenny continued, "we see how stingy Aris is. You've got dresses that could pay college tuition, and enough shoes to wear a different pair every day. You drive a new car every year and carry no less than three or four credit cards. I wish my husband was half as stingy as Aris is."

Another round of laughter followed.

"Whose friend are you?" Gina probed. "Mine or Aris's?"

"I'm your friend," Jenny replied instantly. "A friend who will not lie just to please your ego. You have the perfect man. The truth is, you are torturing him. Most of us have to babysit our husbands. They cannot make so much as a cup of coffee, never mind cooking or doing their own laundry."

All three nodded in agreement.

Gina pushed back from the table. "I don't believe I'm hearing this."

Adamant, Jenny rallied on. "You better. I don't know any man who has Aris's principles and values. He doesn't drink, he doesn't gamble, he's not a womaniser. His family and his business are all he cares about."

"Ha! That's what you think!" Gina glared. "Of course he's a womaniser!"

Jenny's smile was friendly but uncompromising. "What happened that time when you and your sister sent different girls to flirt with Aris, to test him out? He refused all three! All of them sexy young things. Does that seem like a womaniser?"

Unrepentant, Gina laughed. "Just because he refused those girls, it doesn't mean he refuses others. Probably he realised it was a setup."

Mary couldn't hold herself back. "Or Aris was already busy with other girls and couldn't cope!"

Everyone giggled except for Jenny.

Gina gave Mary a high-five. "Yes! That's more likely!"

Maintaining a stern face, Jenny lectured, "We all know Aris is a one-woman man. That means he loves you, like no other man will ever love you. Wake up, Gina!" With conviction, Jenny was on a roll. "Aris is a rare breed of a man, dedicated to his family, his children, his wife, his work. You'd have to be blind not to see that."

The three girlfriends' expressions turned serious.

Jenny cleared her throat. "Would you like a husband like Aris, ladies?"

"I wish!" blurted Mary.

Gina was still pouting. "Other men cook and clean the house. They do whatever their wife wants… and they treat them like real queens. Aris is a peasant. He doesn't even know how to give a proper compliment."

Jenny shook her head. "Gina, you are my friend and I love you, so I'm gonna tell you the truth. Many women succeeded at making good husbands walk out on them, only to bitterly regret it soon after. Open your eyes!"

The other girls nodded in silence.

"It's like I'm listening to my grandmother." Gina grimaced. "You like to be a slave to your husband and your children. You're the one who needs to wake up, Jenny. This is a new world we live in. Women have rights to pleasure, too."

"Well, being with my husband is quite the pleasure." Jenny smiled coyly then stood. "Time for me to go slave for my husband, ladies. I love this kind of slaving!"

18 Partners & Friends… Dead Weights

Peter and his brother stood in front of Aris's desk. "Dad, many businesses merge to grow. We've been approached by a larger company, so what do you think? If we partner with them, we'll get cash plus shares."

Aris leaned back in his chair with his hands behind his head. "You boys already know my views. *Partners, like most friends, are dead weights.* I'll only consider it if we maintain full control. Otherwise I'm not interested in dead-weight partners… or friends."

"Maybe we don't need partners," Gerry added eagerly, "but we all need friends."

Aris smiled. "Partners or friends, the minute you run into trouble or danger, they turn and run from you. Or worse, stab you in the back for their own gain."

"You need friends, Dad."

"Of course, we need to socialise and have fun. But unless you want to be disappointed, expect nothing from these acquaintances you call friends. You're lucky to be good brothers and friends to each other. That's not always the case with family."

Gerry leaned on Aris's desk. "Everyone says you're a genuine friend to them. Even Uncle Jeremy. He admires you."

"That's one of my faults," Aris chuckled. "I may be a good friend to him, but I can't say the same for Jeremy."

"So what if some friends let you down? That's life. You move on."

"I do not hold a grudge, Gerry. But I don't forget, nor do I forgive betrayal." Aris placed his hands on the desk. "We do move on, but we also have to learn from our mistakes!"

Peter looked puzzled. "Are you not even curious to see what this other company has to offer?"

Aris rose to his feet, slapping his upper thighs. "We stand on our own feet."

Gerry tapped the desk. "We can only grow so much by ourselves, Dad."

"Majority control holding," Aris confirmed. "That's the only thing I will consider. I built this company to last for you and your children." Then he sat back down. "As for growth, the sky is the limit. We can broker business nationwide, or even go global. We can start our own insurance underwriting company. We have the power of consumer demand in our hands. It will be a piece of cake. You are young. You can grow as far as you can reach, as much as you want."

✦ ◇ ✦

That afternoon, Aris backed out of his space in the company parking lot and turned to exit when a girl in her mid-twenties jumped in front of his vehicle. He slammed on the brakes.

Tall with golden blonde hair and blue eyes, her miniskirt left little to the imagination. *Melany…* Aris reached across to open the passenger door for her. She climbed in and Aris maneuvered into a parking spot further down and switched off the engine.

Melany's voice cracked. "I d-don't care about your age." A tear fell down one cheek. "You are the only man who can touch my soul as well as my body."

Aris sighed and handed her a tissue from a box on the console. "This is for your own good. I was clear from the beginning. I told you I have a family. Any good times we have together will only be short lived."

She wiped her eyes then crossed both feet on the seat in lotus position. "But you're entitled to some happiness. You

83

haven't slept with your wife in years. I'm the only one who can make you happy. I brought the smile back to your face."

"Melany, you're just twenty-four. You have your whole life ahead of you. The time has come for you to reach out and find your own prince—a young man to build a family with."

"But you do love me!" she insisted. "Don't lie to me!"

"Of course I love you." Aris could not dispute this. "But it's because of this love that I have to be strong and show you the way to free yourself."

"Every time we're together, the dogs bark three floors up and three floors below! It's like the Greek gods are making love! Are you telling me you don't want to be with me?"

"I miss you like crazy," Aris confessed with a slight smile. "Not just making love. I miss your intelligent conversation, your sweet smile, your golden heart. You are a glowing diamond in all—"

"If you believed that," Melany interrupted, "you wouldn't cut me off."

He caressed her cheek with his hand. "Use your intelligence. I cannot allow my personal pleasure to stop you from having a life."

She leaned into the warmth of his fingertips.

"Six months," he sighed with regret. "No calls, no messages. You'll see. In six months' time, any feelings you have for me will dissolve."

She sandwiched his hand in both of hers. "You are the best thing that ever happened to me. I will never find another man like you."

Aris could feel his jaws grind, forcing restraint. "Give yourself a chance, Melany. I never lied to you. Follow my prescription and take the bitter pill."

"Why are you refusing this perfect love? Stop dreaming. You will never find another girl to love you like I do. What we have is the ultimate love!"

"I know I will regret it," he groaned. "My age, my circumstances… I don't want you to become a widow before you even blossom, my flower."

She turned in the seat and pulled his hand to her bosom. "Even if I find a younger man, he could die the next day in a car accident. There are no assurances in life or death. Even I might die before you."

Both sat silently, tears returning to Melany's face in full stream.

Eventually Aris pulled her close, leaning forward to plant a tender kiss on her forehead. "Please, gorgeous. For your future." Then with both hands on her shoulders, he pressed her away.

"That was the traitor's kiss," she keened, shifting her long legs in front of her. Then Melany opened the door and was gone.

With pain in his voice, Aris called after her, "Remember, in an emergency, I will be there for you. No matter what. But otherwise, we will speak after a year."

⸻ ✦ ⸻

Mr. Whiteman entered Varo's office. "Where are we with the insurance proposal?" she asked without looking up from the papers in front of her.

"Concluded. The proposal from Secure Services is far superior, at a much lower premium. We have a win-win situation."

Varo looked up. "Which company is that?"

"The Greek gentleman you met the other day."

Relief flooded her face. "No hidden clauses?"

Mr. Whiteman chuckled. "To the contrary, he exposed hidden clauses he discovered in our previous policies."

She smiled softly. "And what did *Mister* Aris say about me?" She raised a finger to point at him. "In his own exact words."

Mr. Whiteman hesitated. "He said you are a stunner, and that your beauty makes a man choke!"

Varo raised an eyebrow at this. "Is that all?"

"He also said we were lucky to have the perfect boss—intelligent, fearless, compassionate, wise."

Unable to hide her pleasure, she stood and stepped to the side of her desk. "And what about his company?"

Mr. Whiteman spoke with conviction. "Solid family business, over twenty years run by him and his two sons." Varo listened attentively. "Steady growth, good financials, organic growth, no loans. Most amazingly they have high customer retention—ninety-eight percent!"

"That's great," Varo smiled. "You seem to have achieved another win. Send me the full proposal, in print, along with his company report and contact details. I would like to go through everything over the weekend."

Mr. Whiteman nodded then turned to leave.

"Let's invite Aris to come in next week to sign the agreement," Varo added.

Mr. Whiteman stopped mid-stride. "But… he is with us right now. We are signing agreements today."

Varo's mind spun. "I see. When the signing is done, bring him over then."

Mr. Whiteman stepped out of the office, and within a few minutes, he returned with his assistant and Aris Theo.

The assistant handed over a copy of the paperwork. "All agreements signed, Miss Chase!"

"Well done." Varo made a motion to dismiss them. "Leave us. I need to discuss another matter with Mr. Theo."

Her staffers made their way out. Varo eyed Aris appreciatively, then mechanically flipped through the contracts on her desk. "Mr. Aris, you have been avoiding me. The other day at the restaurant, you pretended not to even notice me until I spoke to you first."

Varo traced the steps of Mr. Whiteman and the assistant, then closed her office door gently, returning to stand in front of Aris. "You signed all these documents, yet did not even come to say hello to your new customer. Not to mention your number one admirer!" She flashed him a bashful smile. "Let's go to dinner. I promise not to drink."

This caused Aris to laugh. "But I thought you never drink."

Varo's smile split the heavens. "So you did hear me then!"

He nodded silently.

"Listen, Aris. I took your advice… and the advice of others. I slept on the matter. But I am still captured by you. This is not a temporary admiration, or hormonal attraction."

Aris bit the inside of his lip.

Varo looked deeply into his eyes. "The more I find out about you, the deeper I'm drawn. I want you! I cannot be straighter than this. Let's get to know each other… no strings attached."

"I told you I am in love with my wife," Aris politely declined. "I admire you, but I don't have those kinds of feelings for you. Open up, and you will soon find the right man to fall in love with."

Frustrated, Varo returned to her desk. When she finally spoke, her voice came out at a higher pitch. "I don't want any other man. I want you! Stop patronising me. I never felt this way for anyone else."

His smile was sympathetic. "Merely temporary. Confused feelings of transference. Give it a few days more and you will not even remember my name."

"I know what transference is." Varo's gaze penetrated him. "I did not even know you were in the building, yet I felt your presence. You are the one for me! Sooner or later, I will have you. Stop opposing the unopposable and get to know me."

She crossed to Aris who now looked like prey caught in a hunter's crosshairs.

"Like you, Aris, I was born with certain gifts. I am sure you are lying about being in love with your wife. Give us a chance."

He dry swallowed and took a step backwards. "Thank you for your business, Miss Chase. I must be going now."

Varo's confident smile grew wide. "Stop pretending! I can read you. You want me, too."

When he'd disappeared past the office door, Varo slumped her head against the back wall, hangs pressed to her forehead, in a mixture of embarrassment and frustration. "What is wrong with me? That's the second time I've humiliated myself in front of this man. This *married* man. Stop it. Stop it!"

A knock at the door caused Varo to suck back a deep breath and brush the wisps of hair from her face. "Come in," she called.

Victor entered, bearing a huge file. "Full info on your insurance man."

"He has a name." Varo took the proffered folder. "It's Aris. And he is not my man. Not yet anyway! He just walked out on me… for the second time." She flipped through the file's contents, visibly excited. "Do you have this in electronic format as well?"

"All in the special folder."

Varo let a satisfied sigh escape. "Gina is a pretty woman in any outfit… sexier than many half her age!"

"You will see. Interesting photos! This is just the first quick search. Soon I will have more." Content, Victor turned to walk to the door.

"I felt something wasn't right." Then Varo added sharply, "Search his past as well. Let's see if he really is the one-woman man he claims to be."

"He's a lying hypocrite," Victor declared. "His mobile calls and text messages show he's been having an affair with a student, less than half his age. It's all there."

"Is he now?" Varo fumed. "The scoundrel!"

Victor instantly switched into mentor mode. "This man is trouble. You should stay away from him." Just as quickly, the security chief swooped back into control. "Shall I take care of him?"

19 You Can Have Him

Late the next morning, Varo stepped out of a chauffeur-driven white SUV in front of Aris's house.

Gina answered the door. "Oh, it's you! I was expecting friends."

Varo took no notice of the slight. "Good morning, Gina. I'm here to talk about Aris. May I come in?"

Gina grimaced. "I'm on my way out." But then her voice softened. "I don't get involved in his business. What could you and I possibly have to talk about?"

"He doesn't know I'm here."

"Well, if Aris didn't send you," she began suspiciously, "why are you here?"

Varo pulled out a set of glossy photos from her leather portfolio. They showed Gina dancing and kissing another man in vivid colour. "I know about your affairs. You don't love Aris. But I do. I want you to leave him to me."

"Ha!" Gina puffed herself up. "The lying bastard lectures me on morality, all the while having an affair with you!" She took in the smile of satisfaction on Varo's face. "Now he has me followed. I already told him he could leave any time he wants. He's a coward."

"We are not having an affair." Varo licked her lips. "At least not yet. He said he's a one-woman man. If you leave him, he'll come to me."

Gina's anger dissipated. "He doesn't have any money, you know. All the companies and properties belong to our sons in a trust. No woman can touch it! Not even me."

Varo's expression gave nothing away.

Gina went back to scanning the glossy photos. "A man without money is nothing. He is of no use to any woman. Now that you know the truth, I'm sure you'll change your mind about him."

"Money?" Varo scoffed. "I have plenty of my own! Leave Aris to me, and I will make you financially secure."

Gina threw her head back and laughed. "Probably you're renting a big house for a few days as bait, to show off. All you gold diggers are the sa—" A car horn out front interrupted. Gina shoved the photos into her handbag. "I have to go now. But you can have him. You'd be doing me a favour!"

"That I will." Varo smirked. "Aris deserves better."

Gina practically steamrolled Varo out the door, closing and locking it behind her. "You think you're better than me? You won't last a week. Aris is a peasant. He has no idea how to have fun. We haven't even had sex for years now. He is a useless zero."

Varo's expression remained unchanged. "Pleased to hear that."

"Men chase after me in droves. I'm never short of admirers… unlike some women who have to go after old men!"

Varo raised her hand and waved goodbye, then climbed in the passenger seat of her SUV.

⸱ ◇ ⸱

As soon as Aris stepped into the house that evening, Gina pointed a finger into his sternum. "You can't scare me into staying at home."

"Never did, never will." Aris settled his briefcase on the foyer table.

Gina stamped her foot. "You had me followed. Then you had them hit my car. I could've been killed!"

"What are you talking about?" He unbuttoned his jacket and began to loosen his tie. "As if I cared enough to have you followed." He placed his right hand over his heart. "There is nothing left here for you. Empty!"

"Go look at my car. Some big white monster vehicle pushed me off the road then ran away. No doubt you put your whore up to it to scare me."

Aris's face went white before he recovered. "More likely you bullied some other poor driver out of your way, and in the process you hit them." He took off toward the kitchen before she could see the truth about Melany in his eyes.

Gina followed on his heels. "It was a clear hit and run. Don't pretend you don't know all about it."

He opened the refrigerator and pulled out a bottle of juice. "I know what a bully driver you are."

"You can pretend all you want, but I know you were behind it. It was the same vehicle that woman from the charity drives."

"What woman?" Aris visibly waved away her accusations. "We'll know the truth when the other driver files a police report against you."

Gina's fists clenched. "It's hardly a coincidence. The leggy gold digger came this morning asking me to leave you to her."

Aris's expression fell. "Who?"

Gina poked him again with that same bent finger. "The one you're having an affair with behind my back. She's half your age."

He raised one eyebrow but remained silent.

"How long have you two been sleeping together? Why don't you just go to her? Move out. I don't care. You're nothing to me."

Aris's mind scrambled for solid ground. "If another car hit you, did you get the license plate number?"

"How could I? My car spun a full circle. I'm going to report you to the police!"

Aris stepped hesitantly toward his home office. Stopping short he turned. "Who did you say it was who visited you?"

"Ha! You're probably confused. Too many leggy whores." Gina couldn't contain her sarcasm. "It was your latest victim— that supposed new client."

Relief washed over Aris's features. "Why didn't you tell me that Varo visited you?"

"What was there to tell?" Amused, she continued. "She wants me to leave you. Said she'd even buy me off! Not that she quoted a dollar amount."

"What else?" Aris stood his ground.

"Well, I told her she could have you… if she wants a peasant!"

"Will this poison never cease? I don't know what to believe from you anymore." He changed his mind about going to his office and instead headed for the stairs.

Gina chased behind him. "She showed me those photos you took of me. Now I have proof that you had me followed."

Aris spun round. "What photos?"

"Photos of me and…" She paused as understanding dawned. "In my car. Photos of me with my… girlfriends."

"Where are these photos?"

"I… I don't know," she backpedalled. "I didn't keep them!"

Aris turned his back on her once more, climbing the stairs to escape. Behind him, Gina raised her middle finger in the air.

⟡

Varo's voice practically purred over the video call. "Aris is on his way, Granddad. He phoned wanting to see me."

"Open your eyes, my angel. He refused you twice, but now he changed his mind? That doesn't make any sense."

"I told you, Granddad. Aris and me… we connected from moment one. I've seen it in his eyes. I can feel him."

"Bah," he scoffed as she closed out the online session.

Victor knocked and entered Varo's office. "The insurance man is here. He seems upset. Shall I sort him out?"

"No! I've been waiting for him. Bring him in!"

Victor's posture drooped but he made no argument.

"No one else comes in. No phones. No interruptions," she yelled as Victor departed.

A moment later Aris appeared in the doorway, teeth bared. "If you ever come near my wife again, I will not be nice. Stay away from my home."

Varo took a moment to compose herself. "Wow. I see you're in a good mood. Maybe I could soothe your tension. Help you relax." She strolled casually across the room to him, arms raised to offer an embrace.

Aris grabbed both wrists and shoved her backward. "This is not a joke. I'm warning you. Stay away from me and my family."

Varo stepped even closer, her face just inches away. "Or what?"

"I have my limits, but woman or not, for my family, I will hit you."

Amused, Varo landed a soft slap on Aris's cheek. "Come on then, hit me."

She could see his teeth grinding as he struggled to control his urges.

"Come on," she repeated. "I'd love to feel your hand hitting me."

Now his nostrils flared.

Varo was relentless. "What's the matter? Finally realise you like what you see in front of you?"

His patience exhausted itself. In a flash, Aris's left hand scooped her armpit while his right swooped under her knee, lifting Varo into the air like a weightlifter. He took two steps forward, then paused as if ready to throw her out the office window."

Varo wrapped her arm around his shoulders and giggled. Victor's reflection became visible in the glass. With a gesture she motioned him back.

Aris turned from the window, and with a quick release planted Varo flat on her back on top the desk. "You are intolerable! A sick, arrogant woman. Next time, I might not be able to stop myself. I could hurt you." His breath was coming in thick waves, the tension obvious in his arms and torso.

Varo lay dormant on the desktop, her arms hanging loosely over the sides, a small blood stain blotting the desk behind her head.

Taking in the sight, Aris's face paled. He placed one hand behind Varo's head and lifted. His hand came back with even more blood. He poked her shoulder. "Wake up, you stupid girl. Your head is bleeding!"

Varo lay motionless.

Eager to revive her, Aris tried a few chest compressions. Failing to rouse her, he closed her nostrils with two fingers of one hand, ready to give mouth-to-mouth resuscitation.

He leaned forward, lips touching hers for a split second before Aris felt himself lifted into the air. The security guard Victor clenched him in outstretched arms then thrust him violently across the room toward a plate glass wall. "Kill him!" Victor instructed the two guards who swarmed into the office.

Luckily the glass wall held strong. Aris fell to the floor, dizzy. Still in pursuit, Victor followed up with a hard kick to Aris's crotch.

"No! No!" he heard Varo scream. She shoved Victor out of her way then let loose a series of martial arts moves on the two guards. "Leave now. All of you!"

Victor's chest was heaving, but he did as asked and retreated with the other two men.

Varo offered her hand to help Aris up.

He refused, first rolling then stumbling to his feet.

He'd barely taken one step when Varo slid in front of him. "I proved it to you. You kissed me! You do care for me!"

Aris could taste blood. He removed a tissue from his pocket, wiping his mouth and nose. "You are one sick woman. Pull your dogs back." He sidestepped Varo and headed for the door. "Stop probing my wife and stay out of my life."

❖

Aris climbed into his car, still fuming, and pulled out of the parking lot. Immediately, a big white SUV pulled out behind him but trailed at a discreet distance. He turned onto a scenic route, tree cliffs on one side. Tissue in one hand, Aris wiped more blood from his nose, straining to calm his breathing.

The white vehicle accelerated into the passing line. It came up even with Aris's driver's side door, then swerved hard, scraping his vehicle, pushing him to the berm.

Aris grabbed the steering wheel with both hands, struggling to maintain control and stay on the road. Out of the corner of his eye, he caught sight of the brilliant white SUV, now veering toward him a second time.

This hit punched his smaller vehicle like a lightweight in the championship ring. Aris's car smashed through the guard rail and careened down the steep cliff bank, finally brought to a dramatic halt by the sturdy trunk of an enormous pine tree.

20 ᴇscaping ᴇlixir

In her office, Varo pushed the speaker phone button. Victor's voice was unhappy. "Your insurance man just stormed into reception again. He's demanding to see you."

She tossed her long mane behind her. "Bring him in."

Aris stomped in, trailed by Victor and two guards. "First you tried to frighten my wife, now you try to kill me? You've gone too far!" His fists were clenched in rage, his shirt and jacket stained and torn.

Victor grabbed Aris from behind and, despite Aris's larger size, lifted him with ease, preparing to again smash Aris into the glass wall.

"Put him down." Varo rose and moved in front of Victor.

With the bodyguard distracted, Aris sneaked a hand into his shirt pocket and removed a pen, stabbing out at Victor's ear where a birthmark taunted him like a target.

The man howled, then clenched Aris tighter, throwing him across the space onto a couch near Varo's desk. Touching his ear, Victor's hand came away bloody. He reared up to attack Aris a second time.

But Varo blocked his way. "I can look after myself. This man is a welcome guest! Get out, all of you."

As Victor and the other guards retreated, Aris made his way to his feet, still raging like a bull.

Varo stood tall in front of him. "You are a vicious man. What's wrong with you?"

"You tried to kill my wife," he grunted. "Then you had your dogs try to run me off the road in that same white SUV. It can't be a coincidence."

"What? Is this some Greek conspiracy theory of yours?"

Aris didn't back down one iota. "After I left your office a few hours ago, your lackeys nearly drove me off the cliff."

"If I wanted you or your wife killed," Varo said, arms outstretched, "you would be buried under concrete by now. I told you, I'm in love you. Why would I try to kill you?"

"Explain that to the police. I've already filed an official complaint." One of Aris's feet scraped the rug, like a bull trapped in a holding pen before a rodeo.

"Stress must be making you hallucinate. You're only embarrassing yourself. Sit down."

Aris tensed the muscles in his face. "I don't need your business. I'll cancel our contracts."

"You can't." Varo smiled. "Remember our special non-termination clause? To cancel, it will cost you millions… which you can't afford."

His anger boiled helplessly, fists tightly clenched at his sides.

Varo remained calm. "I admit, it would be nice to get rid of your wife. But why would I want to get rid of you? I would never harm you. I love you."

Instinctively, Aris threw a punch at Varo.

As if playing cat and mouse, she easily dodged, then made a fast swiping kick to the back of Aris's leg, sending him to the floor. The heel of her stilettos tickled Aris's throat. "You are no match for me."

Removing her foot, Varo offered to help Aris up.

He refused, using the couch for leverage to push himself to his feet.

"Victor could have killed you with one punch. He's an undefeated freestyle fighter. I just saved your life! Besides, the cameras will show you attacked me. I could've legally killed you in self-defence."

Aris scanned Varo from head to toe, then his eyes darted around the room, noticing cameras strategically placed to capture every moment since his entrance.

"I also saved the recording of your first attack on me here in my office. Who do you think the courts will believe?"

Undeterred, Aris shook his head. "You are a psychopath, a spoiled, arrogant rich g—"

"I am a good person," Varo interrupted.

Still facing her, he began backing toward the door. "You and your bullies, stay away from me and my family! I told you that I'm in love with my wife. I have no interest in another woman… especially not a devil like you."

Varo's tone became sarcastic. "Oh, so much in love. Your wife told me I could have you. She doesn't want any part of you. Why are you lying to yourself?" She took two measured steps towards Aris. "I know all about you and your wife. Not one day goes by without arguments. Except when she isn't home. She's often out with other people." In a coup attempt she added, "And according to her, you haven't slept together for years."

She could see his face fill with tortured pain.

"No wonder you're so full of anger." Varo then tried to turn on the charm. "I truly love you! It hurts to see you this way. Sooner or later you'll have to wake up to reality. Get to know me before you refuse me."

Aris lashed out. "My wife and family are none of your business."

Varo shifted back to her desk, toying with the edge of a folder in a stack there. She transferred weight to one leg, jutting out a hip in Aris's direction. With two fingertips, she extracted a photo from the folder by its corner. It vividly showed Gina kissing another man. Varo momentarily raised her gaze back to Aris, but his eyes were glued to another part of her.

"Just because I think you have a sexy bottom does not mean I have to sleep with you."

She couldn't hide her wide smile. "So you do fancy me."

Aris shrugged, raising his hands palms up. "Unlike you, I have ethics and principles. I don't need an extramarital affair. That's it!"

"Ethics and principles have nothing to do with it. Even if you are a one-woman man…" Varo's eyes went wide. "…your wife is the wrong woman!"

They stood in a staring match of sorts until Varo broke the silence.

"What loving wife would tell another woman she could have her husband?"

His chuckle was bitter. "Gina forgot to tell you that I'm neither for hire nor for sale. Personality and character are more important than sex appeal."

"Then we're a perfect match," Varo cooed. "You need a woman who loves you and matches your charisma. And I am that woman."

"You are an egotistical spoiled girl who thinks she can have anything, and anyone! Only love wins love. You have no such love currency in you!"

Varo raised her voice. "Don't you dare call me names. I succeeded in a man's world. Many charities rely on my generosity. You don't even know me." After a short pause she added, "Sooner or later, you'll find out who I really am. And then you'll come to me begging."

"You'll still be waiting for that on the day you go to your grave." He stretched out a long finger towards her. "Stay away from my family."

Varo slapped her desk. "Or what? All I have to do is snap my finger, and you and your family will vanish."

Aris paused by the door then turned back to face her. "That's more like your true self. You're an evil woman with a devil's mark."

In a sudden mix of frustration and regret she apologised. "I didn't mean it that way! You make me say and do things I wouldn't normally do. Damn you!"

And with that, he walked away, leaving the door standing wide open behind him.

Varo reached for the phone to summon Victor. A minute later he was standing in front of her, his ear now bandaged.

"Did you have anything to do with a couple of car accidents?"

Victor's face was stoic. "If I do a job, I do it right. That insurance man will blame you for anything that happens to him now. You should stay away from Aris Theo. He's trouble. Focus on your upcoming fight. The freestyle ring leaves no room for outside distractions."

She dismissed Victor but couldn't stop the locomotive of thoughts. *Aris's wife didn't show him the photos. And like a fool, I hesitated to show him, too. Aris will regret this. I'm not finished with him yet.*

21 On Your Mark

The next day just before lunchtime, Aris saw his taxi pull up in front of the house since his car was still out of commission. On his way out, one of Gina's tarty-looking girlfriends parked in the driveway and sauntered towards their front door. Without a word, she started to laugh at him.

Aris reached out for her arm and dragged her forcefully back to her vehicle. Pushing the girl inside, he slammed the car door and waved her off without a word. The girl's features looked frightened as she shifted into reverse and drove away.

The older neighbour lady called, "Good morning, Aris," and gave him a thumbs up sign.

As Aris climbed into the taxi, even the cab driver let out an amused snigger.

⋄

Aris waved to summon Epi to his office while the other hand held the mobile phone to his ear. He no sooner ended that call than the phone on his desk started ringing. He pushed the speaker button and shrugged off his jacket, hanging it from the coat tree in the corner.

Epi stood in front of his desk, notepad at the ready.

"How dare you send my friend away!" Gina's fuming voice boomed. "This is my house. I can invite anyone I want. You abused my friend. You are subjecting me to psychological abuse. Next time I will call the police."

Aris's head drooped.

"Even better, I'll lock you out. You are a peasant with no manners. A nothing! A zero! You should go away and never come back!"

Aris picked up the handset to soften the verbal tirade, then gave Epi a sheepish half-smile and waved her out of the office.

"You're pushing me beyond my limits," he replied in measured tones. "Maybe that's exactly what I should do. Just get as far away from you as possible." He plopped into the desk chair. "You're neither a wife, nor a friend. You've become a cancer… and the only solution to cancer is to cut it off."

He looked up in time to see Epi tug his office door shut behind her, a look of sadness overcoming her ever present smile.

After several minutes of continued shouting and banging his hand on the desk, Aris dropped the phone back in its cradle. He yanked open his tie and shirt collar button. Finally able to breathe again, he summoned Epi back. "Now what was it I originally wanted to call you in for? I forgot."

"Maybe you should do that for a while!" Epi suggested impulsively.

"Do what?"

"Like I advised you many times. Go away. Take a long break. Travel the world! This has been killing you for years now."

Aris just shook his head.

"Even Gina told you to get away. Why not do it?" Epi had nothing but sensitivity in her voice. "It's not like she's going to miss you."

Aris took an unusually long breath, angling his head towards her. "It's not that easy, Epi. I can't just abandon my family and the business."

With one hand she smoothed her skirt as she sat in the chair directly across from him. "You trained the boys. You've always said they could manage the business as well as you can, maybe better. If they need advice, they could always call or email you."

Aris picked up the stack of incoming mail, resisting the call to adventure. "And my little girl Liza. She's still a teenager. I can't leave her with that monster my wife has become." Aris clutched his stomach as pain roiled through his gut. "Can you bring me those stomach upset pills?"

Epi fetched the medication and a bottle of water, worry lines creasing her face.

He swallowed two pills in one gulp and chased them down with the water. "Where's that smile, Epi? Don't stop smiling because of my mess."

"I can't when I see you tortured like this. Where's *your* smile anyway? You used to say the office was your paradise. You are a king here and always happy."

Aris nodded silently.

"You should go!" she encouraged. Epi pointed to the wall behind his chair. "Look at your slogans."

He spun slowly, wanting to at least humour her.

"If you can't take the pain, don't expect the gain!" Epi chanted. "If you want to gain, you have to put in the pain. And in conclusion… You have to earn it!"

Gracefully she slid out of her seat and circled around the desk. "I know you don't want to break up your family. You've taken the pain for your family's sake for years now. Isn't it time to look for a little gain? Maybe if you followed your own philosophies we would all benefit."

"It's not that easy, Epi, but thank you for being concerned." He looked up and felt a different kind of pain in his chest at Epi's expression. "Are you sure you don't want to marry me? What I really need is a girl like you."

Her soft smile returned. "Too late! Your previous assistant, Leoni, warned me about your harmless sweet talk. Besides, I just got married."

"Lucky bastard. That playboy never worked a day in his life. If he doesn't change, you should get rid of him before you end up like me!"

"Uri is not a playboy. He was looking for a home to roost," she teased. "Wait and see!"

Aris sighed. "You're my lucky star. You can always pull me out of a funk. Thank you, Epi."

Epi rewarded him with a high wattage grin, then reorganised his stack of mail and made her way out.

— ◇ —

At home, Aris stared into the refrigerator. "Empty again."

Gina sat at the table filing her nails. "Then go shopping. That's what normal men do. I'm not your slave."

"The mother of my children. Nothing more," he muttered. He grabbed a pen and paper to compose a shopping list.

"What do you want from me anyway?" Gina clucked.

Without a beat's pause Aris replied, "You are totally incapable of what I want. Just the simple things… a smile now and then, some positivity, no arguments, no insinuations."

She twisted the bottle of polish closed and blew on her nails. "I am always happy and positive… when you're not around!"

In agitation, his pen scratched off the edge of the paper, marking the countertop. "Selfish monster!"

Unrepentant, Gina rallied. "I woke up! I found my true self. I am not a slave anymore! I will do as I please. Like my father used to say… I only have one life, and I intend to enjoy it."

Aris opened a cupboard to check the coffee status. "You think that messing around means you're enjoying your life. Look where it got your father. He died alone, penniless and miserable."

"Flirting does not necessarily mean sex, mister."

Back to the refrigerator, Aris pulled out the vegetable drawer to take stock. "Kissing another man is more than flirting."

"Nothing wrong with a kiss!"

Aris chuckled. "And I suppose a blowjob is just another kind of kiss?"

"You have no evidence," Gina spluttered.

"I know who you are now. I don't need evidence."

She opened and closed the fingers of one hand imitating small talk. "Just because you don't know how to enjoy life doesn't mean I will imprison myself."

He clenched the pen to avoid throwing it at her. "I am holding this family together by a thread while you seem determined to destroy it."

"I'm not afraid of you! The law protects me. I have rights, you know. You're like a barking dog with no bite."

Aris ground the nib of the pen into the notepad. "I will walk away from you."

"You don't have the guts. What would you say to the children?"

He looked down to see a pool of ink like blood on the paper. "They're grownups. They're not blind." And with that, he headed out the door.

22 Final Call to Adventure

"What do you say now that you've seen the evidence?" Varo's voice boomed from Aris's speakerphone.

"What evidence?" Aris volleyed back. "I don't manage your account anymore. I don't want any dealings with you."

"The eye-opening photos of your wife kissing your lawyer!"

Aris's blood boiled. "I don't know what you're talking about. Stop interfering with my family affairs." He jammed his thumb against the button to hang up the call.

When he looked up he could see Epi at her desk struggling to pretend she hadn't overheard. His sixth sense kicked in and he made his way out to stand in front of her.

Guiltily she looked down.

Aris reached out a hand expectantly.

In slow motion, Epi opened her second desk drawer and pulled out a large envelope. She mutely handed it to him.

"You don't get to play judge and jury about what mail comes to me."

"I d-do apologise," she stammered. "The envelope was open and I didn't want the boys to see what was inside. I didn't want you to get hurt."

Shaking his head, Aris retreated to his office, closing the door behind him. In one swift motion he poured out the contents onto his desk.

Frozen, not in surprise but rather with anger, Aris collapsed into his office chair. The top photo showed Gina kissing his firm's top attorney. Another showed the two of them walking arm in arm. A third pictured them together at the entrance to a hotel. But perhaps even worse was the glossy photo of his wife held tight in a slow dance… at a bar with an entirely different man.

Aris stopped looking. Tendrils of cold rage filled his veins. His heart beat erratically, wishing he could un-see what he'd just been forced to look at. Not that it was any surprise.

A movement outside his office window drew his attention. Epi stood silently watching over him. He waved her in.

She came with notepad and pen in hand, as always, but more reserved than usual.

"Close the door behind you," Aris instructed.

She did so and turned to him expectantly. "It's not worth opening Pandora's box of pain, you know."

A sigh escaped Aris's lips. "The pain finished long ago. It's the demons within that I have to worry about now. How can I ignore the truth when everybody else knows?"

Epi's gaze dropped to the floor, evidence that what these photos shared had not been news to her either.

"Who brought the envelope?" Aris wondered.

"Miss Chase," Epi spat.

"And you're sure the boys didn't see these awful photos?"

"That's why I hid them in my drawer. Well, one of the reasons."

"If this happens again, make sure the boys don't see anything like this."

She nodded. "But they need to be prepared. Sooner or later, it will come out." In a more timid voice she added, "Gina's not exactly discreet."

"A straying wife is one thing, but finding out your mother's having an affair is a knife in the heart for any son."

He saw Epi staring down at the final photo of Gina dancing with yet another man and felt the condemnation she would never utter.

"Go." Aris waved her away.

After just two steps she turned around. "Don't allow this to demonise you. Maybe it really is time…"

He knew what was coming.

"…to follow your instincts and take some time off."

Like the movement of a glacier, Aris planted his feet and rose from his desk, donned his suit jacket one painful inch at a time, then stuffed the photos back into the envelope. He crossed in front of Epi, heading out the office door.

"I suppose the demons were unleashed a long time ago. Maybe this time I will take your advice."

⋄

When Aris arrived home early, he found Gina reading a magazine on a stool at the kitchen counter, nursing a cup of coffee. Without a word he threw down the foul pictures in front of her.

"What are these?" she asked nonchalantly.

To hide his bitterness he opened the refrigerator door and stared inside. "Evidence. The whole world knows."

"This is just more proof you had me followed." She pushed the images away like rubbish. "It's nothing serious anyway. Just a flirt for fun. A friendly kiss."

Aris spun like an angry top. "Sooner or later our sons are going to find out. Do you have any idea how humiliating it will be to find out their mother's a slut?"

Gina shot to her feet. Moving faster than he'd ever seen, she circled the counter and slapped him with a resounding *thwack*. "Stop spying on me. I can come and go as I please. You said so."

Aris felt the sting but kept his cool. "You can do as you please, but—like everyone else—you are responsible for your actions."

"Stop threatening me." She stomped her foot. "I'll call the police if you touch me!"

"Touch you?" he hooted. "You've burned even the ashes in my heart. I'm totally immune to you!"

With rebellion in her eyes, Gina grabbed the stack of photos and started tearing them to bits, shredding them onto the counter.

Aris only stared at her, rigid, like he was standing in wet cement.

Gina grabbed up the shredded pile and with a shriek threw it at him. The scraps littered the kitchen floor like snow. "Don't you dare show such photos to my sons. That's blackmail!"

Leaving the detritus of her tantrum behind, Aris undid his necktie and beat his usual retreat up the staircase.

The next day at the office, Aris summoned his assistant. "I've decided to take your advice."

"You're getting a divorce?" Epi gasped.

The laughter came on its own. "That may be the next step, but no. I'm going on a search."

"A search?"

"Taking time out." Aris bundled up some papers from his desk and straightened them into a neat pile. "I was thinking I might travel for a year or so… then see."

"And what is it you're searching for?"

"Not sure. Answers, maybe. True love?"

She smiled. "It'll do you good to take some time off and clear your head. True love does exist, but…"

Something made Aris reflect. The smell of olives and summer sunshine came to him in a flash, along with the memory of a certain cemetery. "Do you know that there's a love secret?"

"A secret?" Epi repeated.

"As in… how to make someone fall in love with you."

Epi giggled. "Now I know you need a vacation."

Fire kindled in his mind. "Maybe I'll search for that special woman to fall in love with."

She reached out and put one delicate hand on top of his. "You are a dreamer, Aris. Don't go fooling yourself."

"Dreams cost nothing, Epi."

"Besides, you don't need any love secret! Look how Miss Chase has fallen for you. And remember that hotel girl who fell down the stairs because her knees trembled at the sight of you?"

"Maybe, maybe not."

"What's wrong with you men?"

Aris chuckled. "What's wrong with *you*? You've been telling me to take time off. Now that I've decided to do just that, you still aren't happy."

Epi expelled a long sigh. "I'm happy you decided to take time off, to travel and clear your mind. But you don't have to go making a fool of yourself looking for some love secret that doesn't exist."

Aris remembered his grandfather's words, and how vehemently his grandmother had argued against them. "Don't be so sure. I knew a lady who knew the secret of love. It's just that she died before I could ask her. But she had a granddaughter I could track down."

Epi giggled like a teenager. "Do yourself a favour, Aris. Don't tell anyone that you're looking for such a myth."

Aris drew an imaginary 'x' across his heart. "I only told you because you're a special friend. And when I find this love secret, I'll tell it to you so you can use it on your Uri."

She pursed her lips. "Uri loves me," she insisted. "He's just afraid to accept it yet."

"And how did you reach that conclusion?"

"Go on then. Go find whatever it is you're looking for. Do it. Don't just say you will then not follow through!"

Aris made fish lips and sent a teasing air kiss to Epi.

She fake snatched it out of the air. "I'm glad to see you in high spirits finally. The true you." She turned to leave.

"Don't tell anyone," Aris called after her. "I haven't announced anything yet, even to the boys."

"My lips are sealed." When she reached the door she paused and turned back. "Just don't forget to find the thing you really *need*… not just the thing you *want!*"

23 Crossing the First Threshold

Aris answered the door at his house. Two couples faced him—the newlyweds Epi and Uri, and Aris's former assistant, Leoni, along with her husband John. The men stood practically the same height, but where John was slender and fragile looking, Uri had a pumped chest and a long, crooked nose.

Surprised, he invited them in. Gina made a production of welcoming the guests. "Have a seat," she offered.

"No time," Uri proclaimed. "We need to pack. We just wanted to ask Aris a few details about what to take with us."

Aris looked from Uri to Epi and back. "Where are you going?"

Uri rubbed his palms together. "Me and John are going with you on your travels."

Gina's eyes flashed.

Aris took a small step backward, not wanting to subject his friends to a bout of Gina's verbal diarrhoea. When nothing happened, he stared into Epi's eyes, then Leoni's. Both girls simply shrugged as if to say they were equally surprised by the turn of events.

"I don't remember inviting anyone," Aris hedged.

Gina merely stood there with a pasted smile.

Aris turned on Uri. "This is a sacrilege! You just got married!"

"Yes, but I don't want to wait until I grow old like—" He grunted when Epi elbowed him in the ribs. "I want to do this now, while I'm still active!"

Aris crossed his arms over his chest and turned to John. In a sudden move, he leaned into the second man's face and shouted, "Haaaa!"

John took a frightened leap back.

"I don't mean to belittle you, John, but I don't even know where I'm going or how long I'll be gone. I like you, but you always say you're scared of things. I don't think this trip is for you." Then he turned to Uri. "And you. Even if I wanted to, I wouldn't take you away from your bride just weeks after your wedding. Epi waited a lifetime for you! You're not single or a playboy anymore."

Uri tilted his head. "Epi gave me her consent. I'm strong, and I'm good company. I have travelled the world. I will be an asset." Then he bent close to Aris's ear and whispered, "I can also pull in the girls."

Aris turned to Epi.

She cleared her throat. "I told him he could go with you."

Aris shook his head. "I'm not a babysitter."

"Maybe you're the one who needs watching out for," she smirked.

John remained silent, but Leoni spoke up. "All his life, John has wanted to go on an adventure like this. He's only willing to dare it now with you. John trusts and admires you, Aris. Besides, I remember how my father rebelled when my mother clutched too tightly. Plus, you could use a good and reliable friend."

"A friend?" Aris scoffed. "Gorgeous Leoni, you worked with me more than ten years. You know I think friends are nothing but dead weights!"

"A marriage without trust is dead weight, too," Leoni countered.

In an unexpectedly high voice, John asked, "What if something happens to you, Aris? An accident. You might get sick in a foreign country. Someone needs to look after you!"

Aris laughed dismissively. "I know you're a good person. And I know you mean what you say, John. But are you serious? You think you can look after me?"

"Why not? You need a buddy, like when we go diving." John's voice began to return to normal. "I'm not useless. I can fix any engine. I have other skills. I can even read lips!"

"Two buddies!" Uri added.

"I already feel suffocated." Aris used two hands to part the tightening crowd around him, like doing the breaststroke mid-air. "Forget it. No one's coming with me!"

"Why not?" Gina scorned. "Are you afraid they'll stop you from taking a young girl along?"

He ignored her and turned back to the others. "Guys, thank you for your concern, but I'm going it alone." Then he motioned them all back towards the front entrance, opening the door.

Uri turned to Epi. "He's not as friendly as you made him out to be."

Epi sighed and grabbed Uri by the hand, followed by Leoni and John, everyone in a mixture of embarrassed disappointment.

Unconcerned, Gina asked, "Where are you really going?"

Aris didn't answer.

Leoni fixed her with a hard gaze. "Gina! You've done enough for one day. Just shut it!" Then she wrapped Aris in a sympathetic hug and kissed his cheek. "We had no right to impose on you and your holiday. We just love you!"

24 Love Timeout

The next day, backpack ready, Aris walked out the front door. Astonished, he saw John and Uri waiting with their packs beside Leoni and Epi. All sported wide smiles, like loyal pals waiting for their leader.

Gina appeared, leaning on the open door frame with a contented grin, hands crossed over her bust.

John reached out to shake Aris's hand. "I'm glad you changed your mind. You'll see, I really am good company."

Aris scanned their faces looking for clues, but saw nothing other than John's usual expression of disbelief.

"You won't regret it," Uri picked up the enthusiasm. "We're going to have a great time!"

Gina finally stepped forward, waving her arm. "Hi, guys. Right on time!" Aris blinked twice, three times. Gina shrugged one shoulder and looked triumphant.

Aris nodded to himself, finally comprehending what happened.

Leoni must have also put the puzzle pieces together. She kicked a spot on the grass, clearly embarrassed. "Sssugar. Not again!"

Epi caught on then, too. "Aris, I thought you gave in and agreed for John and Uri to come with you."

Aris pursed his lips.

She looked like a pot about to boil. "I am so, so sorry. We never wanted to impose."

"What's going on?" John squeaked.

Epi's ferocious gaze turned on Gina. "You had no right to do that. You are a selfish manipulator. You embarrassed us yesterday. And, unrepentant, you lied to us twice now."

"Just a bit of persuasion, nothing wrong with that." Gina was downright jubilant.

"Aaaah! You're a two-headed snake," Leoni hissed. "Let's go, guys."

Uri seemed confused. Then he burped. "Why? Has Aris changed his mind again?"

"Aris never agreed to it in the first place," Epi muttered.

Feeling terrible on behalf of his wife's bad behaviour, Aris reached for Epi's arm to stop her. He stared deep into her eyes.

"You were right, Aris," Epi explained. "Uri is afraid of marriage. But he loves me. And he is a very good man—fun, good company, reliable." Uri's face lit up like a circus clown at the praise. "Just a bit of a mouth sometimes. Time with someone like you would do him all the good in the world."

Aris let go of Epi's arm and turned to Leoni.

"It would be a dream come true for John." The corners of Leoni's mouth turned upwards. "You know he has a great heart. Responsible to his obligations. He'll go the extra mile to be your best buddy."

Aris waved both hands outwards. "Guys, I am spontaneous. I don't have plans. Moreover, I don't want to make plans. And I won't stand for arguments. If you don't agree, you split."

John couldn't help himself. In a half girlish voice he yelped, "No problem! Wherever you go, we follow."

Aris sighed and shook his head. "I know I'm going to regret this." He looked to Uri. "I don't want any dead weights. I'm not a babysitter. If you're an arrogant playboy, you won't last a week!"

"No plans! As long as it may last." Uri beamed. "That's what excites me."

"You'll have to bring your own spending money. Or earn it along the way."

Uri pulled a bunch of credit cards from one pocket and a wad of cash from the other.

"I'm not lazy," John affirmed. "I know engines and electrics. I have many skills."

"John has golden hands," Leoni laughed, "but just don't trust him to handle money."

His face drooped at his wife's disclosure.

Tightening his backpack, Aris nodded consent, which sent John and Uri into ecstasy and caused them to hug their wives.

"You see?" Gina taunted. "I told you."

Epi reared up against her. "Forcing your way on Aris by manipulating us all was not right."

"It's for his own good." She patted Aris on the shoulder like a youth.

Leoni raised one finger into the air. "I will *never* trust you again."

"Last night you were begging me." Gina's voice turned sing-songy. "You wanted Aris to take your men away from you. I got Aris to say yes. Look, now they're all happy!"

"It's never right to manipulate people," Epi chimed in.

"What you should be telling me is *thank you*."

Epi's and Leoni's jaws dropped.

Gina smiled coyly. "Don't you know? Men like to be manipulated. They deserve it too!"

◆ ◇ ◆

John pulled out of a deep, long farewell embrace with Leoni. "I don't want you to go," she told him. "Stay!"

He kissed her on the lips. "At first, you pushed me to go. Now I want to." He wrapped her tight and hugged her again.

She pushed back hard. "You weren't even invited. Plus I don't know if I can cope without you." Panic-stricken she slapped John.

"It's only for a few months. You said we needed a rest from each other."

This time Leoni slapped him twice.

Disturbed, the rest could do nothing but watch. Leoni ran a few metres away and covered her face with her hands, bursting into spasmodic tears.

John glanced over at Aris. "I've never seen her behave like this." Gently, he stepped over and cradled Leoni in his arms. "It's okay," he whispered. "I won't go!"

She buried her face in his chest. A loud sob escaped before she admitted, "I'm so embarrassed. First my father and now you. Why do the men in my life keep leaving me?"

Unable to help herself, Gina barrelled in. "Leoni's right. You're all male chauvinist pigs, leaving your wives and families just to travel and fuck about. How would you like it if we took off for a year?" She turned on Aris. "This is all your fault. You'll get no tears from me. As far as I'm concerned, you can go to hell!"

A burst of laughter escaped Aris's lips. "*You* are the only hell in my life."

John looked over at Gina. "It was Leoni's idea for me to join. I don't know what happened."

Aris appeared sympathetic. "Leoni is distressed. This isn't for you, John. Take her home."

His hands sandwiching Leoni's face, John gazed deeply into his wife's eyes. "Love, you have to make up your mind now. If you want me to stay, I'll stay. I'm not taking one step without knowing you're okay with it. It's your decision."

She sniffled, then placed her hands on his cheeks and pulled him in for a kiss. "No! You go! I don't know what happened to me. It was a momentary emotional outburst. I'm fine now. Go enjoy yourself. Besides, despite what Aris says, he does need a buddy. And you are the best."

Leoni wiped the last of her tears and kissed John on the cheek. "Go, my love. Fulfil your dream. Explore and enjoy yourself. We'll be waiting for you."

Epi sidled up and threaded her hand through Leoni's arm. "And you be true to yourself, Uri. Just come home safe and well! One month, one year is nothing. You're worth a lifetime's wait to me."

Aris felt his chest puff up on Uri's behalf. "Did you hear what Epi just said, Gina?"

His wife again crossed her arms over her bosom. "That's because Epi is stupid. Just married and he's already abandoning her… before the honeymoon is even over."

To soften her comment, Aris laughed. "Of course! Epi and Leoni are both idiots… the *adorable* kind of idiots!" He pointed from one to the other of the girls. "Look how stupid. Gentle, sweet, full of love and understanding, supporting to their men."

Gina just tapped her foot on the trim strip at the doorway, making no move to hug Aris goodbye. "Go to hell. I'm not a nun, and I'm certainly not going to sit and pray for your return. Safe or otherwise."

25 No Escape

Across the street from the three men preparing for adventure, a nicely dressed couple in their thirties paused in front of the neighbour's home. "We're interested in that house across the road, next to where those people are talking. Looks empty. Would you know if it's up for sale?"

The older lady was polite. "The bank repossessed it. Not on sale yet, as far as I know."

The female stranger smiled sweetly. "Looks like your other neighbours might be headed on vacation."

"Aris and Gina? Oh no. He came and said goodbye last night. Lovely man. Said he's taking some time off—for a year or so. Just between you and me, I don't blame him. Things are not so great between him and his wife."

"Well, thank you. We'll do some more research on the other house." The young couple retreated to their car.

Inside the vehicle, the woman immediately placed a call.

Varo's voice answered. "What did you find out?"

"Important news, Miss Chase. Aris Theo is leaving on extended travels. Some troubles with his wife. Looks like two other men are going with him."

"Aris is going away?" Varo gasped.

The woman confirmed. "According to the neighbour, they're leaving today. Right now. Carrying nothing but backpacks."

Varo's commanding tone echoed in the car. "Track them! I want to know wherever Aris goes!"

"But we don't have any idea of his itinerary. The neighbour lady said he might be gone for a year."

"I don't care." The boss's tone left no room for arguments. "Get a team. Get *ten* teams. Spare no expense! I want tracking devices on their bags, their phones… even their goddamn balls if you have to! Just do it, and keep me updated."

The phone line went dead. The two in the car stared at each other, speechless. Then the man asked, "Can we even do that?"

"Well…" the woman sighed. "We're not going to plant tracking devices on their balls, if that's what you mean. But we can definitely make some money on this one. And see the world, maybe. You heard what she said. No limits! Let's send a proforma invoice for fifty thousand, plus another fifty for travel expenses. If she pays, we go. If not, we pull out."

The couple sat and observed the men across the street a few minutes longer, pretending to look up things on their cell phones so the old neighbour lady would not grow suspicious.

"Those other guys don't look very professional," the woman said. "Should be easy to track them. Just need to place a bug or two now, and then you can stay on their trail. At least until I get a team together."

The man handed her a small box. "Okay, but if I'm going to follow them, then I shouldn't show my face now. You go attach the tracking devices."

With the tiny electronics clenched in her hand, the lady left the car and crossed the street, headed straight towards John while Epi engulfed Uri in a tearful embrace.

⸺ ⬩◇⬩ ⸺

Backpack fitted snugly, Aris stood waiting on the couples to finish their umpteenth hugs and farewell kisses.

A lady who looked mid-thirties stepped onto his walkway and waved. "Excuse me. I asked your neighbours, but they didn't know. Could you tell me who owns this house next door that's standing empty?"

"The bank," Aris answered without pause. "It's in foreclosure."

"Thanks," the lady replied. She took a couple of steps, pausing behind John. "Heavy bag you've got there. Are you travelling far?"

"No clue!" John practically trilled.

"Wow." Her face registered surprise. She stepped closer to Uri and his bag. "What will you do?"

"No plans!" Uri answered happily. "More exciting that way!"

The woman waved and bid farewell.

— ◇ —

Her partner started the car and pulled away from the curb while the woman pressed buttons on a navigation screen. "Do you have them?" he asked.

"Already activated," she replied and pointed at the screen. "There they are."

He stopped the vehicle next to another parked car around the corner. "Those backpacks feel too temporary. I don't want to lose this big meal ticket. We'll need to place more permanent devices later."

"Use my car." She handed over her car keys. "They've seen this one."

— ◇ —

Aris was still standing on his front stoop when a newish red SUV pulled up. A flashy man in his thirties hopped out, pointing to the car. "We can drive anywhere in this," he announced. "Into any country. Global insurance coverage!"

Aris recognized his cousin Dory's husband, Jim Darrant, but that didn't mean he was happy to see him. The man had a habit of doing and saying exactly the wrong things in any situation.

"Well," Aris sniggered. "I won't say I'm glad to see you, but I suppose we could use a ride to the station." He signalled Uri and John to mount their packs and the three headed to the curb.

"I'm coming with you!" Jim popped the back hatch for the men to deposit their backpacks, then held open the passenger door for Aris. "As soon as I heard about this trip, I dropped everything. I'm a strong team player!"

"You are not, you selfish, arrogant bastard. You wouldn't last a day." Aris relented and climbed in, then pulled his own door shut behind him.

Jim just smiled and trooped around to the driver's side. "From one you became three, and three is better than one. But do you know what's even better than three? Four!"

"F off. You weren't invited." Aris did not look amused.

"But I was invited," Jim insisted. "I spoke to Gina!"

Aris rolled down the car window and shouted to his wife, still perched in the doorjamb with her arms crossed over her chest. "Who else have you invited?"

She smiled triumphantly. "Ask your cousin! Just be thankful you're getting a free driver."

Uri was still settling in, playing with all the buttons and gadgets as he reached up between Jim and Aris to the dashboard. "Gotta confess… this is one sweet ride!"

John tugged at Uri's sleeve. "It's Aris's decision, not ours."

Uri turned a knob and the GPS panel swivelled. "Aris, you told us you'd drop us if we didn't hold up our end of the bargain. Why don't you do the same with this guy? We could use the ride."

Aris slapped Uri's hand to get him to retreat to the back seat. "Good or bad, I don't use people, Uri."

John remained silent but gave Aris a thumbs-up signal.

Meanwhile Jim punched a number into his cell phone then handed it to Aris. "Here, speak to my wife."

Aris held up both palms to refuse until he heard his cousin's loud voice booming from the device. He snatched it up and yelled, "Dory, find another way to get rid of your idiot! Don't loan him to me!"

"Aris, my most beloved cousin," Dory crooned. "You owe me. It's time to pay. Remember how I persuaded the bank to finance your first venture? Please, please, please. I beg you. I will make a statue in your honour. Take the bastard away. Even if it's just for a few days." Aris rolled his eyes then looked out the window at his wife who hadn't budged from the door frame. "Of course, I'd prefer it to be a few years."

Ever since they were children, Dory had been able to get her way. But not this time. "I'm escaping my own devils with this trip. I don't need another one perched on my shoulder."

"I beg you. Save me!" Her voice dropped in volume. She sounded desperate. "If I don't soon get some space, I'll either kill him or kill myself."

Jim tapped Aris on the shoulder and whispered, "It was hard work to get Dory to agree to me joining you." Obviously Jim hadn't overheard what his wife just said. "Don't spoil it for us, Aris."

Undeterred, Dory kept whimpering in Aris's ear. "You are my only family. Please! I'll do anything for you."

Aris couldn't take much more of this torture. Besides, he was anxious to get on the road. Gina was still giving him some combination of a triumphant look plus the evil eye, while Leoni and Epi embraced tearfully.

"Okay, Dory. But only because I owe you. Understand, I will take your cancer away for the time being. And you will not call in any more markers on this debt. Understood?"

"I love you, I love you!" Dory's shriek caused Aris to yank the phone away from his ear. The sound reverberated around the SUV.

When she'd finished the screeching, he inched the phone closer again. "Don't expect much. If I don't kill him first, he'll probably be back by nightfall."

He heard the sound of kisses smooching through the device. "Take him somewhere far away," she sang. "Maybe lock him in a jail for a few months."

"I thought you said you loved the idiot." Aris simply could not understand the way some women treated their supposed life partners.

"I do love him!" Dory confessed. "But putting up with him all day long is another thing. I need a break. A looooong break."

Aris hung up the phone and cast a stern gaze on Jim. "You'll probably be thrown out within twenty-four hours."

Jim practically leapt up in his seat. "Fine with me!" He high-fived Uri then turned the ignition. "Where to?"

All three men waited for Aris's answer.

After looking from one face to another, then casting one last sad glance at Gina, Aris said, "South!"

Uri's and John's faces beamed.

"South where?" Jim asked.

Aris slapped his forehead. "Just shut up and drive."

"But I don't know which way is south." Jim started fiddling with the buttons on the GPS.

Aris slapped Jim's hand down the same way he'd scolded Uri earlier. "Drive before another dozen idiots decide to tag along."

Jim started laughing, but when Aris's expression didn't soften, his left hand began to shake on the steering wheel. "I n-need to know where I'm going. I am miss-directional!"

Grinding his jaws, Aris saw a way forward. He jumped out of the car and circled round. Yanking open the driver's door, he bellowed, "That's it! You lasted one minute. Get out!"

Aris made a move to pull Jim out by brute force, but the cunning devil was too quick. He scooted across the front seat and buckled himself in. "Nope! You said at least twenty-four hours!" Jim's face was now radiant.

Behind the wheel, Aris put the vehicle into gear and drove away from the curb without another thought, while John and Uri waved happily to their wives.

26 The Vengeance

As Aris departed across town, Victor accompanied Varo into the arena where twelve pairs of fighters were about to vie for massive money. Dressed in a Lycra jumpsuit with a matching black mask, only Varo's eyes, mouth and nostrils were visible. But her clothing made it no secret that she was the only female fighter.

In the last round, it would be Varo versus a mountainous Indian-Pakistani fighter.

"She may be a girl," the other fighter's coach told him, "but she is intelligent and has skills. This makes her more dangerous. You need to remain focused. It's not over yet!" After a brief reflection the coach added, "Pretend you're protecting your right rib cage. She may fall for it."

The fighter nodded once. "I didn't come here to lose! Especially to a girl."

Across the way, Victor advised Varo, "He has strong hands and arms. His feet too, but his real strength is in his arms. Pretend to be protecting your right shoulder. Whatever you do, don't expose your left shoulder."

Varo gazed steadily ahead, taking in her opponent's stance.

Victor followed her sightline. "He's sticking his left side forward to make you think he's wounded on the right. But I've been paying attention. Go for his left ribs and hip. Both weakened."

"Final round!" the commentator called. "Winner takes all! The pot stands at a massive $232 million dollars!"

Incited spectators yelled to place last-minute bets as Victor walked Varo to the fighting cage. "This one also uses his brains. He can take multiple knocks and still stand strong. Don't be a fool. Concentrate on his weak points. Speed and surprise will be your secret!" At the entrance, Victor whispered, "Imagine this fighter is connected to the men who killed your parents. Today you can begin to exact your revenge."

A glimmer of a smile graced Varo's lips.

———— ◆ ————

Seconds before the bell, both fighters exhibited signs of exhaustion. But Varo was only faking. In a final move, she lured her opponent to the ground then sprang to her feet and jumped into the air, landing with bone-shattering force on both his kneecaps. Seismic applause rang out around the room.

Victor rushed to the cage's gate clutching Varo's black satin robe. As she exited he whispered, "Hold on! Don't show weakness." He wrapped the garment around her.

"Hurts like hell," she muttered but raised her arm to wave in victory at the crowd, smiling through clenched teeth.

"Just one minute to the car." He deftly maneuvered her out the door and into the waiting vehicle. Once she was safely tucked into the back seat he let out his concern. "This is your last freestyle fight. You're not built for this." Then he closed the door and made his way to the other side. "Even if it means giving up the search for your parents' killers."

Varo pushed his words away. "I won't stop until I fulfil my goal. I *will* find them."

———— ◆ ————

Victor's mobile phone rang. After checking caller ID he pushed the button and continued circling to the other side of the vehicle. "Another lucky day for your girl." The voice was male. "She made me some money today. But you've overtrained her. This is not good!"

"I am in total control."

"Many made that mistake. They paid a heavy price."

"Every little detail is taken care of. We're on track."

The man's voice grew firm. "Then stay focused on the plan! Don't get distracted by her womanly charms. Never forget what we had to endure. Never!"

The door handle within his grasp, Victor grunted. "I've never been distracted. And I never will be. The plan is on track. We will take it all back."

"Stick to the plan," the caller repeated. "I'm watching!" With that the signal ended.

Victor climbed into the rear seat to find Varo's head drooping, a line of blood leaking from her mouth.

"She doesn't look good," the driver noticed. "Are we still heading for the airport?"

Victor met the other man's gaze in the rear-view mirror. He unzipped Varo's fitted suit and removed her mask to reveal the extent of her injuries. "Full speed," he replied. "To the nearest hospital!"

27 Watering Hole

Lamberton, North Carolina

Early in the evening of the first day, Jim Darrant couldn't disguise his yawn. "My eyes can't take any more. I need a nap."

Uri seconded the thought. "Why drive nonstop? Let's get some rest. What's the hurry, Aris? Aren't we supposed to be having fun?"

The traveling heroes pulled off at a roadside bar to wash down the day's dust with some drinks. A couple of steps inside, they came face to face with three provocatively dressed women.

Uri was already salivating.

Aris exchanged a look with John, as Jim followed the girls like a tomcat on a leash.

Uri was right behind him. "Might get lucky the first day out!"

Reaching for Uri's arm, Aris yanked him back.

"What?" Uri balked. "I told you I can pull in the girls."

Aris shook his head. "Go sit in the car, you moron. You haven't even been married thirty days yet."

He attempted to march Uri out the door, but one of the three ladies brushed a manicured hand down his sleeve. "Are you ready for business, boys?"

John probably thought he was being helpful and stole her hand for himself. "Sorry, we're not here on business."

Aris had to shake his head again. How had he managed to get strapped down with these mental lightweights? "What my friend means is that we're all married. Unavailable for… *business.*"

Uri was trying to wiggle out of Aris's grip, but the older man strong-armed him towards the exit.

"I don't see any wives!" the girl giggled. Her friends broke into spontaneously laughter.

Outside Aris gave Uri a hard shove.

"What?" Uri brushed himself off and stood up straight. "Are you made out of stone? Or have you no male urges left?"

"They were business girls," Aris pointed out. "Hookers."

"So?" Uri seemed undeterred.

John sputtered. "H-how can you even contemplate such a thing?"

"If you ask me, you're both morons…" Uri stood by the door waiting to be admitted to the back seat. "All pretence, living in a dream world."

Aris unlocked the vehicle. "Uri, you have absolutely no moral character."

Uri merely scratched his crotch. "You don't have to be in love to sleep with a woman. It's nature. And a man's human right, for that matter!"

"Just get in the car." Aris climbed behind the steering wheel and awaited the rest of them.

"Over seventy percent of couples divorce within the first ten years," Uri shouted above the traffic noise. "The rest of them only stay together because they can't afford to get divorced."

Jim and John each took two steps back.

"Take you, Aris." Uri opened his door and leaned over the seat to speak directly in Aris's ear. "You want a divorce, but you worry too much about your children and what other people will say. When was the last time you got laid?"

John's eyes went wide as Aris clenched his fist.

"A man without values is nothing but a drifting animal." Aris shook that fist at Uri. "Like you."

"I'm right, you know. Teenagers confuse hormonal attraction with this thing you call love," Uri persisted. "As they grow up, they come to find there's no such thing. One day they wake up and realise they made a big mistake… bang! Divorce, drama, pain, misery! Not me!"

"Now that you put it like that…" John stepped closer. "Maybe that's what happened to me."

Aris lowered his arm. "Selfish, spoiled, arrogant men like you simply can't understand. Family is more important than self-interests or superficial pleasures."

"I'm not selfish!" Uri hollered. "Just realistic."

Aris smirked. "Do your parents have a strong marriage?"

Uri's chest puffed up. "My mother knows her place is at home. She understands that my father has sexual adventures with other women. They don't live under an illusion of perfect love or any of that monogamy crap."

Aris was reluctant to let go of the topic. "Yet they stay together, despite your father's womanising. Why?" His question hung in the air. "Obviously they believe in the power of family. Your mother is the strong one."

Aris stuck the key in the ignition while John, Uri, and Jim quickly climbed in.

At the first motel along the roadside, Aris parked the car. "Dinner and straight to bed. Early start at sunrise tomorrow. We have a long drive ahead of us!"

Uri threw up his hands. "Guys, final analysis here. Either you're realistic about man's animal nature, or you're living a lie."

Aris's head drooped. "How do idiots like you find the most loving persons… like Epi?"

28 Pet the Antagonists

"Granddad," Varo called out as she and Victor entered the mansion just before sunset. It had been two full days since the bout in the ring, yet her ribs still ached. Clever concealer hid the scars to her face. "Look what Victor has for you!"

An old man with a head of dense white hair rolled into the foyer in an electric wheelchair. Even at home, he dressed like an executive—striped shirt and tie. His wide face looked expectant.

Victor handed over a small square box.

The older man sniffed the container, nodding appreciatively before opening it. When the lid was removed, he inhaled again, more deeply. "Coconut with cinnamon! My favourite Italian delight. You devils know how to excite me!"

Victor and Varo appeared relieved. "Anything for you, Granddad."

"But these delights don't come without the other part of the memory. It was when I took Grandma to the musical that we first discovered this treat."

Varo planted a kiss on the old man's forehead. "How about some music then?" She turned to Victor and pointed to the white grand piano. "Doubles?"

Victor immediately took a seat at the bench. "Let's see if you can keep up with me!"

A look of delight filled Granddad's face. He wheeled himself and the box of coconut-cinnamon pastries to the side of the piano.

The two dove straight into fast, happy music. The old man danced with his shoulders and hands, following the rhythm.

The second song found all three singing along. When it ended, he applauded. "Hard to say which of you is the better piano player."

"Victor's a good teacher…" Varo let the phrase trail off.

"But in piano…" Victor filled in what Varo was too polite to say, "…the teacher has long been surpassed by the student."

"And soon," Varo lit into another of her grandfather's favourite tunes, "I will also surpass my master's martial arts skills. Age is catching up with him!"

✦◇✦

By midday, the entourage stopped at a highway bar and parked alongside a couple of tractor trailers and a large SUV covered in some sort of glossy signage.

They walked inside and Aris noted a few truck drivers congregating, a couple snuggled up in the far corner, and a company of five well-built men of various ages, two with shaved heads and one with a ponytail.

Jim Darrant was staring at the youngest of the group who appeared to be mid-twenties with a reddish face.

The skinhead pushed back from the table and towered above Jim. "What're you looking at, asshole?"

Jim scanned the room, sensing he had become the centre of attention. "You think I'm afraid of you?"

The young man smiled. His reply came in the form of a surprise punch that sent Jim flying backwards.

John shrank back, peeking out around Aris's shoulder.

The rest of the customers went silent, ready to watch the spectacle without getting involved.

Jim threw the next punch, but it only made his adversary laugh louder. The guy's friends started cheering as he almost playfully tossed Jim around the bar.

Aris took in the scene but made no move to assist.

With the next punch, Jim landed on the floor in front of Aris's feet. Aris gave in and reached down to pull his cousin's husband up.

Closing in, the bullish young man threw yet another punch, but this time Jim ducked.

With lightning reflexes, Aris's palm shot forwards, stopping the punch and tightening around the other man's fist. "Time out, guys."

Shaken, Jim lifted to his feet. The group of friends stopped laughing, now waiting like everyone else to see what would happen next.

Aris felt John's knees quaking behind him. When everything remained still, Aris released his grip. After just a second, the red-faced guy reared back for another punch. Again, Aris stopped him. "You had your fun, young man. He learned his lesson. So let him buy us all a drink."

The angry guy's expression morphed to bulldog fury. His friends pushed back from the table. This time the younger man took aim at Aris.

One of the friends, apparently the leader, caught him from behind and pulled him back. "Drinks on this douche bag? Sign us up!"

Aris released his breath and nodded.

The young man started to relax then pushed back from his friends. "Yeah, free drinks sounds good to me too."

Aris called to the girl tending bar, "Drinks on him!" and pointed to Jim.

She set out a series of glasses on a silver tray and started to pour. The shaved heads and ponytailed guy wasted no time lining up at the bar.

Recovering his senses, Jim put a hand on Aris's lapel. "Let me get this straight. So instead of helping out, you threw me under the bus?" He took in Aris's stern gaze. "What if I don't pay?"

To everyone's amazement, Aris smiled coolly. "The young bull will be unleashed!"

The guy who had stopped the last punch gave Aris a fist bump. "Good move. I'm Paul."

Aris introduced himself then pointed to the rest of his gang. "This is John and Uri... and the *douche bag* is Jim."

Paul gave reciprocal introductions, ending with, "And the *young bull* is David."

Aris picked up a glass from the bar and raised it in toast. "I'm glad drinks saved the day. So are you guys football players or something? You're all enormous."

Paul snorted. "Seriously? That's an insult. Don't you recognise us?"

John shrank back further, his voice even higher than usual. "I'm not really into body building."

"Don't you watch TV?" the bartender asked, holding up a glass just for him. "They're champion wrestlers. Well, except for David."

Uri let out a burp. Then another and another in a chain.

"That explains it." John accepted the glass. "I didn't recognise you with your clothes on."

"Is that your enormous SUV parked outside?" Uri asked and sidled up to the wrestlers, facing off against Jim. "You certainly picked the wrong guys to start a fight with."

Jim's lips drew into a thin line. "I could've had him. I was letting him get tired!"

A round of laughter accompanied another round of drinks. David flexed his muscles for Jim's benefit.

"Come on then." Jim clearly couldn't let it go. "Let's head outside, just the two of us!"

The young bull looked to Paul for approval.

Paul glanced at Aris then shook his head.

David's nostrils flared, but he made no move to defy the leader.

"You see?" Jim tapped Uri on the shoulder. "He is afraid."

Paul's hand slid to the silver tray in front of him.

Aris placed his own hand on top, discreetly removing the last glass then grasping the empty tray. "Allow me!"

Paul gave a knowing smile.

Jim didn't see it coming. Aris landed a hard hit on top of his head and he crumpled to the floor unconscious.

John instantly shifted to hide behind Uri instead.

The other wrestlers laughed and slapped Aris on the shoulder.

Afterwards, Aris turned to Uri and John. "Lay him on the bench over there. It's time we parted ways."

Uri let out a short chain of burps, but didn't dare question the command. He yanked once on John's sleeve, then the two carried Jim and laid him out as directed.

The bartender took her tray back and set her sight on Aris. "Unusual choice to do that to your friend."

"He's not my friend!" Aris knocked back the last of his drink and reached into his pocket for the car keys. "He's a dead weight!"

She polished the tray with a rag, but kept her gaze levelled on him. "I overheard you saying you were traveling without plans. I always wanted to do that… just hit the road. How about you take me with you? I can throw a punch or two."

Uri came back just in time to catch the gist of her request. "Perfect replacement for the idiot!"

"No women." Aris was insistent. "It's bad luck to have one woman amongst many men."

Uri's face filled with disappointment.

Paul stepped in and held out a hand to Aris. "Time for us to go."

Aris placed the keys in his pocket and accepted the handshake.

"Where are you heading?" John managed to ask.

"To a tournament. Another 200 miles away."

Aris's eyes lit up. "Which direction?"

"South."

"We're heading south too," Uri chimed in. "But nowhere specific."

Aris took the bait. "I don't suppose you have room for three more in that big SUV out there? Maybe you could give us a ride to the nearest car rental office."

Paul pointed to Jim, still unconscious on the bench. "What about the douche bag?"

"He lasted longer than I thought he would."

Paul turned to the rest of his team. "Guys, any objection to some company on the road?" When no one replied, he shook Aris's hand again. "Seems you have a ride."

Aris pulled the car keys out from his pocket and handed them to John. "Get our bags. We're parting ways here."

Uri went with him then they both returned holding the backpacks.

Aris grasped the keys then handed them to the bartender. "When the douche bag wakes up, don't give him his car keys until after he pays."

She still seemed miffed to not be allowed to join them.

"You can tell him we joined the wrestlers… but that we're heading *west*. Knowing him, he won't believe you and he will go east!"

Inside the giant eight-seater, Uri stretched his legs. "Aris, it's not nice to just leave Jim like that. He was one of us."

John flinched.

"First off," Aris pointed, "Jim was unwelcome company. And second, he picked a fight, thinking we'd automatically back him. I refuse to get pulled into a fight because of that idiot." Uri cleared his throat, ready to launch further into Jim's defence but Aris didn't give him the chance. "And third… watch out. You're next in line!"

David laughed. "All you have to do is slide open that door. I'll gladly do the rest."

The other wrestlers burst out laughing while Uri secured his seatbelt and let out a chain of burps.

— ◇ —

Inside a nearby vehicle, a woman poked the person asleep on the passenger seat. "They're on the move."

Half awake, he looked out through the window. "But the red car's still there."

She pointed to the monitoring screen. "Look! One of the backpacks is moving. Not fast, but it is moving. Quick, go find out."

He wiped the sleep from his eyes then headed inside. Catching sight of Jim, flat out on the bench, he headed to the bartender. "What happened to this guy's friends?"

"They dropped him for a better ride. What can I get ya?"

Shaking his head, the man turned and raced out. Reaching the red car, he bent and scooped his hand back and forth in the dirt below the trunk. In seconds he jerked up holding a tiny square device.

He climbed back in beside the woman and slapped the dashboard. "Go! Follow that other beacon. They've swapped rides."

29 Love Secret Clue 1

A few miles before town two days later, Aris parked outside a road motel. Room keys in hand, he said, "You guys eat here. I'm going into town after a shower."

"I want to eat in town too," Uri protested.

"I will be eating at a distant cousin's restaurant. And you need to sleep."

With hair still wet from his shower, Aris climbed into the car by himself. At the sound of the engine, Uri and John jumped in the back seat.

Aris stared silently into the rear-view mirror.

"We fancy eating Greek food as well," John explained.

"I didn't say it was a Greek restaurant."

"Whatever," Uri chuckled. "If your Greek cousin owns the place, it will be better than motel food."

There was still plenty of good daylight when Aris pulled the car to a stop outside a house.

"This isn't a restaurant!" Uri gawked out the window.

"Stay in the car," Aris instructed. "I will just say a quick hello to my aunty."

At the door a lady greeted Aris while Uri and John watched from open car windows. As soon as Aris crossed the threshold, the lady motioned for Uri and John to join them.

Inside, they caught Aris whispering to a girl in her late twenties who held a young baby in her arms. "I know why you want to see my grandmother," she said. "Like many others, you are too late. She died and she took the secret to her grave."

Uri looked to John, who just shrugged.

"She could not share it with her daughter or me," the girl said aloofly, "because there is no such stupid love secret."

A loud bang caused the girl to startle. A shirtless man with bulging muscles and hairless chest stormed in. His bare arms were covered in tattoo sleeves featuring angels and hearts. Quickly the girl handed the baby to her mother who wasted no time heading for one of the bedrooms.

"What's this?" he shouted. "Now you bring men into our house."

"My house!" the girl barked in reply.

Thwack! He slapped the girl and grabbed her by the hair.

The girl's mother stepped out of the bedroom, no longer holding the baby, but instead double-fisting a hand gun.

Using the back of his hand, Aris struck hard directly at the tattooed guy's Adam's apple.

The man released his grip on the girl's hair and clasped his hands to his throat, gasping.

"Watch out!" the girl screamed. "He knows Kung-Fu."

Red faced, now regaining his composure, the tattooed man stepped into a martial arts posture.

The girl's mother kept her gun raised, but clearly relaxed when she saw Aris reach for one of the dining room chairs and begin to swing it in attack.

The wooden chair smashed against the bully's torso and Aris was left holding a long stick in each hand. "Oh yeah?" he said. "I know Greek-Fu," and without pause, he struck out at the other man's hands, thighs and head.

The tattooed man retreated several paces, snot beginning to drip from his nose. "S-stop it, man!" he said with a slight lisp.

Aris turned to the girl. "Don't you see? He's just a fairy in disguise trying to look like a tough guy."

Pushing the man to the front door, Aris motioned to the girl to kick him in the rear, which she happily did, then dusted off both hands like she was brushing away an annoying fleck of dirt.

With hands protecting his behind, the man escaped down the sidewalk before turning back to ask, "Who are you?"

Aris replied, "A friend. That's all you need to know."

But the girl pushed past him and yelled, "He is the brother I told you about. The one from the mercenaries' army. Come near me again and he will kill you."

Aris smiled his approval. "In fact, I plan to circulate your photo around town. If me or my friends see you anywhere at all, you will be buried alive."

The tattooed man fumbled with his car keys then climbed into his vehicle. The tires screeched as he sped away.

The girl slammed the door and turned to see John with his red face and Uri burping nonstop.

In a thin tone John asked, "How did you…?"

"How did you know he's gay?" The girl finished the question still hanging in the air. "But he fathered my baby."

Aris helped the girl's mother who was cleaning up the shattered chair. "Angel and heart tattoos? Not to mention the wax job on that one? Definitely a Volkswagen."

"What do you mean?" the girl asked.

Uri and John stepped in closer.

"You know," Aris replied. "A Volkswagen… the engine is *in the rear.*"

Uri shook his head. "Porsches also have engines at the rear."

Aris turned to him and said, "And Porsche is owned by…"

"Volkswagen!" John responded, practically bouncing on his toes like he'd just won on a gameshow.

Aris and the girl's mother deposited the wood fragments in the kitchen trash. "How long ago did your mother die?" he asked her.

"Not long," was the reply. "She was over one hundred."

Aris remained silent but attentive.

The lady pointed to her daughter. "Cali told you the truth."

Intervening the girl said, "I told you she didn't tell anyone the secret. Obviously, because there is no such thing as a love secret. It is stupid. How can there be something which can make anyone fall in love with you?"

"Even if there was," the mother said, "and my mother knew about it, she wouldn't have been able to tell us. She was not in her right mind. Just repeating some ancient Greek words and calling for her sisters all the time."

Aris took a tight step closer to the mother. "Like what ancient words?"

"Words we could not understand."

"Like?" Aris pushed.

The lady recited a sentence in Greek as if by rote.

Aris pulled out his notebook and scribbled down a rough translation. *Ploughed streams distil to Earth.* He levelled his gaze back on the older lady, ready for her to continue.

She continued her recitation in a sing-song voice.

Aris copied down *I crossed two banks sitting in the mouth of the bay. Two nymphs are the owners of Aphrodite's secret.*

Then the lady crossed her arms over her chest.

Aris's pencil paused and he gazed up at her.

"Most likely it's just a poem Grandmother memorised," volunteered the daughter. "But I remember how it ends." Then in a stilted voice, she finished the Greek.

Aris wrote swiftly. *Two nymphs in paradise... the sides of the small bank is paradise'."*

"It doesn't even make sense," the older woman said. "It seems to be mix of two or three languages."

Aris pocketed the notepad. "How many sisters did your mother have?" he asked.

"Six. Four were brought to America by their uncle. But one died a week or so after arriving. Two others too young to travel were left at home to care for their parents."

"So six sisters. Where are the other two who made it to America?"

The mother gave a quick glance to her daughter. "Probably dead by now."

Aris's gaze fixed on the girl. "Do you remember anything else your grandmother used to say?"

He could see Cali's jaw grinding before she replied with two more lines of a foreign-sounding poem. "In paradise... two nymphs... owner... *Rose* and *Liki...Lampi tou Omirou ee als.* Shiny is Homer's sea." Then there was a short pause before she added, "I don't remember any more. Grandmother knew both modern and ancient Greek as well as Spanish and Italian."

Aris remained silent for a few seconds, then asked, "What was her name?"

"Cali. I'm named after her."

"Her full name?"

"Calliope," the mother said.

"And the other two sisters?" he asked her.

"Their names were Droso and Garoufalia."

"Garoufalia is a rare name," Aris observed. "But I've heard it once before. Droso is a new name to me. Who were the two sisters left back in Greece?"

The older woman looked down at the floor. "Mother resented them for crying too much. She never talked about them."

The daughter shrugged. "Aphrodite was the one who died upon arriving in the USA."

Aris nodded and reached out a hand to the girl. "Are you okay here? Do you need anything?"

A sad smile graced her face. "We're okay now... now that he's gone." Her blank stare trailed to the front door.

"How about money?" Aris prompted.

The mother chuckled. "You must be a good man. I am sorry we cannot help you."

Aris reached for his notepad again, this time writing his telephone number on a sheet and handing it to the girl. "If you need anything, call me."

Then he turned to the mother. "And if you remember the names of the other two sisters... or really anything about the village... please, I would like to know."

The girl motioned for Aris to give her his notebook. She wrote down their number for him. "You already know our address, but if you manage to find any living relatives, I would like to know. Especially anyone from Granny's village."

Leading the way out of the house, Aris called to John and Uri, "Come on, boys."

The daughter followed them to the car, carrying an embroidered cloth she pulled from the coffee table. At the driver's side, she pushed the embroidery into Aris's hand. "Granny lived in Mexico for a time. She was many things— even violent to strangers after she was tortured. But she was not crazy. Anyone would have broken under the torture she endured."

"Torture?" Aris balked.

"Twice," Cali nodded. "The police dismissed the case, saying she'd hurt herself, but she would never do that. And I swear to you she never revealed anything about a love secret to us. Probably because she did not know it herself. If you go looking for such a thing, my advice is that you don't let it be known what you are searching for. Many nasty ones will come after you."

Aris fixed his eyes on hers. I feel your hesitation. Your mother cannot hear you now. Why not tell me what your grandmother revealed to you?"

Squeezing her lips together, Cali glanced to where her mother stood at the door. After almost a full minute, she leaned close to Aris and whispered, "I don't know why I trust you. But Granny already died so maybe I should tell you what I know."

Aris took out his notebook and pen and focused on Cali's every word.

"I don't know if it's true, but Granny told me only the two sisters in the village knew the whole secret. The rest knew only a small clue. She said her clue was that you must be near the other person for the love secret to work. That's all Granny revealed to me."

Cali stepped back from the window and watched as Aris gently folded the embroidered cloth and tucked it into an inside jacket pocket along with his notebook. Aris nodded a silent thank you before pulling away from the curb.

The three men remained silent until Aris parked outside a restaurant. Uri looked up from the passenger seat. "This is Italian, not Greek."

"It is a restaurant," Aris grunted.

"So…" John began hesitantly. "I take it you didn't want us to know you are searching for some love secret."

"You even lied to us," Uri accused. "That woman wasn't your aunt. And I'm guessing this isn't your cousin's restaurant." Then Uri laughed.

"I thought you were a clever man, Aris. Even I know there's no such thing as a stupid love secret. This is the twenty-first century. Wake up, man!"

Without responding, Aris stepped out of the car. "I'm having Italian for dinner. If you want Greek food, go look for a Greek restaurant."

The guys followed him inside. After they were seated and placed their order, Uri leaned across the table. "Show us what she gave you."

"Nothing." Aris held up an empty hand.

"We heard her," Uri urged. "Are we going to Mexico? Why not Miami? There's plenty of Cuban Latinas." He turned and winked at John, nudging the other with an elbow.

"You two can go to Miami and your Latinas," Aris said. "I'm headed to Mexico."

"Me, too," John chimed in as the drinks arrived.

30 New World...
Princes & the King

The next morning, Aris tossed the car keys to John and took the back seat all for himself. "I'll call the rental company and re-arrange drop-off at the Mexican border the day after tomorrow."

Hours later John pulled the car in at a hotel. Uri stretched in the front passenger's seat. "We've been driving for over ten hours. Let's check the girls here and see how mobile they are."

"What are you talking about?" John asked.

"We're in Mobile, Alabama." Uri winked at him. "Get it?"

Aris rolled up from where he had been laying in the rear seat and stretched. "They pronounce it *Mo-beel,* you dolt," he said. "Anyway, I had my nap. I can drive the next couple of hundred miles."

Uri puffed out his chest. "Come on, Aris. Let's see places... have some fun... check the girls. Mexico is not going anywhere."

John looked sheepishly at Aris in the rear-view mirror. "You always say we must be well rested when driving."

Exasperated Uri, shouted, "Your stupid love secret is not going to go away either. Anyway, there is no such thing."

* ◊ *

After a restful evening of Southern hospitality, Aris woke the boys at sunrise. John and Uri were still yawning when they got to the car, and Aris surmised they had not gotten to bed nearly as early as him.

Aris headed for the driver's seat. "But it's my turn," Uri protested.

"I will take the first shift," Aris insisted. "You're not even awake yet."

They drove along the Gulf Coast, through Biloxi, skirting New Orleans, and passing through Baton Rouge—more towns that Uri mispronounced along the way. Aris pulled the car in at a run-down motel outside of Laredo, Texas. "Wake up, guys. Time to stop for the night."

After pulling their bags out of the trunk, Uri checked his watch. "Man, it's past midnight! I thought we were going to stop in Houston for dinner."

"You're not supposed to drive so many hours without stop," John whined.

Uri hiked his pack up on his back. "Are we in Mexico?" he asked, noting the number of billboards in Spanish.

"Calm down, both of you," Aris soothed. "You were asleep anyway. What's the harm? We're just a few miles before the border."

"What about the adventure, the fun you promised us?"

Aris chuckled. "That must've been Gina's empty words. I promised you nothing!"

By mid-morning the next day, they had returned the rental car and climbed on a rickety old bus headed south. Aris spread himself out across the wide rear seat, resting his head against his backpack. John and Uri each took up seats in different rows.

At the buzz of his cell phone, Aris checked caller ID before putting it on speaker. "Melany! Did you find your prince?"

"Lots of eager young men," she sighed. "Mostly empty heads… top and bottom."

Aris chuckled. "Give them a chance. Give yourself a chance. You'll learn to be more select—"

"I did," Melany interrupted. "None of them can even hold a conversation apart from football and beer. In bed, they're done before I even begin. I have to go to the bathroom to finish myself!"

Uri's eyes went wide and John tried to pretend he hadn't overheard.

Aris smiled. "At least you don't have to wait for them to warm up."

"Oh, that's what I enjoy most."

He heard the conviction in her voice and decided to change the subject. "And your exams?"

"Doing great. I have three subjects left to finish over the next twelve months."

"I never doubted you! Now get back to exploring for your prince. Don't chase them away before the fox even catches the scent. When you find the right one, he'll have staying power."

"I'm losing hope," Melany groaned. "Now I see why girls turn lesbian!"

"Nonsense. But if that's what it takes along the way to searching for your prince, why not? At least girls know how to take their time."

"You're awful!" Melany cackled. "First you push me to find another man, now you're telling me to sleep with women! What about you? Are you going to sleep with men until you find that special person?"

"Too late for me," Aris laughed.

"Are you involved with another girl?"

"You were the exception, my dear. Now I'm taking time out to travel and clear my head."

"Alone? I should join you. You know… look after you!"

"I've already been loaded with two mules who don't know what they are in for."

"You mean two *bodyguards*," John shouted.

"Chasing the dream of perfect love, no doubt. You're blind to what's right in front of you."

"I'm not sure anymore that there's such a thing as perfect love. But if I do discover the love secret, I'll make a dozen girls fall in love with me."

"There's no such thing as a love secret," Melany huffed. "Your dream is here, waiting for you. You're just running away.

At some stage, you'll have to stop and face reality. You're still my king."

Aris couldn't help wondering why no one could believe in his quest. "Kings are old and past their expiration dates. What you need is a young prince."

She went quiet for a moment. "Can I call you, now that you're travelling?"

Aris didn't hesitate. "Anytime. If I don't answer, I'll call you back."

"Can I say I love you?"

He heard the not so subtle challenge in her tone. "No, but I can. I do love you! Take care, and don't forget to have fun in between books and work." He ended the call and looked up to see Uri and John both ogling him.

"*I do love you…*" John mimicked. "That wasn't Gina's voice on the other end."

"Ha," Aris scoffed. "The word *love* does not exist in her vocabulary."

"So who's the girl?" Uri prodded.

"Just a friend, someone I mentor!" Aris brushed him off.

"Mentor, my ass. Whoever that girl was is taken with you."

"I guide her; I do not mislead her."

Uri turned to fully face Aris. "If you're talking to her about some perfect, true love nonsense, you're most definitely misleading her. There's nothing more to it than a man and woman's passionate sexual urges."

Aris met Uri's gaze. "What about all those millions of people around the world who are in love, irrespective of age, race, colour, religion or culture, willing to kill and die for each other?"

John leaned in to hear Uri's reply.

"Illusions!" Uri spat. "A man needs a woman for sex on demand, and to raise his children. A woman needs a man to provide for her, and a secure dick. It's an exchange."

Aris shook his head. "Erotic love is always short lived. True love is something else entirely."

"Beyond sex, a wife is just to make children, and to cook and clean up. In between, you have other women for crazy sex."

John cleared his throat. "I um, I sort of agree with Uri. But can't there be a friendship love, somewhere between the two, like I have with Leoni? We both fell for abusive partners before. Not even love at all."

Aris stretched then folded one leg atop the other. "Just because you both chose the wrong partners the first time, it doesn't mean there's no such thing as true love."

"I disagree. Leoni and I are friends first. We never argue. No jealousy, no demands, no arguments." John's eyes dropped to the seat beside him. "But for sex, I agree with Uri. Romantic love is just a false pretence."

"That's what most guys say until they experience the real thing." Aris placed both arms behind his head, interlocking his fingers. "When you love the whole person—their character and mind—looks don't matter anymore. That smile, that warmth, that spark is still there. You still want to kiss… and be kissed."

"You're living in a dreamland, Aris. You don't have to be in love to sleep with a woman. Welcome to the new world." Uri reached over the seat to poke Aris's thigh. "We make love for joy, not just to have children."

Aris stretched, clenching and unclenching his fists. "I do like to dream. But you're the one living an illusion. I want to like the person behind the looks. Otherwise, it's just like two empty bodies masturbating each other."

Uri's laughter erupted. "If I was a dreamer like you, I'd still be a virgin."

Aris took a sip of water from his bottle. "I think there are some people who truly cannot love. Or at least they have no capacity to love anyone besides themselves… selfish bitches and bastards… like you."

Uri pounded his chest like Tarzan. "At least those bastards know how to enjoy themselves!"

— ◇ —

Peter and Gerry arrived at their family home to find their sister Liza straddling a boy on the couch, while a different girl was kissing another boy across the room.

Gerry cupped his hands and made two thunderous claps. "Time to go, boys."

The young men startled, but so did the other girl. Peter held the door and allowed them to leave before he turned to accuse his sister. "What is this, Liza?"

She straightened her top self-righteously. "Mum gave me permission."

"And where is dear old mum?" Peter asked.

"Out!"

Just then the door popped open and Gina came toppling in, visibly intoxicated. She opened her arms to hug first Peter then Gerry. "My good boys looking after their sister…"

"Someone has to." Gerry's voice was cold.

Gina waved dismissively. "Liza can look after herself."

"Mum, we found her kissing a boy on the couch!" Peter said, planning to shield Liza from worse embarrassment.

"It's okay. I gave her permission to bring her boyfriend home."

"We found them practically on top of each other," Gerry blurted. "Luckily still dressed."

Gina just shrugged. "That's how teenagers learn. I never had that chance. They locked me in a nun's school, then got me married, not far from her age. I knew nothing. I knew no other man. She has to experiment to learn."

"She's too young, Mum," Peter looked back and forth from Liza to Gina. "Father would not approve."

"Tell that to the man who abandoned his daughter and all of us!"

Gerry took his mother by the arm. "Dad didn't abandoned Liza. He was running away from you."

Crocodile tears sprang to her eyes. "You always take his side. You never understand me."

"Don't play 'poor me' on us." Gerry tightened his grip. "We've seen this charade a thousand times before."

Gina's eyes lit with fire and she yanked out of her son's grip. "You're a male chauvinist just like your father. You made my head spin. I'm going for a shower."

"It's the drinking that made your head spin, not us, Mum."

Peter stepped next to his brother. "Anyway, we're only here because you invited us for dinner. What are we having?" He looked sceptically into the kitchen.

Indifferent, Gina headed for the stairs. "Did I? Well, order something for delivery. I'm starving!"

Gerry tapped Peter on the shoulder and motioned to the door. "Come on. I'm not staying for this."

Gina's tone sweetened. "No reason to go, my loves. Give me five minutes to take a shower and some aspirin. Then I'll cook whatever you want."

Gerry pointed a sharp finger at her. "I'm warning you. If you don't pull yourself together, I'm going to take Liza home and look after her myself. I promised Dad I'd keep an eye on her."

Gina stomped down the stairs and pointed her own finger into Gerry's chest. "You will do no such thing. Liza wouldn't want to go with you anyway."

"Oh yes, I would!" Liza shouted. "I can be packed in five minutes."

"Enough. Go to your bedroom, ungrateful little lady." Liza's shoulders collapsed. Then Gina spun to her sons. "You can't tell me how to raise my daughter. Nobody tells me what to do!"

This time it was Peter who prompted Gerry to leave.

Sudden understanding dawned on Gina. She chased behind them. "Don't go, my loves. My head is not right today. Stay. I've missed you."

Peter opened the door and kept walking, but Gerry turned back for one last parting shot. "Goodbye, Mum. We'll be back when you're sober."

"This is all your father's fault!" Gina shouted. "He never taught you to respect your mother!"

31 Good Mood

The three amigos disembarked at high noon in the centre of a small Mexican town. John spotted the local hotel and they all checked in for separate rooms.

Aris smiled at the receptionist then pocketed his key and turned to his companions. "Do not disturb me. I'm crashing for a long overdue sleep. A month on the road with you bozos has worn me out."

"I think we'll sleep even longer than you," John replied.

After a refreshing three-hour siesta, Aris changed clothes and headed to the hotel lobby where he found Uri and John waiting, both clean, fresh, and apparently re-energised.

"I'm starving," Aris announced.

John's face lit up. "What about a pre-dinner drink?"

Aris looked to Uri, who shrugged indifferently, so he turned towards the front desk. "I can ask the receptionist to recommend a good restaurant."

John whipped a paper out of his back pocket. "I already asked. I even walked round and checked out the restaurant and found a good bar not far away."

On their way, Aris noticed an obvious working girl dressed in a flashy red fitted dress that left her shoulders bared sauntering toward them. Unseen by his companions, Aris raised his arm behind them and pointed to John's head.

The girl sidled up to John and threaded her hand around his arm. "Ready for business, Mr. Bang-Bang. French, Greek, open to all."

As soon as John figured out what she was insinuating, he pushed her away. "No, no!"

She placed both hands on her hips and pouted as both John and Uri continued walking.

Slowing, Aris took out some cash and waved it to her, then grabbed his crotch and pointed to John again.

Her heels clicked on the pavement as she scurried to catch up. "Sexy, sexy mister…" When John turned she made no bones about fondling his crotch right there on the busy street.

Embarrassed, John's girly voice cried, "No! I'm gay. I'm gay!"

Bursting into laughter, Aris handed the cash to her out of sight from his companions. She tucked it into her cleavage and took off in the opposite direction.

Aris caught up and levelled his gaze on John. "If I was to tell Leoni that in the middle of Main Street you started shouting, 'I'm gay,' I would not be lying, would I?"

"It's true," Uri seconded. "I witnessed it."

John's cheeks flushed. "It's not true. I just wanted to get rid of that… girl."

"I don't think your wife would like to hear that you let a hooker grab you by the balls."

John stopped in his tracks, all colour now draining from his face.

Aris and Uri kept walking. When John still didn't move, Uri turned back and called, "He's just joking. Come on!"

John blew out a long sigh then skipped to catch up. "Bastards!"

◆

Varo adjusted her blonde wig and skilfully applied bright red lipstick before stepping out of the chauffeur-driven SUV around the corner from the surveillance shop. She pushed through the storefront entrance then turned to lock the door behind her and flipped the window sign to *Closed*.

She saw two men at beat-up tables that passed for desks, stationed behind an unmanned receiving counter. Clearly a janitorial staff was not in the budget either. She wondered where all the money went inside these necessary but somewhat reprehensible surveillance companies she had been forced to use lately.

"We talked on the phone." Varo dropped a box and a stack of cash on the empty counter. "Here's your deposit. Fifty grand in unmarked bills."

The larger of the two men stood. "You still haven't explained the whole job."

"I will send you a location forty-eight hours before the fight. You will install multiple nano cameras along the ceiling so we can record every view of the ring."

"Why do you want the cameras overhead? That's more complicated," the second man interjected.

"The fight takes place in a cage which blocks the side view at waist height. I need to see everything this mystery killer does. He hides his moves."

The same man picked up the cash and riffled through the stack. "Okay, but the balance is due on delivery. And payment comes only to me by hand."

Varo was nonplussed. "In the box you'll find CIA-grade nano cameras no scanning machine will detect. If you're caught, this man and his lackeys will kill you. It's imperative that you're discreet."

"And what if we refuse?" asked the shorter partner.

Varo shifted her gaze to him and tucked a blonde curl behind one ear. "My boss will then have to inform the killer that you recorded his fight. He will first torture you, then most assuredly kill you. Most likely he will kill your families too." She swung her hips as she turned and headed to the door, waving behind her. "Ciao, boys!"

⸻ ◆ ⸻

Aris was surprised by the clean, bright space inside the cantina. Even the music was soft enough to allow easy conversation. He and John and Uri found seats at the bar and placed their orders.

A well-dressed Mexican took one look at the beverage in front of John and said, "What're you looking at, you American fairy?"

John spun around to face the tall man. "I'm s-sorry?" His voice cracked into a high pitch. "I wasn't looking…"

The Mexican shoved John so hard he bounced off the counter, putting Aris between the two of them.

Aris watched the scene unfolding in the mirror above the bar. With two heavy steps, the Mexican closed in on John while Uri began letting out a series of burps. Aris held up a hand in front of the tall man.

"I have no quarrel with you. It's the fairy I'm after. I heard him shouting in the street that he was gay!"

Uri released a gigantic burp then stifled a giggle.

A small group of locals at a nearby table burst out laughing. They were the only other patrons in the establishment.

Casually Aris remained on the barstool. "You're wasting your time on this one. My friend doesn't fight. He's a lover boy."

"Old man," the Mexican towered above Aris. "Move aside. Go take a seat with the geriatrics."

John puffed up his chest as if trying to appear more manly. "Listen, Mr. Mexican. We came to enjoy your lovely country. Come have a drink with us." He glanced from Uri to Aris and then back to his would-be opponent. "We'll buy."

The Mexican spat in John's face. "I don't drink with fairies!"

Aris rose and backhanded the man, causing him to take a sidestep, while John ducked behind.

The locals from the next table sprang to their feet. The Mexican grabbed Aris by the collar. "What did you just do, old man?"

Uri looked on, mesmerised. "It's their country, Aris. Don't fight. I'll pay for drinks tonight."

Without answering, Aris slapped the Mexican on the other cheek.

The barmaid made no pretence about stepping back from the scene and picking up the telephone.

The tall man clenched his fists and punched his own chest. "You did it again!"

Aris played it cool. "I see you are a man of principles. You will not hit an old man. You also wouldn't hit a fragile lover boy like my friend." Instead Aris pointed at Uri and added, "So if you have to punch someone, punch him."

"Why…" Uri let out a shocked burp, "…me?"

The locals gathered round them, squeezing in.

Aris smiled at Uri. "Because you're the one with the hard head and iron fist. If he punches you, he'll break his hand."

The Mexican looked back and forth between Aris and Uri, then squinted at John still hiding like a little girl. He flared his nostrils, aware that his friends were watching him.

"H-how did you do that?" John whispered to Aris.

"Just making friends," Aris declared.

The Mexican reared back. "I am not your friend."

"Oh, but you are," Aris replied. "You just don't know it yet." He reached for the taller man's shoulder with one hand and brought John out from behind him with the other. Surprisingly, the Mexican allowed Aris to position him as desired. Aris looked into John's eyes. "No fear, my old friend. Just slap him."

John's hands visibly shook. "I think I just pissed my pants."

Aris scowled. "Slap him hard, I said. Slap him now, or I'm going to let him loose on you!"

Some of the locals pulled cash out of their pockets like they were placing side bets.

John nervously bounced on his toes. In a moment of quick decision, he flailed out and landed a sharp slap against the Mexican's face. He pulled his hand back to shake out the sting then darted behind Aris once more.

As if released from a catatonic state, the Mexican threw a jab at Aris. Swiftly side-stepping, Aris pushed the man's arm away towards Uri and dealt a sharp kick to his stomach.

Uri looked up into the face of the now raging Mexican and burped. Without hesitating, the Mexican drew his fist back and punched Uri in the head.

This stopped Uri's chain burping, while the Mexican turned to shake out the pain. But the reprieve lasted only seconds. This time he threw another punch, but to Uri's stomach. "You may have an iron head, but you've got a weak belly."

The impact sent Uri folding to the floor, gasping in pain.

The Mexican spun on John, who squealed and ducked. Aris wasted no time and landed a forceful backhanded slap to the Mexican's throat.

The tall man let out a choking sound, holding his throat, while the locals around them began exchanging money.

Aris yanked John out from behind him and pointed him at the weakened opponent. "He's all yours. Hit him now!"

John hesitated.

"Punch him before he lifts up, or he'll smash your face."

With a loose fist, John cuffed the Mexican on the shoulder.

Like a bull facing down the matador, the Mexican snorted once and reared back with a punch that landed squarely on John's face.

John flew backwards like a feather, landing on a table.

The locals now swarmed Aris and Uri, ready to join the fight.

Aris raised one arm with an open palm and shouted. "Hold it!" He pointed to the closest of the locals and said, "If you can knock Uri down by punching his iron head, then all the drinks tonight are on us."

Uri quickly tucked his chin and pushed his forehead out to absorb the punch that came almost instantaneously.

Like the first Mexican, this man cradled his hand screaming out in pain.

Surprised, Uri tapped on his own head to see if he felt anything, while another Mexican levelled him with a punch to the stomach, forcing Aris to re-join the fight.

Letting loose, Aris toppled three Mexicans fast and furious to the floor, then landed a sidekick into the first Mexican's stomach. The blow pushed the man rear first toward John. Aris commanded, "Kick his ass, hard!"

John's right foot booted the man's bottom, sending the Mexican hopping up and down like a rooster with its throat cut.

Aris pushed him back into John, this time face to face. "Finish him," Aris directed.

Encouraged, John kicked again, aiming straight for the Mexican's crotch. As the taller man folded, much to his own surprise, John punched the Mexican hard in the face, sending him to the floor.

The one local left standing ran fast for a head bang against Aris. Again sidestepping, Aris's movement forced the Mexican's head straight into the bar counter. While he was reeling, Aris called, "Yours, iron head. Get him!"

Like a soccer player after a header, Uri landed a good head bang into the Mexican's chest, sending him flying backwards before he fell flat on his back.

Seconds later, a group of six policemen stormed into the bar, weapons drawn and pointed at Aris, John and Uri.

"He s-started it!" John protested, pointing at the Mexican who'd called him a fairy.

The head officer stepped forward. "If they started it, you can press charges."

Meanwhile, several of the locals climbed to their feet.

John and Uri looked to Aris for a lead, who smiled cordially. "Press charges? Against our friends? We were just playing around."

The officer's words dripped with irony. "If they're your friends, what do you do to your enemies?"

Aris extended his arm to help one of the other locals to his feet. "We have no enemies. We are all friends here."

The weakened man clenched his broken nose and in a nasal voice, began, "We're not—"

The first Mexican kicked his buddy lightly. "Of course, we are not friends."

The police officer eyed him up, as if waiting for the fight to continue.

"We are *brothers!* Our American brothers here just invited us for drinks on them." He pointed to the woman behind the bar. "Did you not hear them invite us?"

"*Si,* I heard this invitation," the barmaid confirmed.

"Well then," the officer set his sights on Aris. "You are friends. You are not friends. You are brothers. You are not brothers. Do you want to press charges? Yes or no?"

With conviction Aris bellowed, "Of course we are brothers! And we did invite them for drinks. We do this all the time!" He summoned the bartender. "Drinks for our brothers, please." Then he motioned to the policemen. "And drinks for our new friends, too!"

"Wise decision, Mr. American. This mule is my real blood brother." The officer returned his gun back to its holster and patted the first Mexican on the back. "If you had asked to press charges, those charges would have been pressed against you! But today you earned our respect. We can call you friends now. Let's drink!"

The first Mexican placed an arm around his brother, the officer. "Who's buying?"

"He is!" Aris said pointing to Uri.

"Why me?" Uri protested.

"To show our brothers that, contrary to popular belief, the Jewish are generous, not stingy!"

A round of laughter preceded the drinks which flowed swiftly. After a while, Aris made his way around the group bidding goodnight to their new friends so the three amigos could finally make their way to the restaurant.

Just before he reached the door, the busty barmaid called, "Mr. Aris!"

Uri and John watched as she slipped a small piece of paper into their leader's shirt pocket.

"You dropped your receipt!" She winked up at Aris coyly.

Aris pulled out the paper to see a phone number. Gently returning it to his pocket, he whispered, "I'm a married man."

She pushed her ample bosom forward and laughed. "Even better!"

Uri gave her a thumbs up. "Absolutely. Aris needs to be educated."

＊◇＊

John had trouble putting one foot straight in front of the other as they left the bar. "Aris, that girl was so nice to chase after you to give you the receipt."

"Lucky bastard," Uri laughed. "I pay, but Aris gets the receipt. Hopefully he won't waste the opportunity to thank that busty bar wench." He winked at Aris, then rubbed his scalp. "By the way, how did you know I had an iron head?"

"Everyone knows you're hard headed," Aris joked.

"Come on. Tell me the truth. How did you know? You never punched my head before."

Aris kept walking. "The important thing is that they believed it."

"But their hands hurt afterwards." Uri offered John a steadying shoulder to lean on.

"Exactly," Aris replied. "Because they believed it! Subconsciously, to avoid what they thought would be a painful impact, at the last second they took all the force out of the punch, resulting in them hurting themselves."

John reached up to pat his companion on the top of the head. "So does Uri have an iron head, or not?"

Aris just smiled. "All empty heads are iron heads!"

Uri ducked his head forwards. "Want to give it a try, John?"

He waved off Uri's suggestion. "What I don't understand is how Aris got away with slapping the Mexican. How did you know he wouldn't strike back?"

"Simple, I read his facial expression. He was just playing with us. This gave me the advantage of surprise. It's my formula of three—preparation, no fear, and follow-through. Although I do admit, we got lucky on the latter."

"I don't understand." John paused in the street. "You were not even ready for a fight."

Aris took him by the elbow and prodded him forwards. "Oh, I was ready. I knew there would be a fight. It was the Mexican and his buddies who weren't prepared for our response. When I slapped the ring leader while smiling, I instilled fear into them. Then the threat of Uri's iron head was the icing on the cake."

"Weren't you afraid?" John wondered.

"Let's just say I don't get scared in the face of danger."

John marvelled at their leader.

"But a few days later," Aris continued, "when I think back about what happened, I usually realise how stupid I was."

"I don't understand you either," Uri exclaimed.

Aris turned to John. "You were afraid to hit the Mexican at first. But after you received your first punch, you let him have it, in his weakest spot, sending him to the floor. You even got your voice back to normal! Did you notice that?"

John beamed. "I surprised myself with that!"

"Your survival instinct took over. You came out your true self."

"I've always been afraid of fights and bullies," John confessed.

"No," Aris pointed out. "You were just afraid of being embarrassed."

"Well… I'm still not sure," John hedged. "I get what you're saying, but… I do have to admit it. Afterwards, I felt good kicking his ass."

Uri polished a knuckle on his forehead. "I've never been in a fight before. Maybe that's why I didn't know I had an iron head."

Aris just smiled. "Let's keep it our little secret!"

❖

"Shall I see you tonight?" Aris whispered to the busty girl about to leave his hotel room the next morning.

"Absolutely!" She gave him a kiss on the lips. "You're good for business. Your friends the Mexican brothers will be there again too."

Aris squeezed her tush and smiled happily, then opened the door for her to leave before he got dressed.

In the breakfast room, Aris piled his plate full and joined John and Uri where they had already snagged a table.

"You're hungry this morning," Uri observed. "What happened?"

"Overworked my bottom last night." Aris rubbed his gut. "Stomach bug, you know."

"I had stomach problems last night too," John said. "We should go to a different restaurant tonight."

Uri gave John a light tap on the arm. "Let's see first if the general has decided whether we're staying or going."

John gazed up at Aris. "Well? Are we staying or going?"

Aris took a sip of the fresh-squeezed orange juice and thought about spending another night in the company of that barmaid. "No rush. This is a friendly town. Let's stay a few days or a week. Then we'll see."

Uri looked surprised. "I thought you wanted to find that love secret as soon as possible."

Aris stabbed a fork full of eggs and bacon. "But now we've made some good friends." He smiled at the thought. "We even have friends on the police force. That gives us protection. No rush."

※ ◇ ※

Waiting for the bartender's company, Aris laid out the embroidery given to him by Cali, granddaughter of one of the six sisters.

One end featured a small group of houses, streams, hills and a boat at the bottom. In the middle were Greek words. He sounded them out to himself, then translated it aloud. "Paradise, the *ktitor*."

Searching on his mobile phone, Aris whispered, "Ktitor? What does that mean?"

When he looked back to the fabric, he noticed the right side contained a design that resembled a map of the U.S. and Mexico. At about mid-Florida on the Gulf side, the shape of a woman with long hair had been embroidered, next to the letter K. Placing his finger on that spot, Aris whispered, "Tampa. Cali."

Running his finger down to the Mexico portion of embroidered map, he saw no similar mark, so he raised the fabric up to the light bulb. Seeing nothing but a deep brown blob, he flipped the cloth over and focused his sight. Turning it back to front, a soft smile filled Aris's face. "Just dirt. Probably a coffee stain."

Pulling out his toiletry bag, Aris grabbed a cotton swab and his travel shampoo. Gently he began to clean the area mapped as Mexico.

As the stain lightened, an image formed beneath it. "There you are… the second sister who came to America." Squinting, Aris declared, "So she has red hair? Is that even possible? But there is her initial. The Greek delta."

Aris placed the fabric next to an open paper map on the bed. Trying to match the location, Aris's hands shifted to the northwest corner of Mexico.

The door opened and Aris watched the lady from the bar saunter in and begin to unbutton her blouse. She sidled up next to Aris. "Will you rub my back in the shower?"

Sceptical Aris tried to remain focused on the map.

Not to be dissuaded, she touched her pointer finger to Aris's chin and drew his gaze. "*Helloo*, I am up here. What are you looking for on the map?"

Her smile was captivating so he gave the girl a quick kiss. "Hi, Antonia. Somewhere there is an old lady—probably with red hair—named Droso. I need to find her, but I do not have a clue as to how to start."

"Are you chasing a lover?" Antonia pouted.

"More like a grandmother."

"You're not exactly a teenager yourself. Are you sure she's even alive?"

"That I do not know. But I will find out. Tomorrow I will get a car and go on a search."

"I have a car," she volunteered. "I can drive you."

"I may need a few days there to find her."

"I can take the week off. My sister can fill in for me." Antonio rubbed her fingers skilfully along his crotch. "I like exploring… especially when I have good company."

Aris could no longer resist. "Then I will rub your back the next few nights."

"We will be sweating," she giggled. "We will need to shower night and day."

"Then I will rub your back after breakfast, lunch and dinner!" And with that he led the way to the bathroom.

———— ◇ ————

Next morning the receptionist passed a note to Uri when he and John reached the lobby for breakfast.

Reading the slip of paper, his expression turned sour. "That two-faced bastard dumped us here in the middle of nowhere. Didn't even have the guts to tell us to our faces."

Eager, John grabbed the note. "It says, 'I will be back in a few days.' That doesn't sound like we're being dumped."

Uri spun on him. "What constitutes a few days? Two? Five? Maybe a hundred?"

"But where did he go? And why didn't he want to take us with him?"

"Where else?" Uri mocked. "He's chasing clues about that stupid love secret."

The receptionist interrupted to say, "He didn't leave by himself. He was with the girl."

John's eyebrow arched. "What girl?"

Grabbing John by the arm, Uri pulled him away. "Never mind. You are still asleep. You obviously don't notice a thing."

"Aris," cooed the barmaid, "we have been searching for ten days now. Sunrise to near midnight. I have to get back."

Silently Aris ground his jaw, staring into Antonia's eyes.

"We searched every small village, spoke with all the mayors, asked at the police station, and even checked church records and talked with old people." She caressed his hair. "If there was a red-haired lady with such an unusual name like Droso, someone would have remembered her. You must know it's time to give up."

Aris nodded softly, feeling the truth in her statements. "I know. But there is still one small church about five miles from here. Let's check that first and then we can head back."

"Your friends will be cursing you, making them wait more than a week without so much as a message. They may have left."

"Not a concern. In fact, I'd be glad if they were gone."

"That's cruel," Antonia said. "They're your friends."

"Mere acquaintances… dead weights. I did not invite them."

Aris loaded their luggage into her car and Antonia drove them the few miles to a building that locals said was once a monastery.

Twenty minutes later, Aris resigned himself to the truth, but it didn't remove the sting from this latest failure. Standing by the door of the church, the priest politely waved goodbye as they drove off.

"Okay, we'll head back now. Then I will search further south on my own. Perhaps the lady who made my map was no good at geography."

Antonia's eyes flashed. "Maybe she misdirected you on purpose."

Pondering the possibility, Aris mumbled, "Probably wanted to protect her sisters."

"Protect them from what?" Antonia dropped the car into gear and pulled onto the dirt road. "Were they criminals?"

Absent-mindedly Aris whispered, "The love secret…"

With a jolt, Antonia slammed her foot on the brake. "What love secret? What are you hiding from me?"

Aris kept his expression neutral, realising his slip of the tongue. He sighed deeply to buy himself extra time before replying. "I mean… they love each other, so she would want to protect them. Let's head back now. I've kept you away too long."

◇

In the hotel lobby, Uri met up with John to head to breakfast. "It's been nearly two weeks now. Face it. Aris is not coming back. He's dumped us. We should move on."

John's shoulders slumped. "Only ten days. Besides, Aris would not have dumped us without saying so."

Uri smacked his friend on the arm with the back of his hand. "Oh yeah? Then why hasn't he sent even one text message? And why didn't he reply to any of our messages or calls?"

"Maybe he just wanted to relax for a couple of weeks by himself."

This time Uri's smack was less gentle. "He's not alone, you doofus. He's got that girl with him. But he's just using her. I bet Aris is looking for those sisters to find out about that goddamn love secret. He is possessed by that lunacy."

John pushed Uri away. He headed off briskly towards their favourite local restaurant, calling behind him, "It's not as if you aren't enjoying yourself! You already had three different girls. Why are you complaining? Besides, I know Aris will be back. Just be patient."

Uri scrambled to catch up. "If he's not back by tomorrow, we have to hit the road by ourselves."

John just shook his head.

◇

Antonia's driving had been erratic ever since Aris's accidental disclosure about the love secret. "Pull over," he demanded.

"Why? So you can leave me on the side of the road like you did your so-called friends back at the hotel?"

Aris grabbed the wheel and twisted it to the berm. Antonia's reflexes were too slow. The car slid off the gravel road and swooshed into the knee-high grass outside a farmhouse at the edge of a village. Finally she slammed on the brakes, but not before the right front tyre rolled over a pointy pitchfork laying forgotten in the field.

Aris could feel the puncture before he heard it. Thankfully the car had slowed and only swerved a few more feet to the right before coming to a halt. He hopped out into the tall grass to check the situation.

Down on all fours to inspect, he yelled to Antonia, "Put it in reverse. Just enough so I can get this pitchfork out."

When the tool was freed, though, the damage was obvious. "Open the boot," he called. "I'll grab the spare."

He rolled up his sleeves while Antonia popped the trunk. She leaned up against the side of the car to watch him work.

Aris grunted in the heat, but resolved himself that nothing more could be accomplished until the tyre was changed and he could get the barmaid back home. He pulled out the spare then rooted around for the jack. "Where's your tyre jack?" he demanded. "I don't see it anywhere."

Antonia's hands flew to her face. "Oh! My sister borrowed it last spring and never gave it back!"

Exasperated, Aris rolled his eyes and shook his head. He let his sight drift to the farmhouse up ahead at the end of a dirt driveway. "We will have to ask at the house for help. Come on."

Aris led the way, and brushed dirt from his pants and wiped the sweat from his brow before knocking.

A teenaged girl opened the door.

"We have a flat tyre," Aris explained. "Could we possibly borrow a jack?"

The girl tilted her head to the side. Antonia repeated his request in Spanish.

The girl replied something, then closed the door behind her.

"She says she'll ask her mother," Antonia supplied.

When the door re-opened they stood facing a woman who looked to be about fifty. Her complexion looked more Mediterranean than Mexican. "My daughter says you need help with your car." Her English was flawless, but had a familiar accent to Aris.

Focusing on the task at hand, he explained, "We need to borough a car jack."

She held out a hand. "Give me your keys. I will have my husband change the tyre. He has all the tools in our garage."

Antonia handed over the car keys at the same moment as a man approached wearing dusty overalls and wiping his forehead with a red bandana. The woman immediately passed him the keys and the man assessed Aris from head to toe before closing his palm around them.

"Maybe you two would like to sit inside and cool down with a drink while you wait," she said. But instead of motioning them inside her house, she pointed towards a building next door at the edge of the village. "We have an excellent cantina just there."

That seemed to please her husband, and he headed towards the barn to fetch some tools.

Antonia peered into the distance to see the proffered oasis, then with more strength than Aris expected, she practically dragged him the short distance to the bar.

When they reached the arch of the porch, Aris grunted. "I better go and help that woman's husband. It's not right to take advantage of strangers."

But Antonia wouldn't release his arm when he tried to pull away. Instead she used her opposite hand to smack him on the shoulder. Then she pointed up to the sign above the entrance.

Drosita's.

Aris's face lit and suddenly he was no longer tired.

An old woman's voice boomed from inside, "*Ela!*"

Aris recognized the Greek word for *come* and took two hesitant steps to the saloon-style swinging door. His heart began to pound.

The lady kept speaking. Aris translated easily in his mind, the language of his childhood flooding back to him. Her words beckoned, "Come in. I've been expecting you for years now."

Elated, he pushed open the door and found himself staring at an old woman with long, pure white hair. She stood surprisingly tall in front of the bar, though wrinkles lined her face and arms. Her nose was bloated with black and brown spots. With slow and ginger steps she moved to a nearby rocking chair and sat heavily. The floor beams creaked as she rocked forwards and backwards.

Because Aris was still holding the door open, a beam of sun hit her in the eyes. She reached into a pocket and retrieved a paper fan, waving it to cool her face.

Mesmerised, Aris stood with his gaze fixed on the old woman.

The lady from the farmhouse pushed Aris from behind, and he stumbled into the cantina. "This is my bar," she explained. "I'll fix you both a drink." She ushered Antonia to a table and pulled out a worn wooden chair. "Welcome to Drosita's."

Aris's stare turned from the old lady to the woman before him. Surprise morphed to shock. *Drosita? Little Drosa?*

Instead of joining Antonia at the table, Aris found himself stumbling over to the older woman who continued to fan herself.

"Don't mind yia-yia," Drosita continued as she pulled out clean glasses behind the bar. "She used to speak seven languages and often gets confused."

Still enthralled, Aris found it impossible to shift his gaze from the old lady.

The woman gave her fan one more hard wave, then held it out to her side and dropped it at Aris's feet.

Instantly he bent down to retrieve it. Folding the splayed fan, he placed it gently back into the older lady's hands. A ray of sunshine again struck her face as the cantina door swung open, and she raised the fan quickly to shield her eyes.

The girl who had answered the door at the farmhouse waltzed in. She made her way directly to the bar and picked up a tray, balancing the drinks her mother had just finished preparing.

With practiced ease, she carried them to Antonia's table and placed both on the tabletop. She stepped back from the still empty chair beside Antonia and motioned for Aris to take a seat.

The old woman resumed fanning herself and in a wobbly but sure voice, continued in the language so close to Aris's heart. "You have good manners. Your eyes are bright and warm. You have a good heart."

Drosita made her way out from behind the bar and knelt by the older woman's side. "Yia-yia, speak American. These strangers, they do not understand."

The old lady nodded and smiled, but continued as before. Aris interpreted easily. "You must respect, you must love, you must have good manners!"

Aris's head swam. He reached down and braced a hand on the straight-backed chair next to where the old woman was seated. "The three ancient Greek elements one must have to be civilised." His voice was practically a whisper.

Drosita spun on her heels, now facing him directly. "You speak Greek?"

Before he could answer, Antonia shouted, "Aris, Aris! Look!" He turned to see her pointing to an old-style portrait on the wall that featured a beautiful woman with flowing red hair standing next to a young girl whose face resembled Drosita's daughter.

Aris could no longer hide his elation. He followed Antonia's direction and approached the portrait, examining it in detail.

After a long minute he turned to Drosita. "And who is this beautiful redhead?"

Drosita's chest swelled. She pointed to the old lady in the rocking chair.

"Your mother?" Aris's voice was still tinged in surprise, but he could feel his own excitement rising.

Smiling, Drosita said, "No, my grandmother. Mamma died a few days after giving birth to me. Yia-yia raised me."

Aris made his way back to Drosa and knelt at the old woman's feet.

Drosita reached out to shield him. "Stay back. She doesn't like strangers!"

Ignoring the warning, Aris gently embraced the old woman's hand and softly kissed it.

"Huh," Drosita laughed. "That's strange. Usually yia-yia tries to run and hide from strangers. Once she even attacked someone."

Drosita stood and turned the wooden chair that Aris had used to brace himself a few minutes earlier, offering him a seat next to her grandmother.

Aris accepted and exchanged sweet silent smiles with the old lady.

Time paused while he looked into her eyes. Memories flooded back of his grandparents at their village table, of fresh bread and olives warm from the sun.

"Aris…" the old woman's voice still wobbled. "The name becomes you. Tell them who I am."

Drosita stumbled backwards. "Yia-yia, so you can still speak American!"

"Of course," she replied immediately, facing her granddaughter. "I only speak to you in Greek so you will learn the mother of all languages!" Then she turned soft eyes back to Aris and prompted, "Tell them who I am."

Drosita placed a hand on the old woman's shoulder. "Yia-yia, this stranger does not know who you are."

Aris could barely contain his pleasure. "She is Droso, sister of Calliope and Garoufalia. Four were brought to America by an uncle; one sister died soon after; two more were left back at home."

Droso shook her head. "Maybe she died. But maybe they lied to us!"

Drosita's jaw had dropped. "How do you know such things? I do not even know of these other sisters."

"Finally, someone with a pure heart," Droso warbled. "And brains."

The world faded around Aris as the old woman scooted her chair next to him and gently caressed his face. In his native tongue, her voice was melodic. "You are not searching for gain nor for abuse. You have been hurt. That's why you seek this secret."

A subtle frown formed on Aris's face.

"You alone are worthy to know the answer," she continued.

Aris allowed a glimmer of hope to spark in his soul.

"But alas," she sighed. "I don't know it."

He pulled the embroidered fabric out of a pocket and unfolded it to show the section marked *Paradisos*. "Where is this place?" he asked her in Greek.

Droso nodded. "It is between two *ochthos*—banks—at the mouth of the water. The grandmother was the owner of Aphrodite's secret."

Aris whipped out his notepad and began scribbling, then he flipped back a few pages and told Droso, "Your great niece Cali says your sister Calliope would sing a song that used this unusual word." He read the lyrics aloud and watched her expression for clues. "In paradise, two nymphs should hold the love secret—Triantofilo and Angeliki."

Droso merely patted his hand when he'd concluded. "Cali was jealous of her two younger sisters."

"Where are they now?"

Droso made the sign of the cross. "Only God knows."

"Do you remember the name of your village?"

She shrugged. "It was only called *village*."

"But where… in which area is the village?" Having come this far, Aris was impatient to unearth his next step.

Droso patted his leg and sat back in her rocker. "Garoufalia is older than me. She has something like this embroidery you are holding."

Aris prodded eagerly. "Where is Garoufalia?"

"They separated us after we arrived here in Mexico. She was taken to the next country."

Drosita moved right next to her grandmother, focused on every word.

"Which country?" Aris practically begged.

Droso went silent. The squeak of floorboards beneath her rocker was like a metronome ticking away Aris's life force.

After an expanse of time, Droso finally said, "I don't know why I am revealing everything to you. I'm tired of waiting. Perhaps because my time is up, and I will go to paradise now as well." She turned to her granddaughter. "Drosita, bring me the portrait from the wall."

Drosita fetched it willingly. She placed it reverently into her grandmother's hands.

Aris moved in closer to view the picture in detail, but the old woman flipped the frame over on her lap. "Open it, Aris. Remove the wood."

All the air seemed to go out of the room. Aris's heart was pounding like never before. He looked up to notice everyone was staring at him, eager to discover what was hidden in the frame. He glanced up at Droso and when she nodded for him to proceed, he pried back the cover, revealing an embroidered cloth tucked behind the portrait.

It was similar to the one Cali had given him, But when he pulled it out he saw this map focused only on Mexico and a much smaller country at its foot, embroidered with a blue mark.

"Sololá," Droso pointed. "A village near a lake. My second daughter knows better."

Drosita's eyes practically bored into those of her grandmother's as the woman shared, "I ran away many times. They beat me and imprisoned me as a slave, until my husband found me. We fell in love and he took me away. We built this house."

"Yia-yia!" Drosita sobbed.

With pain in her face, old Droso lifted her long, flowing hair and began speaking in Spanish, her gaze focused on Drosita's teenage daughter. "The fifth time I ran away to find my sister, they cut a portion of my ear and broke my little toes."

"Yia-yia!" the younger girl screamed, while her mother Drosita burst into tears.

"Why have you never told us this before?"

Antonia, who had been sitting silently nursing her beverage, reached into her handbag and brought out a pack of tissues and handed them around. She whispered a quick translation to Aris of what Droso had just spoken.

"These memories are not easy, my love." Droso's hands dropped from her hair and with the fingertips of one hand she reached out to caress Drosita's cheek. Then with her other hand she motioned for the younger girl to come around to her other side.

Aris noted her melodic voice did not waver this time, and he listened intently as Antonia translated the Spanish for him. "You have family. Many people. You must learn our language to speak to them. This man will find them for you!"

With this declaration, Droso's energy seemed to drain. But she mustered a deep breath and continued. With her sight set on Drosita, she commanded, "Give Aris the address for Chrisafina."

Drosita went to the bar and retrieved a tattered and yellowed page filled with handwriting.

Droso stretched her hand out to the embroidery on Aris's lap. "Safina lives in a small village outside Leon. I remember it because it sounds like *léon*, the ancient Greek word for lion."

Aris didn't hesitate when she wrapped her gnarled hand around his fingers. "Many came looking for this," she whispered to him in Greek. "I trust you. Garufalia knows where the village is. If she is still alive… and you find her… show this to her," she said, now pointing to the cloth. "And tell her I love her very much."

Aris folded both pieces of embroidery and placed them in his pocket, then reassembled the wooden frame and carried the portrait back to hang it in its place on the wall.

Drosita handed him a slip of paper with an address and a phone number. "I don't care about whatever this *secret* is that you and yia-yia have between you. But if you find any of my relatives, please give them my number."

Aris tucked the slip in the back of his notepad, then ripped out a blank page where he scrawled a Tampa address. "You have an aunty, a cousin, and that cousin's baby. They live at this place in Tampa, Florida."

Droso had obviously been listening closely. She called, "What about my sister Calliope? Did she die?"

Aris nodded solemnly while Antonia used the last of her tissues to wipe down the table where she'd been seated, then carried the glasses—one empty and one full that Aris had never even sipped from—to the bar. Aris could understand her desire to do something with her hands. After all, working behind a bar was an everyday job to her.

A beam of sunlight flashed across Droso's face as the cantina door swung open. The man Aris assumed to be Drosita's husband clomped in and handed the car keys to Antonia. "All done," he said curtly. "Your car is right outside."

Antonia was obviously ready to go. She claimed the keys and kissed the man on both cheeks, thanking him. Then she turned to Aris. "Shall we go?"

Aris knelt one last time beside old Droso, again respectfully lifting and kissing her hand.

Her expression melted. "You are blessed and courageous, dear Aris. Keep your heart clean, and always be alert! Be warned! Deadly demons await you."

Aris nodded and began to stand. Droso's hand pulled him back. When he was again kneeling before her, she sandwiched his face between her two palms, staring deeply into his eyes, as if examining Aris's soul.

In a pained whisper Droso said, "Before we left the village, our granny gave each of us one clue."

Aris nodded.

Droso let out a soft smile. "You have the first one."

Aris nodded again.

"Then here is mine," she said. "You must be touching the other person."

32 The Devil Round the Corner

The next morning, Aris came down from his hotel room to find Uri and John in the breakfast area.

"Wh-wh-where have you been?" John's voice shook. Then he pushed back in his chair and stood to give Aris a slap on the shoulder and a big grin. "When did you get back?"

Uri didn't even make a move to stand or greet him.

Aris mentally calculated how long they had been on the road and said, "Guys, it's time to move on."

"Where to?" Uri finally looked up.

"Leon," Aris answered quickly, remembering the lion Droso had spoken of. "A town which famously has the most beautiful women in all of Mexico."

Uri cracked a wide smile and slapped Aris a high five. "Now you're talking my language!"

They hopped a bus and rode south through the central part of the country. Upon arrival in Leon, they checked into a hotel right off the city centre.

Aris yawned. "Guys, I'm going for a nap. Don't disturb me. I will see you tonight for dinner."

"We have good *masseurs* in town if you are tired, Mr. Theo," offered the girl at the reception desk.

Aris shook his head and walked away. "I need to sleep."

Less than half an hour later Aris approached the reception area with freshly washed hair. "Can you call me a taxi, please?"

"Where to?"

"A small village near a lake."

"There are many!" the receptionist balked.

Aris showed her a note, to which the girl replied, "Ah, this is not far." Uri laughed triumphantly, sneaking up behind Aris. "You can't fool me. You slept most of the way in the bus. I'm coming with you this time."

John stepped out from the shadows. "Me too."

With a deep sigh, Aris lied, "I had a shower and it woke me up. I'm just going to explore a bit until my hair is dry. We'll party together tonight."

"No," Uri insisted. "We will not let you disappear for ten days again, searching for that stupid love secret."

The receptionist instantly looked up at Aris, now completely focused on their conversation.

"Seriously," Aris told the boys. "I'm just going to visit my aunty. I don't need any babysitters."

Uri coughed and said something under his breath that sounded like, "Bullshit." Then he said, "You mean like those people we visited in Tampa?"

Aris's patience was running out. "Listen. Go explore the town. Get a massage. Just get off my back."

"You are still searching for that myth of a love secret," Uri hissed.

The receptionist came around her desk and tapped Aris on the shoulder. "Your taxi is outside now."

Adamant, Aris pushed Uri away. "I mean it, or I will grab my bag and we'll part ways right now."

John tugged on Uri's arm. "Come on. Aris needs some space to do his thing."

Aris gritted his teeth and left without even saying thank you to the receptionist.

— ◆ —

In the back of the cab, Aris looked up from the slip of paper. "Stop here," he said. "I'll only be a few minutes. Wait for me."

Outside the house, Aris knocked on the door. A man answered.

"I'm looking for Senõra Safina," Aris said.

A mature heavyset woman appeared behind the man at the door. Curious, she looked out. "I am Safina. Who are you?"

Aris smiled politely. "Drosita gave me your address."

Safina gasped for air. "Has my mother died?"

"No, no," Aris soothed her. "Droso is well and she sends her love."

"Ha," the woman before him scoffed. "Her love? Mother refused to speak to me. She never forgave me for leaving home."

"Droso never stopped loving you."

"She sent you to tell me this?"

"No," Aris replied.

"Why are you here then? What happened? You never said who you are."

Aris found his smile again. "You can say I am a distant relative. I am Greek as well."

Unconvinced, Safina asked, "A distant relative?"

"Your mother wants you to give me the address of your aunt—Garoufalia, who lives somewhere near Sololá in Guatemala."

Safina took a step back and began shutting the door in his face. "You're just using my family's names to gain trust. I bet you're another one here looking for that cursed secret."

Aris stuck his foot out to block the door from closing. Pulling out the embroidered fabric Droso had given him, Aris volunteered, "When I met your mother, she gave me this."

Safina looked from the fabric to Aris's face a few long seconds.

Aris brought out the other embroidered cloth. "And Calliope's granddaughter gave me this as well."

Safina's voice grew scratchy. "Mother told me she burned it."

"It was hidden inside the frame of her portrait."

"Mother never trusted us. She never trusted strangers either. So why did she trust you?"

Aris refolded the embroidery and placed it back in his pocket. "Droso is a lovely lady and very intelligent. With very strong instincts reading people's characters. Would you please trust me the way she did? Your niece Drosita is waiting for me to find Garoufalia and any other living relatives."

"I don't believe you. You are looking for the devil's love secret."

"I'm looking for your mother's village back home. Your aunty may be the last one who knows where it is."

Safina's expression was pained. "How is my mother?"

Aris reached out tentatively, covering Safina's hand that still rested on the door frame. "She is sound and well. Full of spirit. But she said she is tired."

"That sounds like her." One corner of her lips turned up in a smile. She sighed and said, "I don't even know if Aunty Garoufalia is still alive. She is older than my mother."

"I can let you know after I find out," Aris offered.

Safina squinted and her gaze drilled into Aris. "Indeed, Mother always had strong instincts about people. One look and she could read a person's character. If she trusted you with her embroidery, you must not be a crook."

"Please," Aris begged.

"Aunty lived in the only village on top of Sololá lake."

Aris pulled out his notepad.

"I will write it down for you." Safina took the pen and paper from Aris's hands. "The house has a cross on the roof with an arrow pointing east. And here's my number. I want to know if she is still alive. I know she has two daughters."

Aris reclaimed the pad and copied down two sets of numbers, tearing out the sheet and handing it to Safina. "This is your niece Drosita's number. And this is Calliope's granddaughter Cali's number in Tampa. Both will be happy to hear from you. Call them!"

Aris waved goodbye while Safina stood silently staring down at the paper in her hands.

◆ ◇ ◆

The hotel receptionist entered the salon where four stylists were working. She made her way to an attractive woman who ran the shop but sat reading a magazine.

With an indifferent sideways gaze, the lady said, "Open your mouth before you explode. What is it?"

"Katerina, I cannot afford a haircut today, but I need one."

Shaking her head Katerina told her, "It all depends what you have to say."

The words tumbled out. "Three Americans checked into the hotel earlier."

"Big deal." Katerina flipped pages in her magazine. "What do I care?"

"They had an argument in front of me." The receptionist was practically beaming.

"And you think that's worth a free haircut?"

"No. But what they fought about will be!"

Indifferent, Katerina flicked past the feature article to stare at the pictures.

"One of the Americans asked for a taxi so he could go see a distant aunty outside town."

Katerina didn't even look up. She just raised a manicured hand and pointed to the door.

"The one with the hooked nose challenged him… said that he was lying."

Katerina's patience was growing thin. "You stupid girl. Why would I be interested in two Americans arguing?"

"The crooked nose accused the other one of going to search for the love secret."

Katerina's eyes finally raised from the magazine. "So the American has a Mexican lover. So what?"

The receptionist's left foot tapped impatiently on the floor. "After the first guy left, I asked the crooked nose about this love secret… and he said it was supposed to give power so you could make anyone fall in love with you!"

Katerina's eyes flashed. "What do you mean?"

"The secret is apparently thousands of years old. Greek queens used it to make men fall in love with them."

Katerina set the magazine down and now stared openly at the receptionist, whose face took on a dreamy expression. "Can you imagine? To control the most famous, rich men, and never have to work again!"

One of the other stylists turned. "I'd like to know this love secret."

"Me too," the others chimed in.

"Get back to work," Katerina glared at them. She stood and pulled the receptionist outside by the hair. "Tell me about this American."

"Ouch! I don't know him!"

"What is his name? What does he look like?"

"He checked in under the name Aris Theo. He has our same skin colour. Tall with wavy black hair."

"What about this aunt?"

"Crooked nose said she wasn't really his aunt."

"But who is she?"

"I don't know her name, but I remember the village because he asked me to call him a taxi."

"Who's taxi took him?"

"One of the locals. Marino."

"Get me his phone number."

"What about my hair?" the receptionist pleaded.

"You can have your free haircut."

The receptionist giddily pushed the door open to go back inside. Once her locks were freshly shorn, she got brave enough to address the salon owner again. "But Katerina, I should tell you the American's friend said the love secret is just a myth."

"Myth or not, I want to know everything they say. And everywhere they go." Katerina shoved the receptionist outside and reached for the phone. Perhaps her no-good brothers could also be of help for once.

33 A Coincidence?

Late that afternoon, the receptionist watched as Aris met John and Uri in the lobby. Before heading out, the tall one turned to her. "Thanks for your help hiring the taxi earlier. Any chance you can recommend a good bar and restaurant for us?"

She circled a couple places on a small tourist map for him.

"Thanks again." Aris smiled at her. "Say, your hair looks really nice this afternoon. Did you just get it cut?"

The girl blanched, but as soon as the men stepped outside, she dialled a call. "Katerina, the Americans just left. I gave them directions to a bar just across from your salon."

⋄

The three amigos were already enjoying the atmosphere of Leon. Locals passing by happily greeted them, *"Buenos días."* Soon, the three took the initiative to greet the locals first.

Up ahead, Aris took note of a curvy brunette standing in front of a hairdresser's shop. Four other younger girls stood nearby chatting.

"Buena sera, señorita," Aris greeted.

The curvy woman stepped in front of Aris. "Who do you think you are?" Her brows were knit together. "First you come into our home, now you think you can fuck us in the middle of the street?"

John panicked and stepped into the road to distance himself. Uri just stood staring at the woman.

She grabbed Aris's collar. "What's the matter, you lost your charming tongue?"

"S-sorry, lady," John stammered an apology. "Everybody was greeting us, so we were just trying to be polite."

Aris placed one hand on the girl's forearm and pried her grip away, gently pushing her aside. Before his foot could take another step, the curvy girl grabbed him by the arm and yanked. Her face transformed. "You're no American gringo. You have dark skin like mine."

"Greek-American," Uri offered.

"El Greco!" the Latina exclaimed. Messing up Aris's hair, she trilled, "Come, I give you free haircut!"

Aris flattened his tousled hair. "I like it just fine as it is. Thank you."

"Why are you in such a hurry?" she asked. "Come, relax! This is peaceful town. We do not shoot Americans here."

"We are just hungry," John interrupted. "Our hotel doesn't offer dinner, only breakfast."

The hairdresser met Aris's gaze and held it. "My house has better food than any restaurant."

Aris smiled mutely.

She dropped his arm and retreated. "I will see you tonight, El Greco!"

A few steps away, Uri ribbed him. "I see why they call it the town with the most pretty girls. They're all stunners!"

"Pretty but strange." John scratched his head. "One minute they want to kill us, the next minute they're inviting us for a home-cooked dinner."

"Oh, they're devious," Aris observed. "Make no mistake. In their minds, we are their tickets to America."

After a rather quick pre-dinner drink at the bar, the three friends made their way to a restaurant and ordered up a dinner worthy of champions.

A curvaceous woman in a black dress, with a scarf covering her hair and cheeks, seated herself and her male companion at the next table, never letting the gentlemen out of her sight behind her dark sunglasses.

When the three returned to their hotel to turn in, the night shift male receptionist picked up the phone after they'd passed.

The call was answered immediately. Just four words was all she needed. "The Americans are back."

——— ◇ ———

Instantly recognisable without her sunglasses, Katerina entered the hotel. At the reception desk she opened her hand. The night clerk placed a key in her palm. "Number 29."

Outside Aris's door, Katerina knocked. No one responded so she let herself in.

Apparently hearing her entrance, Aris appeared from around the bathroom door, dripping wet, with a towel wrapped around his waist. "Excuse me! I'm in the middle of having a shower."

The hairdresser flipped the lock on the door behind her. "Good! I want you clean and fresh."

Taken off guard, Aris stepped backward. "I'm sorry, pretty lady. I'm not looking for company. I'm married."

With practiced poise, she stepped towards him. "Aren't we all?"

Aris waved both hands to stop her, but couldn't help noticing her cherry-red lipstick. "I uh, I don't sleep with... working girls. My friend Uri across the corridor will gladly pay you."

"If I fancied your friend, I would be in his room right now. It's you I've fallen for."

——— ◇ ———

Aris had had about enough of women's fanciful ideas of love. Pointing to the door he said, "You don't understand. I'm in love with my wife. And I am a one-woman man."

The intruder ran her tongue over those bright red lips. "Practically a virgin. That makes you even more desirable. I can show you some tricks!" She paused long enough to eye Aris from head to toe, still dripping on the tile floor. "I see you do not recognise me. I offered you a free haircut earlier."

Aris stepped his way carefully around her to unlock the door to the hallway. He could hear shuffling in the corridor outside and wondered if Uri had overhead the conversation. "Thank you again, pretty girl, but I'm not into tricks. And I don't pay for sex!"

The sound of Uri's door opening but not closing was all Aris needed for confirmation.

"Please go." Aris swung open his door and gestured for the hairdresser to leave.

The smile faded from her face. "I'm not a whore!"

Aris caught sight of Uri peeking around his partially closed door. "Go there to Uri." Aris pointed. "He has a big one made of iron."

"If I wanted a big one I would've found a mule. At the restaurant, I overheard you saying that sex is just the icing on top of the cake. That surely means you know how to make love to a woman. Plus… I hear El Grecos are passionate lovers!"

Aris couldn't help but smile at this. All the same, he gently pushed her over the threshold into the hallway, then closed the door behind her.

Frustrated, she banged on his door. "No man has ever refused me. I know your name, El Greco. Mr. Aris! You will regret this!"

She kept thumping for a full minute, but eventually gave up.

Uri opened his own door wider. "Hey, *señorita*. Why not come to my room?"

She paused to give him the once-over. "You're no married man." Then she turned to leave.

"I am married." Uri leapt at the opportunity to share. "But you are so beautiful I would gladly sin for you."

She raised her middle finger and started walking away. "One night, two stupid Americanos! I will get the man I really want. He will go on his knees begging for me."

Disappointed, Uri couldn't help watching her shapely curves as she walked away.

— ◇ —

Maybe thirty minutes had passed. Aris was near sleep in a t-shirt and boxers when his door burst open with one hard kick. Four Mexican men flanked the hairdresser.

Aris wiped the sleep from his eyes and sat up in bed. He could see through the open doorway that Uri was once again peeking out to see what was going on. But then Aris's attention became diverted.

One of the Mexicans raised a gun and pointed it straight at Aris's head.

A string of uncontrollable burps burst out of Uri before he slammed his hotel room door and bolted the chain.

To the Mexicans' obvious surprise, Aris looked amused.

The hairdresser stood with one hand on her waist, the other holding a handbag. She had moved to the side of his bed, looking down on him.

Another of the men, this one with long dark hair, stood directly in front of Aris's bed. "You insulted our sister. She said you called her a *puta*."

The man holding the weapon lowered his aim to Aris's crotch.

The long-haired brother spat, "Either you're crazy or you're a *pousta*."

Aris shifted his gaze from the first to the second.

A shorter third brother spoke. "Normal man, we shoot once. But *pousta*, we shoot twice—front and back!"

"What's the matter, gringo?" asked the long-haired brother. "Our sister not good enough for you?"

Aris raised his arms in submission, chuckling now.

"Oh, you think we're funny, do you?"

The leader of the pack was fuming. "You humiliated our sister. You offended our family!"

Aris shook his head and lowered his hands. "That's exactly what I was trying *not* to do. Not to humiliate your gorgeous sister. Not to offend your family."

Puzzled, the brothers exchange glances.

Aris sat up straight. "In my country, they will kill you if you sleep with someone's sister—at least without having permission, or getting married first. Here you brothers want to shoot me for *not* sleeping with your sister? We're two worlds apart, I'm afraid."

The older brothers laughed. "You must come from a very stupid country if you have to get married just to have sex!"

Uri's door crept open just an inch. Aris could only imagine that Uri approved of what he was hearing.

The hairdresser smacked her red lips together and took a step closer, offering her hand to Aris. "What will it be, El Greco?"

Aris caught her hand, and kissed it charmingly, then pulled back the bed sheets to invite her in. "Just a cultural misunderstanding, gorgeous. Now that I have your brothers' permission, how could I refuse the most beautiful girl in Mexico? Hell, in all of Latin America. Probably in the world!"

The long-haired brother smiled. "I like this guy. He is respectful. Wanted our permission!"

Unconvinced, the shorter brother warned, "We'll be watching outside the hotel. If our sister comes out and she's not happy, first we'll shoot you in the balls, and then you'll die like a dog!"

Aris heard another string of burps giving away his friend's anxiety.

Catching sight of Uri, the brother with the gun raised his weapon and pointed it straight across the hallway. Uri wasted no time slamming and locking his door.

The hairdresser waved her brothers away, snuggling into bed beside Aris, and blessedly they closed the door behind them.

⊰ ◇ ⊱

She leaned in for a kiss, but Aris pushed her back.

"Need I remind you my brothers are right outside?"

"I'm allergic to makeup," Aris explained. "Why don't you have a shower? If I kiss you while you're wearing makeup…" Aris looked down at his crotch, "…my boy will go to sleep."

Then he playfully slapped her rear. "Hurry up, my gorgeous. I'm burning for you!"

She rose from the bed, partially unzipping her dress. "You like?"

Aris nodded emphatically. "I love!"

She swung her curvy hips all the way to the shower. "I knew you would love me."

Once he heard the shower turn on, Aris hopped out of bed and nudged the curtain to one side. It only took one quick look to see one of the brothers had taken up station across the street with a couple of thugs in tow.

Deciding to make the best of it, Aris climbed back into bed.

The dazzling Latina appeared nude, revealing deep curves and chocolate tan skin. Magnetised, Aris nodded his approval.

She spun a full circle, exhibiting her beauty. "You really like?"

"Like?" Aris lifted the bed sheet again, inviting her in. "You're stunning!"

"I knew you liked me when we met in the street."

Aris raised his arms and pulled off his t-shirt. "No more talk. Show me your Mexican tricks."

Delighted, she climbed astride, kissing Aris passionately, while he ran his hand over her rear.

"Ooh," she murmured. "I like that you are hungry." She reached for the light switch beside the bed.

Aris stopped her. "I like to watch what I eat," he teased. "Especially when the menu is as delectable as you."

— ◇ —

The next afternoon, Katerina directed the taxi driver Marino to pull up outside the door of the house where he'd brought the American.

Katerina stepped out wearing a stunning form-fitting dress and knocked on Safina's door, leaving two of her brothers in the car.

When the chubby older woman opened up, Katerina said, "My fiancé came to see you earlier."

Safina looked from Katerina to the taxi and back, but otherwise remained silent.

"Aris, my Greek-American fiancé… he came to see you?"

Taking her time to notice the two men outside, Safina's voice wavered when she replied, "Yes, he did come to visit."

Katerina nodded to encourage the woman's trust. "Aris told me you know the ancient love secret."

Safina laughed aloud. Pointing to her enlarged belly, she laughed. "Do I look like someone your fiancé would share a love secret with?"

Katerina would not be fooled. "Then why did Aris come to see you?"

"He was looking for a distant relative from back home."

"Where?"

"Greece."

"I heard him mention a visit to your aunty?" Katerina asked rather than said, batting her eyelashes.

"She died a long time ago," Safina quickly supplied.

"Is she buried nearby?"

"Oh no, she moved to Guatemala when I was a baby. No one knows why or where."

Katerina pounced on that answer. "So she may not be dead yet."

Safina just shook her head. "If my aunty still lived, she would be over one hundred and fifteen years old. How many people live to that age?"

"So you did not invite my fiancé in?"

Instantly fearful, Safina pulled the door open wider. "What a fool, I did not even invite you in. Please come in and have a drink."

"Thank you, but I have to head back." Katerina turned to leave. "I apologise for troubling you. I am a bit jealous… you understand."

Back in the car Katerina kicked off her heels in the back seat. "A waste of time. The lady knows nothing about a love secret. She actually thought I was implying that she was Aris's lover! Can you imagine?"

"Maybe the American's friends were lying about him because he didn't want them to come with him."

Katerina flipped the hair back out of her eyes and looked out the window at passing scenery. "Maybe… but if Aris knows this love secret, I'm going to find it. I will poke his eyes out, I will hang him by his balls, but I will make him talk!"

34 Hungry Latina

It was past mid-morning, yet Aris was still asleep face down. The hairdresser zipped up her dress and leaned over to run her tongue in Aris's ear. "You were very hungry, El Greco! I do believe you are a one-woman man. You sent me to glory so many times. Now I'm in love with you for real."

Aris rolled and opened his eyes, letting a smile escape.

"I've been looking for a man like you for so long. You know how to take your time, how to touch and love a woman. I want you to be my one-woman man."

He stretched an arm to gently caress her arm.

"But are you someone to grow old with? Young and stupid men have their eyes on *babysitas*, or should I choose a mature man or a young widow? Difficult choice."

Aris shifted up to rest his back on the headboard. "Age is just a number. A girl once told me, 'I'd rather spend a few happy years with a mature man who loves me than a miserable lifetime with a young man who doesn't know how to appreciate a woman'."

The hairdresser nodded. "I like this girl. Young men tend to shoot before they're even undressed. Every minute, I love you more now, El Greco!"

Aris pulled her hand to him and lavished it with a kiss worthy of a queen.

"How can I convince you to stay one more night for me? I will show you more magic tricks…"

"Only one more night?" Aris teased. "I thought you loved me!"

Her face lit up. "I do love you very, very much!" She took a step towards the door but paused. "Are you sure you can stay one more night for me?"

Aris's eyes twinkled. "We paid ahead for seven nights."

"Ooh!" This time joy radiated from her whole being. "You rest then, and I will see you tonight!"

Opening his arms, Aris beckoned her back. "One more of your sweet kisses!"

"No! I already put on my makeup. Tonight I will have many, many more kisses… everywhere!"

Coyly, Aris pointed to his crotch. "The boy isn't allergic to your makeup!"

She giggled. "Now I know I made you love me." When she opened the room door, she signalled the guard in the hall. "You can go. He's in love with me!"

The hairdresser practically floated down the hall, all the way to the receptionist's desk.

"How long did the Americans book to stay?" she asked.

Looking at the register, the girl replied, "Seven nights."

Another smile spread across her face. She murmured, "El Greco did not lie. He really loves me!"

⸻ ◇ ⸻

At noon, Uri and John had still not seen Aris. They knocked on his door, and it swung on its hinges. "Wake up, Aris," Uri called, pushing it the rest of the way open and stepping inside.

Aris was still collapsed on the bed, eyes glued shut. "Go away. I need to sleep!"

"We can't leave. There are Mexicans guarding the hotel. What should we do?"

"Why do you want to leave?" Aris yawned. "We already paid ahead for the whole week."

"Well…" Uri kept his voice low. "I did see that luscious Latina's brother pointing a gun at you last night. In fact, he pointed it at me twice. This place is too dangerous. We should go."

Aris pushed himself to sit up. "They're good boys. They just wanted to make sure their sister would be looked after."

"Um, they're guarding the place inside and out," John sputtered.

"Relax. That girl has endless energy in bed. I'm thinking of staying. She has a big plot of land with stables. I like horses. Maybe I could manage it for her."

Uri and John exchanged curious looks.

"Warm climate." Aris yawned. "I think I'll drop anchor here and see how we're getting on in a few months. You boys can continue travelling by yourselves."

"I knew this would happen," Uri fumed. "So inexperienced. After the first whore who fucks him, he thinks he's in love."

"Hey, watch it. This girl is brilliant. And she's no whore. I still feel her on my boy."

Uri grabbed Aris by the shoulders. "You are a total fool. As soon as she's had enough of you, her brothers will shoot you. Then they'll kill us too so there are no witnesses."

"Uri's right, Aris." John started pacing the room.

Aris rolled away from Uri's grasp and clawed his way out from under the tangle of bedsheets. Wearing nothing but his black underpants with a red elastic stripe, he made his way to the bathroom. "Relax, she loves me. And now that I got to know her, I really like her too. Maybe I'm already in love." He shut the bathroom door in Uri's face.

"You idiot!" Uri shouted. "How can you love her after just a night or two? You're twice her age. She's only using you."

Aris spoke through the door. "You can feel a woman, from the way she touches you, the way she kisses you all over. She even kissed my ass!" He flushed and returned to the bedroom. "I'm telling you, she makes me laugh. I felt something strong with her. I want her."

"You're endangering our lives," Uri persisted. "We better get away from here before they kill us all."

John stopped his pacing for a second. "Think about what Uri is saying. He's more experienced with women than you and me."

Aris grabbed up his trousers and a fresh shirt. "So you bugged me to hook up with a random woman every night for nearly two months. And now I find a woman who loves me—a woman I like, and whose touch excites me—and suddenly everyone is revolting." He buttoned the shirt and pointed to the door. "I'm starving. Let's go eat."

The three made their way downstairs, with Uri and John casting suspicious side glances. As they exited the hotel, Uri said, "Look, guards everywhere."

"They're f-f-following us," John stammered.

Aris waved a dismissive arm. "Think of them as bodyguards. This is a dangerous country."

Inside the restaurant, Aris chose a table in the centre. Two of the guards seated themselves at a back table while two more claimed a table near the front.

"You see?" Uri pointed. "They've surrounded us. We're prisoners."

Aris summoned the waiter. "Please send some beer to those two tables. Put it on my account." Smiling, Aris waved to the guards.

After lunch, Aris hailed a waiting taxi. One of the Mexicans jumped out and sent the cab away. Waving his arm, he summoned a car parked nearby. "Where do you want to go?" he asked Aris. "We'll drive you."

"We can't even go where we want by ourselves," Uri muttered in protest.

Undisturbed, Aris grinned. "Private limousine. We have no need for dirty taxis."

The Mexican held the door for Aris. "We have orders to protect you. It is dangerous for Americans to be by themselves here. Many thieves, many murderers in Mexico."

Aris shrugged. "You see? We have protection... and a free ride. I could get used to this kind of service. I love this girl." He climbed into the backseat. "A quick tour around town, please."

John and Uri reluctantly climbed in on either side of him. Uri leaned across Aris to whisper, "Probably they're taking us somewhere to kill us."

"Ah! Stop worrying. I love the girl." Aris leaned back, taking in the view. "If she accepts, she will be my new wife. She has a brilliant personality and is a tiger in bed."

Uri balked. "If she accepts what?"

Aris smiled. "If I had a ring, I would propose to her tonight!"

John and Uri exchanged worried glances.

Aris continued to take in the sights. "What's that up ahead?" he asked the driver.

"The station."

"Bus or train?"

"Both."

A few metres down the road, Aris pointed to another building. "What is that?"

"A factory," came the reply.

They turned a corner. "And that?"

The driver looked proud. "This is our football stadium."

Aris clapped his hands together. "And what is your town most famous for?"

The driver laughed. "Beautiful girls and football!"

Aris continued asking about the sights, complimenting the beauty of the city, while John and Uri stewed in silence.

───◇───

Back at the hotel, the three friends climbed out of the chauffeur-driven car. Uri pointed to several men positioned both outside and in. "See? We're still prisoners."

"Stop moaning," Aris roared. "These guards are here to protect us! I am in love with this girl."

The middle-aged receptionist watched the interaction, taking in every word. She nodded and smiled along.

Aris continued his rant. "You've seen her. She's gorgeous, and she's intelligent too. We will have beautiful children together."

John shook his head in disbelief.

"The two of you are free to go." Aris pointed to the exit. "If you pack and leave right now, you will see the guards will not stop you. I'm going to propose to the girl tonight."

Out of the corner of his eye, Aris saw the receptionist smile.

"If you want to die in Mexico, be my guest." Uri brushed his hands. "A Mexican Cleopatra bewitched you. You're a damn fool."

Aris walked straight over to one of the guards, and in a sudden move, slapped him hard on the face, sending him off balance. "You're supposed to guard us, not fall asleep!" *Bam!* Aris landed another hard slap on the man's face.

The Mexican ground his teeth, but kept himself from hitting back. In Spanish the man declared, "As soon as Katerina finishes with you, I will be the one who kills you! Your hours are counting backwards. I will uproot your genitals and feed them to you."

Aris smiled softly then walked over to the receptionist. "What did he say?"

Uri and John leaned in when she lowered her voice. "My cousin Katerina has instructed me to look after you. We all love you. If your friends are problems just tell me, and I will uproot their genitals and kill them."

Uri let out a series of burps while John shivered in his shoes.

Aris merely started up the stairs, calling out, "I'm going back to bed. I'm going to need plenty of energy for tonight. My gorgeous Katerina is coming."

The guard motioned with his gun for John and Uri to follow Aris.

Meanwhile, the receptionist dialled a number. "Hi, Katerina? The American just told his friends he's in love with you. He wants to stay with you. He will propose to you tonight!"

The hairdresser's squeal caused the receptionist to pull the receiver back from her ear. "He did? I knew he loves me!"

"Yes, the American is brave. He slapped Pablo twice!" she told Katerina. "Pablo said he would be the one to kill the

American, but I translated that Pablo said he would protect him."

"Put Pablo on the phone now!"

The receptionist called the guard over to the desk. Hesitant, he took the phone. "*Si?*" His face turned stone cold, and he too held the receiver back from his ear.

"You touch one hair on my El Greco's head and I will skin you alive. And then I will eat your heart!"

35 Planting the Love Secret

It was past the witching hour, and Katerina had spent each of the last five nights in Aris's bed, keeping him up late but with orgasmic rewards.

As the sun rose, she was still enjoying his feather touch, spreading ever so slowly from her neck downwards. Like a teasing game, each fractional movement only excited her more, driving her crazy for his hands to reach her waist… and beyond.

Supporting his weight on his left arm, Aris lifted his torso to extend his reach. In slow tantric motion, each finger stretched, one sliding through the partition of Katerina's creamy rear, causing her to writhe in place.

Aris's fingers continued their path as he angled his hips and upper body so he could caress her inner thighs. Her hips jerked and she moaned softly.

Leisurely passing the inner fold of her knees, then down to her calf muscles, Aris stroked with a light pressure. In time he reached the arch of her foot, then ran his thumb across the top, giving a light squeeze to each toe in its turn.

He could see Katerina's eyes roll back in her head. She released a long, torturous sigh.

Soon her moans turned to groans as he began the arduous return journey of tantric caresses.

Somewhere mid-thigh, her eyes popped open, rising to meet Aris's gaze. "You're not saying anything tonight."

"I am enjoying you. Talk spoils the pleasure."

She turned her head, leaving her left cheek open to Aris's soft kiss.

Leaning in to plant another on her left shoulder, Aris whispered, "I don't know how it happened. I am just in love with you."

Her face lit up, though he could tell she still harboured some scepticism.

Aris continued his tantric motions on her back. "You said you knew magic. I didn't expect falling in love to be like this. I've never experienced such magic before."

"Ah, now you believe me." She squeezed her eyes shut as he planted a soft wet kiss along her spine.

"Perhaps you used that magic to make me fall in love with you, Katerina!" Aris suggested.

"Or perhaps you use that love secret to make me fall in love with you, my Greco!" she mused, arching her back into his kisses, which began to descend.

His eyes sharpened. "What love secret?"

"There is an ancient love secret," she murmured. "Those who know it can make anyone fall in love with them."

Aris chuckled. "There is no such love secret. It is only a myth."

"Not according to your friends! You went to visit someone to find the love secret."

Disguising his alert with amused laughter, Aris rolled to his side. "The lady there knows nothing. I was looking for her aunty but probably she died by now."

"Where is the old lady?"

"Somewhere in Guatemala. She left many years ago."

"And why are you looking for her?"

Aris took his time responding. "This aunty is one of my few remaining relatives. I wanted to ask her if she knows the origins of my family."

Unconvinced, Katerina lifted her head. "Do you know this love secret?"

Aris's mind started spinning. "Maybe."

"You will tell me then!"

Aris grinned like the Cheshire cat. "It can only be told to one person in a lifetime. I think it is too early for me to share it!"

Katerina rolled to her back and placed her hands around his cheeks. "If you really love me, you will tell me, Aris!"

"First I must make sure you love me. What if I tell you the secret, and then you kill me? You will be able to make any young man fall in love with you."

She rose in fury. "So there is such a love secret that makes someone fall in love with you!"

"I wouldn't be so sure about that," Aris said, again stroking the inside of her thigh.

With her thumbs on his eyebrows, she brushed from the centre of his forehead out to his temples, ever so slowly. "Then I will torture you until you tell me the truth."

"Then I will not tell you." Aris caught her wrists and flipped her back over on the bed. "Because you can only reveal the secret to someone you trust... someone who loves and trusts you as well."

"But you promised to tell me."

"Before I die! That is the tradition."

"What if you had an accident and died before you could tell me?"

"I am not the only one who knows the love secret."

"Maybe you don't know this secret at all and that's what you want the old lady for." Katerina bit her lower lip as Aris's hands once more began their excruciatingly pleasurable circuit.

"Maybe I do not know it!"

She chuckled. "Ha, you do not fool me. You already know the love secret. Or maybe you at least know part of it and you went looking for the old lady to tell you the rest."

"No one can fool you, my little fox!"

"Your friend said that thousands have died searching for this love secret. Wars were waged, and millions more died in its pursuit."

"My friend believes in myths."

"Myth or not, I will wait then," she sighed, "until you feel my true love. But you must promise to tell it to me someday."

"I promise," Aris swore, surprising even himself. "You are very special. I love everything about you, especially the scent of you."

Again she arched into his touch, but couldn't resist teasing him with her words. "This explains why I've fallen in love with you so quickly. You used this love secret on me."

He nodded absently. "It takes a few more days to work. I am not sure you really love me yet." He bent over her naked body and rubbed his nose on her back, sniffing deeply. "I can't get enough of your natural fragrance. You are amazing."

"What about in bed? Do you love me in bed?" Katerina asked.

"The most magical of all! The way you kiss me, the way you touch me… the way you take your time and enjoy me." A shaft of sunlight broke through the curtains, cascading across Katerina's curves. "You awaken my lion, even when I'm tired."

She giggled. "Oh yes, I enjoy you!" Then with a sudden push sending Aris tumbling on his back, Katerina leapt out of bed. "It is time for me to go. I have an important rendezvous at the shop. Then I will speak to my brothers… They will get us married."

Katerina began collecting her garments, strewn around the room.

Aris tried to pull her back. "Can't someone else cut the hair this morning?"

She paused, clutching a pair of sheer stockings to her bosom. "Oh, my Romeo. I am no hairdresser. That shop is just a front for my brothers'… well, for my family's business."

Aris cocked his head. "What do you mean? Family business?"

"We're in the *distribution* business," she answered coyly. "White powder, you know?"

Aris's smile was subtle.

"I will come back, earlier tonight. You rest up for me. Maybe eat a double portion of steak." She put the finishing touches on her hair, then headed for the door.

"But I haven't proposed to you yet!"

She stopped midstride. "No. No," she repeated more softly. "You must ask me in front of my eldest brother, and then you ask for his permission as well. Respect, you know?"

She turned to blow a kiss then opened the door to the hallway.

Again pausing, she turned back to look at Aris who was still naked in bed. "But how are you going to propose to me if you don't even know my name?"

Aris chuckled. "Of course I know your name."

She pursed her lips in a pout. "You don't. You're bullshitting me."

"Gorgeous," Aris laughed. "Your name is gorgeous!"

A bittersweet smile covered the Latina's face. "Ha! They warned me El Grecos were bullshit sweet talkers."

Aris opened his arms wide, inviting her back. "You are the gorgeous Katerina De Kapal!"

Katerina's face beamed but she kept her footing. "You do know who I am!"

"But how should I ask your brother? Should I say, 'Please, can I marry your sister with the sexy bottom?'"

She just shook her head, but joy was in her eyes. Katerina blew another kiss. When she finally turned, she swung those luscious hips that were her birthright, tantalizing Aris and leaving him to close his own bedroom door.

⋯ ◇ ⋯

Outside the hotel exit, Katerina brushed past one of her brothers, waking him with a not so gentle touch.

"You stayed too long," he muttered. "I go kill him now."

"No. No! You mustn't." She spun to face him. "Aris loves me. He will propose to me. He will stay in Mexico for me!"

"Bullshit!"

"He said he likes my magic. I made him fall in love with me." Katerina's eyes became glassy. "I love him too!"

Her brother looked unconvinced.

"We need to go now. We're already late… but El Greco loves me. He will propose to me in front of Pietro. He is staying for me."

"We agreed. One night," he protested. "Then one became two became five. It is enough. I go kill him now."

"Ask!" she yelled, pointing to the receptionist's desk. "They paid the hotel for seven nights." Her expression was euphoric. "I am in love with Aris! He is so good, and so very hungry. He touches me like a queen. Maybe, we won't kill this one. He loves me!"

"Maybe I kill you as well, you fool!"

Katerina's eyes went wild. "I need a man! This one loves me. I feel him. He says I am magic. He wants to marry me!" But she could tell her words had no effect, so she added, "I will test him. I need more time to get him to tell me the love secret."

"Kat, don't fall in love again. The American will just run away."

She held her head high and proud. "My king is no Americano. He is Greco-Americano."

"Italiano, Spaniolo, Germanio, Americano…" He spat on the sidewalk. "All bastardo! And Greco-Americano is two times bastardo!"

Katerina yanked his arm, now practically begging. "I need more time with this one! If he truly loves me, I will marry him. We can make such beautiful, strong, clever children. And tall!"

"Stupido," her brother hissed.

"You're the one who's stupido. He knows the ancient love secret," she tempted. "Once he tells me, I will tell you, and you'll be able to make any girl fall in love with you."

A roguish grin spread across his face. "Women always love stupido."

"Hurry," she said, snatching at her brother's sleeve. "We have a shipment coming this morning. Leave Pablo here but bring the others."

"Only one guard? If he falls asleep, the Americanos will disappear."

"We can't make a mistake with this shipment. If something goes wrong, Pietro will kill us both." Katerina flipped her long locks over one shoulder. "No worry! El Greco is mine. I make magic on him!" Then she looked her brother in the eyes. "And if not, I will let you kill him."

⸻ ◇ ⸻

Aris let the curtain fall when Katerina and one of her brothers finished their conversation out front. He watched discreetly as the guards followed them.

Quickly pulling on his pants and a shirt, Aris threw every item he owned into his backpack. In the hallway he pounded on Uri's door.

Uri opened it just a crack and peeked out, probably expecting to see a gun pointed in his face.

Aris raced to Uri's window to see that the guards from the hotel rear had gone as well. "Get John and pack," he commanded. "We're leaving immediately."

"What? You're not in love anymore?" Uri burped once.

"Shut up, you fool! She's a nympho. I had to fake my last orgasm. I'm starting to pee blood."

Uri slapped Aris on the shoulder conspiratorially. "But what about her brothers? They'll kill us!"

Aris put his hands on Uri's shoulders as well. "This morning Katerina confided to me that the hairdressing shop is only a front for drug distribution."

"Ah! That explains why all her brothers have terrible hair. What about the guards?"

"At least the guards in the street have gone. I convinced her that I would stay and marry her."

Uri burped twice. "What if they set a trap? Maybe they'll let us try to escape, then shoot us from behind?"

"No time for that. Take my backpack. Tell John to get ready. Cover our packs with bed sheets, so they look like piles of dirty laundry. Take the back stairs to the emergency exit. You and John wait for me there. I'll get a taxi and come to pick you up."

"Are you sure all the guards have gone?" Uri asked.

"We'll soon find out. If I come back with a ride, she believed me."

"And if not?"

"Then you and John run as fast and as far as you can."

Aris took two steps but turned back, pulling Uri in by the shoulders. "Go now. If I'm not there in thirty minutes, you two leave! You know where the station is."

36 The Escape

Aris donned his sunglasses as he walked over to the hotel receptionist. Without turning his head, he noticed a guard the others called Pablo snoozing on a chair with his legs stretched out. "Excuse me," Aris greeted the lady at the desk with a charming smile. "Can you kindly tell me where I can find a pharmacy? Or somewhere that sells protection?"

"Protection?" the girl asked, glancing over at Pablo.

Aris pulled his sunglasses down and dropped the volume of his voice. "I mean condoms. Please?"

The young lady covered her mouth with a hand, perhaps trying to disguise a snicker, but then she gave him quick directions.

Outside Aris spotted a suspicious Mexican standing alone on the corner. Aris crossed the street lazily but scanned his surroundings. After passing the man and turning the corner, Aris glanced back to make sure he wasn't being followed. When no one else came around the corner, Aris stretched his steps.

The receptionist picked up the phone and dialled. "Your Americano from Room 29 went out."

From the other end of the line, Katerina asked, "Only him? Where is he going?"

The receptionist giggled. "To buy condoms."

Katerina gave a throaty laugh. "Then I better prepare for tonight. Those Greeks have interesting appetites! Okay, no worries."

After several blocks and two more turns, Aris noticed a small pickup truck delivering supplies. He checked behind him once more to verify that no one was following. Satisfied, he approached the driver as the man hefted a heavy bag onto his shoulder in front of a shop. "If you'll drive me to the bus station, there's fifty U.S. dollars in it for you."

The Mexican just stared at Aris then hoisted a second bag onto his other shoulder and carried both into the shop.

When the man returned to his truck, Aris tried again. He pointed to his watch, then held up five fingers. "Five. Just five minutes to the bus station."

"Take taxi," the driver mumbled and swept Aris out of his way.

"We have bags that won't fit in one taxi."

"You have a bag?"

"Three of us with bags. Not a big load."

The driver's eyes gleamed as he said, "Fifty each!"

Aris looked stunned.

The man stretched out his palm as if waiting for payment. "Gas more expensive than tequila here!"

Aris passed over one bill. "Fifty now. Another fifty when we get to the station." Then he climbed into the passenger seat.

The driver followed Aris's directions to the back of the hotel. "You skipping out on the bill? More fifties!"

Aris shook his head. "We paid ahead. But the receptionist wants me to take her to America and I don't want her to chase after us."

"Bring her, too," the driver grinned. "I can keep her for myself while you run away to America."

Gina looked at her family gathered around the dinner table—Liza, Peter with his wife and their two children, and Gerry with his partner and young son. She raised a wine glass.

"I want to apologise, my children, for the other week. I was out of line to have invited you for dinner but forgotten about it."

Peter's expression softened, but Gerry still looked contrite.

Gina's voice sweetened. "I was also wrong with my language. It was awful how I treated you. Aris was right on this one thing… you children must always take priority."

Peter raised his glass in toast. "We love you, Mum!"

In a surprise move, Gerry raised his glass as well. "You are our priority, too."

Peter's four-year-old daughter squealed. "Where is Grandfather? I miss him."

"He's gone," Gina said dismissively. "You should forget about him because he's never coming back."

She noticed the reproachful gazes from each of her children. Then her granddaughter burst into tears.

"You can't even be nice to our child," Peter's wife scowled. "Your jealousy poisons everything."

"I'm only telling the truth. It's not my fault Aris ran off."

Gerry shook his head. "One minute you're apologising and agreeing with Father, then the next you stab him in the back."

"I apologised to *you*," Gina explained. "Not to your two-bit father who abandoned all of us."

The four-year-old swiped at her tears with the back of one hand. "Grandfather will come back. He promised! He'll come back for me!"

"Of course he will," Peter's wife consoled.

"When Grandfather comes back, I'm going to ask him to sleep in our house, Mum. He can sleep in my room."

Gina opened her mouth, but Peter stopped her before the sarcasm could escape. "Don't even think about it!"

⋯ ◆ ⋯

The truck rolled to a stop in front of John and Uri.

Aris pointed to the white bundles. "Leave the bed sheets, but throw the packs in the back and jump in. Lay low till we get to the station." Once the guys were safe in the truck bed, Aris urged the driver, "To the bus station!"

Upon arrival, Aris handed over a second fifty dollars while Uri and John unloaded.

At the ticket office, Aris instructed Uri, "Be discreet, but check to see if that driver is watching us."

Uri set his pack down and peeked around the side of the ticket booth. "Yes, he's still there, and he's definitely watching."

Aris spoke loudly to the ticket man. "Three tickets to the American border, please."

The vendor told Aris the total and collected the fee. "*Ocho*," he directed, pointing to the number eight blue bus.

"How long until it leaves?" Aris asked.

"Three hours."

Taking the tickets, Aris handed one to John and one to Uri. "Follow me."

"Are we going home?" John asked.

Aris grabbed his backpack. "Just follow me. We're being watched."

They loaded their bags into bus number eight and climbed aboard. Aris claimed the second window seat. From that vantage point, he saw the truck driver speeding away from the curb.

Immediately Aris hopped up. "Okay, guys. You wait here, but keep watching me. On my signal, grab all three of our packs and follow."

John stood up at his seat, then sat down, then stood back up again. "What are we doing? I don't understand. I thought we were going home."

Aris shot him a stiff look and John dropped on his rear to the seat. Stepping off the bus, Aris stared at the destination board and saw that the next departing bus was bound for Guatemala. He caught the attention of a teenage boy nearby. "I'll give you ten bucks if you go buy me three tickets for the Guatemala bus… the one leaving soonest."

The young Mexican raced off and soon returned with three tickets. "Bus 22, green, over there. Departs in five minutes."

Pleased, Aris slipped the kid a twenty-dollar tip and waved to summon John and Uri.

— ◊ —

A couple miles outside of town, Katerina's brothers waited, guns pointing towards the blue number eight bus headed their way.

Pietro flagged down the driver, who brought the bus to a grinding halt at the side of the narrow road.

The brothers climbed aboard, searching faces for their quarry.

"Where are the three Americanos?" Pietro called to the driver.

"No Americanos," the man spat.

Pietro pressed his pistol to the driver's head. "Don't fuck with me. Three Americanos boarded this bus."

"No Americanos," the man repeated.

Another brother pointed his weapon at the head of a female passenger. "Where are they?"

The woman trembled, clutching her handbag. "No Americans on this bus."

The brother looked to Pietro who shook his head. They all climbed off and regrouped around the car.

"They must have switched buses. First they lied to my little sister, now they fool us as well. I will kill all three of them!"

"I told you to let me kill them," the youngest brother whined. "Americano and Greco, two times *pousta*, two times *bastardo!*"

"Where to now?" asked the third brother.

"Back to the station. We'll find them and shoot their balls off."

They hopped in the car and made a sharp turn, headed back to town. The brother in the passenger seat dialled a number and Katerina's voice boomed from the speaker. "Are you bringing him back to me?"

"The cheating bastardo outfoxed us. But we'll find him."

"I told you, Aris is intelligent," she cooed.

"Intelligent, maybe. But he's still *bastardo*," the younger brother yelled. "When we bring him back, he won't be good for anything."

"You don't touch him!" Katerina screamed. "I want him alive. I will torture him until he tells me the love secret. Then you can do whatever you want to him."

"You believe those lies?" the younger brother laughed. "There's no such secret."

"The goddess Aphrodite gave this secret to Paris of Troy," Katerina recounted. "Paris used it to make Helen fall in love with him. She abandoned her children and even her husband the king to follow Paris. Troy went to war for ten years… all because of this love secret."

"Don't be stupid, sister. I'm telling you there's no love secret."

"There is," she argued. "Everything began in Greece—the alphabet, music, medicine, computers, astrology. El Greco told me. And I watch the History channel, so I know it's true. These Grecos have clever minds. They keep the love secret for themselves."

"Maybe our sister is right," Pietro said quietly. "I want to know this love secret too. I can make Dolina… or any other girl… fall in love with me."

"It's a trick!" the younger brother argued. "But at least I'll get to torture the bastard."

"If you touch one hair on El Greco's head," Katerina screeched, "I will pull your eyes out and eat them for lunch. You bring him back to me alive. After two more nights in bed, I will have convinced him to tell me the love secret."

The brothers all cringed at the pitch of their sister's voice.

"But after that," Katerina softened, "then you can flay him alive."

Just a few blocks up the road, Katerina's voice screeched.

"What happened," Pietro asked.

"I know where El Greco is going. He is going to find that old lady in Guatemala. Hurry up before he gets across the border."

"What old lady?"

"I tell you later. Hurry up!"

* ◇ *

The three friends climbed onto the green bus at the last possible moment and took seats near the back.

After they were underway, Aris questioned another passenger to find out the itinerary.

"That guy said it's forty minutes to the nearest town. We won't need to change buses. One stop, then we go straight for the Guatemalan border."

Uri and John looked positively terrified to be on the run.

Aris could give them no reassurance. "If that lunatic woman's brothers take offence to me leaving her, they will find out where we're going."

John scratched his head. "What if this girl truly loves you, Aris?"

Uri laughed. "What she's got isn't the kind of love Mr. Dreamer is looking for."

"I'm no longer convinced there's such a thing as true love," Aris mused. "It seems love is always a compromise."

John arched an eyebrow. "I can't believe I'm hearing this from you. Up until a few days ago, you always believed in true love."

"Well, even if I could find it, I'm beginning to suspect it's usually one-sided." Aris pointed at Uri. "Look at this idiot. Epi truly loves him…. but he doesn't care one iota."

"I love my wife," Uri defended. "But I don't believe in this myth of undying love. My love is for all women. That's why I can never say no."

"Hmph," Aris grunted. "As soon as a better alternative appears, he jumps into another bed. It's as if people would rather be with someone… anyone… than be lonely." After a short pause he added, "I remember a couple of girls telling me that their partners loved them. When I asked if they loved their partners, they answered, 'Well he loves me.' So I asked, 'But do you love him?'"

John was hanging on Aris's every word while Uri pretended to stare out the bus window at the passing landscape.

"One of the girls answered, 'He's a good father.' The other replied, 'He's a good provider.' So I pushed harder. 'But do you love your husbands?' Neither one of them so much as opened their mouths again."

Uri turned back to the conversation. "*If a better alternative shows up…* now that's a motto I'll subscribe to! That's why we need easy divorces. Like the Arabs. They can just say to the girl three times, 'I divorce you,' and it's done. No courts. No drama." Uri punched Aris in the shoulder. "You do have to admit these last few nights with the hairdresser were pretty great, right?"

"She had the curves, and she was a tiger in the sack. But it was only hormonal pleasure without emotions. At the end, I was just waiting to become the tiger's next meal."

"But you enjoyed it!" Uri insisted.

"Yes, I enjoyed it. Still, it was empty of any emotion. I did kind of like her. Under different circumstances, who knows?"

Uri clapped his hands triumphantly. "That's what it's all about. Enjoyment! You don't have to marry the girl to enjoy her company. Finally, you're learning something! You should thank me."

Aris looked from Uri to John and then back again. "Maybe I should go back to her."

37 Black Widow

Without looking up from his desk, the Chief of Police barked, "You have two minutes. Not a second more!"

Detective Joanna Bear may have been a rookie, but she seemed unintimidated. She deftly laid out four photos labelled Missing Persons. "All four of these men vanished. No notes, nothing. None had money worries. All were single. No ransom demands were made. But each of them had one common connection…"

The Chief raised his head and motioned for her to get on with it.

Detective Bear stared into his eyes. "Varo Chase."

The Chief cleared his throat and lifted to his feet. "What are you insinuating, Detective?"

"You tell me. Each one of these four gentlemen had an affair with her."

He cast his gaze out the office window. "Are you telling me Varo Chase is some kind of black widow, killing her lovers after mating?"

"I don't know anything about murder, or spiders for that matter, but she's just become a prime suspect in all four cases."

"Prime suspect?" the Chief laughed. "Missing persons cases have victims, not suspects."

"Yes, prime suspect," Detective Bear assured him. "Just by accident, my department stumbled across two other cases—recent complaints made against Miss Chase by another successful businessman, that Chase tried to run him and his wife off the road on two separate occasions."

Stone-faced, the Chief merely examined each of the four photographs spread across his desk.

"I reached out to the detective in charge. The complaints were reported about a white SUV in each case. The claimant, an Aris Theo, says he refused Chase's sexual advances, and the attacks were meant as retaliation."

The Chief rubbed his chin with thumb and forefinger and waited for what must ultimately come next.

"Varo Chase owns a fleet of white SUVs."

Collecting the photos, the Chief took a few steps around his desk to stand next to the detective. "Do you know who Varo Chase is? She has connections all the way to the top. The highest seats of our government. So these accusations better have grounds or all our heads will fly."

Detective Bear arched her neck proudly. "Two of the missing persons were last reported seen in the company of Varo Chase. There is a pattern emerging here, sir."

"Something just does not feel right about this," the Chief mused. "As a matter of transparency, I must inform you that Miss Chase is a close personal friend. I view her like a daughter to me."

The detective took two steps back to distance herself.

"Varo could have any man she wants. Why would she resort to violence?"

"Perhaps these men did not want her attentions."

A bitter smile graced the Chief's face. "She's also a generous philanthropist… many charitable organisations, including our own police benevolence fund."

He started to pace in front of his desk.

"Why would Miss Chase kill her lovers? She has the highest security clearances. She can walk in and out of even the President's office. It just doesn't make sense. Your accusations will make us look like fools."

The rookie cop didn't flinch. She reached out to retrieve the photographs which the Chief handed over reluctantly.

"I can name three of her ex-boyfriends who are alive and well. Off the record, one is our current Vice President. If she's hell bent on eliminating such men, why did those three escape her? Where is your pattern?"

The Chief could tell he was getting nowhere. He needed to appeal to the detective's feminine side. "I knew Miss Chase's parents. They were murdered when she was just nine years old."

"Yes, sir. I know." Detective Bear's voice softened. "That's why I came directly to you."

He pointed a finger. "You are not to mention their death to anyone, especially to her. She gets very upset."

"Perhaps the abused becomes the abuser?" The detective wisely bit her tongue before sealing her own fate. "But just because Chase is your friend, that shouldn't stop us from investigating."

"I don't intend to stop anything." The Chief circled his desk and sat back down. "I want you to make this case a priority so we can clear her name ASAP. But make no mistake, if you botch this, I will have your badge. I want solid evidence, no speculation."

Detective Bear appeared unmoved. "Your connection blinds you, sir."

"And inexperience clouds your judgement. Dismissed, Detective."

"One-hour stop for re-fueling," the bus driver called. "Get something to eat and don't be late."

John led the way, followed by Uri then Aris.

"Mmm, I smell sauteed onions." Uri licked his lips. "Mexican for dinner again."

Aris turned the other direction, heading for a small store. "Not for me. I've had it with onions. I'm allergic."

"You're allergic to the two best things in life then," Uri chided. "Onions and women!"

Aris kept to his path and raised a middle finger behind him, passing a young mother and her four-year-old son who was playing cops and robbers with a plastic pistol.

Forty-five minutes later, John and Uri took their seats, while Aris paused beside the driver. "How long to the border?"

"Two hours, give or take." The man yawned. "Depending on how many pick-ups we have to make."

"You're sleepy," Aris noted.

"I'm used to it."

"Wait, I'll get you some coffee." Aris stepped back off the bus.

"With plenty of sugar," the driver called behind him. "Or a sandwich would be even better."

Aris returned some minutes later. "One super-size coffee with plenty of sugar, and something called a *mulita*. They told me it was like a quesadilla on steroids."

The driver stashed both on the console at his side and started up the bus. "*Gracias a Díos, señor.* Today just got better."

⁕ ◇ ⁕

Katerina's brothers met up with a second car of lackeys at a bus station in a nearby small town. "Spread out," Pietro ordered. "The supervisor said they got on the #22 bus."

The youngest brother stood grinding his jaws. "When I get my hands on them, I'll kill them. I'll kill them two times."

"The bus isn't here," another brother yelled back from the end of the lot.

"Maybe it's not here yet," one of the lackeys suggested.

Pietro pointed to the buildings next door. "Two of you go to the shop and two to the restaurant. Ask around if anyone's seen three Americanos. I'll check to see if the bus has come or not."

Before Pietro even finished speaking to the old man at the small ticket booth, his youngest brother was panting at his side. "The Gringos were here. Two eat at the canteen, one took nuts and sweets, then he went back for coffee and a sandwich. They left maybe half an hour ago."

"More like an hour," said the old man in the booth.

Pietro shook his head. "Katerina was right then. They're heading for Guatemala. It will be touch and go to catch them before the border."

"Come on then!" the younger brother shouted, bolting for the car.

Pietro uncurled a map from the glovebox. "There's a shortcut, but the road is narrow."

One of the middle brothers chimed in, "We should stay on the main road. If we get stuck behind a mule we'll never catch them before the border. Probably the bus has regular stops along the way. We need to make good time."

Pietro thought for a moment then reached for his cell phone. "Pablo," he said to one of the men in the other car. "There's an old road about five miles from here. Take that shortcut toward Guatemala."

"Good idea!" the younger brother shouted.

"If you get to the border crossing before us, grab the Americanos," Pietro continued. "Do nothing. Wait for us. Full speed, Pablo."

The brothers raced headlong down the main road. "Pass this *pousta*," the younger one roared. The driver pulled into the opposing lane, coming head to head with cars travelling the other direction. Bumps in the road sent the vehicle flying, and dust rose on the landings.

A storm cloud passed overhead, and the sky darkened. A few miles later drizzle coated the windshield, already splattered with bugs. The driver switched on the wipers, but they couldn't compete as a heavy rain filled the gullies and drenched the road. The driver dropped the car into a lower gear.

Pietro banged his fist on the dashboard. "Don't slow down! We didn't come all this way just to lose them."

"You're going to kill us," the driver protested. "If we miss them at the border, we can chase after them in Guatemala."

"You forget we're not welcome there, thanks to that bad shipment last month. If word gets out, we'll be taco meat." Pietro's phone rang and he checked caller ID. "Be quiet, it's Katerina." He answered on speakerphone.

"Did you catch them?" she screeched.

"We're close. You were right. They are heading for Guatemala."

The younger brother leaned over the back seat and shouted towards the phone. "You'll know when we catch them. You'll hear their dying screams!"

"Do not touch El Greco. Not before he tells me the love secret…"

"Don't worry, sister," Pietro soothed. "I will chase him to the end of the world myself." With that he ended the call.

The driver flipped off the windshield wipers as the rain eased. "Remind me why we're risking our lives for that stupid bitch."

The middle brother from the back seat slapped the driver's head. "She's the smartest out of all of us."

"Sure, chasing some mythical love secret."

"What if it's true?" Pietro wondered. "Wouldn't you like to be able to make any girl fall in love with you?"

The driver laughed. "Just so long as they fall in front of me with their legs open, I don't care what else they fall into."

* ◇ *

The Chief called Detective Bear's supervisor into his office. "David, I want extreme confidentiality on these missing persons cases. No one gets wind of it. Are you on this?"

"Joanna's a good detective," the supervisor shared. "Young and eager, perhaps, but I can ride herd."

"Well, I want more. I want you to investigate this claimant who filed about the car accidents. I want to know everything about him."

"I'm telling you, Joanna's got a one hundred percent success rate so far. If someone can close the cases, it's her."

"Don't misunderstand me, David. I want you on this every step of the way. Check the missing persons again to see if they secretly had any financial troubles… or any connections with the companies Miss Chase took over in the last few years."

"Speaking of connections to Miss Chase—" David began.

But the Chief interrupted. "Check their motives and find out exactly where and who they were last seen with. From now on, you report directly to me, with the utmost discretion.

The supervisor cleared his throat. "As I was about to mention, there is someone else with a connection to Varo Chase that you should know about."

The Chief cocked an anxious ear.

"Detective Bear was adopted after her policeman father was killed with a machete while he was defending a young mother."

The Chief's face lit with recognition. "You mean Sergeant Woodcroft was the detective's father?"

"Yes, sir. After his death, Miss Chase's donations to our benevolence fund supported Joanna and her mother. That money paid off the house loan and covered all the mother's psychiatric care… until she died as well. Joanna still lives in that house."

"You know the rules, David. None of the sponsored police orphans are to be notified that Miss Chase is their benefactor."

"Are you aware that the fund also sponsored Detective Bear's law studies with a full scholarship?"

The Chief spoke through clenched teeth. "Make sure neither of them finds out. I'm positive Miss Chase cannot be involved with these disappearances." He motioned to dismiss the supervisor. "Get out. You've raised my blood pressure enough for one day."

— ◇ —

John had been staring out the dirty bus window, counting donkeys on the long road trip. He'd grown accustomed to crazy Mexican drivers trying to overtake the bus on the straightaways, but it still unnerved him when some would pull out to pass in the curves and bends of the single-lane road.

The sound of a honking horn drew his attention down to another such idiot. This time it was a car filled with four men who appeared to be shouting at each other and pointing up at the bus.

Oncoming traffic forced the car to retreat behind the bus, but mere moments later, they made another attempt. This time John looked straight into the black eyes of Katerina's eldest brother.

He jumped over to where Uri was seated and shook his friend by both shoulders, pointing out the window. "Th-th-they're here."

"Who's here?" Uri asked. "Still counting jackasses?"

John shoved Uri's face up against the glass. A string of burps escaped his friend's mouth as Katerina's brothers once more narrowly avoided being squashed by oncoming traffic, retreating behind the bus.

Uri jumped up and threw himself over the seat back to poke Aris in the shoulder. "Aaah! Aris!"

Aris groggily shoved Uri's arm away. "Can't you see that I'm sleeping?"

"Th-th-they're here," John repeated, louder this time.

Aris opened his eyes and followed Uri's panicked pointing out the back window.

Lazily lifting his torso, Aris turned. The sight of Pietro in the front seat waving his pistol woke Aris faster than a double espresso.

"Don't look back," he instructed John and Uri. Fast on his feet, he made his way to the front of the bus.

John couldn't help himself. He perched on the back seat gawking out the rear window.

Two quick shots pelted off the metal screen that wrapped the back of the bus. John and Uri ducked, crashing to the floor together in a jumble of limbs.

"Aris!" John squeaked in a girlish voice. "They're shooting at us!"

"I told you not to look back!" Aris continued making his way up the aisle. The four-year-old boy had apparently tired of cops and robbers and was now asleep in his mother's arms. Aris borrowed the plastic pistol and dug out his wallet with the other hand.

When he reached the front of the bus, Aris pointed the toy gun at the back of the driver's head and waved cash. "Fifty bucks if you don't let that car overtake us."

The driver snuck a peek in the rear-view mirror. Seeing Aris he grabbed at the money. Then he looked out the side mirror and caught sight of the brothers' car angling once more to pass.

Grinding some gears, the driver moved his bus into the middle of the available space.

Katerina's brothers swerved to avoid being forced off the road. No guardrails lined this stretch of pavement. The road was still damp from recent rain, and made it even harder for the brothers to regain control of their vehicle.

At the sight of oncoming cars and a small pickup truck, the bus driver moved back into his lane.

Sure enough, the brothers managed to catch up again. The bus driver tried the same manoeuvre, but an old man and his donkey had wandered into the far lane in a patch where rain had washed out the side of the road.

But on one final attempt, the brothers were successful, easily overtaking the bus, then veering back in front of it so quickly it made the driver slam on the brakes.

Several passengers were thrown into the aisles, and a chorus of groans went up all around. Aris himself had clung to the back of the driver's seat and had dropped the toy pistol which rattled its way several rows back where its owner was now wide awake and screaming.

The bus driver's knuckles were white as Aris looked from the man up and out the windshield to see the brothers speeding away into the distance.

Indifferently the bus driver declared, "Not looking for us."

Aris knew better.

Several hundred metres ahead, the brothers' car spun around, blocking the roadway. Car doors flew open and four men hopped out, aiming handguns directly at the bus.

Aris dug into his wallet. "Fifty more if you don't stop."

The driver again snatched the cash. "This is only a ten!"

Aris reached into his pocket and pulled out a big wad of bills, handing across another fifty-dollar bill.

"They'll shoot us," the driver advised.

"No, they want me alive," Aris assured him. "Step on it!"

The sound of two shots echoed through the air, but neither hit.

"Just warning fire," Aris encouraged. "Try and take out the front wheel of their car as we blow past."

As the bus got closer and closer to where the four men staged their standoff, Aris could see two of the brothers exchanging frightened glances. But the younger brother in the back held his ground, as well as Pietro up front.

When the large vehicle was a breath away, the brothers scattered like flies on a donkey's swishing tail. The sound of metal on metal caused the bus passengers to shout in panic and clutch at each other. The brothers' car went spinning as the bus shook by it. Aris raced to the back of the bus to keep it in sight as the vehicle toppled over the embankment, somersaulting end over end down a hill.

Guns raised once more, Aris saw one brother take aim at the back of the bus, while Pietro used his weapon to hijack the only other vehicle on the road.

38 Race to the Border

Pietro's brothers looked at him like he'd lost his mind.

"A tractor? Seriously?"

By the time the brothers all climbed on, the vehicle could hardly budge, what with the heavy forklift attachment on the front and a crammed-full trailer it was already towing.

"Full speed ahead!" Pietro shouted.

"No full speed," the farmer replied. "Trailer loaded."

The younger brother hopped off and unhitched the connection. "Let's go!"

⋄

"How far to the border?" Aris asked the bus driver.

"About fifteen miles."

"How fast can you make it?"

The driver stretched out his hand. "Fifty!"

Aris smiled and laughed. "And another fifty when we're safely at the border."

The Mexican driver shook his rear and settled into the seat, down-shifting and jamming his foot on the gas pedal. He moved into the passing lane as if it belonged to him. "About time I see some action!"

The other passengers were less entertained. An old woman pointed her knitting needles at Aris's behind, while the young child's mother clamped onto her offspring to keep him from flying around the bus.

Four minutes later a semi hauling two tandem trailers was headed straight at them.

"Out of my way!" the bus driver shouted, but at the last minute Aris grabbed the steering wheel to manoeuvre the bus into the normal lane.

"I would have pushed him out of our way," the driver complained.

"And we'd be pancakes. You don't get the other fifty bucks until we get to the border... alive."

Pietro fished in his back pocket and pulled out some cash. "We have to get to the border before that bus."

The tractor driver stuffed the money in his shirt pocket. "Hold tight, and don't shit your pants!"

He spun the tractor away from the main road and into the field. Two of the brothers tumbled off the back and had to run to catch up. The other two clenched with white-knuckled hands.

After a few minutes, they came to a spot where the main road made a big bend. The tractor crossed the road again and headed into the next side field.

This time the first two brothers clung tight, but the youngest plunged into the gulley when the tractor driver refused to slow to negotiate the drop off the main road.

"Stop!" Pietro yelled. "We have to go back for my brother."

"Let him run like you did when we fell," one of the other brothers shouted. "We don't want to miss the Americanos!"

Undeterred, the tractor driver continued his straight path.

Pietro pulled out his gun and took aim at the driver's head. "I said, go back and pick up my brother."

The tractor driver spun them around and they circled back, but still the younger brother had to sprint to jump on board.

Aris could see the border crossing about a hundred metres ahead, with several cars and two buses stopped in line. He raced to the back of the bus where John and Uri were still glued to the rear window.

John pointed, but not where Aris expected. "Over there," he squealed. "In the field."

Aris caught sight of an enormous cloud of dust rising behind a tractor overflowing with dark-skinned Mexicans, poised to intersect the main road ahead of the bus.

"They're going to try to cut us off," Aris muttered. "Get all our backpacks and come up front." Aris quickly headed to the driver. "Get us as close to the border as possible. This time I don't care who you have to run over."

The driver held out his palm, and Aris graced it with yet another fifty-dollar bill.

In seconds the bus swerved to the side and, with one set of tyres dragging the gravel berm, they passed the line of cars and buses. Several passengers screamed, and the little boy took aim out the window with his plastic pistol.

Aris followed the young man's line of sight to see Katerina's brothers and their hijacked tractor had reached the border crossing as well. But the tractor had to drive parallel to them since a deep gulley separated the field from the main road.

Pietro's gun was aimed at the bus driver, while his brothers unsuccessfully tried to shoot out the bus's tyres.

The bus driver let out a cackle and shouted, "Emergency spin stop!"

With a hard pull of the hand brake, the tyres gave out a long loud screech. Passengers and their belongings flew into the aisle, and Uri came smashing into Aris's back. "Stop! We're gonna crash!" Then he burped twice.

The bus continued its swivel, as if in slow motion. Aris took in every detail of the action, from the old lady with the knitting needles now laying in the aisle in a tangle of yarn, to Pietro and the brothers looking fierce but helpless on the tractor.

Just ten metres from the border crossing, now facing the wrong direction, the bus came to a grinding halt.

"Super-sized coffee worked! Now it's time for my sandwich." The bus driver reached over to the console to retrieve the *mulita* Aris had purchased at the previous rest area.

Aris donned the backpack Uri had brought up for him. "We're gonna have to run for it!"

The bus driver opened the door for them, probably sad to see the rich Americanos go.

Aris spotted another familiar face peeking out of a blue car at the side of the road. In that same moment, all four doors of the blue car opened and Mexicans holding pistols hopped out and took aim. "Pablo and the other thugs are here, too."

He glanced behind to catch sight of Katerina's brothers aboard the tractor, now climbing its way up onto the main road at a spot where the gulley wasn't as deep.

Aris turned to the bus driver, his arm stretched with more cash. "See that blue car with the four men? Angle the bus with your side in front of it."

The driver wasted no time dropping the sandwich into his lap and reaching for the money.

⁕ ◊ ⁕

Aris, John and Uri bolted off the bus as the driver took pleasure in following Aris's instructions.

The three stayed hidden on the far side of the bus as it angled around. Passengers were glued to their windows gawking at the activity taking place all around them.

When the bus could move no further, and was blocking the path of bullets from the blue car, Aris yelled, "Run, guys!" and took off frantically towards the border patrol.

⁕ ◊ ⁕

The tractor driver braked to a stop beside the #22 bus. One of the middle brothers stuck his hand in the driver's shirt pocket and swiped the money Pietro had bribed him with, then landed a hard thump with his pistol to the man's head, rendering him unconscious.

Meanwhile the younger brother raced after John and leapt onto the man's back, pulling him to the ground, pack and all, in a jumble.

"Aris!" John yelled in a high pitch.

But there was a queue of people waiting to cross the border, and Aris was far enough ahead that the hubbub covered up John's plaintive cry.

Uri grabbed him by the pack and yanked. "They got John!"

Turning around, Aris saw all four of Katerina's brothers standing over John, who was huddled in the foetal position on the ground. Pietro waved, sporting a big smile.

Uri let out a chain of burps. "Wh-wh-what are we going to do?"

Aris exhaled a deep sigh. His teeth ground together and he could feel the muscles in his back and thighs flex as adrenaline coursed through his entire body.

"Take my pack," he told Uri. "You and John cross the border and check into a hotel in the nearest town. If I'm not there in forty-eight hours…" He looked deep into his friend's eyes before adding, "… go home. Tell my sons I drowned somewhere at sea and you couldn't recover the body."

⸺ ⬧ ⸺

The bus driver carried a bottle of water and the rest of his sandwich over to the tractor driver. The man was still unconscious, so the bus driver poured water over his head.

Fisting his skull in agony, the tractor driver shook himself awake. He scanned left then right, taking in the action and slowly piecing together what had happened. "Bastards took back the money they paid me."

The bus driver pulled out a wad of cash from his pocket. "My Americano didn't. And he has more!" Smiling to his friend, he recounted Aris's kindnesses. "Americano bought me treble coffee and sandwich, without me asking. He good person. Plenty of cash!"

"Did the gringos get across the border? Or did those awful brothers catch them?"

"Two of them got across. But the brothers got my Americano. Took him in a blue car with a white stripe down the middle. Left two minutes ago."

The other driver started up his tractor and whipped out his mobile phone. "Thanks!"

The bus driver hopped off and took a bite of what remained of his sandwich, watching as the tractor crossed back into the fields.

⸻ ◆ ◇ ◆ ⸻

Aris was crammed in the centre of the back seat between Katerina's middle brothers. The younger brother was now driving, with Pietro in the passenger seat. Pablo and the other lackeys had been left at the side of the road to catch a bus back to town, as the brothers commandeered the blue car.

"We should've brought them all," the brother on Aris's right whined.

"No room," Pietro answered. "Greco is the only one we need."

The brother on Aris's left tried to knock him on the head, but Pietro stopped him with a stare as he wrenched the cell phone up to his ear.

"Yes, Katerina. We have your El Greco." Pietro gave a wry smile at Aris in the back. Then he let out a deep sigh. "No, he did not tell us the love secret." He hung up before his sister could launch into another tirade.

The brother on Aris's right raised his gun and pointed it at Aris's head. "Tell us the love secret!"

"Never mind," Pietro crooned. "Sister will make him speak the secret."

"Of course I will tell Katerina," Aris grumbled. "I was just taking my friends to the border. I had every intent to return to my love, to my Katerina."

The brother on the left slapped Aris in the head.

"After all," Aris said, tapping Pietro on the shoulder. "I had to come back to ask your permission to marry her."

"*Pousta!*" shouted the younger brother as he slapped the steering wheel.

"Ask Katerina," Aris assured. "I tried to propose to her this morning but she stopped me. Said I needed your permission. Call and ask her!"

"Hmph." Pietro grunted but made the call. "Sis, I don't suppose your El Greco tried to propose to you this morning, did he?"

Her squeal could be heard throughout the car. "*Si*, he did!"

"Katerina, my love," Aris shouted to be heard. "Did you get my message? I was just taking my friends to the border and coming back to you."

"No," she pouted. "Who did you give this message to?"

Pietro turned to Aris. "She wants to know who you told to tell her."

"I left a note in my room on the bed."

Pietro relayed the information.

"I will check. If he's lying you cut one finger from each of his hands for me." Then she disconnected the call.

Six minutes later, Pietro's cell rang. He put it on the speaker. "So was there a message?"

"*Si!*" Katerina squealed again. "El Greco loves me. Said he would marry me when he returns!"

The younger brother slapped the steering wheel again. "That's bullshit. I say we cut off all his fingers now."

"No!" Katerina raged. "But first, he must tell me the love secret."

"Fine," the younger brother seethed. "The *bastardo* tells us the love secret now, or I shoot him."

"Only to Katerina," Aris declared. "I'm sworn to tell the love secret to only one person—someone I love and trust. I will only reveal it to my beloved Katerina."

"Yes, yes. Only to me, my El Greco!"

"I love you, Katerina!" Aris shouted.

"You see?" Katerina practically glowed through the phone. "He is coming back to me. Nobody touch my man." Then she switched to Spanish and added, "But after I get the love secret, I will skin him alive myself."

Pietro ended the call.

"*Mierda*," the youngest brother cursed. "Why is there a roadblock out here in the middle of nowhere?"

Pietro looked up from his cell phone.

The brother on Aris's right yelled, "Look! Our tractor man is hauling ass across the field."

Aris ran all the possible scenarios through his head while the brothers reacted. Five police cars blocked the road ahead, with just one ancient pickup truck and a motorcycle rider separating them from inspection.

Pietro turned to the brother on Aris's left. "Stick your gun on the Americano's kidney to keep his mouth shut."

The other middle brother stammered, "Um… maybe we should um, turn around and um, use the old road."

"Don't be stupido," Pietro said.

Aris watched in amusement as the tractor tried unsuccessfully to negotiate the gulley to climb up on the road ahead in line with the police cars.

"Well…" the same middle brother hedged, "I kinda knocked out the tractor man and took back the money you paid him."

Pietro squinted and shook his head like a wet dog. Turning to the driver, he instructed, "Spin around! We'll take the old road."

They were close enough to the roadblock that Aris could make out a plain clothes cop wearing a sheriff's badge give a friendly wave to the tractor driver.

"Back!" Pietro now shouted. "Turn back!"

Tyres screeched as the youngest brother slammed the breaks and spun the wheel, leaving scorch marks on the road, before pinning the gas pedal to the floor.

Aris heard sirens begin their wistful wail as four cop cars joined the chase. Even the tractor driver gave up his fight against the landscape and turned to follow them.

The youngest brother whirled the blue car into the passing lane, causing Aris to jostle into the brother with a gun already stabbing into his side.

After breezing past an old VW Beetle that looked like it was held together only by rust, the driver reeled them back into the other lane.

Aris could see the tractor making good time as the blue car approached a bend in the road ahead. Meanwhile lights and sirens filled the road behind them. But wait! What did Aris see on the road ahead?

A green bus with a destination indicator that read "22" came rushing around the curve, headed straight towards them. When Aris recognized the sound of its air brake, he braced for impact. The bus tyres began their long, loud squall.

The enormous vehicle came to a swivelled stop across both lanes.

"Fuck! Cut across the field!" Pietro shouted, and the youngest brother twisted the steering wheel, muscles bulging under the adrenaline.

At their present speed, the blue car flew over the gulley, landing with a jolt in the open field.

Aris seized the moment of surprise, pummelling the driver with a massive punch to the head, sending the youngest brother folding into the wheel.

A devastating backhand to the throat of the brother on Aris's left made the man drop his gun and gag for breath, while Aris stuck a hard elbow in the throat of the brother on the other side. While that one clutched at his neck, choking, Aris sloped himself over the body to thrust open the door.

The blue car was still racing unbridled as the youngest brother's foot had become jammed on the gas. With a manic shove, Aris pushed the Mexican to his right out of the car.

He took note of Pietro yanking his youngest brother's body back against the driver's seat and grabbing for the steering wheel to try to bring the car under control.

Aris felt the vehicle slowing, and knew time was of the essence. He throttled the one remaining brother in the backseat, rendering him incapacitated. Again he levered himself across the body to heave open the left door, but this time flung his own weight instead.

Aris rolled into a ball to absorb the worst of the impact, but heard the chugging of the tractor at top speed, arcing itself into a beeline for the blue car.

The soil here was soggier, probably due to the recent downpour, and Pietro's attempts to keep speed were waning as his car's wheels sucked mud.

The next sound Aris heard was the whir of machinery as the tractor driver lifted the arms of the forklift. With its big tyre treads, the tractor made short work of catching up to the muck-drenched blue car.

Aris watched the tractor driver expertly angle the forklift's tines through the open car windows, then another mechanical whir followed as its feisty driver raised Katerina's brothers high into the air. The three were caught like Mexican fish in a net!

Aris inspected his body for damage. Feeling none beyond a bruised ego, he looked back towards the road where police officers had raced to the field and were already apprehending the brother who had fallen out of the car.

Then he saw the driver of the #22 bus loping into and out of the gulley, heading his way. When the man reached Aris, huffing and puffing, he pointed back to one of the policemen dressed in plain clothes but sporting a sheriff's badge. "Nice to have a son in high places," he grinned.

The sheriff and several of his officers were already closing in on the blue car's occupants, weapons drawn and aimed. "Lower the forklift," the sheriff called to the tractor driver.

Once all four brothers were handcuffed and led back across the field, the sheriff and one of his officers remained, chatting with the tractor driver. Aris and the bus driver made their way over to join them.

The sheriff turned to Aris. "You're lucky my father informed us. This is a known drug cartel with many murders left unprosecuted. We've been hoping for just such a break. We'll take your statement back at the border station."

The tractor driver reached with a handshake for Aris. "Your friend tells me you good man," he said, pointing to the bus driver with a toothless grin. "And you have many fifty-dollar notes in pocket."

Aris dug into his left trouser pocket while shaking the man's hand with his right, then discreetly clasped hands together to slip a few bills into his saviour's fist.

Turning back to the sheriff, Aris saw that the officer already had a keen understanding of what had taken place. He snaked a hand back into his trouser pocket.

The sheriff held up a cautionary hand. "Please. It is an offence to bribe an officer of the law."

Aris smiled in surprise and stole a glance at the proud bus driver. Then remembering details of all that transpired, Aris warned, "Sheriff, there are four men—thugs of Katerina's brothers—back at the border."

The plain clothes sheriff turned to his father the bus driver. "We'll ride with you. I'll phone ahead for more support and we'll arrest them there, while my sergeant takes the American's full statement."

Aris accompanied the policemen and the driver back to the bus, passing four cop cars where Katerina's brothers had been restrained in the backseats.

He took note of the youngest brother, writhing against handcuffs and growling in Aris's direction.

"Your sister is gorgeous," Aris taunted. "A half-hour BJ and she still rides me like a bucking bronco! If you hadn't threatened to kill me and my friends, I would've stayed and married her."

Turning his sight on Pietro, Aris said, "You have more brains, and you actually love your sister. Tell Katerina I do love her, too. And tell her I will send for her to come to America to marry her because I do not trust your brothers."

"You lying *pousta!*" the younger brother shouted. "You won't send for Katerina and you're not coming back. When? When are you coming back?"

"In my village, we eat when we are hungry," Aris laughed. "We sleep when we are sleepy. We make love when we are horny. Wherever we are, whatever the time. We have no watches. When I come back means… when I come back."

The sheriff opened the rear door where the youngest brother was restrained. Reaching into a shirt pocket, he retrieved some cash. "I think this belongs to one of my father's friends."

One of the middle brothers yelled from the rear of the next car over. "My brother's stupido. Back in our car we have a lot of cash. We can arrange even more to you."

The sheriff motioned to his sergeant who pulled out a notepad to consult.

"We found and searched this car well, sir." The sergeant peered up at his superior as he announced, "We found no money. Just one bag of white powder, Evidence enough to send you to jail."

"What?" the same brother fumed. "We had a duffel bag full of cash! And twenty kilos ready for delivery."

Aris could see Pietro bang his head against the seat in front of him in the next police car over.

Joyfully the sergeant made a fresh note in his pad. "There were lots of witnesses around the car when we arrived at the scene. I guess someone must have stolen it all. But now that you've confessed…"

40 THE SAMARITAN & FIFTY-DOLLAR BILLS

Aris and the sheriff boarded the #22 bus. The driver broke into a wide grin. "How many fifties you slip the tractor man?"

"None," Aris confessed.

"What? No, I saw you."

"I offered but he refused."

"He refused?" The driver carefully negotiated a three-point turn to get the bus headed back towards the border. "Either he's a rich farmer, or he's stupid."

Aris reached into his wallet and started to peel out some bills.

"No, man. You're a good friend. You bought me coffee *and* a sandwich."

"How many children you have?" Aris asked.

"Five, including this one." He threw a nod towards the sheriff.

Aris counted out five fifty-dollar bills. "You give one of these to each of them." Then he turned to the sheriff. "It's not a bribe if it comes from your father."

The driver pocketed the cash. "I've got three more children by my wife's sister."

Aris slapped his knee. "You moron! You slept with your wife's sister?"

"What can I say?" the driver shrugged. "She is a young widow. I do what I can to help her in the kitchen…" Then he made eye contact in the rear-view mirror and winked at Aris before adding, "…and the bedroom."

"Go slow, Dad," the sheriff coached the bus driver. "Aris, let me know when you see the four hatchet men."

Scanning the area, Aris pointed to two Mexicans. "There! The guys leaning on the red bus. The short one is named Pablo. I don't see the other two, but if they catch sight of me, I'm a dead man."

"Dad, pull the bus up next to that other police car."

The driver brought the bus to a glide stop and opened the door for his son. Pocketing his badge, the sheriff stepped out and summoned two other men in civilian clothes who carried themselves in a professional demeanour. Aris followed discreetly, trying to stay out of Pablo's line of sight.

"One of you take this witness to the station. Walk him slowly in front of those two men leaning on the red bus." He pointed to Aris who was visibly shaken by this news. "Don't worry, sir. We'll be right behind you." Summoning a middle-aged man dressed like he was ready for a night at the club, he added, "When I tap your shoulder, Detective, give one of your loud sneezes."

The sheriff stuck his head back inside the bus and called, "Dad, pull into your normal parking position for this route. If the henchmen come on board, excuse yourself and tell them you're going to the bathroom."

Aris tried to refuse, having only narrowly escaped the previous ordeal. But the sheriff would not hear his excuses, pushing him out in front of the bus.

After taking just a dozen steps, a series of loud sneezes erupted behind Aris. Despite forewarning, he turned to see what was the matter, only to get the evil eye from the sheriff. Aris faced forwards and continued the march to his likely execution.

Pablo and his friend had also looked up to see the source of the bizarre sneezing. They were currently elbowing each other in the ribs and laughing, but when Aris resumed walking, the taller Mexican's expression changed. This time he grabbed Pablo by the shoulders and whispered something.

Aris didn't need to read lips to know his presence had been noted. The sight of Pablo drawing his pistol sent Aris scurrying for cover on the far side of the queue forming for the border crossing.

But Pablo's friend was also quick, blocking the way and indiscreetly clasping his own handgun under the loose shirt front.

Aris didn't bother to look for the sheriff or his deputies. Clearly in Mexico it was every gringo for himself. Aris prepared to launch one of his trademark rear kicks, but stopped short.

"Where's Pietro?" Pablo asked, glancing around like a student desperately wanting to earn the teacher's praise.

Instead of the cartel leader, what Pablo saw behind him was a middle-aged man out with a buddy, probably heading over to Guatemala for an evening of debauchery, out of sight of any wife at home.

Pablo turned back to Aris, whose eyebrows were now climbing onto his forehead. "I'm like a fox on the scent with you, and you are the chicken who won't get away again."

Aris saw Pablo's back stiffen, and the next thing he heard was the sheriff's voice booming. "And I am a wild coyote who would like nothing better than to rip the fox apart limb by limb and eat him alive."

Pablo slowly raised his arms, revealing the sheriff's gun pressed into his spine.

Pablo's friend angled his body to flee the scene, but two deputies had already circled behind him and grabbed an arm from either side to secure him while the sheriff force-walked Pablo to bus #22.

Aris followed dutifully, hopeful to soon be on his way to offer a well-earned night of debauchery of his own to his two faithful companions across the border.

The sheriff led Pablo to the front seat and handcuffed him to the safety bar, directing the other officers to do the same with his buddy on the opposite side of the bus.

"You." The sheriff pointed to Aris. "Sit beside our little friend here and keep him company while we wait for the other two to take the bait."

Aris perched on the edge of the seat, catching the bus driver's reassuring smile in the rear-view mirror. Meanwhile the sheriff struck up a seemingly casual conversation with the deputies a few seats back, arguing about which team would win an upcoming football match. Aris recognized another of the plain clothes detectives take up station, slouching outside the bus door with his lips wrapped around a cigarette.

Each second ticked by interminably. Aris wondered what Katerina would think when she learned her brothers had been imprisoned and the love of her life had fled the country. Such a shame. The lady was a hellcat in bed, but Aris's tastes were ready to turn to something a bit less feral.

Aris flashed back to his present situation when two men tripped out of the makeshift saloon next to the border station. They looked around as if to find someone they knew. Seeing the green bus, one man's eyes lit up and he slapped his friend on the shoulder then pointed.

The first man made his way onto the #22 bus, followed on the heels by his buddy. "Shit, Pablo! Where'd you find the Americano? Pietro's gotta be out of his mind by now looking for him."

"Like lambs to the fucking slaughter," Pablo mumbled and rattled his hands in the cuffs at them.

The henchman in the rear was the first to figure out what was happening, but the cop at the bus door had already stamped out his cigarette and drawn his weapon at the man's back.

"Time for a trim and a shave!" the sheriff laughed merrily. "Eight of the hairdresser gang's members in one day!"

The other cops escorted the four men out and into police cruisers that pulled up to the border right on time. Aris gave a handshake to the bus driver, and a hopeful wave to the sheriff. "Well, now that you have the whole gang, you won't be needing me anymore."

"We still need that statement," the sheriff smiled. "I'll need to know of any illegal activities you may have witnessed."

Aris caught himself grinning. "I'm not entirely familiar with Mexican law, but that Katerina certainly did some sexual wonders that haven't yet been legalized in all of the fifty United States."

The sheriff just shook his head as his father fought down a belly laugh. "All right. You're free to go. Just try to keep your pecker away from any more chickens or foxes on the other side of this border, eh? This coyote won't always be there to protect you."

Aris didn't give the man time to change his mind.

"Where to now?" Uri asked when Aris arrived at their hotel.

"Sololá, the town with the most beautiful girls in Latin America."

"Lying bastard. You said that about the last town. The only girls that wanted me were all short with massive rears and stomachs."

John burst into laughter.

"No, no. This one is spectacular, situated next to a lake. The girls are tall, slim, and lightly tan. No comparison with Mexican girls," Aris insisted.

"You don't fool me," Uri said. "You're still chasing that cursed myth the love secret."

"How far away is it?" John asked. "Look at these ancient busses—a tractor would be more comfortable."

Aris appeared sceptical at first but then agreed. "It's three to four hours away. Let's splurge for a taxi."

Uri tapped Aris on the shoulder. "Why is it that you listen to John but not to me?"

"Because John doesn't nag like an old woman. Plus he is right. Remember, you both said you would go where I go… no questions asked."

Nodding his submission, Uri said, "As long as you don't land us in a death trap again."

◆ ◇ ◆

The next morning in the hotel in Sololá, the three friends stood taking in the spectacular views of the Atitlan lake.

John sighed. "This is just as amazing as you promised, Aris."

"Well, I don't see any girls," moaned Uri. "Only old women."

"But beautiful!" Aris laughed. "In truth, I expected a much smaller village. Let's explore. To save time, John you go east, Uri you go west, and I will go north. Then we meet back here in a couple of hours. Ask around for the best bars and restaurants. And any interesting places to visit… maybe some fishing trips."

Uri grunted. "You want to get rid of us again."

"You are nagging again, Uri," John warned. "Aris is right. It will save time."

Aris went off in search of a house with a giant cross and an arrow pointing east, meanwhile stopping to ask locals about an old Greek lady named Garoufalia.

Up one hill, Aris saw a lady struggling to carry her shopping bags. Volunteering, Aris carried the load to the top of the steep path where she lived.

From that vantage point, Aris spied the house he'd been looking for at the peak of the north end of the village.

When he finally made his way to the home, a young boy answered the door.

"I am told an old Greek lady named Garoufalia lives here."

The boy shouted something and raced deeper into the house. Shortly a woman who appeared to be in her sixties appeared. She searched Aris's face for a few long seconds. "No old woman, no Garoufalia." Without further discussion she shut the door.

"Her sister Droso from Mexico sent me."

After only one second the door reopened. Suspiciously the lady asked, "Who are you? What you want?"

Aris was equally suspicious. "Just to meet Garoufalia, to find Droso's family."

"Who are you?"

"My grandfather was from the same village back in Greece, but I never learned more about it. Droso does not remember either. May be Garoufalia will know. She is the eldest. Do you know her?"

"You still haven't answered me. What is your name?"

"Aris."

"Aris what?" she prodded.

"Aris Theo."

"So you are Greek?"

"Yes. Greek living in America."

"Well, Aris Theo, you are a liar. Droso does not know this house."

"No, but Droso's daughter near Leon gave me this address."

The lady only continued to glare at Aris.

"The sister Calliope died in Tampa. Her granddaughter sent me to Droso, who is still alive. Her granddaughter Drosita wants to find all her relatives. She asked me to pass along her telephone number."

Unconvinced the lady folded her arms in front of her chest.

Aris reached into his pocket and pulled out the two embroidered cloths. "One is from Droso and the other from Calliope's granddaughter. The image on the left is the same. It is the village where they were born."

This got the woman's attention. She delicately fingered the two pieces of fabric. Finally she invited him in. "You are not lying, Aris. Mother had similar thing."

After a long coffee Aris passed the lady a slip of paper. "This number is for Drosita, Droso's granddaughter. She would love to speak with you."

She tucked the paper under her saucer but remained silent.

"So Garoufalia is your mother," Aris prompted. "Is she around?"

"Hmph," the woman came to life once more. "Many came looking for Mother."

"I know," Aris agreed. "Droso told me the same."

Unresponsive, he could see bitterness drawn on her face.

"Do you happen to know the name of my grandfather's village?"

Earnestly the lady shook her head.

"Is Garoufalia alive? At least tell me this one thing so I can stop searching for her."

"Mother died!" the woman said.

Nodding with a saddened face, Aris pocketed the two pieces of embroidered cloths and headed for the door. "Thank you. I will be going."

But the young boy stood by the door. In fair English he spoke. "Grandmother, I want to know where great granny came from. It is our…" he struggled for the word, then added, "roots."

Encouraged, Aris looked expectantly from the boy to the older woman.

"There's not much I can tell you. Mother migrated with my younger sister to an old Greek island called Sardinia."

"That's Italy!" Aris corrected.

"She died a few years later. My sister just sent a letter with those exact words—'Mother died.' Maybe you can find my younger sister there. Last I know, she stayed in Sardinia and married late."

Aris's notepad was already in his hands. "Where in Sardinia? A town, a village, an address?"

"The letter was postmarked from a port town. That's all I can tell you."

"What is your sister's name?"

The lady hesitated, but the boy tugged on her sleeve.

"Korona."

"Have you spoken to her since then?"

With tears welling in her eyes the lady confessed, "I was so upset when she and Mother packed to leave, I told them both to never speak to me again." A cry ripped from her throat. "They never did!"

With sympathy, Aris offered her his handkerchief. "Anything else you can tell me? Anything at all that would help me find her?"

Nodding, she wiped her tears. "Once when I was angry as a child, I attacked my sister with a knife."

The boy pulled his hand away, clearly shocked. Aris nodded for her to continue.

"I cut a long deep wound on her left cheek. She will have a scar."

Aris thanked the woman for her help then added, "If I find her, would you like me to give her your number? Say anything?"

This prompted even more tears. After some time, the lady said, "It is too late for my mother. But if you find my sister, tell her I never stopped loving her. The day she speaks to me again will be the happiest day of my life."

Offering his notepad and pen, Aris said, "Write down your telephone number and address."

The boy grabbed both and pressed them into his grandmother's hands, silently urging her.

Hesitantly, she wrote the contact details.

"Can I give this to Drosita?" Aris asked.

With one quick nod Garoufalia's estranged daughter approved.

"So you are Chrisafina," he said.

Her smile was subtle but proud.

"Your aunts, Droso and Caliope, each revealed to me the one clue they knew. Has your mother ever revealed hers to you?"

"I was a wild tempered child. Mother never trusted me with anything." Chrisafina's tone was regretful. "What kind of clues?"

Aris decided it would be best to encourage her trust. "One said you must *be close*, and the other said you must *be touching*…"

Chrisafina sucked in her lower lip and shook her head.

"Does anything come to mind," Aris asked.

"Nothing," Chrisafina replied. Then her gaze shifted up and to the right like she was trying to recollect something just out of sight. "Unless it was a clue and I never realised."

"What?" Aris said quickly, but then tried not to act too excited. "Let's see. It could be."

Chrisafina seemed unconvinced. "Often mother would point her finger at my younger sister and say, 'Remember, you must look the other person in his eyes'."

Aris took out his notebook and jotted it down next to Droso and Cali's clues.

"I don't think it means anything," Chrisafina continued. "Mother was always pointing her finger at my sister and telling her to notice people's eye movements."

Aris added that second part to his notes. "Anything else like this? Don't worry if it makes no sense to you."

Chrisafina shook her head. "Nothing else. But I do remember a time when my sister saw me listening in. She started acting suspicious after that. But I still don't think these are clues."

"Maybe not," Aris agreed, tucking away his notepad with a smile. "But maybe there is something to it."

41 Into the Lion's Mouth

The guys had been lazing in Guatemala for ten days before they boarded another bus. "Sololá was nicer," Uri conceded, "but I'm still not impressed by the girls."

Aris jabbed him in the gut. "You were not impressed because they all refused you!"

"Not *all* of them."

John laughed a girlish giggle.

"Prostitutes do not count!" Aris clarified.

"Even the older ladies there were pretty," John admitted.

"We will be in Guatemala City in a couple of hours," Aris consoled Uri. "More prostitutes in a big city!"

The bus stopped at the next small plaza and the driver shouted, "Americans, we are here."

Uri looked out through the window. "This is not the centre of Guatemala City."

"You take another bus for the city centre, mister," the driver explained.

Aris took it upon himself to examine the nearby offerings and led the way to the closest bar.

A short distance from the entrance, three well-dressed men started pushing, punching and kicking a peasant who was already on his knees.

"Stop!" a boy of six or seven years bawled at the men.

An older girl wrapped the child in her arms. When it looked like the worst was over, the two children fell on top of their father, shielding him from more blows.

A small crowd had gathered around Aris and Uri and John. Oddly, no one stepped in to help when one of the well-dressed men forcefully yanked the children up and lobbed them backwards.

"Aaah!" Both children's cries echoed down the street.

The peasant took the beating without uttering a single word, as blow upon blow landed upon his body.

Aris slowly inched forward, closing the gap to the peasant.

"This is not good." John's girlish voice gave away his nerves.

Uri burped twice. "What's that fool Aris doing now?"

Aris used his body to block the two children's view of the beating. He clenched his jaw and pondered his next move.

"Aris!" John waved his arm like a flag. "Come back!"

"Help us," the girl cried to the crowd that stood watching in mute horror. Then she reached up and wrapped her arms around Aris's thigh. "Please, sir. Please help our father!"

Aris caressed the girl's hair. "Go back to your brother."

She slipped away and Aris took off his backpack, dropping it unceremoniously to the ground. With deliberate steps he placed himself next to the peasant and stared hard at each of the three abusers in turn.

With renewed hope, the young girl sucked back her tears and rushed to her father's other side.

One of the three men said something in Spanish.

"Speak English!" Aris commanded.

The same man pointed a finger into Aris's chest. "It's none of your business, American. Walk away."

The man standing closest to the daughter grabbed her by the hair and started pulling hard.

Aris angled his body and issued a hard chop to the man's forearm, instantly freeing the girl. He could hear Uri's chain burping nearby, followed by, "Shit. These dudes kill people in gang wars. Aris, come back!"

Suddenly the girl stopped crying, her sight fixed on her father's mangled face.

Several people in the crowd groaned.

John and Uri exchanged glances in even more horrified disbelief. "What do we do now?" John whimpered to his friend.

Aris took matters into his own hands and let loose a fierce punch to the man who appeared to be the ringleader.

The girl's face morphed in surprise. Then her arm raised to point at the other men poised to attack. "Mister! Watch out— "

Out of the corner of his eye, Aris caught sight of the second well-dressed man pulling an arm back for a punch, while the one closest to the girl was still shaking out the sting of Aris's previous attack. Viciously, Aris kicked back like an unhappy donkey and sent the second man reeling with a grunt into the third.

The two wound up in a jumble on the ground. After they sorted themselves, the third man reached inside his jacket and pulled out a pistol.

"Eek!" John squealed, and joined the fray from behind to bat the weapon out of the third man's hand.

Turning to watch, Aris could not believe his eyes when John landed a second kick to the gunman's head, throwing him flat on the ground.

Uri trotted over and picked up the pistol while Aris helped the peasant to his feet. The children practically flew into their father's arms.

"Go home," Aris urged the peasant and his children.

The poor man just shook his head. "They will punish me even more now. You must run, mister. They will kill you for sure."

Aris reflected on his recent escapades. Life and death situations were becoming the norm. "Don't worry," he coached. "Take the children home."

The man and his kids shuffled up the street as quickly as his wounds would allow. The young girl, however, turned to look back at Aris. She was holding one of her father's hands while her brother squeezed tight to the other. With her free hand, she touched her heart and mutely mouthed, "Thank you."

"Drop it!" Uri's voice pulled Aris back to the present. Aris saw Uri wagging the pistol he'd retrieved, pointing it back and forth between the other two men, who slowly pulled out their guns and dropped them to the ground.

John appeared to be in some sort of post-stress shock, staring out into the distance.

"Pick up the guns," Aris instructed.

"B-b-but I can't shoot anyone." John's voice cracked.

"Just pick them up and move them away."

What had previously been a tightly clustered crowd loosened with whispers of "Stupid Americans," and "Don't know who they're dealing with." One man pulled out his cell phone and appeared to be giving some sort of report.

The ringleader of the well-dressed men shouted, "We will bury you alive, then I will piss on your grave." Instantly, the crowd dispersed, disappearing behind closed doors.

Aris pulled on his backpack then took the guns from John and Uri, pocketing the bullets, then tossing the weapons far out of reach.

"Come on," he motioned to the three well-dressed men. "We'll buy you a drink."

John nodded crazily. "Yeah, drinks on us! We're all friends."

The third man hooted. "Drinks on you, all right. Soon you'll be drinking our piss!"

Aris motioned for John and Uri to don their packs and follow him into the bar. But at the entrance, Aris looked through the glass door to see the owner locking it from the inside, refusing them entrance.

The three seated themselves on the door step and waited.

The sound of an Army jeep roared into town, followed closely by a personnel carrier. Aris flashed back to his childhood when the Epikouriki had taken his father away.

"Walk away, guys," he whispered to John and Uri. "You're not with me."

At the sight of a dozen soldiers hopping off the vehicle and forming a line, the colour drained from John's face. But neither John nor Uri moved to run.

The soldiers formed a semi-circle around the Americans, and as a unit, lifted their rifles.

Even Aris was now frozen in his spot, but gave a hoarse whisper to his buddies. "Move on, I said. Pretend you don't know me!"

Uri let out an enormous burp. "Too late. You should've thought of this before you interfered in other people's business."

The sergeant in charge tipped his rifle up, indicating Aris and his friends should stand.

Instinctively, mechanically, the three raised their arms in surrender and struggled to their feet under the awkward weight of the backpacks.

The soldiers circled closer, rifles still aimed like a firing squad. Speechless, Aris watched as the three abusers approached, now with happy grins.

They each took position, one in front of Aris, and the others in front of John and Uri. The ringleader let loose a punch to the stomach and Aris buckled and grunted under its force. The other two unleashed punches and kicks, and soon the three friends had been forced to their knees.

Not unlike the scene with the peasant being kicked mercilessly, now Aris and his buddies were on the receiving end, only no children or foreigners were going to plead for their rescue.

An officer stepped forwards and ordered, "Sergeant Leo, arrest these men!"

A skinny man with a worn wrinkled face and flat nose stepped out from the group. Turning to the others, he called, "Bring the American bastards. We'll take care of them at the camp."

John clutched at his stomach as he was pulled to his feet. Uri moaned and let out a whimper, but Aris rose under his own determination, keeping silent.

Sergeant Leo pushed him from behind. "I guess your mama didn't tell you not to mix with the chicken food."

Aris thought of the peasant and hoped the man had made it back home with the children.

"You're about to learn!" Sergeant Leo prodded again, this time with the tip of his rifle. "The chicken is going to eat you alive."

— ◆ —

The next ten days did not pass as lazily as the previous ones. Aris, Uri and John found themselves jailed in an Army camp, bruised, unshaven, and filthy.

"You are lucky," Sergeant Leo reminded them daily. "The General is not here yet to carry out death sentencing."

But one of the maids in camp lent more hope. "Relax, our General is friends with your government. At least you will be given a choice."

It was easy to notice the change in the soldiers' behaviour when the General arrived at camp.

John appeared despondent, but Uri rallied around. "I wonder if the maid was right… and what choice we'll be given."

Sergeant Leo accompanied three soldiers who came to fetch Aris and his friends at gunpoint, parading them through the camp, then dropping them to their knees in front of a large man in military regalia seated in a camp chair under an expansive tent awning.

"Americans," the General scoffed. "Good! I will give you a choice."

A loud sigh escaped John, and Uri's eyes appeared brighter for the first time in over a week.

The General and all the soldiers laughed. "You can choose—death by firing squad… or death by hanging." He looked expectantly from Aris to John to Uri, positioned side by side in front of him.

Uri's head drooped, and a series of burps escaped unbidden.

"There is also the option of man-eating dogs. Food is sometimes scarce here, you see." Another round of laughter ensued.

John flopped forwards into the dirt, sobbing uncontrollably.

Aris glanced over at Uri. The two reached out to help their friend back up to his knees.

The maid who had once brought a hopeful voice to the friends, now set a cool beverage in front of the General and beat a hasty retreat.

The General downed half the drink in one swallow, then wiped his mouth on his sleeve. "Your American government is friendly with our President. Who are you spying for?"

"We're nobody's spies," Aris spat. "We don't get involved in politics."

"Politics?" Uri cackled, motioning to Aris. "He just likes to play the hero."

"You didn't stop me," Aris replied coolly.

"You didn't ask!"

Aris cleared his throat and looked into the General's eyes. "We would like to call the American embassy and engage a top lawyer."

"Good idea!" the General praised. "But in this country, the judge and jury are the same man. And so are the lawyers."

"So who's that?" John managed weakly.

"Me!" the General laughed triumphantly. "The General President!"

John collapsed to the dirt once more, and even Aris could not suppress his own feelings of defeat.

"No way," Uri protested, pointing to Aris. "No way we're going to lose our lives over this moron defending some stupid peasant. I didn't do anything. I was just watching."

John gulped audibly and snorted back his tears. Still prostrate in the dirt, he turned his face to Uri. "I kicked the gun out of the guy's hand, and you took it. Aris didn't have to ask us to get involved. That's what friends in danger do! We help each other."

"You're both idiots," Uri laughed bitterly. "If Mr. Samaritan here hadn't jumped into other people's affairs, you'd be sipping a cold beer right now." Uri slapped his own forehead. "And I'd be in bed with a Guatemalan girl."

42 GUESTS OR PRISONERS

"Ten days with no movement! How is that even possible?" Varo barked into her office phone. "Only dead people don't move."

"Guatemala is a military state," the woman's voice answered. "We are unable to get anyone on the ground there for surveillance."

Varo shot to her feet, slapping the desk with her palm. "I only asked you one thing… not to lose sight of them!" She thought about hanging up on the inept woman, but changed her mind. "I want you personally on the next flight out. Build your own local team, and send me Aris's exact locations daily. Day or night, I want to be kept informed!"

After disconnecting, Varo made her way down the hall and into the security monitoring room. Her appearance sent employees clambering to their feet, military style.

"Show me what you've got."

Within seconds, a large screen on the wall lit with the image of some sort of camp with tents.

"What's that?" Varo asked as she examined the overhead view.

"An Army holding camp," the monitoring engineer answered.

Varo's eyebrows knit together. "Whose Army?"

The door opened and Victor entered. "Either your boys have business with the Guatemalan Army, or they're messed up with something they should've better left alone."

"My sources say they've been stationary for ten whole days." Varo turned to him. "Do you think they're being held prisoner?"

"Guatemala is an American ally," Victor countered. "Dozens of ex-military bases have been converted into holiday camps. Maybe they fell into a bottle of rum and can't find their way out."

Varo appeared unconvinced. Her face filled with anger. "You knew Aris has been in this military camp for days? And you did not even think to alert me?"

"No military would want to harm American citizens," Victor explained. "Unless your boys got into some illegal activities."

"What if they did do something wrong? Something against the government?" Varo's mind reeled.

"Best guess?" Victor shrugged. "They'd already be dead and buried. Guatemala has a nasty general as president."

Varo spun on her heels and stood inches from the monitoring screen. "What if they found the surveillance bugs on the backpacks and presumed Aris was a spy?"

"Too many possibilities," Victor assessed. "You need boots on the ground to verify."

Varo sighed deeply then left the room.

✦ ◇ ✦

Back in their prison cell, Uri began talking to himself. "I'm Jewish. They wouldn't dare kill a Jew."

John burst into spasmodic laughter. "Oh, don't worry. Most of the world's presidents and prime ministers are Jewish. They'll protect you."

"Really?" Uri turned to him.

"Yeah, didn't you know?" John's voice became manic. "President Bush is Jewish, even President Clinton's a half-Jew."

"What about Reagan?" Uri asked.

"Oh no, Reagan could not possibly be Jewish," John giggled. "His dongle wasn't crooked."

Aris took the small bit of humour where he could find it.

Another prisoner, reclining in the dirt, raised up on his elbows. "You'll die happy," he stated. "I've seen this before.

Right before a man is about to die, he's overcome by this stupid kind of… What do you call it in English? Euphoria?"

"Feels like I'm already drunk," John explained.

The sergeant named Leo appeared outside the cell. "Good news!" he called.

"We're being freed?" Uri hopped to his feet.

Sergeant Leo smiled. "By evening, your wait will be over."

John exhaled loudly. "Oh, thank God!"

Not buying into it for a moment, Aris met the soldier's gaze.

Sergeant Leo stood with his feet apart, clasping his hands behind his back. "The General has passed his sentence. No torture, no broken necks. You are very lucky indeed!"

John's face lit with joy. He embraced Uri and cried, "We're saved!"

Again Aris was hesitant. "What exactly was the General's sentence then?"

Sergeant Leo grinned from ear to ear. "You are to be shot at sunset. No more waiting to suffer!"

Uri and John dropped their embrace, their expressions like children who'd just learned the truth about Santa Claus.

"At sunset?" Uri burped. "Why does it have to be at sunset?"

"Because the General is taking his siesta now," Leo explained giddily.

Aris knew it was now or never. "Sergeant, you must inform the American embassy. It is our right as American citizens."

Leo started walking away. "Your embassy has already agreed to the General's terms."

Uri flung himself up against the metal bars. "Please! My family will reward you well. We have money!" At this last, Leo turned back as Uri added, "I'm Jewish, you know."

"Oh, I did not know this." Leo rubbed his palms together. "For sure the General will not shoot you if you are Jewish."

"Yes!" Uri pumped an arm in the air.

"Instead, he will feed you to his dogs."

—◇—

The elegant lady sat in the driver's seat while a mechanic adjusted the passenger's seat next to her.

Casually he said, "I heard the new American prisoners fight about something they called the love secret."

Indifferent, she said, "They are about to die and yet they speak of their love secrets. They're just confessing their sins."

"No. One of them said the only reason they'd come to Guatemala was in search of Aphrodite's ancient love secret. It was supposed to have the power to make anyone fall in love with you."

She extended long lean legs and pivoted in her seat. "What do you mean, Pepe?"

"Apparently the tall one is on some sort of quest to find this ancient love secret. They began in Tampa, then went to Mexico. Then their leads brought them to Guatemala."

She touched the mechanic's hand. "I want you to find out everything you can about this love secret. Find out where they have been in Guatemala. Places, people, everything." Celia pointed a sharp fingernail into his chest. "But whatever you learn… don't tell anyone else!"

❖

Within minutes Celia entered the office of the intelligence officer, dismissing everyone except the three star-colonel who stood by a filing cabinet.

The man crossed his arms over his chest, but remained silent.

"I have a secret mission for you," Celia began. "Fail me and you know where you will end up. You can kiss that pending promotion goodbye."

Celia moved towards him and he stepped away from the cabinet. She circled behind him as if assessing him from all angles, then came back around facing him.

"The three American prisoners were searching for an ancient mystery—Aphrodite's love secret or something. That's why they came to Guatemala."

The colonel squinted one eye, listening without interrupting.

"Speak to the toolmaker, Pepe, first. He overheard the Americans arguing. Then interrogate each of them separately Find out where they have been in our country... places, people's names."

"That will be easy," he said.

"Play it friendly," she ordered. "You are not to kill them. Not yet!"

"And if they refuse to talk?"

"They were arguing openly in prison. Why would they refuse? Start with the two shorter ones. Offer them a drink. Play the nice guy. The tall one is the one who is supposed to be searching for this love secret. He's more likely to resist."

She turned to exit but then paused at the door.

"Find out who they visited in Mexico and Florida. I want your report within the hour. And not a word of this to my husband, the President General!"

43 Impatient

Back in her office, Varo stood at her desk and pressed the speed-dial button. "Tracy, get me the Vice President. Now!"

She started pacing, left then right, until the phone rang.

"Miss Chase," a familiar voice greeted her. "To what urgent matter do I owe the pleasure?"

"Mr. Vice President, I just texted you coordinates for what my team believes is a military camp in Guatemala. Three Americans are being held there against their will, for ten days now. Their wellbeing is my top priority. I want them released immediately."

"Guatemala?" the man scoffed. "How do you know they aren't there under their own freewill... mercenaries, drug traffickers, or something?"

"Don't be silly. These are family men," she dismissed.

Not a stranger to difficult conversations, the man was not easily persuaded. "So why are they being held? Are they criminals, murderers, or thieves?"

"Not a chance!" Varo fumed. "These are normal people. American citizens who need your immediate protection. You even met one of them at my last function—Mr. Aris Theo."

"Ah," the Vice President assessed. "So at least one of them is an old flame."

Varo sensed his twinge of jealousy. "Mr. Aris Theo is my company's insurance broker."

He made her wait, cognisant that one did not necessarily exclude the other. "I don't remember him," he finally said, "but an action like this requires diplomacy."

"You are the Vice President of the United States of America. You people make and break governments all around the world whenever you want. All I'm asking is that you get some people on the ground and bring these men home."

"I see you are eager. Right now I have a meeting with the President, but after that I will do my best."

"No!" Varo shouted. "The President can wait. I want you to make this call right now!"

"Don't expect miracles, my dear," he cautioned. In the background Varo could hear an aide summoning him to the Oval Office. "Things in that country move very much at their own pace."

⁂

Aris sat in their cell with his back against the wall. Judging by the position of the sun, it was already mid-afternoon.

John had retreated into himself even further than usual, so Uri sought out one of the other inmates for conversation. "Why are you in here?"

The tan-skinned man with dark eyes and hair looked up. He had not uttered a single word the entire time the three friends had been imprisoned. "I make engine parts…" he began, "but they accused me of making bombs."

This must have evoked John's sympathy. He seemed to awake from whatever place he'd vanished to. "Are they shooting you too?"

The man shook his head. "Maybe no. Sometimes they need me to make tools for them."

An explosive sound tore through the air. *Rifle shots*, Aris thought.

The three Americans jumped to their feet, surveying the area for movement. Seeing none, their gaze turned to the toolmaker.

"Do you th-think they s-started the executions already?" John bleated.

Another deafening round of rifle shots ripped through the heavens.

Uri smacked his friend on the shoulder. "It's not even dark yet!"

The toolmaker just laughed. "File a complaint."

◆◇◆

Sergeant Leo arrived with five soldiers. He waved to signal one of them to open the cell door, and three more accompanied him inside to stand behind Aris, John and Uri.

Upon another signal, the three soldiers grabbed the Americans and led them out of the cell and down a long stretch to where it opened up in front of a stone wall. The stone was riddled with pockmarks and holes. It took Aris only a moment to determine this was where the firing squad would face them down.

The Americans were positioned facing away from the stone, with Aris on one end and Uri on the other, with John holding the centre spot.

Aris scanned the view. To the left was a high platform, accessed from the balcony of what appeared to be an office building. The General and a younger attractive woman came out and took seats on the platform.

To the right stood a variety of other army officers. Directly in front of them were five soldiers bearing rifles.

A couple minutes later, two other prisoners were escorted out to join the Americans. Neither made any noise or protest.

John made a noise as if trying to clear his throat, but it came out as a squeak. Then in a high girly pitch he exclaimed, "Sergeant, I demand to speak to the General."

Sergeant Leo turned to the platform. "Sir, one of the Americans is *demanding* to speak with you."

The General's gaze was caught in the cleavage of the lady beside him. "He can demand nothing. Get on with the execution."

Celia had been married to the General for only a short time, but she'd known him her whole life. In truth, they were half-siblings, children of a man with strong character and military bearing. Her hips were wide, like those almond-shaped eyes that always got her what she wanted. And if that didn't work, then her ample bosom could provide.

Today she was dressed in leather riding gear, carrying a bull whip, prepared to witness the spectacle. She took a seat next to her husband, whose scrutiny did not appear to rise any further than the deep vee of her custom-made blouse beneath an open leather jacket.

She set her own sight upon the three men below, kneeling in front of the firing squad. "Who are they?" she asked as two more men—locals, by the look of it—were led out into a similar position.

The General momentarily made eye contact. "Some stupid American drifters. They attacked our secret service officers."

His lack of concern for others' life was no surprise, but Celia assessed each of the Americans with renewed interest. Her eyes settled upon the one at the far end, older and taller than his peers, but with regal bearing, and the same dark skin, hair, and eyes of her family.

"Mount rifles," Sergeant Leo called.

Instantly the five soldiers raised their weapons.

"Take aim!" came the next order.

The men leaned into their rifles, taking sight on the prisoners, fingers poised on the triggers.

Celia saw the Sergeant turn to her husband, awaiting his final signal.

But the General instead placed a hand between her thighs and squeezed. Obviously his mind was on other things that day.

Celia placed a fingertip beneath his chin and tipped his head back to look at her, then angled his head towards the Sergeant. In mute anger, the General gave a nod, then returned his attention to the leather-clad sight that held him as another sort of prisoner entirely.

—⟡—

John looked from Aris to Uri. "Are we going to paradise or to hell?" he whispered.

Aris angled his head towards this dear friend whose biggest dream had been to accompany Aris on an adventure. *Some adventure this turned out to be.* He noticed a trail of wetness stream down the front of John's pants, soaking the man's trousers and leaving a puddle beside one foot.

"I don't know about you," Uri answered bravely, "but I'm going to paradise."

Aris could not help but be proud of Uri's bold outlook in the face of such deadly danger.

"But I swear," Uri added, "that I will cross over to hell and find Aris so I can kill him a second time!"

—⟡—

Celia took another look at the three Americans and two locals her husband had just condemned to their deaths. Again she was taken with the vision of the man at the far end of the line-up.

"He looks like our father," she murmured with admiration.

"What, my love?" the General asked.

The Sergeant drew a deep breath to issue the final command, and Celia knew she must seize the moment. "No!" she yelled firmly, rising to her elegantly boot-clad feet. "Wait!"

All eyes, including her husband's, turned to her.

She motioned that the soldiers should lower their weapons. Then she turned to the General and again sat down beside him, gripping one of his hands and returning it to rest on her warm thigh. "Look at the tall one on the end. He looks like you and our father."

The General cocked his head, but did as asked, taking in the final American with only a cursory glance. "So?"

The Sergeant took measured steps, placing himself directly below the platform, awaiting instructions.

Celia placed her own hand high upon her husband's thigh and squeezed. "He can be the one."

"What are you talking about, woman?"

Celia lowered her voice. "Tall, dark skin… resembling you and Father. Everyone will think the child is yours…"

The General once more looked out at the American on the end, this time squinting.

"I want a baby!" Celia pleaded. "You agreed. And you know I love you. This man has such a resemblance to Father that no one will need to know you can't…"

She let the implication hang in the air.

The General's eyes burned fire. He pulled his hand away from her as if she'd scorched him.

Celia knew she'd taken the wrong approach. "Then afterwards, you can still shoot him. No one will ever know."

The General's expression softened a bit. Once more he turned his face on the Americans below, scrutinizing each in turn.

The Sergeant cleared his throat, waiting for a fresh signal.

Celia threaded her hand through her husband's arm. "We will never find someone else who looks this much like Father. I know how much you want a child, an heir to carry on your name…"

"No! I hate Americans!" Turning to the Sergeant, he motioned to proceed with the executions.

Again with measured steps the Sergeant returned to his spot behind the soldiers.

In a less adamant voice he ordered, "Mount rifles!"

The firing squad raised their weapons once more.

"Get on with it, you fascist Nazi pigs," the American next to the locals shouted.

The Sergeant looked up at the General, then to Celia, taking his time. With no further visual prompt or instruction, he did what he was required to do. "Take aim!" he commanded.

The soldiers leaned in and sighted one prisoner each, fingers now twitching above the triggers.

Leo raised his arm, then turned to look at the General.

Celia also turned to look at her husband. His expression was stony and cold.

"Come on, you pussies!" the same American shouted. "Get it over with already."

In a loud and proud voice, the American on the end declared, "Uri, mind your tongue… and John, hold your head high! Don't give them the pleasure of seeing your fear." Then he reached out and grabbed the hand of the companion next to him.

Celia clutched both of her husband's hands in hers. "Look!" she cried. "He is not scared. He is a born leader—like you!" She pulled the General's hands to her heart, aware that they would wander of their own accord, but she was not above using her body to get what she wanted. "This child would be brave and intelligent—like you. You can finally have the son you've always longed for." She kissed him on both cheeks and added, "Plus he will look like you."

The General let out a short huff. "Only a stupid man wouldn't be scared in the face of death."

As if reading Celia's mind, praying for some further delay, the Sergeant made his way over to the prisoners. Standing in front of the American at the centre of the five, he asked, "Do you have any last wishes?"

The man called Uri spat at the ground. "Fuck, yes. Just finish it!"

The Sergeant angled his body in front of the next American and asked the same question, but this time any response was too soft to overhear.

With excitement, the Sergeant turned to the platform. "Last wish, General!"

Celia's husband looked out, unamused.

The Sergeant shouted, "This American's last wish is to fix your motorcycles, sir. They know motorcycle mechanics!"

— ◇ —

"What?" John squeaked. "I wasn't even scared of death anymore. Now someone wants me to fix something?"

"Oh, yeah?" Uri laughed cynically. "Do you always pee your pants when you aren't scared?"

Aris came to John's defence. "It's not urine," he protested. "John ejaculated in the face of danger. It is a common, natural outburst. Animals do it as well."

The Sergeant had stepped over to the platform again, but Aris could hear him say, "Sir, you've been wanting to get those motorbikes running again. It's like two wishes granted."

"Why would they want to do that?" the General scoffed.

The Sergeant shrugged. "How can I understand stupid Americans? But it is a last wish…" He pointed to Uri and said, "That one was a young motorcycle champion but gave up after an accident." Next he pointed to John. "See this one? He is the best mechanic in the world. He told Pepe the toolmaker that his whole life revolves around fixing engines—especially motorcycles. He was the champion's personal mechanic. And the tall one with the darker skin?" The Sergeant pointed to Aris. "He is their manager and financier. A Greek-American."

"A motorcycle champion?" Uri grunted. "I think I'm already in hell!"

— ◇ —

Celia noted the Americans' looks of surprise, but the General's full attention was now riveted on the Sergeant's words.

Seizing the opportunity, Celia whispered, "Manager and financier? Definitely means he's intelligent as well as handsome—like you," she deftly added. "We don't want a stupid son."

The General squeezed the bridge of his nose, clearly caught in the conundrum. Even if he could manage to impregnate Celia—a deed she sorely doubted—a child between two half-siblings wasn't likely to rise to great intellectual heights.

Still, sensing his hesitation, she softly suggested, "My love! Why not shoot them after they fix your beautiful motorcycles? You've been promising to teach me how to ride them. This way you will gain two things at the same time."

The General grunted. "You mean after you sleep with him."

Celia raised both palms in the air. "If it means so much, I won't touch him. We can call in a doctor to take a sperm transfer."

The General kicked the base of the platform. "And then the whole world would know."

Celia expended all her energy to hide her smile. Now she knew she had him. "You can shoot the doctor too."

The General turned back to the Sergeant. In a louder voice he called, "How will they fix my motorcycles without parts?"

Celia's lips parted in a full smile. She could see the Sergeant's mind whirring.

"Pepe the toolmaker can make them."

The General leaned back in his chair, rocking it forwards and backwards on just two feet. After a long minute, he stopped, planting the chair firmly back on the platform. Exchanging a glance at Celia, who did her best to smile seductively, he told the Sergeant, "They have one week. Give them Pepe and anything else they need. If they succeed, I may spare their lives."

Celia saw looks of disbelief forming on the face of two of the Americans, while her chosen Greek-American prize remained more thoughtful, analysing, giving nothing away.

"If not," the General concluded, "I will shoot you too, for offering stupid Americans a last wish."

Celia squeezed her husband's arm joyfully. "Let's celebrate, my love, before you leave. Postpone your departure until the morning!"

"No," the General replied flatly. "I leave immediately. Better to surprise my enemies."

But it didn't really matter to Celia. She'd already gotten everything she truly wanted.

Leo's face was grim as he turned back to the Americans. "Why didn't I listen to my mama? I mixed with the chicken feed, and now the General will eat me."

44 The New Ordeal

"Lower rifles," Sergeant Leo commanded, then marched briskly to the Americans. "Come quickly, before the General changes his mind." Then he instructed the other soldiers to return the two locals to their cell.

"Are we not being shot?" Aris asked in disbelief.

"Not today," Leo informed them. "Come, I will explain."

"Moses has answered my prayers!" Uri exclaimed. "I am alive! I will pray every day from now on."

Leo spat in the dirt. "Pray hard, but work harder. My life is at risk if you fail this task."

He led the Americans to a small outbuilding, then opened a garage-style door along one side. Aris counted five ancient motorcycles parked in a line, but caked in mud and covered in cobwebs. Apparently they had not been ridden in quite some time.

"You have seven days to fix the General's motorcycles," Leo explained. "If not, he will cut off your balls and feed them to you. Then he will shoot you."

John gulped audibly while Uri let out one long burp.

"But he will do the same to me if you fail," Leo shared. "So I believe we must plan an escape, because there is no way you can succeed at this task."

"I don't understand." Aris walked inside the makeshift workshop, noticing a wooden bench to the side and a set of shelves holding rusty tools and parts.

John and Uri followed Aris, and the Sergeant trailed after. John ran a hand over one of the motorcycles, brushing off a layer of dust, then kneeling for a closer inspection.

"I told the General your last wish was to fix his motorcycles—his dearest love," Leo said, pointing to John. "Well… after his beloved wife Celia, of course."

Aris turned and stared hard into the Sergeant's eyes. "Why would you do that?"

The man stared back, seemingly looking right through Aris. "I don't know," he confessed. "Something told me there's a reason you were brought here, to this camp. I could not keep my mouth shut. Now I will die because of it. Mixed in with the chicken feed."

John made his way down the line of motorbikes, one at a time, sighing here, nodding there.

Leo circled around behind John. "I told the General you were the mechanic for a famous champion motorcyclist."

"I do know everything about engines," John confessed, "but why spare all three of our lives?"

Pointing to Uri, Leo explained, "The General thinks he is the champion you work for, but that he stopped after an accident. Perhaps he believes he can learn something."

"And what about Aris?" John asked.

Leo's head drooped. "I told the General he was your manager and financier."

Uri balked. "And the General believed all this bullshit? You've just prolonged our agony."

The Sergeant strode across the room and landed a stinging slap across Uri's face. "Ungrateful bastard! Better start praying to your Moses right now."

Aris stepped thoughtfully around the dilapidated motorcycles and circled over to stand near Uri and the Sergeant. "You risked your life to save us, for what reason I can only imagine. But at least now there is hope of escape. We thank you."

After inspecting all five motorcycles, John was now back kneeling in front of the first one. "With the right parts…" he muttered, "I can make this work, I think."

"What?" Leo's eyes went wide. "But no. Even if you fix the engines, the General will still shoot you. And then he will shoot me. But you must appear to be working, and quickly now, as the General's wife has said she will come to check on your progress."

John didn't need any further prompting. He grabbed a screwdriver from one of the shelves and started disassembling an engine case, laying pieces and screws out along the dirt floor in an orderly fashion. "Do you have any spare parts somewhere?"

Leo shook his head. "It is hopeless, but I will bring Pepe, the toolmaker. Perhaps he can try to make some replacement parts while the rest of us work on an escape plan."

⸻ ◇ ⸻

Aris watched the Sergeant make his way back to the holding area. Already he was forming a plan of his own. Motioning for Uri to join him next to John, he whispered, "There are five bikes. If you can scrounge together enough parts to fix just two, then we'll be able to have a ride out of here."

Uri's glum expression lifted, but John only became more focused. Like an assembly-line worker, he moved from bike to bike, removing screws and placing filthy, rusty parts out on the ground in a straight line.

After ten minutes, the Sergeant returned with Pepe in tow.

"Seven days to perform a miracle," the other prisoner assessed.

Aris smiled hopefully. "The world was made in only six!"

John wasted no time pulling Pepe into his work, pointing to various bits and bobs of metal, and making requests.

The Sergeant grabbed Aris by the arm and pulled him to the far side of the workshop. "Now I understand why the General accepted this proposal," he whispered. "Today is your lucky day. She has asked to see you."

Aris tried to comprehend what the Sergeant was telling him. "Who wants to see me?"

"The general's wife!" Leo's face grew rosy. "Señora Celia!"

Aris pushed away from the Sergeant. "Tell her I'm busy. We don't have time for women's foolishness."

Leo softly kicked Aris's foot and craned his head to the side. "Tell her yourself."

Turning his sight, Aris witnessed the saucy Latin beauty, still in leather riding gear, a bull whip in her hands. Her every step appeared calculated to intoxicate. But Aris knew better after his recent Mexican encounter.

The General's wife sidled up beside Aris, stroking the tip of her whip across his shoulder. But almost instantly she pulled away, scrunching up her face. "You stink!"

Aris held himself tall and proud, meeting her gaze. "We don't all have the luxury of a hot bath and clean clothes."

But his insurrection didn't have the desired effect. Instead she circled behind him. In an instant, he heard a crack and felt the tip of her whip sting his buttocks. He reached behind him to rub the spot, but a second crack followed against the back of one of his knees, folding him to the ground, kneeling.

All conversation ceased. John, Uri, Pepe and Leo stood frozen in their spots while Celia completed her wide circuit around Aris. With a delicate flip of the wrist, her whip grazed his cheek, drawing blood.

Aris silently fumed at being made to play the submissive, but knew there was nothing to be gained from taunting this woman further. He reached up and wiped a streak of blood from the corner of his mouth.

The General's wife wrapped a length of whip in one hand and lightly flicked the tip against her opposite palm, again circling Aris. "Beg for your life!" she said to him. "My husband the General would cut out your tongue for being so rude to me."

Aris maintained his silence, but puffed up his chest and kept his eyes focused straight ahead.

Celia completed another loop then raised her right foot, planting a leather boot against Aris's chest. He couldn't help but notice the powerful thigh muscles bulging inside her tight leather pants. With a firm shove from that leg, she toppled him backwards.

Marvelling at the woman's confidence, Aris let her tower over him, hoping to be finished with this little game so he and his friends could soon get back to plotting their escape.

"However, I will not mention your extremely rude behaviour to the General… *if* you can fix my problem."

Aris let out a slow exhale, wondering what she could possibly be leading up to. Maybe some twisted sexual favour based on the way she still toyed with the bull whip.

"Sergeant Leo informs me that you are a plumbing and air-conditioning expert."

Huh? Aris clamped down on all his emotions. The Sergeant had saved their bacon once that day, and Aris would not betray the goodwill.

"You will come tonight," she ordered.

From the corner of his eye, Aris saw Pepe give a tiny knowing nod.

"You will fix my system…" Celia spun out her words. "I need to *cool down*."

Before Aris could raise an objection, Leo stepped in. "Of course, Señora Celia. Aris has many years of experience in the business of *plumbing and air-conditioning*. Many years' experience," Leo repeated, nodding pointedly to Aris.

Celia turned to the Sergeant and lowered her voice. "Have the American bathed and shaved, and give him new clothes. When I return from my ride, I will reverse the car. Put him in the trunk. It is imperative that no one knows about this. If you speak…" she let the phrase dangle mid-air as she raised the tip of her whip and wagged it in Leo's face "…you will be shot."

Aris noticed Uri leaning in, trying to eavesdrop, but he stumbled over motorcycle parts, causing a loud metallic crash as several banged together on the ground.

Celia shifted her gaze to Pepe and elevated her voice slightly. "You too, toolmaker! One word and I will cut out your tongue myself."

Aris remained silent, kneeling rigidly.

Celia now squatted before him, powerful thighs once more flexing under the tight leather. "Try to escape," she cooed, "and I will shoot your friends." She brushed the tip of her whip slowly across Aris's abdomen. "Do not disappoint me…" Her dark eyes met his.

Aris was revolted by the spark he saw there.

The next instant, Celia rose and strode regally back to her waiting vehicle, speeding off into the distance with a cloud of dust.

Aris climbed to his feet. "What, exactly, did you tell her, Sergeant? I don't know shit about plumbing and air-conditioning."

Leo raised both palms into the air. "I didn't say anything of the sort! But we must not upset her. No matter what, you must keep her happy. Not even the General says no to Señora Celia!"

Aris made his way over to stand by John and Pepe.

John looked up, his face radiating in a way it hadn't since they left home nearly three months earlier. "I think I can already get one bike to start, maybe by tomorrow, and with Pepe's help, we'll have another ready in a few days."

The grin that Pepe shot Aris was somewhat disconcerting.

"First I have to figure out this plumbing and air-conditioning problem for the General's wife." Aris frowned at the toolmaker. "I doubt I'll be joining you this evening."

John looked up, encouragingly waving a screwdriver and putting it into Aris's hand. "Don't worry! If I can fix all these bikes, you can surely fix a little plumbing."

45 Into The Goddess's Nest

Aris willed his cramped muscles to relax, folded into the trunk of Celia's car next to a toolbox stuffed with a variety of ancient but hopefully still usable tools. He had no idea what might be needed, or why someone in the position of the General's wife could not simply call a specialist repairman.

He felt the vehicle slow, then heard the horn beep twice. The sound of feet scurrying and grating metal led him to believe some sort of gate was being opened.

The car pulled forward, then moved slowly for a number of minutes. Then Aris heard a mechanical whirring like a garage door sliding open.

With a click, the trunk of the car popped open above his head.

Aris looked up to take in his surroundings. They were inside an expansive garage, which held a number of shiny vehicles that cost a small fortune.

Celia once more towered above him expectantly.

Aris stretched his back and began the process of climbing out without assistance. When both feet were on the ground he reached into the trunk to lift the toolbox.

"Leave that here," the General's wife instructed. "Follow me and do not speak."

Puzzled, Aris obeyed.

The woman named Celia ran her fingers along the side of a box on the wall at shoulder height. When she found the spot she was looking for, she squeezed hard for a number of seconds.

Aris felt rather than heard a small popping sound. To the side, a secret door emerged from what he'd previously thought to be a solid wall. Beyond the door, a light automatically turned on. He squinted through the crevice to discern the hint of an oak staircase with a thick carpeted runner.

Celia took Aris by the arm and led the way. When Aris's feet touched the second step, the door sealed shut behind him.

Up the stairs they climbed. At the top of the narrow passage, Aris noticed Celia kick at the riser of the last step.

Another door popped open ahead of them.

Celia guided Aris into a plush and massive bedroom. With a quick assessment, he decided it must be nearly ten metres in each direction. But the focal point was clearly the enormous four-poster bed covered in an emerald-green tapestry spread, and draped with gauzy curtains. Beside it stood a champagne bucket on a stand, filled with ice and a bottle chilling lazily inside. At the far end of the room, a pair of French doors led out to what Aris guessed must be a balcony overlooking the grounds of the General's estate.

Trying to gauge his next move, Aris licked a finger and held it to the air. "The room seems cool enough to me. Maybe your problem has fixed itself."

Celia reached back to him and spun herself into his arms. "This problem is somewhat more involved," she hinted, clasping one of his hands and dragging it up to her bosom, forcing his fingertips to graze across one breast. "I'm burning up from the inside!"

Aris did his best to maintain his composure. What he'd previously seen of this woman did not indicate that her sexual appetites ran to anything available on his menu.

"I just saved your life today," she purred. "You could appear a little more grateful."

Aris remained unamused. "Postponed our execution, more like."

Celia threaded her arms around Aris's neck and gazed into his eyes. Reaching down, in a surprisingly slow and soft motion, she twisted one button on Aris's shirt to release it. Deftly she moved to the next and then the next until his chest was completely exposed.

"Execute your duties well… perform to my satisfaction…" Her voice was now like gossamer, weaving a spell around Aris. "… and I will make sure you fly back safely to America."

Aris felt her hands delicately caress then tug at the hair on his chest.

"Your skin is the perfect colour, just like mine."

With a flick of her thumb, she grazed one of his nipples and lit a spark inside Aris. He began to wonder if maybe this was indeed a plumbing situation for which his prior experience would be a good match!

Ready to test the waters, so to speak, Aris placed his hands on Celia's upper arms, caressing then squeezing gently. "Promise you will save the lives of my friends too. If so, I will satisfy all your needs."

Celia arched her back. "Daring to make a demand?"

Aris instantly lightened his grip, letting his fingertips merely brush against her skin.

"A rare noble man," she said next, relaxing into his embrace once more. "Trying to save your friends' lives, but not yours. You showed courage and leadership before in front of the firing squad. However, you are in no position to make demands or set terms."

With a feline gait, Celia stepped away and pulled Aris along behind her. She opened a door to a bathroom with a sunken tub, brimming with bubbles. "Let's refresh together!" Then she closed the door behind him.

Aris felt his face turning beat red. The perfume from the bubble bath was unbearable. "I… I…" Aris raised one hand to his breastbone, massaging to try to encourage his throat to release.

"You have no need to be shy," Celia tittered. "Undress for me." Then she turned away and began to peel off her own leather clothing seductively.

Both hands now raised to his own throat, Aris started to choke, gasping for breath. There was no way she could possibly mistake his noises for anything seductive, yet the General's wife seemingly remained oblivious to his struggle for air.

Fully nude, Celia turned sideways, exhibiting superb curves, narrowing at the waist to a wide but flat belly, tapering to long sculpted and muscular legs.

But Aris had no time for anything other than self-defence. His face was on fire, and he grasped helplessly at the doorknob, struggling with the other hand to scratch at the burning itch enflaming his body.

Finally he felt the door click open and he raced across the bedroom to where he saw double balcony doors. He needed to get to fresh air immediately!

"No!" Celia called. "The guards will shoot you on sight!"

Aris stopped in his tracks, turning to Celia and realising he could never communicate the problem unless he could first regain some semblance of control.

Once more he spied the champagne bucket next to the bed. Clumsily he stumbled to the stand and grasped the open bottle to his lips. He managed to swallow some of the liquid, but most ran down the sides of his chin, dribbling onto his chest.

But at least that little sip helped ease the clutching in his throat. Aris then plunged both hands into the bucket, seizing ice cubes and rubbing them all across his face.

The General's wife remained unfazed. Standing nude at the foot of the bed, she watched his every move with curiosity but no concern or urgency.

After a few moments of relief from the ice bath, Aris choked out the words, "Door... perfume... *allergic!*"

At this, Celia tipped her head back knowingly, but made no quick moves. Instead she made sure Aris first had a good view of her firm breasts, and the trail of light hair leading from belly button downward to her clean-shaven triangular mound.

"Shut the bathroom door, *now!*" Aris roared with as much strength as he could muster.

Quickly now Celia glided across the room and closed the door on the offending bubble bath she'd probably meant to entice him to her bed. Next she reached for a pink silk gown, hanging from a hook next to the bathroom door.

"Water... fresh air..." Aris practically begged.

Celia nodded once. She dimmed the lights and moved to the secret door panel by which they had entered the bedroom.

"Do not try anything stupid."

Aris pushed his way through and collapsed on the top step. Drawing on all his mental reserves, he forced himself to slow his shallow breaths, to allow his pulse to stop racing, and to focus on just the next critical moment of air.

It took several minutes for Aris to regain control over his functions. Just when he thought he'd managed it completely, a bit of saliva caught in his throat, causing him to cough.

"Shh!" Celia threw a hand across his mouth. "I will get you more champagne."

Aris clamped down on the urge to cough. "No..." he again choked on his words. "Water... *and whiskey!*"

Celia spun towards the bedroom, returning with a tall glass of water and a bottle. "As you like." She settled onto the top step next to him, the silk of her dressing gown parting over tanned legs.

He ignored the water but reached for the whiskey, downing a large gulp followed by another. It burned its way into his system, but after what he'd just endured, it was a good burn.

Aris looked over into Celia's wide dark eyes. "Black label. Nice." The twitch of her lips gave away just a hint that she had indeed been worried about him. At least a little.

He set the bottle down and took the glass of water she still held in her other hand. Celia rose to her feet and once more disappeared behind the panel, returning with a flute of bubbly champagne for herself.

"Go empty the bubble bath and turn on the fan to clear out the fumes," he instructed.

Aris took a few more deep breaths, followed by a hefty sip of whiskey. The burn was still good, but it caught in his throat. Aris reared back with a massive cough.

Before he could squeeze it out, Celia's hand clasped over his mouth. "The guards will hear!"

Aris again looked into her face, this time sensing her panic, not necessarily for his well-being, but perhaps for her own. He clamped down on the urge to cough while reaching for the glass of water.

Celia nodded sweetly and placed her hand, palm open, on the centre of his back, rubbing in a soothing motion.

Aris allowed the gesture to calm him. Time seemed to slow. He concentrated on one breath after the other, allowing his mind time to process all that had happened since arriving in the back of Celia's car.

After many minutes of her warm touch, Aris felt close enough to recovery to chance more conversation with his newest jailer. "So…" he smiled to Celia. "You like my colour?"

Her expression melted and, after setting down the champagne flute, she wrapped both arms around him. The silky gown felt cool against his chest, but Aris could still sense the flame lingering inside the General's wife.

"I like your colour, too," he joked. Where the silk parted between Celia's legs, Aris brushed with the back of his hand. "I think perhaps you will need a lot of air-conditioners to cool the fire I'm going to light."

Celia's response was surprisingly gentle. She placed her palms against both of Aris's cheeks. "Your face is still burning. I doubt you are ready yet for what I had in mind."

Aris measured every expression that crossed Celia's face, hoping to parse the true reason behind her actions.

"Once the bathroom air clears, I just need a cold shower. Between that and the whiskey," Aris whispered, "the allergies will clear. Then I will be even more energised than before." He added a wink for good measure.

"Wow!" The word came out as a whisper on the air. "But you don't have to wait. We have a second room for the shower."

Pulling him up, Celia led Aris across the bedroom to another door. It opened into a room dominated by a white marble shower with glass doors.

Aris had enough forethought to bring the whiskey bottle, and raised it to his lips for another sip.

Celia whisked it out of his grasp. "No more. I don't want you getting drunk and making noises."

She nudged him into the marble enclosure, flipped on the cold water only, then stepped back to avoid being splashed while Aris shivered under the chilly spray.

"I like my showers hot," she declared. "I'll have mine next door."

As much as Aris relished the thought of trying to escape, he knew he needed the recovery the cold shower would provide. And who knew? Perhaps Celia was merely baiting him into trying to flee to test him in some way. He wouldn't risk it. Not again while his friends' lives floated in the balance.

Aris braced himself against the chill and lavished this shower more than the perfunctory one he'd been given earlier that evening under Sergeant Leo's watchful glare back at the camp.

Afterwards, Aris turned off the water and reached for a pure white towel, its soft plushness feeling fresh against his skin. He dried off then wrapped it around his waist and walked back into the bedroom.

Steam was emanating from the other bathroom and Aris could hear the shower pulsing there. Still craving fresh air, he made his way towards the French doors. Peeking through the matching gauze curtains, he saw that it did indeed lead to a balcony. He gripped the door handle and prepared to twist.

"No!" came a cry from behind him. Celia stepped out of the other bathroom wearing nothing but what God gave her. "We cannot risk the guards or the maids hearing our noises."

Aris turned to face her, letting his own towel fall to the bedroom floor. This time he allowed himself to savour all the visual delights of her body before lifting Celia into his arms. Now that the allergic reaction had subsided and the shower made a new man of him, clearly his body appreciated what she had to offer.

"Oh, I thought you might be a bull! I can see I'm in for quite a ride."

"I'm not sure I can contain myself," he teased.

"I'm counting on it," she replied coyly, snaking her fingertips through his chest hair again until he laid her down atop the emerald bedspread.

Aris angled his body on top of hers, meeting the length of her tip to toe. He wasn't sure how to handle a delicate part of the conversation that would soon be necessary. He cleared his throat. "Your Sergeant… um… didn't warn me I might need… *protection.*"

Aris wondered if Celia would produce a pack of condoms, or what her response might be.

Rolling to the nightstand, Celia retrieved something. But it wasn't a box of any sort. It was a remote control. She switched on the television to a music station and turned the volume up before tossing the remote casually to the side.

Aris began kissing her neck and stroking her with a feather-light touch. His lips followed his fingertips south until he felt Celia's powerful thighs clench in excitement.

"I have a feeling I won't be able to contain myself either," she moaned. "It seems you do know a few things about heating and cooling."

46 Hateful Friends

The phone rang just as the General lit his cigar. He tried to ignore it. Checking caller ID, the General took a deep drag of the cigar before answering. "My dear Ambassador, how nice to hear from you."

"This is not a social call, General. I'm told you're holding three of our American citizens in your camp. Surely you realize they must be released."

The General's mind flashed to the day Celia had persuaded him of her ludicrous plan. His sister had a voracious appetite, and honestly, he was glad to have a few days away from her bed. "What prisoners? The Americans are my guests. I hired them to fix my motorcycles. When the bikes are ready, the men are free to go."

"General, this is not a casual matter. One of these men is highly connected… to both our VP and President."

"Ambassador, I am out of camp two days now, but these Americans are under my protection."

"We know you've been away. That's why it's imperative that you call back to camp now and make sure these men are protected."

"I return in three days. Nothing will happen to them."

"I have no reason to doubt you," the Ambassador replied smoothly. "But you don't want any accidents…" He left the words hanging in the air, then after a significant pause added, "This comes direct from our President."

The General stubbed out his cigar, all the enjoyment quickly draining from his day. "But of course. Anything for my great friend." With that, he ended the call before he could say something he might regret.

Aris climbed out of the car's trunk and headed straight to the small room off the workshop for the second time in forty-eight hours, collapsing onto the mattress. Despite utter exhaustion, his expression was joyful.

"Poor man," Pepe snickered. "Fixing plumbing all night. No wonder he needs to sleep." He shook his head then returned to shaping the metal piece in front of him.

John and Uri followed Sergeant Leo to where Aris was bunking. "Aris," Leo called, poking his shoulder. "My friend Rita who is Celia's maid says you've been enjoying yourself these last two nights."

Aris grunted and rolled over, leaving them to talk to his back.

"Don't fall for the devil," Leo continued.

"Aris always falls for the devil," Uri chimed in. "It's his specialty."

Knowing he'd get no sleep until he answered his friends, Aris rolled back over. "Our lives depend on how well I please this gorgeous devil."

"When Celia's done with you," Leo said, "she'll happily pull the trigger on you herself."

Aris opened one eye, squinting at Leo to measure the truth of those words.

"Remember what happened last time you fell in love…" Uri began.

Aris looked up at his two American friends, recalling their life and death departure from Mexico. He saw Pepe now standing behind John, grinning a bit, trying to listen in.

Indifferent, he shut his eyes. "I'm doing my best. Nothing wrong to enjoy it. Deep down, she's just a girl looking for some warmth. Maybe you misjudge Celia."

Leo kicked the bottom of the bed. "Shake yourself out of it. Others have made that mistake before. They are dead and buried!"

"Relax, guys." Aris yawned. "Judging by her tenderness, I'm convinced there's a golden heart under that… *leather* exterior."

Aris saw Leo's gaze turn to land on Pepe who quickly scurried back to his workbench.

Leo leaned in and whispered to Aris, "Something's wrong with that one. He never gets punished, and he often gets assigned to new prisoner's cells. I don't think we should trust him."

"I'll see what I can find out tonight." Aris rolled onto his side. "Now can you stop punishing me so I can get some sleep?"

⸺ ⬩◇⬩ ⸺

On the third night in voluptuous Celia's bed, a quick knock came at the door followed by the entrance of a maid in a short black dress.

Aris had been just about to send Celia shooting over the edge of ecstasy. His concentration was intense. He took in every response of his lady who immediately turned from a pussycat to a fearsome tiger.

"Get out!" she yelled, throwing a pillow at the maid, thrusting out with her feet as if she could boot the woman off the planet.

Aris soundlessly took the brunt of the kick in his belly.

"I swear, madam…" the girl began. "I have seen nothing. I know nothing!" The door slammed behind her and the sound of racing feet confirmed her flight.

"Stupid girl!" Celia yelled, climbing out of bed and reaching for her dressing gown. "My maid Rita has seen you in my bed. We will have to dispose of her."

Aris reached for Celia's hand to try and soothe her back to bed. "She will surely know she'll be punished if she tells. Why would she risk that?" He climbed to his knees and pulled Celia towards him so they were chest to chest. "We have something good going between us. I would not like to be the cause of this girl's death."

She melted into him then rolled back into bed. "It's just that if anyone finds out about…"

Aris put a finger to her lips, then wrapped a protective arm around her shoulders and hugged her tight. Celia's entire body was vibrating with tension. He knew he needed to disarm the situation and fast.

"Forget her," Aris suggested. "She wouldn't dare talk. But what about the prisoner Pepe? He's seen you pick me up every day now."

Celia drew a sharp breath then chuckled. "Pepe is a cousin from my mother's side. I use him as my spy."

Aris gave her one more tight squeeze so she wouldn't notice his eyes flare wide.

"*Ay Díos mio!*" Celia slipped out of his grasp and rolled on top of him, her hands pushing Aris into the mattress. "Don't you dare tell a soul. No one!"

Aris knew his every gesture would be scrutinized. "Relax," he soothed, allowing Celia's hands to roam free across his chest. "No one will ever know. I will protect your secrets."

Celia's expression softened a bit, but with one hand she pinched his nipple as she whispered, "Perhaps I trust you too much. What you know could get me killed."

Aris clenched his chest muscles against her tweak of his flesh. One word from this minx could get him killed even quicker. "Don't you realize we have something special?" he asked. "Our bodies seem to know exactly what's right. I crave your touch. I hunger to be near you."

Her face broke into a smile, and she released his nipple, only to rake her fingernails through his chest hair. "I fancied you the moment I laid eyes on you." Shrugging out of the silky dressing gown, she dragged the soft material over his erection, taking pleasure in his evolving expressions. "I saw you as handsome, intelligent and fearless. Like a bull facing down the bull fighter. But these last few nights you changed me, Aris."

"How?" The single word came out as a sigh.

"You make me laugh. I enjoy every moment with you. All day I have to be mean. Everyone here hates me. But when we are together, I feel…"

"What do you feel, Celia?" Aris asked, looking deeply into her eyes.

"I feel—"

"Loved?" Aris finished her sentence for her. "Love should not scare you. You make me feel special, too."

"Is it possible we are falling in love?"

Aris used the tender moment to roll her over face down into the centre of the enormous bed and slide lower. He traced a path of kisses from her lower back to her bottom. "I'm definitely in love with these gorgeous cheeks."

Celia giggled like a schoolgirl. "Get serious. If my husband finds out, he will cut you to pieces. Are you not worried?"

"What better way to die than enjoying you, my love?"

"The General says only a fool doesn't get scared."

For days Celia had avoided even the mention of her husband, but tonight she brought him up twice in quick succession. Aris knew he must turn the conversation quickly. "Shh, my darling. Don't worry! My team will finish his bikes this week and the General will be happy."

"The bikes… I'd almost forgotten." It was as if a timer suddenly flipped on in Celia's mind. One week to repair the motorcycles. "This is the first time I've ever worried about anything… or anyone," she confessed.

Aris took advantage of her admission, feeling conflicted about his own strong feelings for Celia at the same time. "But I have something that will make you even happier," Aris said, teasing her with his continued kisses.

Celia's body instinctively bucked into his. "Oh! Make me forget, Aris. Just make the world go away, my bull!"

⁂

Varo clicked a button on her steering wheel to answer the incoming call. "Vice President, it took you a long time to return my call."

He sighed. "I told you things move slowly in that part of the world."

"My sources tell me the Americans are still in that camp. What have you accomplished?"

"Good news. The ambassador was informed by a high-ranking officer that your friend and the other two have been contracted to repair some motorcycles for the President General."

"Motorcycle repair?" Varo scoffed. "Aris is no mechanic. He's an insurance man."

The Vice President became defensive. "Apparently at least one of them knows a thing or two about motorcycle mechanics. Or they better. The President General has a violent temper."

"You call this good news?" Varo shook her head, trying to stay focused on the road.

"They're alive and they're not prisoners. I call that obvious good news."

Varo ended the call without saying goodbye, then dialled another number.

47 Beware of the Seductress

The sun was already high in the sky when Aris woke the fourth morning. He gave Celia's shoulder a gentle nudge, then stood to pull on his trousers. After another moment and Celia hadn't roused yet, Aris gave her shoulder another gentle squeeze. "Wake up, my love."

Celia rolled onto her back and smiled up at him. Then her eyes fell on the clock above the dresser. "Oh no! We're late!" She bolted upright and raced to the bathroom. "Hurry! We leave in two minutes!"

Aris appreciated the view, like some Renaissance piece of art sprung to life for his benefit.

When she slammed the bathroom door shut behind her, he turned to look at the items displayed on her dresser next to the clock.

A framed portrait took him by surprise.

"Who is this man?" he called.

He could hear the sound of Celia brushing her teeth. Perhaps she hadn't heard his question.

"This man in the photo," he said when she returned to the bedroom. "He looks a little like me."

Celia yanked opened dresser drawers in front of him, pulling out lacy undergarments and clothing for the day, flinging them onto the bed. "You are his spitting image, no?"

"There's an obvious resemblance," Aris agreed. "Who is he?"

"Our father!" Celia replied quickly, then corrected herself, "I mean, the General's father."

"Handsome bastard!" Aris admired the portrait a few seconds more then set the frame back on her dresser so he could take in more of the real-life artwork while Celia dressed.

Through the secret door, they vanished outside. Aris returned to his spot bent over in the trunk. Two honks of the horn before each guard gate, and Aris heard the usual metallic noises as soldiers instantly swung open the gate for her. Then he recognized the crunch of gravel as Celia's car entered the camp and reversed in front of the workshop.

No sooner had his feet touched the dirt than Celia sped away, with two honks at the gate again.

Drained, Aris stumbled inside to John's workbench where Uri and Leo were ensconced in an argument over sports. "Where's Pepe?" Aris asked.

"Gone to fetch some parts," Leo answered unconcerned.

Aris lowered his voice and pulled all three of the others into a tight circle. "I just learned that Pepe is Celia's cousin. She uses him as her spy."

Leo slapped a hand against his thigh. "That explains it!"

"You didn't mention anything of our escape plan to him, did you?" Aris looked from Leo to Uri and finally to John, knowing the latter was too trusting for his own good.

"N-n-not yet," John confessed. "But I didn't want to leave him here to die."

Aris shook his head. "Pepe is in no danger from Celia. But we are!" He turned to the Sergeant. "Leo, you have to get word to your friend, Rita. I'm afraid for her now, too, because she saw me in bed with Celia last night. I made Celia promise me she wouldn't hurt the girl… but I don't know if I can believe her. Rita needs to disappear!"

"Are you sure it was my friend?"

"Celia called the maid Rita." Aris made a motion as to describe height and looks then added, "Wavy black hair, full lips."

Leo rubbed his hands together in satisfaction. "Rita! We could use her help. I have a plan, and now she'll have a reason to go along with us."

Curious, John turned and stood. "We have a plan?"

"Have you finished two bikes yet?" Aris asks.

"Mid-day today, hopefully." John's face was proud in a way Aris hadn't noticed since they left home months before. "But we'll be hard pressed to salvage a third. If we have to take the maid, we'll need three bikes."

"I'll think of something." Aris turned to Leo and instructed, "Bring Rita here."

"What about Pepe?" Leo asked. "He will most certainly be back."

"Give me a few hours to sleep first." Aris turned to head to the mattress in the small adjoining room.

"Sleep fast," Uri said. "Celia seems to come for her 'bull' a little earlier each night!"

— ◇ —

Late that evening, Celia rested her head on Aris's bare chest as they recovered. Her finger caressed his belly button. "Ar-is." Her voice was sing-song. "I can't seem to get you out of my mind, not even for a single second." After a short pause, she raised her head to look into his eyes. "I never expected to fall in love with you. Truly in love."

Aris smiled softly and stared deep into those dark pools. "I confess, I'm surprised by my own strong feelings for you. But you belong to the General. You're his wife. You'll soon forget about me."

She rolled and placed both hands on his chest. "Don't believe me? I will prove it to you."

Aris brushed a tender kiss on her lips. "You don't have to prove a thing to me, my gorgeous tiger. You've marked my heart. I will treasure you… for the rest of my life!"

Celia shifted, now sitting up in bed beside Aris, but still looking deeply into his eyes. "The General knows you are sleeping with me."

Aris's body practically jumped. "What?" He pulled back then shifted to also sit up.

With a look of regret, Celia said, "I'm risking my life to tell you this. It's a secret you must take to your grave."

Aris leaned in and placed a hand on both her shoulders. "Of course."

She shot him a stern glance. "The idea was mine. I've been wanting to get pregnant, but the General cannot give me a child. That's how I stopped him from executing you—I convinced him you were the best candidate because of your similarity to our father. No one would know the child was not the General's."

Aris noticed she had chosen each of her words carefully, but still he wasn't entirely sure what she was confessing. "So you're using me as a sperm donor."

Her face turned sad. "That was the plan. But I feel for you now. I am in love with you. By revealing this, it should prove how very much I love and trust you. If the General found out that I told you the truth, he would shoot me even before he shoots you!"

Aris smiled bitterly. "Either way, I get shot."

"I am sorry." Celia nodded in pain. "That was the plan."

Aris squeezed her shoulders lightly, then caressed his way down her arms until he held her hands together in his lap. "If you love me too, is there a way we can change the plan?"

"We are being closely guarded," Celia said. Aris saw a fire spark behind those dark eyes. "I already thought of a new plan."

"A plan for what?"

"You must tell no one what I am about to reveal. Promise me!"

Aris would have promised anything in that moment. He leaned forwards and planted a long wet kiss on Celia's lips.

She caught her breath then began. "See father's picture over there?" She pointed to the framed photo he'd noticed that morning. "He is not just the General's father."

Aris looked from the image of the man he resembled back to the woman in front of him.

"He is also my father."

Aris could feel his jaw clench.

This time it was Celia's turn to squeeze Aris's hands and then caress her way up his arms to his shoulders. "Do you see how closely father's photo, in his younger years, is the spitting image of you?"

Intrigued, Aris nodded.

Her hands sandwiched Aris's face. "All we have to say is that you are father's *true son*, the true heir. You have come back to liberate your country from the tyranny of your half-brother."

Aris just smirked and shook his head.

"The General's mother had you imprisoned, but we all thought she had you killed."

Unconvinced, Aris rolled his eyes.

"I'm serious!" Celia pressed her warm hands against his cheeks. "We tell the people how the General has kept me prisoner—his half-sister! Abusing me. The people will believe us. Everybody fears him."

"This is a dangerous plan, Celia."

"To make sure I couldn't run away, the General blamed many executions on me. He made people fear me, but also hate me."

Aris remembered how Leo always said Celia was more cruel and dangerous than the General.

Persisting, Celia continued. "Listen. Listen! We'll dress you in Father's uniform, and many people will think you are him, returned from the dead!"

"And what about your brother, husband, president, general?" Aris wondered.

Without hesitation she blurted, "We kill him. I'll poison him. Or even better, I'll sedate him, then you hide here and you kill him. You will claim victory and take your rightful place as heir!"

This time Aris laughed out loud. "You're crazy! Then what?"

"Then you govern the country! You'll release political prisoners, or at least some of them. You'll give money to the poor, and you'll announce a housing project to give people homes. You'll assign a parliament and I will select its members. The people will see you as their liberator!"

"That's some fantasy," Aris frowned.

She kissed away his pout, now thrilled with the telling of her adventurous plan. "You will inherit all of Father's riches, and you will have me. Together we will have money, gold, land. We will get married, and have many children together!"

"Wow! But we'd still be half-siblings. How could we marry?"

"Easy." Celia sat back on her heels. "You'll pass a law that half-sibs can marry. After all, you will be the leader!"

"The church would never allow that!"

"No problem. I know all of the archbishop's secrets!" Celia smiled joyfully. "He likes little girls… and boys!"

"Tempting," Aris sighed. "But I don't see how it can work."

Celia smiled radiantly. "I love you, Aris. No man has touched me like you have. We were made for each other. And the whole country will thank you. The whole world will respect you. I will help you. I know all the politicians, all the ambassadors. And their secrets."

"How well do you k-n-o-w them?" Aris asked leadingly.

"Be serious! Not as well as I know you!"

"But I still don't understand. Why do you want to kill the General?"

Celia's gaze fell to the mattress. "You don't know my pain. He raped me. He humiliated me. He was going to kill me." She clutched a bit of fabric and started kneading it between her fingers. "Only because no one else loves him, he allowed himself to fall in love with me."

Aris's heart began to ache for Celia's struggle, for her past, for her present.

She unclenched her fists and then reached out with renewed hope to touch Aris's chest. "I will tell you how to make everyone love you."

How to make everyone love me? That sounded mysteriously like the love secret of his quest. Aris leaned in closer.

Celia's face was now practically glowing. "You and me running the country. You'll make me your Vice President. We'll release all the political prisoners. I will go around the country giving out money, food, clothes to the poor. We'll re-open schools which were closed. We'll build hospitals. Together we'll become everybody's hero. I know you will make the best leader ever. And I will help you!"

Aris took a deep breath and held it. That was not the love secret he'd imagined. Not at all. "What about my friends?"

Celia tipped her head to one side. "You pardon them, of course. They will worship you for saving their lives."

After all the three amigos had been through, Aris laughed at the irony of John and Uri thinking he'd saved their bacon.

48 Falling for the Temptress

Back at the garage, Aris didn't stir until well past mid-day when Pepe was away again. He gathered his friends, who listened with their mouths agape, as he revealed Celia's plan.

They looked from one to the other in disbelief. "It's a good plan," Aris concluded, turning to Leo. "I will pardon you all, and make Leo a well-compensated commander. Seems like a win-win, with no danger of being shot while trying to escape."

Leo worked his jaw muscles then bit his upper lip. "I'm wondering which part of you is doing the thinking… your dick or your asshole?"

John and Uri nodded their agreement.

"Celia loves me! And to tell you the truth, I love her too," Aris confessed. "She makes me laugh. Even when I'm tired, she awakes my body."

Leo spat into the dirt. "I thought you were smart, but you're a goddamn fool."

Again John and Uri nodded like bobbleheads.

Aris rested a hand on Leo's shoulder. "I tell you she loves me. Celia trusted me with her deepest, darkest life secrets."

"For starters," Leo said, shaking off Aris's arm, "everybody knows they're brother and sister."

Aris raised his eyebrows while John and Uri's heads just about sprang off their bodies.

"All right. Half-brother and sister, whatever," Leo scoffed. "But Celia can't love anyone. She's an evil snake… the one who turned the General into a monster. Assuming you go along with her, the next day she'll have you killed so she can take over completely. Then she'll burn this whole country to the ground."

Aris took in all this new information, processing it alongside what he'd learned over a lifetime of studying people… and women.

"Don't sell us out for some sex tricks," Uri broke the silence. "Leo's idea is the only way out. We're nearly there. Stick to the plan."

Aris let the words and the schemes tumble through his brain. Even if they could escape the camp, there was still a good chance they'd be caught and shot on the spot.

This time it was Leo who placed a hand on Aris's shoulder. "I can't believe you've fallen for that siren. She's lured many to their deaths. She is only using you to get out from under the General's thumb. We won't see the daylight after you kill the General for her. You'll be the first one she has executed, claiming to be the hero for exacting retribution for her husband's… well her… whatever… his death. Then she'll be in charge. She already has half the Army Generals in her pocket."

Aris's voice was thick. "I'm sure Celia truly loves me. She is not evil. She's just an abused girl. The General raped her."

Uri shook his head. "Pay a whore and she'll kiss you everywhere, tell you anything you want to hear."

"What if Aris is right?" John's sceptical side revealed itself. "What if Celia really loves Aris? Love can happen for anyone."

Leo squeezed his lips tight. "Did Celia ask you not to tell us?"

"Obviously. She doesn't trust anyone."

"If she really intended to let you free us, why not get our support to carry out her plan? We're your friends. We could help!"

Aris's expression froze. "You have some good points."

Uri leaned in and whispered, "Pepe's back."

Leo let out a belly laugh. "Pretend we're joking… and keep your mouths shut!"

— ◇ —

When Aris woke past mid-day after yet another sleepless night, he'd reached some conclusions. He made his way into the workshop. "Where's Pepe?"

"In town for parts again." Leo was standing next to Uri, watching John perform his engine magic.

"We can use the bikes to escape…" Aris said nonchalantly.

"No. No!" Leo threw up a hand. "We're not ready! Bikes make a lot of noise and there's no protection from bullets. I've been thinking about what you said before…"

"One way or another," Aris said, "someone will probably shoot at us. Even if we don't try to escape, the General has already promised he will shoot you too!"

The group shared a few long seconds of silence.

Anxiety clawed at Aris's chest. "We're running out of time. The General will be back any day now."

Uri cleared his throat and looked up. "I uh… don't know how to ride a motorcycle."

"You can ride with me," John offered.

"Nice—death by bullets or by your shitty driving."

Leo shook his head. "We have another problem. No petrol. We're only given enough to test-start the engines. The guards are always watching us."

"Pepe could help steal some gas," John suggested.

"He's Celia's dog, remember?" Leo scratched his chin. "Maybe we go with Celia's plan."

Aris raised a single eyebrow.

John pushed back from his work. "I thought you said Celia would just kill us all after Aris killed the general."

Aris met Leo's gaze. "I think I see where you're going with this. It's a perfect plan. But—"

❖

Celia sat in front of the vanity's mirror while her maid dried and styled her hair. At the ring of her cell phone, she examined the caller ID. "Wait outside," she instructed.

Celia waited until the girl was in the hallway, not paying close enough attention to notice there was no click of the door closing completely.

"My General, my love! I miss you so!"

"The Americans must be shot… before I return." His voice boomed over the speaker as Celia fussed with her hair with both hands.

"Two more nights," she told him. "This is my most fertile time of month."

"No. Tomorrow morning, I'm telling you. They must be shot before I return. The American government's been calling."

Celia set down her brush. "What about the Sergeant who's been helping fix the motorcycles?"

"Shoot him first."

"Okay," Celia sighed. "I'll have him shot alongside my maid Rita. Stupid girl. I like her, but she's seen the American in my bed."

"Shoot her and anyone else you like," he huffed. "But do it before I get back."

Outside Celia's bedroom door, Rita clutched a hand to her mouth and fled down the hallway.

<hr>

Mid-afternoon, Aris sat supervising John's work from a distance over coffee while Leo and Uri hovered like helicopter parents.

Motion from outside drew his attention and Aris watched curiously as the maid Rita raced across the dirt to the workshop. He stood in time to catch her hand as she stumbled inside, breathless.

Leo turned at the noise and made his way to Rita, brushing Aris's protective hand away and wrapping the girl in his arms.

"Madam…" Rita choked out. "She was talking to the General on the speakerphone. He ordered her to shoot the Americans now."

The sound of metal on metal clattered on John's worktable.

Aris didn't turn from Rita, even when Uri let out a long string of burps.

"And then the General ordered her to shoot you and me too," she sobbed into Leo's shoulder.

"Why shoot you?" Leo asked.

"Because I saw the American in her bed."

Leo hugged the girl tight, rubbing her back while sighing deeply.

"When are they going to shoot us?" Aris asked.

"Tomorrow." Rita sniffled. "She wants another night with you. She's in her days… you know, get pregnant."

"Why did the General move up the timeline?" Leo asked suspiciously.

Rita leaned back to look him in the eyes. "The American President called the General."

Leo's face went pale.

Uri slammed a fist against the workbench, sending John's work clattering again. "Bastard! He's supposed to be a supporter of the Jews."

"Maybe you didn't hear everything," Aris considered. "If the American government knew we were prisoners awaiting execution, they should be coming to our rescue."

John rearranged the bike parts on the table in front of him. "Unless they think we've been turned into spies. I saw this movie once where the President and Vice President—"

A lightbulb flashed in Aris's mind. "That bitch! She's connected to both the VP and the President."

"Who? Celia?" Leo asked, wrapping Rita ever tighter in his embrace.

"No." Aris started pacing. "Someone I know. But I can't hardly believe she'd…" After striding the length of the space four times Aris came to a halt. "It doesn't matter who's behind it. What's important is that we've got to move up our timeline. We escape tonight!"

49 Escape Improvise

Aris could see the maid Rita trembling in Leo's arms. "Where do you sleep? At the house or in the camp?"

"Service room at the house. I'm Celia's personal maid. She likes me close."

"Good!" Aris clapped his hands together.

"What's good?" Uri collapsed into a chair next to John, his face red and bathed in sweat. "Finding out we're about to be shot? Again?"

Aris ignored Uri and stayed focused on the girl. "Surely you know as well as Leo that you'll both be executed alongside us."

"Yes!" Rita clung tight to Leo. "We need to get away, and we need to do it now!"

Leo gazed into the maid's eyes. "My darling, I already have a plan. But we'll need your help."

"Anything," she murmured, looking at him adoringly. "You know I would do anything for you, my hero."

Leo blushed. "I did not know. You never told me before!"

This time it was Rita's turn to look surprised. "Then you are blind," she beamed. "Remember the pastries I bring to you? Remember the cakes? Do you think these are easy to steal without attracting attention?"

Aris knew they didn't have time for Leo and Rita to play out the full soap opera just now. "I've been thinking about the original plan. Because of the problem with getting gasoline for the motorcycles, and because the bikes are noisy, and because there are five of us, I think we should keep that only as our backup plan. Escape is not enough. We have to vanish… and fast!"

"I was thinking the same thing," Leo said.

"As for other means of transportation, the only car that can get gas without question is Celia's."

Leo nodded. "Correct! And Celia's car is big enough to hold all five of us."

"Oh! Good idea," John squeaked.

Uri let out a double burp. "Sure, but I'm still not seeing a master plan here. Celia's not exactly gonna hand over her car keys."

Aris snapped his fingers. "Ah, but it is obvious. Celia will come to pick me up again, for our last night t—"

"I know!" Leo interrupted. "In the morning, Aris kills Celia, then along with Rita, they come to pick us up and we vamoose!"

Rita kissed him. "My clever Leo!"

But Aris balked. "I'm not a killer. No way would I kill Celia."

"It's her life or ours." Uri banged a fist on John's workbench.

"Maybe we should keep her as a hostage," John offered.

"Hmm…" Aris hummed. "That's an idea. We could exchange her for our lives at the border."

Leo shook his head. "I don't want to be anywhere near that evil woman. I think Aris should tie Celia to the bed, tape her mouth shut, and steal the car! By the time she's discovered we'll be miles away."

"My intelligent Leo!" Rita gave the Sergeant a kiss on the lips.

"Why wait till morning?" Uri moaned.

Aris shot back, "Because nobody is allowed in or out of camp after midnight. If Celia's car went out late she'd be expected back immediately."

"Lucky you, Aris." Leo smiled coyly. "You'll have to entertain Celia all night long again. Just don't let the devil turn you. We'll be here waiting."

John cleared his throat. When he spoke it was almost in his normal voice. "What if… what if Celia *doesn't* come for you tonight?"

Rita jumped in without pause. "She *will* come. She told the General she is in season to get a baby in her belly."

"Flying bareback?" Uri slapped out at Aris's arm. "You bastard!"

Aris smirked at the inner workings of his playboy friend's mind. Movement outside drew his eye. Pepe was returning, carrying a small pile of parts. "Quick! Rita, go out and stall Pepe while we finish our plan!"

Leo turned to look out the door, immediately dropping his arms from the maid's shoulders. "Please, buy us a little more time!"

Rita smiled lovingly up at Leo. "My hero, anything for you. Till morning!" Then she gave his hand a tender squeeze and sauntered outside, swinging her hips gently for Pepe's benefit.

The gears were already whirring in Aris's mind. "The guards expect Celia's car to come in and out of the gate every morning now."

"Will you tie Celia up before or after you have sex with her?" Uri asked.

Aris waved a dismissive arm. How on earth did Epi tolerate Uri's total fascination with sex? He dove back into the plan. "The guards never fully stop the car, so that's good, but what happens when they see me driving with Rita?"

Leo tapped his temple knowingly. "Very simple. Rita will put on one of Celia's dresses and her sunglasses, maybe a scarf. Then, Aris, you're in the trunk like normal."

"Excellent!" Aris could already picture the rest playing out in his head.

Leo picked up the narrative. "Rita drives into the camp, reverses up to the garage like Celia does each day, but this time we jump into the car instead of Aris jumping out. No soldier will dare stop Celia."

"Celia never stops," Aris confirmed. "She honks the horn twice and as soon as the gate opens, she speeds off."

"Even better," Leo added.

John held up a hand, like a timid grade-schooler. "Um… How do we know Rita hasn't been sent to spy on us?"

Leo flashed an angry glare.

"Rita saw me in bed with Celia," Aris clarified. "Celia wants her dead, just as much as the General wants me out of the picture."

Just then, Pepe made his way inside the garage with a bag on his shoulder.

"What took you so long?" Leo asked, instantly switching to a stern voice. "We've been waiting for hours!"

Pepe handed over the canvas sack. "Everything you asked for. Now I'm going to sleep," he said, heading for the mattress in the small room.

"No, you don't." Leo grabbed Pepe by the arm. "We're ready for a test ride around the camp. Go and fetch us petrol for three motorcycles."

"They'll never give me petrol," Pepe grumbled.

Leo handed off the bag to John and grabbed two large gas cans. "Take these," he said, pushing them into Pepe's hands. "I'll come with you." With a quick wink back at Aris, Leo shouted, "John, I want those machines ready to go by the time we return!"

⸺ ◆ ⸺

The evening sun hadn't yet set when Aris saw Celia's car turning into the camp. *She's early*, he thought, his heart already beginning to pound.

Aris tapped Leo's arm and pointed discreetly. Exchanging sights they continued working on the bikes, a smile spreading on both their faces. John had magnificently fixed two of the General's machines, and a third was getting close. Still, Aris couldn't help but hope all of that hard work would be for nothing.

Aris stood to get into position for Celia's car to reverse back at the garage. But she didn't even cast a glance his way. Instead the car carried on, passing the workshop entirely without stopping.

Leo's breath caught. "*Mierda*, do you think she knows something?" His head motioned to Pepe, standing near the door talking to a patrol guard.

Aris stared after the car, watching it drive through camp and down the road.

"Whew!" Leo whistled softly. "She pulled in to refuel. This really is our lucky day!"

A few minutes later, Celia's car sped back towards them, reversing up to the garage. Deep relief filled Leo's face, but Aris could only take things one breath at a time.

The trunk popped open and John stepped over to help Aris climb in. "Our lives depend on you," he said in a timid voice. "No pressure!"

Aris felt his body tense, once more twisted like a pretzel and hidden in the dark. With a hand extended to keep John from closing the trunk yet he said, "I will be back, guys. And I will get you out!"

50 The Unexpected

*J*ust before sunrise, Aris was exhausted from another night in Celia's bed. But he had work to do.

"My darling," he began, reaching for the belt from Celia's silk robe. "I have an idea for something that should give us both a little extra thrill."

He whipped the slim belt loose and let the bit of fabric dangle above her belly, tracing its tip under and around her luscious bosom, then trailing it down an arm to her hand.

When Celia shivered and her eyes lit up, Aris had all the confirmation he needed.

Working quickly, he tied both her hands together and secured them at the head of the bed, making Celia stretch to reach. Excited, she let out a low groan.

He pulled a pillowcase off one of the many pillows on the bed and used it as a makeshift blindfold. Then Aris set about teasing and tantalising his would-be victim until the time was right.

With a feather touch he stroked Celia's cheeks, planting butterfly kisses all down her neck. When he reached the base of her throat, she was already writhing beneath him.

Aris let his hands roam down her torso, circling her belly button. Sliding further, he grazed her hip with the back of one hand, letting its motion stop above the cleft of her femininity. Again Celia bucked and thrust her hips upwards.

"I think we're going to have to improvise on this next part," Aris whispered.

He pulled the top sheet off, then standing, twisted it deftly into a makeshift rope. Binding her feet together, he tied off the sheet on one end of the bed, caressing her calf muscles and leaning down to nibble on the toes of one foot.

Celia moaned in pleasure. "I like your surprise!"

Sliding upwards and climbing back into bed, Aris kissed his way up her body. He removed another pillowcase before kissing Celia full on the lips, a wet kiss with tongue that left them both breathless.

Then he threaded the pillowcase underneath her head, and before she could think to refuse, he tied it tight and wrapped it as a gag, muffling her lusty moans and groans.

Aris kissed her one last time on her forehead. "Goodbye, my love. Goodbye! It is a great pity the General wants to have me killed. I am so in love with you. I could have stayed with you forever. But if you do get pregnant, please look after our boy until I come for him. I do love you!"

With that, Aris rolled off the mattress and began to put on his clothes.

"Nooo!" came Celia's muffled scream.

"I was supposed to kill you, but I love you too much for that."

Aris switched on the television to a music channel and dialled up the volume. From a dresser drawer where he'd seen Celia stash it, Aris removed a handgun and tucked it into the waist of his trousers.

Rita was waiting outside the room when he opened the door. Aris pulled her inside.

Witnessing Celia nude, tied up, and kicking and groaning, Rita's eyes filled with fright.

Aris riffled through other dresser drawers, selecting a dress and scarf. "Here, get dressed in Celia's clothes. Her sunglasses and lipstick are on the vanity in the bathroom."

Rita seemed to understand and retreated to the restroom to change in private.

Aris leaned down over Celia, tenderly kissing first one nipple then the other. "Goodbye, my twin girls. I love you, but mama wants to kill me! I will miss you!"

Celia jerked her bottom more violently, bouncing on the bed against her restraints.

Aris tightened all the knots once more until Rita stepped out of the bathroom, now dressed and camouflaged perfectly as her mistress.

"Remarkable!"

He grabbed Celia's car keys while Rita flipped a switch at the side of the bed.

"What's that for?"

Rita dropped her gaze to the floor. "It's the do-not-disturb light. No one comes in when mistress has it on."

Aris smiled approvingly.

He opened the secret door to the garage.

Rita marvelled and whispered, "So that's how she does it," while Aris led the way.

When they reached Celia's vehicle, Aris popped the trunk and began to climb in. "Close it behind me. Remember, when you get to the guard gates, slow down and honk twice, but don't stop."

Rita just stared after him. Aris coiled himself up, waiting for her to close the trunk so they could get going.

Instead, after a long moment, she leaned on the car gasping. "I don't know how to drive!"

Aris froze. "Wh-what? What do you mean you don't kn-know how to drive?"

Frightened, Rita shook her head. "No! You must drive. You must dress like Celia!" She unwrapped the scarf and forced the material into Aris's hands.

He remained silent but climbed back out of the trunk.

"I will dress you," Rita continued. "Celia has dozens of wigs and other dresses." With that, Rita traced her way back up the secret stairs and returned mere moments later.

Grinding his jaws, Aris stood wordlessly as Rita yanked at his shirt and pulled down his trousers, motioning for him to step out of them. Then she unzipped a loose dress and worked it over his head and shoulders, leaving the back open as the zipper clearly would not close over his girth.

Next she pinned on a sexy wig then wrapped a scarf around Aris's shoulders and expertly began applying makeup to his face. Taking a step back, she smiled. "Perfect! Let's go!"

Before he could so much as glance down at himself, Rita had gathered up his clothing and tossed it into the trunk where she easily followed and looked up at him expectantly, waiting for him to close her inside.

What could he do? The girl didn't know how to drive, and time was of the essence. Aris shivered inside the ridiculous dress, his head already itching from the pins Rita had used to attach the wig. He shut the trunk and climbed behind the steering wheel.

⋯ ◇ ⋯

Celia's car reversed into the workshop, where three anxious men awaited. The boot of the car popped open.

Sergeant Leo looked in, shocked to see Rita rather than Aris. "What happened?" he asked, helping her to climb out.

"Hurry!" She coaxed Uri and John to load the backpacks in the trunk.

After a few seconds to digest his surprise, Leo commanded Uri and John, "Jump in and scrunch down."

"But you left the bikes on," John pointed back at the workshop.

"The noise will make the other guards think we're still working."

Leo tossed the backpacks on the rear seat, then made his way around to the passenger side, tucking Rita onto the floor space under the dashboard. "Don't make a move until I tell you it's safe."

Taking a short look at Aris, still camouflaged under wig and makeup, Leo formed the sign of the cross against his chest. He shut the front passenger door, then he climbed into the backseat and stretched out across the floor.

⋯ ◇ ⋯

Facing the gate, Aris's sight zoomed in like a falcon.

"You're going too slow!" Leo urged from behind him. "And lower yourself. Celia isn't as tall as you."

Aris honked the horn twice and pressed down on the gas. "Shut up!" he muttered without moving his now bright red lips.

The lieutenant clearly caught sight of the car and driver bearing down on his position. He stepped out of the guard post and stood directly in front of the gate.

Aris blew his breath upwards to cool his drenched forehead, sweating beneath the heavy wig. His foot was ready to nail the gas pedal to the floor.

Raising a hand, the lieutenant saluted the approaching car. "Open the gate!" he commanded.

Accelerating a little, Celia's car drove past the man and through the gate without mishap.

Aris exhaled a deep breath of relief. "We're through!" he shouted excitedly.

Rita began to lift, but Aris pushed her back. "Stay down, military car approaching!"

Once the vehicle passed, Aris gave the all-clear.

Leo sat up in the backseat and leaned his head forwards between Aris and Rita's shoulders. He looked around to get his bearings then instructed, "Take the first left."

"Are you sure?" Aris questioned.

"Yes!"

"Sure, like you were sure that Rita could drive?"

"Tiny mistake," Leo chuckled. "You did fine though. You look very sexy!"

"You are playing with our lives!" Aris's tone was harsh. "We need to get over the border as fast as possible."

"My life, too. But this road doesn't lead to the closest border. For sure they'll start looking for us towards El Salvador or Honduras, maybe even Mexico. They will never ever think we might go east, to the farthest border, for Belize!"

"My clever Leo," Rita bathed the Sergeant in kisses. "You have a mind better than any General."

Aris could do nothing but keep driving, despite the hairpins still digging into his scalp.

51 Escape Hiccups

"Turn here into the woods, on the right," Leo commanded. "Okay, stop."

When Aris turned off the engine, the Sergeant hopped out to open the trunk for Uri and John. Various moans and groans followed as the two men unfolded their bodies and stood for the first time in thirty minutes.

Meanwhile, Aris flung off the scarf and started pulling at the wig to remove the bobby pins. Rita offered to help, so he climbed out and stood patiently while she once more made excellent work of the matter.

Once Uri and John regained use of their limbs, Leo leaned into the trunk space, rooting among the backpacks. "Where are the General's uniforms?"

Aris shrugged. Uri and John looked at him expectantly.

Leo started pacing behind the car. "How are we supposed to cross the border without you in the General's uniform?"

Aris was unamused. "I guess it's your turn to dress as Celia."

Rita caught up to the Sergeant and tugged on his sleeve. "There are three uniforms at the dry cleaners."

"Oh no," Aris grumbled. "Going back into town in this ridiculous outfit is not an option!"

This time Rita practically beamed. "Madam Celia stops her car outside the dry cleaners. I get out and collect the General's uniforms. It's simple!"

Leo stood puzzling the idea for less than a minute. "We go now, before they discover we're gone." He motioned to Uri and John. "Back into the boot." Then turning to Aris, Leo grabbed the discarded wig from the roof of the car and plopped it back on Aris's head. "I have a man's face. Better for you to be Celia."

Aris reluctantly straightened the contraption on his head. "If we're going back into the lion's mouth, we'll find another way to cross the border."

Uri and John struggled back into position and Leo closed them in. "A General is not stopped at the borders. In fact, now we can be three Generals. Even better. The only other way is through the jungle. We have no equipment, no gear. We would die before we even got started."

Before Aris could wave her off, Rita shoved bobby pins back in to secure the wig. "Beauty is pain," she said in a sing-song voice.

◆ ◇ ◆

Two chamber maids stood outside Celia's bedroom. They could hear only the continual sounds of a bed squeaking and their mistress's moans.

Exchanging glances, the younger girl twerked her bottom, bringing a smile to the other woman's face.

The older maid pointed to the red, do not disturb light. "We should inform the General."

"Celia would have us shot!"

The elder woman fiddled with the polishing cloth in her hand. "If we don't, the General will have us shot."

Her counterpart moved down the hall, pausing to dust a flowerpot. "If the General knows we saw his wife with someone else, he will kill us just to keep us quiet."

The older maid continued to stare at the red light with concern. "I've never seen this lit in the daytime. Very unusual! Who does she have in her bed?"

"You're right. Let's get out of here. I don't want to be around when this guy stumbles out after what she's putting him through!"

The ladies covered their laughter and quietly made their escape.

◆ ◇ ◆

In camp, a patrolling soldier heard the last of the motorcycle engines splutter to silence. When nothing started up again, he made his way within sight of the workshop.

Hearing no voices, he leaned his head through the door. "Sergeant Leo?" Scanning left and right, the soldier walked in "Sergeant Leo?"

Still no response. But he heard a light banging on the floor coming from inside the small enclosure where Aris used to sleep.

Rifle mounted, the soldier poked open the door to the small room, expecting to find five men having an unsanctioned siesta.

Shocked, he saw only Pepe laying on the floor on his side along with a wooden chair. Then he recognized the prisoner's hands were tied, his feet bound to the chair, with a wad of fabric duct-taped into his mouth as a makeshift gag.

He yanked at the duct-tape, pulling it off in one painful rip.

"They escaped!" Pepe shouted while the soldier began untying him.

Once his feet were free, Pepe ran for the camp gate with his hands still bound.

He shouted to the Lieutenant on guard, "They escaped!"

The officer remained calm. "Who escaped?"

In a frenzy, Pepe banged the guard box. "The Americans! They took Sergeant Leo with them. You morons let them pass through the gate this morning."

The Lieutenant stared hard at Pepe, unflinching. "No one has passed through our gate all morning. We heard the Americans working on the motorbikes in the workshop."

Pepe now flung himself at the Lieutenant, who pushed him back. "I'm telling you, they escaped. They tied me up and left in Madam Celia's car."

"No chance!" the officer scoffed. "Only Madam Celia was inside the car. I saw her with my own eyes. We all did. She drove in, checked the garage like usual, then a few minutes later she drove out."

Pepe pointed into the guard box at the telephone. "Call Celia at the General's house!"

"No way!" The Lieutenant looked down his nose at Pepe. "I'm not disturbing her. Maybe your friends went to the canteen and didn't invite you."

Pepe squinted at the man and raised his still bound hands. "Why would they tie me up if they were just going to the canteen?"

Hesitant, the officer picked up the phone and dialled. After a moment he asked, "Are Sergeant Leo and the Americans in the canteen?"

The man's face froze. He hung up the phone but kept his hand on the receiver.

Pepe started shouting again, "Call Madam!"

"You're crazy," he said. "Madam Celia will shoot us if we disturb her over nothing."

Pepe bared his teeth like a hyena. "Then you can look forward to being shot by the General when he finds out you let his Americans escape."

Hesitantly, the Lieutenant picked up the phone again. He heard a guard's voice answer from the gate of the main house. "What time has the Madam returned home this morning?" he asked with extreme caution.

Unconcerned the soldier replied, "She's still out, sir."

Pepe was bouncing from foot to foot. "What? What?"

His hand still on the phone, the Lieutenant's face drained of colour. "And what time did Madam leave the General's villa?"

"The usual, by first light," the guard informed.

In slow motion, the officer put down the handset, ending the call. "Maybe she went shopping in town."

Pepe now bounced like a jack-in-the-box. "And I suppose she took the Americans and Sergeant Leo to help her pick out new shoes?"

The Lieutenant remained silent for a few long seconds.

Nervously, Pepe kicked the ground. "Fuck! Fuck! Fuck! They've kidnapped Celia. The General will feed us alive to his dogs."

The officer anxiously dialled another number. "Connect me to Madam Celia."

The call rang and rang without answer.

He eagerly dialled again. "Connect me to the General's maids."

A young woman answered the phone quickly.

"I need to speak to Madam immediately!" the Lieutenant barked.

The maid's voice was flippant. "Madam is *occupied*. She has turned on the do-not-disturb light."

The officer released a heavy sigh and hung up the phone gently. "Madam is at home. No problem!"

Pepe stopped kicking the dirt and instead kicked the Lieutenant's polished shoe. "Is the General back?"

The officer flinched but answered, "Noooo…"

Pepe laughed out loud at the man, pointing a finger to the side of his head. "Are you stupid? Her car never returned home. How can she be occupied?"

Horror filled the Lieutenant's face this time.

Pepe nudged him by the shoulder. "Cut me free then get the Jeep! We'll go check! What if they took Celia as a hostage?"

The officer sliced Pepe's bindings with a pocketknife. Then he grabbed a set of keys from the desk and the two raced to the Jeep.

At the villa guard booth, they slowed while the Lieutenant shouted to the guard, "Open. Open!" The gate raised, and he continued shouting, "High alert. No one leaves. And I mean no one!"

At the villa, they took the stairs two at a time.

Pepe saw the red light, advertising that his cousin wished not to be disturbed. Then he heard her voice practically sobbing, "*Ouuuu. Ouuuu*," and the bed banging against the wall.

Two maids stood further down the hallway smiling to themselves. The younger mumbled, "The love secret!"

Pepe looked to the Lieutenant, but clearly the man was afraid for his life. He knew it was up to him now, so he knocked. "Celia? Celia, it's Pepe. Are you okay?"

The banging got faster. Her answer came out louder, "Ouuuu! Ouuuu!"

The older maid said, "They've been at it all day today!" and the two women shared a shielded laugh.

Pepe knew the risks. No choice was truly safe. He reached out a hand to turn the knob.

The door was locked. He flung a kick at the knob, then another, breaking it open.

Adrenaline pumped through his veins as Pepe shot into the room first, followed by the Lieutenant. He pulled up short at the sight in front of him.

His cousin Celia lay nude, with her arms stretched tight above her head, gagged and blindfolded, and her legs bound together and tied to the foot of the bed.

"Ouuuu! Ouuuu!" she howled louder still.

Out of the corner of his eye, Pepe saw the maids pop their heads into the room, then scurry away.

He and the Lieutenant worked quickly to free Celia, then Pepe covered her with the wrinkled sheet that had been used to wrap her legs.

"Where were you?" Celia rasped. "Stupid maids, I've been screaming for hours."

Instantly the maids backed out of sight.

Pepe took little comfort in pointing to the switch at the side of the bed. "You had the do-not-disturb light on."

Catching her breath, Celia sat up in bed.

Pepe spoke in a soft voice. "Are you okay? What happened?"

"I was attacked by the American." Her voice was scratchy. "And the maid Rita."

"But how did the American get into your—" the officer began.

Celia's fearsome growl cut him off. Her eyes flashed in anger. But she waited before answering. "You tell me," she finally said. "How was he allowed to step outside the camp? Did he walk straight through your gate? Were you all asleep?"

"But… you drove in and out of the camp this morning. I saluted you, Madam."

"Idiot!" she spat. "They dressed in my clothes. If you saw my car, that means they used it to escape. The General will shoot you all. Incompetent."

Pepe's voice was low when he shared, "Sergeant Leo helped them. They knocked me out and tied me up on a chair."

Celia held the sheet around her body as she stalked to the bathroom, returning a couple moments later in her morning robe. She opened the bedroom door and screamed down the hall where the two maids were hovering quietly. "Why didn't you raise the alarm? You helped them. You are part of their plan!"

Horrified, the younger maid answered, "No madam, Rita told us of the *love secret* and we thought…"

With fury in her face, Celia screeched, "What *love secret,* you stupid women? Spreading false gossip. You saw I was tied up." She yanked the Lieutenant's pistol from his holster. Without hesitation, Celia shot first one maid and then the other in the forehead.

Like an angry lioness, Celia pointed the weapon at the Lieutenant's head. "Were you the officer on duty at the gate?"

He stood at attention. "Yes, Madam."

"One word of this false gossip and you'll be next! Alert the governing officer. Unless you find them and bring them back—dead or alive… preferably dead—you won't live to see the morning."

Hesitantly he asked, "Who will inform the General, Madam?"

She spoke through clenched teeth. "I will. Prepare two helicopters fully armed. Now go!"

"B-b-but," the Lieutenant stammered. "The General refuses to get into a helicopter."

"The helicopters are for me," Celia sputtered. "I will hunt those animals down. You begin the land search. Dispatch cars in all directions."

The men turned to head out the door, but Celia caught Pepe's arm and pulled him back.

"Does anyone else know about the American?" she whispered.

"No!" he answered immediately.

She gave his cheek a soft caress. "You are my true blood. You saved me. I will never forget this."

"I owe you everything," Pepe pledged. "If it wasn't for you, the General would have shot me a long time ago. Now let me go bury these two big mouths."

52 THE CHASE

One of the two helicopters landed fully armed. Celia climbed aboard dressed in full military regalia. She handed her mobile to the pilot, showing GPS coordinates for her car. "Follow the tracking on this vehicle."

Within minutes the first chopper was on top of Celia's car. Without warning, she manned the machine gun and open fired.

＊ ◇ ＊

Uri panicked in the back seat, a chain of burps revving up like a motorcycle's engine in response to the ping of bullets off the trunk of the car.

"Wh-wh-what's…" John's high-pitched voice could not even finish a sentence.

"Through the woods!" Sergeant Leo shouted, pointing sideways.

Aris turned the wheel hard. The car bumped and jarred when it left the packed dirt, practically tossing John into Uri's lap. Almost immediately they were under the cover of trees.

Aris slowed the vehicle to navigate the dense canopy and dodge the largest of the rocks. This gave him an idea. When he had them safely under cover, he stopped the car and opened his door.

Seconds later he climbed back in and shoved the automatic's transmission into reverse.

"Wh-wh-what are—" John's voice still cracked.

Once they'd retraced their path almost to the edge of the woods, Aris slammed on the brakes and put it in park. "Out of the car. If they didn't follow the direction we were headed before, it means they've got satellite tracking on this vehicle."

Once everyone had climbed out, Aris dropped the huge rock on the gas pedal. The engine revved like a hornet's nest.

Standing outside the driver's door, with a flick of the wrist and an even speedier withdrawal, Aris sent the car blazing back towards the dirt road.

◆ ◇ ◆

"They've circled back," Celia's pilot informed her. "Almost exactly where they left the road before."

She angled the machine gun at the edge of the woods and took aim. Less than a minute later, she saw the front end of her car emerge from the tree line, tyres spinning like crazy, stirring up a cloud of dust.

With all the hatred she possessed, she squeezed the trigger and let the bullets rain like hail from the front to the back of her car.

One or more of the shots hit the gas tank. She felt the pilot angle the helicopter away in almost the same instant as the vehicle exploded in flames.

Regaining her balance, Celia continued to lay waste to the flaming fuselage, pumping round after round into the heap of metal.

"Go back!" she screamed into her headset when the pilot had guided them out of range.

"No one could have survived that explosion," he replied.

She withdrew a pistol from a holster at her side and pointed it at the pilot. "No arguments."

◆ ◇ ◆

Uri stood shivering in his own sweat. "Now what? We're trapped. They'll send soldiers to kill us."

Leo pulled Uri further back under the tree canopy. "This is best. They'll think we're dead. The river is only a half-mile or so from here. We can get a boat."

Rita wrapped her arms around Leo's waist, pushing Uri out of her way. "My Leo is so intelligent!"

Aris brushed the dirt off his pants and turned back to the woods. "Quick!" he said. "Run. We'll get the boat downstream. Then we can steal a car they won't be able to track."

Leo smiled and said, "Follow me."

◦ ◇ ◦

Celia secured the sighting on the helicopter's rocket launcher. "Hold it steady," she called to the pilot, then pressed the button to fire.

The missile blasted away from the chopper aimed straight at the already flaming car. Celia returned to the machine gun, now squeezing the trigger and guiding bullets like a line of type back and forth across the metal frame.

"Circle back to check if anyone escaped," she ordered.

The pilot guided them in a path around the vehicle, but couldn't get too close because of the flames.

At last Celia seemed happy. "Okay, take me home. I'll send a ground crew to bring me proof of their bodies—I want skulls, rings, dentures… anything that's left of them."

The helicopter immediately rose and turned back towards camp.

With her pistol redrawn and pointed once more at the pilot, Celia's tone was unmistakable. "Those bastards were spies. This is top classified information. You do not even speak about this to your superior officer. Understood? You know nothing about this."

53 Messing with Chicken Feed

Late the next afternoon, the five arrived at the last village before a remote border crossing into Belize. Leo, Aris and Uri were dressed in the General's various uniforms, but on Leo's smaller frame, the uniform made him look a bit like Charlie Chaplin.

"We have to find a different car again. This one would have been reported stolen and they will know it was us.," Aris suggested. "By now, they've discovered our escape and the whole army will know what we're driving."

"How?" Leo scoffed. "We can't buy a car and if we steal one, then we'll have the same soldiers and helicopters surrounding us."

Aris drove them around the small village plaza.

Leo pointed excitedly. "There. Stop by that small canteen."

Aris climbed out and headed towards the restaurant door. "I smell good food. Let's have a nice meal, then we can find another car."

"Or a tractor," John snickered and ribbed Uri in the side.

Inside, the owner and his wife flinched upon sight of the three generals. Fear and apprehension were written all over their faces. But immediately they raced to the kitchen and came out bearing pitchers of drinks.

Aris smiled widely and took a seat at the biggest table.

"Well," Leo said, reassessing the situation. "We are generals after all. I guess we could stop and confiscate any car we want."

Towards the end of their meal, Aris heard yells and screams outside. He looked to the canteen owners, but they avoided eye contact. Approaching the window, he called back, "There's a military lorry, a personnel carrier, an off-roader, and a Jeep. They appear to be loading goods into the lorry."

Leo pulled out a small wad of bills to pay for the meal so the friends could be quickly on their way.

In full terror, the canteen lady clasped her hands in a prayer position. "Please. The meal, drinks, all on us. Your soldiers have already taken most of our stock. We have nothing left."

Uri and John looked quizzical so Rita translated in a hushed voice, then they joined Aris at the window, mirroring his look of concern.

Leo asked, "How often do the soldiers come to collect?"

Aris made his way back to stand beside Leo, pointedly doing his best to pretend he was really the President General.

The canteen couple exchanged gazes.

Timidly the wife answered, "Every few weeks. Whenever they feel like it."

Leo's nostrils flared.

The sound of a *thwack* called them all to the window to see what was causing the latest outcry. An officer had stolen the walking stick from an elderly man and was presently beating him.

"What's he yelling at the old man?" Aris asked.

"Empty handed again," Rita translated. "I will have you shot."

Aris looked over to Leo whose face was frozen. The sound of a string of burps behind him indicated that at least one of his friends already sensed what was coming next.

"It's none of our business," Uri urged. "Remember, that's how we got into trouble in the first place. There's nothing we can do. Stay out of it!"

Leo rubbed his chin. "The bastard! He's collecting anything these poor people have left."

Aris's breath was coming faster. "And he's beating anyone who comes with empty hands."

At that very moment, a woman in her thirties, dressed in black and accompanied by a boy, was pushed to her knees in front of the officer.

The uniformed man pulled her by her long black hair. Aris heard her wail as she burst into tears.

Pulling out a knife, the officer cut a handful of her hair with a sawing motion, tossing the hair into the woman's face.

"We have to do something." Aris's blood was boiling.

The officer then kicked the woman in the stomach and she rolled to the ground, shielding her child in the process.

"Another one empty handed." A corporal pushed a second woman in a black dress into the street with her teenage daughter.

Staring at the beautiful girl the officer let his gaze wander from her head to her toes. Finally, he gave his order.

Two soldiers responded immediately, grabbing the teenage girl roughly and dragging her into the back of the Jeep.

Soundless, the girl looked back at her mother with wild eyes.

On her knees, the mother begged, "Please, she is only thirteen. Show mercy. Punish me, not my girl."

Rita translated and clutched at Leo's sleeve for reassurance.

Aris puffed up his chest and headed towards the door.

"But we're so close to the border, Aris!" John squealed in a girlish voice. "There's nothing we can do for these people. The soldiers will shoot us on the spot."

"I don't want to be fed to the dogs," Uri added. "You can't change the world."

Aris noticed the canteen owner and his wife exchange a glance, then whisper something that let him know their identity was now in question. "Americanos."

Undeterred Aris fixed his wild stare on Leo. "We can fix this," he said. "But you'll need to do the talking, Sergeant. I mean… General Leo."

⸺ ◇ ⸺

The true General arrived at his villa in a cloud of dust, just in time to watch Celia eating her breakfast. After a short outburst and Celia's even shorter response, he plopped into a chair beside her.

Grinding his teeth, he dialled a call and placed it on speaker, staring pointedly at his wife.

In a fake happy voice the General declared, "Tell your President that his wish has been granted. The Americans completed their job and left yesterday. They are on their way to the border."

The voice of the U.S. Vice President boomed across the room. "Our eyes on the ground informed us that they escaped, taking your lovely wife as a hostage."

The General's eyes bulged out of their sockets.

"Which is it, my dear friend?" the voice taunted.

"Nonsense," the General huffed, lips bloated. "Fake news. Propaganda by our enemies. I am having breakfast with my wife right now." He pressed a hand firmly on Celia's shoulder and urged her to speak.

"Good morning to the great American Vice President," Celia oozed in her most charming voice. "When are you going to stop listening to rumours and believe my good husband?"

They heard a sigh of relief on the end of the line. "Madam Celia! I am so relieved to hear you are safe in the company of my dear friend. Pardon me. We were very concerned for your safety."

"Perhaps you'd like me to rev up the motorcycle engines so you'll believe me," the General mocked. "Your boys did a good job."

"Not necessary, my friend," the other retorted. "The world is full of fake news these days."

"Happy to hear this, Mr. Vice President."

"The important thing is that Madam Celia is safe and well, and the three Americans are travelling free. I will inform our President immediately."

The General sneered, "I am happy my friend is happy." He hung up the phone then turned to Celia. "You made sure there is no trace left of them?"

She didn't look up from her food. "Only ashes. No dentures, no mobile phones. The car was collected and scrubbed by a special unit. They covered the spot with wild grass and flowers."

The General huffed. "Overconfidence is a weakness. We'll keep up the search for another week. Just in case!"

— ◇ —

In her office, Varo answered the Vice President's call.

"Good news, Miss Chase. Your three American friends are on their way to the border."

"Thank you, we saw they were on the move, but…"

"But what?" the Vice President questioned.

Her mind spun. "Nothing. I wanted to wait a bit longer before I called to thank you."

"Anything for you, Varo. But be prepared for next week," he said slyly. "It may cost you a little extra!"

— ◇ —

His deep breaths betrayed Aris's rage.

Leo squeezed his eyes nearly shut, pushing his lower lip out to cap the upper one. Raising his stance, Leo threw his head back and donned a pair of dark sunglasses. "Three generals! Of course, we can do something. But the rest of you stay here with Rita."

Shocked, John and Uri dropped onto chairs with Rita, their faces now turning a sallow yellow.

Leo rolled up his uniform sleeves and double folded the trousers at his waist. In a stiff military walk, he followed Aris out the door.

"Attention!" Leo shouted as they approached the soldiers in the plaza.

Witnessing the approach of not one but two Generals, the officer fell into a momentary panic. His soldiers immediately stamped their feet to attention.

Approaching with a stern face, his left arm folded behind his back, Leo shouted, "I said, attention!"

Reeling with surprise, the officer joined the soldiers at attention, his left hand still on the old man's walking stick.

Leo moved into the man's face and kept his voice raised. "My good Captain, I see you are collecting taxes for the Army."

Taking two steps further, Leo stood beside one of the soldiers carrying an automatic rifle on his shoulder, bearing the uniform markings of a Sergeant.

Tugging the weapon into his own grasp, Leo pretended to examine the rifle. "Nice. American and brand new," he said, shifting back in front of the Captain. "You are very lucky we have released these to your units."

Aris noticed a funny glance exchanged between the singled out soldier and Leo, but it disappeared in an instant.

A string of locals peeked around corners and peered out through dirty windows, leaving Aris to look away from their miserable, sad and scared faces.

The two women in black were still on their knees in the street. Aris clasped his hands behind his back and moved to stand directly in front of them, garnering Leo's attention.

With a slight nod, Leo motioned to the teenage girl in the Jeep. "You are so lucky, Captain. There are no such beautiful girls where we've been lately."

Relief filled the man's face. "She is yours, General. You can have her."

In a sudden move, Leo landed a hard slap across the Captain's face. "Since when does the Army steal food from the poor villagers?"

Aris saw wonderment on the faces of the two women before him.

Leo pressed the tip of the rifle under the officer's jaw. The man stiffened, dropping the old man's walking stick.

Shouting his lungs out, General Leo displayed all the anger he could muster. "Since when is the protector of the people, the Army, kidnapping underage girls from their mother's arms?"

Villagers and soldiers alike focused their gaze on General Leo.

Continuing his verbal assault, Leo roared, "Since when does the Army beat and slash the hair of innocent mothers?"

Aris witnessed the two women's faces change to curiosity as they swapped surprised glances.

The soldiers stared straight ahead, clearly afraid to draw the wrath of this General who was verbally assaulting their commander.

Leo reached to the Captain's holster and seized his handgun before continuing the onslaught. "You are an embarrassment to your uniform. A disgrace to our great Army!"

With the rifle still pressed into the Captain's neck, Leo angled to face the soldiers.

"You are all a disgrace! Stealing from the poor is absolutely forbidden by the Army code! What if another unit like yours is stealing from your families in your village at this very moment? Kidnapping your young sisters!"

A number of the men blanched and dropped their sight to the dirt street.

"Drop your guns and step back three metres!" Leo ordered.

The soldiers who still had weapons complied immediately and returned frozen to attention.

"I will court martial you all. That is… if I can stop myself from shooting you right here and now!" He looked up and down the line of men as if selecting which one he would kill first. "Sergeant!"

"Yes, sir! General, sir!" replied the soldier who had shared a curious glance with Leo after being disarmed earlier.

"Order all these soldiers and this excuse for an officer to strip to their underwear now. They are a disgrace to the uniform." Leo turned to Aris and handed him the rifle, pointing to the soldiers before them. "Shoot anyone who still has his trousers on after one minute."

Ecstatic, Rita shouted, "Yes, my Leo. My hero. Shoot them all!"

Picking up the next nearest automatic rifle from the discard pile, Leo raised his weapon to clarify for Aris what his Spanish demands had meant.

The Sergeant turned to the men before him. "Trousers off! You heard the General." At that, he began unbuckling his own belt.

"Excluding you, Sergeant Antonio," General Leo shouted.

With a gleam at hearing his name, Antonio obeyed and re-buckled his belt.

Replacing the point of the rifle under the Captain's chin, Leo called out to the three in the canteen, "General, come join me."

John, Uri and Rita heeded quickly, though a series of burps gave away Uri's current state of mind.

In pointed English, Leo told them, "Pick up the guns and guard the soldiers. Anyone moves… shoot to kill!"

John and Rita were quick to comply, proudly standing with rifles pointed on the trouser-less men before them. Hesitant, Uri stood by motionless.

With his automatic still pointed at the Captain, Leo ordered, "Sergeant Antonio, select your good men… I repeat, only your good men… and order them to put their trousers back on. Then they are to return everything back to the people, right now!"

The two women at Aris's feet sobbed in amazement. A few villagers peeking around the side of a building raised their eyes to the sky as if thanking God. The canteen couple now stood by their door, and the husband gave a very quiet clap of gratitude as his wife clutched her hands to her chest.

With pleasure, Sergeant Antonio called several names and repeated the order. The selected soldiers happily dressed and started unloading the confiscated goods, returning them to the people's surprised delight.

Motioning for Aris to guard the Captain, Leo marched to the Jeep and offered his arm to help the teenage girl. With a warm smile, he held her right hand and personally walked her back to her mother, then helped both women stand.

"My dear lady," Leo said in Spanish. "Please accept my apology. Not everybody in the Army is a criminal pig."

Excited, collecting their various goods, several locals began applauding Leo shouting, "*Viva el General! Viva el General!*"

Aris was overcome with pride.

The Captain must've noticed his moment of distraction. With lightning speed, he pulled out a knife and moved to hold it at Leo's throat. "You're no General. You're that missing traitor, and these are the Americans we were warned about. Sergeant Antonio," the Captain called out. "Pick up the weapons from these men."

Aris's finger itched above the trigger while John and Rita maintained their stance, still pointing rifles on the half-naked soldiers.

The man known as Sergeant Antonio approached Leo first, reclaiming his automatic rifle. The Captain's face filled with achievement.

Rita called to the Captain, "If you touch a hair on my Leo's head, you will die like dogs here and now."

"Sergeant Antonio," the Captain pointed to Rita. "Shoot her."

In the next second, the Captain's right hand dropped the knife. His face turned green, his hands slowly rising, freeing Leo.

Puzzled, everyone watched as Sergeant Antonio pushed his automatic rifle under the officer's jaw. "In case she misses, I will gladly shoot you myself."

All eyes turned to General Leo, who fixed his own gaze upon Sergeant Antonio. "You recognised me."

Nodding proudly, Antonio grinned. "I cannot forget the man who saved my life. Yours is not a face to forget anyway!"

Leo looked down upon the Captain, then motioned for the canteen owner and some other men who gathered closer to join him. "Take this man to the church and tie him in front of Jesus. Feed him only bread and water, once a day, for two months. Make him appreciate what it is to be hungry for a lifetime."

Happily, the locals grabbed the officer, dragging him to the church.

Leo crossed his hands behind his back and took a few steps in front of the soldiers who remained with their trousers down. "You are soldiers. You were supposed to protect the people of our country. Leave your weapons and mobile phones here. Pick up your clothes and go back to your camp now."

One soldier immediately complied, snatching up his pants and flinging his phone to the soil.

"What are the rest of you waiting for?" Leo asked the remaining soldiers.

"We'll be punished if we go back without our rifles," one answered. "Most likely we'll be shot. We don't like this Army anyway. We'd rather stay with you, General."

Leo crossed his hands over his chest. "Listen. I'm not really a General. I'm a wanted man. I can't help you. I am running away, trying to help my friends escape."

Sergeant Antonio turned to Leo and explained, "They're not wrong. We will be punished for not resisting you. I can't go back either. Our only option is to take to the jungle."

Antonio conferred with his fellow soldiers and then returned to Leo's side, clapping him on the shoulder. "We will come with you, Sergeant Leo. Um… I mean General Leo!"

54 Last Hitch to the Border

Aris nudged Leo's shoulder. "These soldiers could help us get across the border."

Pausing, Leo pulled up his oversized trousers and looked around. He seemed to be enthusiastic about the possibilities, but when his eyes met Rita's, they dimmed. Turning to Sergeant Antonio, he offered, "Okay. You want to come with me? Back in your cars. Let's go."

All the remaining soldiers started climbing into the Army trucks.

Leo turned to Aris. "Grab your bags and drive the off-roader." Then he headed to the Jeep urging, "Uri and John, you too. Get moving!"

Rita trailed happily at John's feet, toting one of the automatic rifles.

Leo swung round, clearly dejected about what he had to do. "Not you, Rita. You stay in the village. You'll be safe here."

Her steps came to an abrupt halt and she cocked one hand on her hip. "No! I go where you go."

"I said you're staying here." Leo waved her off.

Adamant, Rita raised the rifle and pointed it at Leo. "I go where you go!"

Aris watched the corners of Leo's lips curl, suppressing a grin. He took several small cautious steps towards Rita, then lightly lifted the rifle from her hands. "I promise you'll be safe here. The Captain will be punished and sent far away—if not shot. Crossing the border with us would be far too dangerous."

Rita wrapped one arm around his waist and looked up into his warm eyes. "Celia will kill me. I want to go to America with you."

His voice softened. "If I manage to get to America, I will send for you."

Aris watched as the lady with the teenage girl made her way to Leo and Rita. "Madam," she said. "I have room for you."

Leo quickly ran a sleeve across his face to cover any emotion. "Go with this woman, Rita." He gave her a slight push. "I will send for you."

Tears sprang to her eyes, and she clung to Leo's neck, weeping.

After several long moments, she pulled back and said, "If you do not send for me, I will still come and find you."

Leo stepped away and retrieved his bag from the car, placing it in Rita's hands. "Look after this like you look after your own eyes. Not for one moment will I forget to send for you." Then he turned and took long strides to the Jeep, narrowly avoiding her seeing his tears.

❖

Leo summoned Sergeant Antonio and whispered something into his ear. Antonio ran to the first lorry and climbed into the passenger seat.

Turning to another soldier, Leo instructed, "You drive the Jeep for me. We're heading straight for the border to Belize." With that, he climbed in the passenger seat, ready to be chauffeured like a true General.

John and Uri piled their bags in the back of the off-roader as Aris started up the engine and fell in at the end of the convoy.

At the Melchor de Mencos border crossing, the Jeep paused in front of the gate. General Leo saluted the guards who clambered to attention.

The Lieutenant in charge held out a hand, palm up. "Papers, please."

Leo's driver interrupted, "Stand at attention when you address the General!"

Leo kept his gaze stern and straight ahead.

"Open the gate!" the driver ordered forcefully.

335

The Lieutenant stood his ground. "We have strict orders that no one is to cross the border unless fully identified."

Angrily the driver spat, "And who do you think issued those orders?" He pointed to General Leo. "Open the gate!"

Red-faced the Lieutenant insisted, "Papers first… from everyone."

The driver sighed deeply and reached into his pocket, pulling out his own papers.

The man examined them then held out his hand again. "And the General's papers."

Leo raised his right arm, as if summoning someone from the vehicle behind them. He stepped out of the Jeep and slowly circled round to stand in front of the border guard Lieutenant, looking straight into the man's eyes, just a hair's breadth away.

Sergeant Antonio and half a dozen soldiers assembled around them, holding their weapons at the ready.

Nodding his head, Leo raised one eyebrow and said, "Bravo, Lieutenant. You are executing orders very strictly."

In a flash, Sergeant Antonio raised his weapon, taking aim at the Lieutenant, while his other soldiers disarmed the border patrol guards.

Leo waved for the off-roader to pull forward.

In seconds, the vehicle was beside him idling at the ready. "Aris, you have made it."

Leo stopped short. John's smile was beaming ear to ear from the passenger seat, and Uri was busy releasing a string of burps into the afternoon air from the back. But what truly captured him was seeing Rita tucked into the backseat, clutching his bag tightly in her arms.

He slapped his thigh. "I thought I told you to stay in the village. Stubborn mule you are, Rita!"

Rita held her head high. "I go where my Leo goes."

This time he slapped the side of the Jeep, half amused. "But Leo isn't going to America."

Instantly excited, Rita passed the bag to Uri just long enough for her to climb out. She threw one arm around Leo and kissed him deeply in front of the whole crowd.

Aris cleared his throat, not wanting to interrupt the happy lovers, but also not wanting to linger at the border crossing. "Are you seriously not coming?"

Leo fixed his sight on Sergeant Antonio and said, "I cannot."

"But the general and Celia… Leo, they will hunt you down!" Rita practically clung to his side.

"It is my people," Leo replied. "I love my country. Plus, I cannot leave…" He took a deep breath then added, "I am no American. You go."

"Are you really staying for your country, or for love?" Aris inquired.

Leo smiled proudly and squeezed Rita tighter. "Every man's first country is his woman! And Rita is mine. I could never leave her."

She planted a huge kiss on Leo's cheek and whispered something in Spanish that Aris could not make out, but it caused Leo's face to blush a deep crimson.

Reaching into his pocket, Leo counted out some money, handing it to Aris. "Enough for a taxi and food until you can get your credit cards replaced in Belize. Go before it's too late."

Aris snagged a piece of scrap paper from the glove compartment and jotted something down, passing it to Leo. "Memorise this number and the address. Call me anytime and I will be there for whatever you might need."

Leo took the paper and gazed hard at his friend's scrawled handwriting.

Then Aris stepped out of the car and embraced Leo. "If you ever make it to America and don't visit me, I will cut off your balls."

"Just don't feed them to your dogs," Leo joked.

"Seriously," Aris continued. "You saved our lives. We owe you, my friend."

From the passenger seat, John stretched out his arm for a handshake. "We'll be waiting for you!"

Uri shook farewell from the backseat window. "You are a born leader. A real General, Leo. Thank you."

Aris stepped one foot inside the car, but Leo pulled him back.

"No! You must walk from here into Belize. We'll need this car," he said pointing to the off-roader and then eyeing up Sergeant Antonio, "…for the revolution!"

This brought a great smile to Aris's face. The three Americans hopped out, each pulling on a backpack and taking quick strides to cross onto Belize soil.

Leo signalled his driver to negotiate a U-turn. Meanwhile he asked the Lieutenant, "Are you aware that losing your weapon results in a death sentence?"

The man's face grew pale.

Leo released Rita from his grasp and moved once more into the Lieutenant's personal space. "Do you know who I am?" he asked.

"You…" the Lieutenant began hesitantly. "You are the escaped Sergeant Leo."

Sergeant Antonio waved the tip of his rifle in the man's face. "Wrong! This is *General* Leo!"

Leo gave his Sergeant friend a soft smile. Returning his gaze to the border Lieutenant he asked, "Have you seen us today?"

After a few moments of silence, the Lieutenant responded, "No, Sergeant. I mean… no sir, *General.*"

Leo nodded happily. He turned to climb into the Jeep but then added one more question. "Have you seen any Americans?"

Without hesitation, the Lieutenant answered, "No, sir! No Americans."

Turning to the other border guards, Leo posed the same question. "Have you seen Sergeant Leo or any Americans?"

"N-n-no, General," one frightened soldier replied while his comrades also shook their heads.

Turning to Sergeant Antonio, Leo instructed, "Take their photos showing they have been disarmed. We'll hold onto this for insurance."

Sergeant Antonio lowered his rifle and snapped a photo with his cell phone. Motioning to his men, he then called them to return to the lorry along with the border patrol's weapons, while he climbed into the off-roader and negotiated a U-turn in preparation for their departure.

Leo helped Rita climb into the Jeep's backseat while the lorry also spun around to follow the convoy back away from the border.

Finally he settled himself in the passenger seat. "We will leave your guns one mile down the road," he informed the Lieutenant. "You and your men can run and pick them up. But remember… if anyone finds out we were here, we will share the evidence of your failure."

The Lieutenant saluted farewell with hope in his voice. "Yes, sir. Thank you, sir!"

Leo gave his driver the go-ahead and whispered, *"Viva la revolución!"*

◇

Aris and his friends turned back to watch Leo's entourage pull away from the border. He gave a hearty wave, then made his way to a waiting taxi.

"Belize City, please," Aris requested, and he and John and Uri piled their backpacks in the trunk and then climbed inside.

"How long?" John asked.

"Half hour to Belmopan," the driver answered, "plus another forty to Belize City."

"Finally." Uri let out one, long, loud burp. "We're free!"

The driver caught Uri's eyes in the rear-view mirror. "Who are you running away from?"

Aris held up a quick hand and answered before his naïve friends could land them in even more trouble. "From our wives!"

The taxi driver laughed heartily, and the three friends let out a collective sigh of relief.

55 We Have Them

Triumphant, Victor entered Varo's office. "We have them. They just crossed into Belize."

"Belize? I thought the VP would bring them back to America."

He shrugged. "Maybe he's flying them from Belize instead of Guatemala."

Varo nodded, now deep in thought. "Get to the agency. Tell them I want two teams tailing 24/7. They are not to lose track of Aris again."

"I already spoke to the girl," Victor confirmed. "She should be arriving in Belize in a few hours, but they also assigned a local team. It's a small country. They will make contact very soon."

Varo let out a quiet sigh.

"We identified two of their cell phones, switched on."

"And the third?" Varo asked.

"Not activated yet, but the other two are together." Victor made his way out of the office.

"He really came through for me," Varo whispered to herself. "The Vice President made the promised call."

⋯ ⋄ ⋯

Aris consulted the micro-calendar above the desk of their small budget hotel. It was day eighty-two of their journey. The friends were sharing a room with three single beds, but after the Guatemalan prison camp, it felt luxurious.

"We made it," Uri laughed, plopping onto his bed. "Let's head for Spain. I'm tired of being chased by drug lords and dictators. I want to hear women speak Spanish without feeling like I'm about to be shot down."

John smiled, reclining on his own mattress with his hands clasped behind his head.

"More women?" Aris questioned.

"You don't have to marry them to have a great time," Uri scolded.

"Earlier you were crying that I was going to get you killed." Aris turned from the calendar to face John and Uri. "It's time to part ways, guys."

"Well, you did nearly get us shot," Uri pointed out.

"Twice," John added.

Uri sat up in bed. "I promise you will love the Spanish girls, Aris."

"Never intended to chase women." Aris opened up his wallet and took out a picture of his granddaughter. "It's time for me to head home."

"You're a hypocrite," Uri shouted. "You never said no to the Mexican hairdresser. Hell, you even wanted to stay with that killer Celia."

John just stared up at Aris silently.

"I only refused Celia because of you two. She loved me." Aris flipped through other photos then returned them to his wallet. "By tomorrow, or maybe the day after, we'll all have our new credit cards." He kept his voice low. "You don't need me anymore. Not that you ever truly needed me. I was just your excuse. You two go on to Spain. Have fun with the sexy girls."

"Come on, Aris," John muttered. "Europe won't be any fun without you."

After a short pause, Aris changed his mind. "Actually I would advise you to go back to the U.S. You've had a taste of what happens around me. Better to go home to your wives."

Uri's laugh was maniacal. "Sure, you spread your *love secret* all around Latin America and then abandon us to finish the journey alone."

"The love secret is real," Aris corrected. "But I fear it's guarded by dragons and monsters who fart fire."

"You Greeks and your myths." Uri pulled a world map out of his backpack and spread it across his bed. "When are you going to figure out there's no love secret to make someone fall in love with you?"

Aris spoke to John as if Uri was no longer present. "This is just one more reason we should part ways. That asshole wouldn't know true love if it bit him on the butt."

"I've had more than a few girls try to bite me there," Uri reminisced.

Aris and John stared at him, momentarily speechless.

"Anyway." Aris brushed off the image. "It's time I made arrangements. You two should do the same."

"After all we've been through together?" John dry-swallowed. "You don't want to come to Europe with us?"

"It's for your safety," Aris answered. "Uri's right. I did nearly get you killed."

"When the going was tough," John countered, "we didn't run or push you away. Now that the danger's over, you're just gonna abandon us?"

Aris smiled lightly. "Let's be clear. If Uri had been given a choice, he would have fled without looking back."

"Selfish bastard." Uri spit on the wooden floor.

"I'm not ready to go home yet," John mumbled. "I feel like I'm just starting to come into my own." He shifted onto the mattress beside Uri and started examining the world map.

"Looks like there's a marina not far from here," Uri pointed to the paper. "We could hire a boat and sail across the Caribbean, then out across the ocean bound for Spain. We'll be like Christopher Columbus, off to explore new territories…"

Aris scoffed, "Christopher Columbus introduced smallpox and nearly decimated the indigenous population."

"You always said you had a fear deficiency, Aris," Uri now taunted. "What happened to 'danger is always around the corner with me'?"

John joined forces. "I always wanted to cross the Atlantic. Count me in."

"Crossing the Atlantic at this time of year is not for virgin sailors," Aris smiled condescendingly.

"John and I are fast learners," Uri said. "Didn't you see how we worked together to fix the General's motorcycles? We're a team now."

"Then your team should do the safe thing and book a flight. The Atlantic this time of year is more life-threatening than the General's firing squad."

John shook his head. "Uri's right. We're a team. And I never abandon a friend."

John let the words hang in the air with the implication that abandoning a friend was exactly what Aris was about to do.

Unimpressed, Aris muttered, "It is a wise man, John, who knows where courage ends and stupidity begins."

"Oh, so now we're quoting dead people?" Uri chuckled. "Well, you can't swim for new horizons unless you've got the courage to lose sight of the shore."

"You've lost sight of a lot of things, *friend.* If you try to cross the Atlantic now, you'll be swimming all right," Aris sniggered. "Swimming with the fishes."

56 The Call

That afternoon, Aris glanced across at Uri and John snoozing in their twin beds. Discreetly he sneaked out and stopped at the reception desk where a girl in her late teens sat browsing a magazine.

"Excuse me. Where is the nearest boat marina?" he asked.

The girl didn't even glance up. "There are a few."

"How far?" Aris prompted.

This time she looked up as if to take stock of who was asking. "Too far to walk," she replied coolly. "Ask the taxi driver." She motioned outside to the taxi stand. Almost imperceptibly her gaze shifted to an American couple sitting on a bench in the corner of the lobby and she nodded ever so slightly.

In a hurry, Aris exited the hotel, ready to part ways with Uri and John.

The American couple rose to their feet. The man peeled off a couple of bills and handed them to the receptionist while the woman made straight for the door to follow Aris.

Turning right outside the hotel's entrance, Aris attempted to hail a taxi. It was no easy feat, but eventually a driver flashed his lights to signal his availability.

Before Aris could climb in and shut the door behind him, Uri and John opened the rear door and joined him. "Going somewhere?" Uri asked.

Silently Aris looked to Uri. A single burp escaped the latter's mouth so John took the lead. "We are both good swimmers!" he proclaimed.

Aris couldn't help but crack a smile. He turned to the taxi driver and said, "To the nearest boat marina, please."

None of them even took note of the American couple.

◆ ◇ ◆

Liza helped carry plates to the dinner table where her brothers Peter and Gerry were already seated. Gina brought the main course and then collapsed into her seat as if she'd made some monumental accomplishment.

"Any news from Father?" Peter asked, piling heaping servings onto his plate.

Gina sighed as if deeply satisfied. "You better forget your father. He has not even made one single call in all these months."

"No news is good news," Gerry laughed merrily.

"Don't fool yourselves," Gina scorned. "Your father has abandoned you. He is not coming back."

Liza kept her head down, gazing at her still empty plate. "He has not abandoned us. He just needed a break from your arguments, Mum."

"Sooner or later," Gina lashed out at her, "you will realise that your father is a family deserter. He cares only for himself."

"Come on, Mum," Gerry raised his voice. "We all know you're the one who pushed Father to desert you. You're the one he really left… not us."

Gina held her head high, shaking out her long wavy hair. With one freshly manicured pointer finger, she poked the centre of her chest. "I am here! Standing by my family. I did not desert you."

◆ ◇ ◆

Aris followed John and Uri into the marina's reception office where two buxom brunettes were seated at a desk surrounded by brochures for excursions to various local sights.

"Good morning, ladies." Uri's playboy smile was broadcasting at high wattage. "Do you know of a boat crossing

345

the Atlantic for Europe that might be in need of a couple strong crew members?" He flexed his muscles and winked.

The elder girl giggled. "No, sir. At this time of year, all the boats are crossing westwards, coming to us from Europe."

The younger girl also smiled, but did not laugh. Instead she circled around her desk and placed an appreciative hand on Uri's bicep. "It is not safe to make the crossing eastwards right now. Even for big, strong men like you."

John's face filled with apprehension, but Uri was practically glistening under the brunette's expert attention.

"I told you so," Aris gloated. "But you didn't believe me. Now you have it verified. Go home."

Uri laughed.

Sighting the toilet sign arrow, Aris headed over. John took a step forwards as if to trail Aris's every move.

"The only place I'm going is to the toilet. There's no need to follow me," Aris said, brushing John aside. "Now head across the street to that café and order me a black Americano."

He and Uri made their way over to the café and staked out a table near the street. A few minutes later, Aris joined them.

"Aris," John began timidly. "Can someone fall *out* of love?"

The question took Aris by surprise. "Where did this come from out of the blue?"

"Answer me," John insisted.

Aris reflected for a while before answering. "When my younger son Gerry asked me this exact same question, some years ago, I could not answer him honestly. But now I can."

At that very moment, a waiter approached the table and stood silently at Aris's side without greeting them or asking for their order.

John was ready to hang on Aris's every word, but Aris knew the waiter would simply leave unless they quickly took advantage of his presence. Aris and Uri placed their order then encouraged John to get a simple coffee for himself.

The waiter gone, Aris started again. "I believe it is possible to fall out of love."

John seemed genuinely taken aback by this answer. "B-b-but—"

"You may still be attracted to the looks of that person," Aris added, "but if you grow to despise their character or behaviour… or perhaps their attitude towards you, then absolutely, you can fall out of love with someone."

The waiter returned with their coffees.

"A betrayal can also cause you to fall out of love with someone," Aris reflected. "In fact, this can make even the ashes of love evaporate. Nothing, absolutely nothing, is left in your heart. As if that person never existed."

Uri laughed out loud. "Absolute nonsense. A person can't fall out of love."

John opened his mouth to reply, but Aris put a hand on his arm to stop him.

"A person can't fall out of love," Uri continued, "because there is no falling in love in the first place! It's just fairy tales and Greeks that try to make love seem mythical."

Aris took a sip of his strong coffee then sat back to await more of the would-be prophet's so-called wisdom.

"Go back to the cavemen," Uri said, "and ask if they fell in love. No! They had any woman they wanted! Go to the Arabs. They have harems with dozens of women."

"B-but that's not r-right, is it?" John stuttered.

"Why not?" Uri's voice strengthened as if he were orating to a crowd. "Look at the billionaires… they all have lovers and children by many women. They do not fall in love! Look at the animals. One male services a herd of females. And if another male should win a fight… well, the females will mate with the strongest. They don't bother with falling in love either."

"How can you know," Aris asked, "if you yourself have never fallen in love?"

Uri's chest inflated. "Look around you. Why are the most beautiful girls with much older men? They think you can provide for them. And then they can have your money to do whatever they want when you're not around anymore."

John's head was ping-ponging back and forth between Uri and Aris. "Hmm… the ladies certainly have seemed to gravitate towards you, Aris. What do you say to that?"

Aris shook his head. "There's not much I can say. You can't explain how to fall in love. It's just something that happens. You have to experience it first hand." With that, Aris finished his coffee and summoned for the check. "Especially to someone with a selfish, empty, iron head like Uri!"

57 THE TROJAN BAIT

Victor placed the call to Varo's private line.

She answered immediately. "Tell me you've found them, Victor."

"They're not coming back to America," he replied coolly. "They're in a marina in Belize. Our operatives say they're looking for a job, to hire themselves out as crew to sail across the Atlantic to Europe. But no one wants to cross at this time of year."

"Aris is persistent. And stubborn," she acknowledged. "If he means to find a boat, nothing will stop him. But how are we going to track them across the Atlantic if it comes to that?"

"Well, this can be your opportunity to track them even better." Victor let the words hang in the air before adding, "Why don't we provide such a boat?"

He could imagine Varo's mind reeling with possibility. "You're a genius," she said. "We can supply the boat and track it ourselves!"

"Next steps?" Victor asked.

"Summon my pilot and meet me at the airport. We're flying to Belize."

"We?" Victor's eyes bulged. "When?"

"Now, Victor! Call our people on the ground and have them start looking for boats for sale. Aris used to own a catamaran, so that would be best. I just want to track him, not kill him."

Victor's reply came quickly. "Consider it done."

58 Mother and the Trojan Plot

At first light, Varo's plane landed on the small runway where she was met by a hired limousine with tinted windows.

"To the marina," she instructed the driver, then turned to the woman from the surveillance crew seated across from her and Victor. "Where are they?"

"Holed up in the hotel still, waiting for their replacement credit cards," the woman replied. "Or maybe they have them by now."

"Did you find a boat to buy?" Varo asked eagerly.

"There are many, but mostly junk or too small for the job. One needs two months to get ready. A second is a power luxury boat—twenty million—but also needs lots of work before it's sea-worthy."

Varo would not let money stand in her way, but any delay might cause her to lose track of Aris forever.

"But there was a third option," the woman added. "A catamaran, a 60-footer, custom made in good repair. It's valued at about two million. The selling agent says we can probably push the price down."

Exchanging glances with Victor, Varo exclaimed, "Perfect! Aris used to own something similar."

Victor nodded slightly.

"Buy it!" Varo announced. "Victor will organise payment and all the documentation."

"Don't you want to see it?" the woman asked.

Varo swished a hand through the air. "No need. Have you found the cook I asked for?"

"No man wants to make such a dangerous crossing. But we did find two girls…"

"We only need one," Varo chided.

"One girl on a boat—with men—is considered bad luck," the lady detective recounted. "Anyway, they're friends, so it's both… or none."

Victor's smile looked more pleased than Varo felt. "Okay, bring those girls to my hotel," she said. "Then start passing the word that this boat needs a worthy crew to cross the Atlantic. Only the strongest and bravest need apply. That should bait the hook sufficiently."

That afternoon at the hotel, two girls followed the lady detective to Varo's corner table where she sat enjoying a coffee with Victor.

"This is Kay, and this is Lilly," she introduced. "I've brought them up to speed on the plan so far. Kay and Lilly, this is…" The lady detective's words hung in the air.

Varo scanned both young women head to toe. The one named Kay was brunette with a subtle Brazilian backside while Lilly was a real golden princess with straight hips. "If you must call me, call me Mother," Varo began. "Your story will be that this boat belongs to your father's company. All you are looking for is a skipper and crew to sail it to Europe."

Lilly looked surprised, but happily sat down at the table. "I thought we were just supposed to be the cook and the mate."

"Yes, of course you must cook and help," Varo clarified. "But you must also be in control, and the only way to maintain a captain and crew's respect is to tell them it is your boat so they take care of you."

Kay raised her arms overhead in a victory salute. "I like that!"

"Yes!" Lilly exclaimed "Girls in control!"

"Accomplish this small task well," Varo goaded softly, "and you will be rewarded." Kay and Lilly's eyes met Varo's. "You will each receive ten thousand dollars. Five, if you get the crew and sail away now, then another five when you arrive in Europe."

Lilly looked to her friend with eyebrows raised, then clasped Kay's hands and pulled the brunette to her feet. They did a full circle dance right there in the restaurant. "Yes! We get paid to travel in style!"

Kay seemed more reticent and quickly returned to her seat. "You'll have to excuse my friend. She's easily excitable. Am I to understand that we don't want just any crew?"

Varo narrowed her gaze appreciatively on the brunette. "Correct. You will negotiate with the skipper and crew, offering to pay double because you want to sail quickly."

"No need to waste your money," Lilly chided. "I know how to attract men!"

Concern drawn on her face, Varo continued. "My associate Victor will provide you with all the equipment, the latest technology to make your voyage safe and comfortable." She nodded to her mentor.

Victor reached into the pocket of his blazer and passed an envelope across the table to Kay. "Here is one thousand dollars, pocket money for you to get ready. Succeed in signing the skipper and crew and you'll get your half-payment immediately."

Lilly ogled the envelope as Kay discreetly opened it just enough to confirm its contents.

Pointing to the lady detective, Victor continued, "This woman will drive you to the marina. Take all your belongings and get settled in. I want you to familiarise yourselves with the boat, so you will be able to convince them it's really yours."

"Who do we have to convince?" Kay asked immediately.

Varo motioned to her mentor and the lady detective. "Take Lilly and leave us for a minute." Victor rose immediately, though the other two were reluctant to depart before the conversation had reached its natural conclusion.

When they had gone, Varo fixed her eyes on Kay. "Your question tells me you are a very clever girl. I'm going to be straight with you, but I want you to promise that what you hear will stay between us."

The brunette laughed lightly. "I'm a great secret keeper."

"It is incredibly hard to find a good skipper and crew these days. You will need to be very convincing. These men must believe the boat belongs to your father's company, and that you need them to sail you across to Europe."

"I understand," Kay said. "So who is this skipper?"

"He will soon be contacting you. His name is Aris, a Greek-American. Only this man and no other. Make sure it is him. He is the best for the job."

Kay nodded cautiously, as if waiting for the *secret* part.

"And I also care a lot for him," Varo added. "But if Aris finds out I'm involved, he will refuse the job. He detests favours. So strictly no mention of me. Do you understand?"

Kay smiled sympathetically "Have no concern. As a woman I understand and admire you completely."

Varo cupped one of Kay's hands. "Good. I feel we are friends already." With her other hand, she placed a business card between them. "Now, memorise my phone number. I have arranged for a satellite phone to be installed on the boat. I will be available to you 24/7… but remember to only address me as Mother."

Kay nodded mutely and squeezed Varo's hand after she studied the number.

Varo removed the business card from the table and replaced it with a small box. "One last thing, Kay. For your safety, I want you to hide this somewhere in the middle of the boat. Somewhere it cannot be seen. It is a powerful tracking device. In the…" Varo paused, "unlikely event that anything happens to you, we will know immediately and be able to send help."

Kay clutched the small box and stared at it from every angle before tucking it gently into her handbag. Varo began to wonder if Kay was smart enough to already sense the danger.

59 Taking the Bait

Aris and his friends returned to the marina café for lunch the next day. A young waiter approached, different from the mute one they'd had before. "Mister, you were asking around for a boat yesterday, right? I found one for you!"

Aris immediately looked up with a gleam in his eye while John and Uri's faces turned sour.

"Some rich American girls," the waiter started. "They're late getting daddy's boat to Europe and they're looking for a skipper." The waiter stared down at Uri and John. "And a crew. They must be crazy."

"Two girls?" Aris cocked an eyebrow. He detected a slight improvement in Uri's mood at this news.

The waiter nodded happily.

"What kind of boat? Where is it moored?" Aris was no longer hungry.

"Here in the marina. I have their number." The waiter stretched out his hand, as if expecting some sort of reward.

Aris tried to appear reluctant but couldn't help himself and graced the man's palm with some cash.

Cheerfully the waiter announced, "Wait here. I will go call them!"

The young man went through a door into the kitchen, but returned to their table within minutes. "The girls are on the boat," he said. "I will take you there now."

This time Aris successfully feigned indifference. He leaned back into his seat, looking off into the distance. "We're not interested. It's hurricane season. That's why no one's touched the job."

Eager to convince, the waiter pulled out a slip of paper which Uri snatched away.

"This says the girls will pay double." Aris watched as Uri's face contorted, eventually computing the benefit of being confined to a boat for weeks with two needy American gals. "This would cover all our travelling expenses for a long time." Obviously Uri's previous reluctance had washed away with the hurricane tide.

"No," Aris ordered, still wondering if there was some catch. "You don't know what it means to cross the Atlantic this time of year."

John looked to Uri supportively. "So we get a bit wet. Maybe we throw up a few times! Aris, you said that after a couple of days, everybody gets used to the motion of the boat."

Uri's eyes practically burned a hole in the slip of paper. "Two *girls*, the waiter said. Not two women. They must be young!" He shrugged. "If two girls can do it, so can we."

John nodded like a bobblehead. "Come on, Aris. I thought you said we should always face our fears."

Aris could feel his jaw grinding. "Oh, I'm attracted by the challenge, but I won't risk your lives again. I have to get rid of you two first."

John recognized this as a concession. He playfully smacked Uri on the arm. "We don't mind a bit of risk. You go, we follow… remember?"

Still indifferent, Aris closed his eyes. "A boat with no experienced crew would make a good meal for the sharks."

Eager to persuade, the waiter shifted beside John to face Aris. "If these girls have their own boat, it means they're experienced. You may even get to like them… Why don't you have a look, then decide?"

John and Uri rose as if to follow the waiter. Uri prodded, "Come on, let's have a look. No commitment."

Reluctantly, Aris climbed to his feet. "If these girls really are experienced," he said, depositing his napkin on the table, "then you two will not be needed. Let's go."

Kay and Lilly stretched out happily under the bimini canopy on the boat as the waiter climbed aboard. His three companions remained on the dock. Stretching his arm out as he had done earlier to Aris, he announced, "Ladies, I have found you the skipper and crew you are looking for."

Kay eyed each of the four men in turn, then placed a tight wad of bills into the waiter's hand and watched him promptly depart.

Aris shook his head and let out a guffaw.

On the opposite side, a smaller catamaran was docked. Aris noticed an old man with only patches of black in his beard who looked up from his work, then shifted as close as possible to take in the conversation.

Lilly waved to the three of them. "Come on board, guys!"

John took a step forwards, but Uri pulled him back, pointing to Aris whose gaze was locked on Kay. "I guess we know which one Aris has picked. I'll take the blonde."

Not to be deterred, John happily climbed aboard, followed by Uri who turned up the wattage on his smile.

Without a word, Aris walked to the end of the portside bow and scanned the left front of the boat. Turning back, he then inspected the aft side before climbing on. Aris raised his gaze to assess the mast and boom. His right hand grasped the shrouds, the metal ropes supporting the mast, and he shook them hard, feeling the tension.

Satisfied, he joined the group under the hard-top bimini to complete his inspection—scanning both girls, top to bottom.

"You must be the captain." Lilly's voice practically oozed as she unsuccessfully attempted to rub up against Aris.

Alternating his gaze between Kay and Lilly, he replied, "You're looking for a skipper and crew to cross the Atlantic to Europe?"

With her own stare fixed on Aris, Kay answered, "Yes, we're late already, so we need to set sail quickly. We're willing to pay…" She glanced to Lilly. "Double the norm."

Aris shifted to continue inspecting the boat.

Uri rubbed his hands attentively, then put one arm around Lilly's shoulder when she pouted at Aris's apparent rejection.

Opening the engine hatches, Aris took note of the clean engines and engine room. Moving on, he gave the starboard shrouds the same hearty tug he'd used earlier on the left. Then the halyards—the mainsail lifting rope—followed by the genoa sheets which control the front sail.

Returning, Aris locked eyes again with Kay before entering the saloon, a stylishly decorated living area surrounded by sparkling clean windows.

Behind him, he could hear Lilly coo, "This skipper is moody. We'll have to teach him how to relax."

Uri and John followed Aris in and watched as he checked the electronics and navigation instruments, all Raymarine brand. Turning the kitchen tap, Aris proceeded to smell and taste the water. A smile creased his face, but he cautiously hid it before turning to his travel companions.

The three men exited and gathered around the table under the bimini where the girls were already seated. With pleasure drawn across her face, Kay said, "It's a strong boat, captain. Custom built, all-weather. It's ready to sail, but we've serviced everything again, and are awaiting the latest model of navigation electronics to be fitted later today and tomorrow."

"Your boat?" Aris enquired.

"Daddy's company boat," Kay confirmed. "But I have full power of attorney to manage and appoint a skipper and crew."

Sceptical, Aris tilted his head back. "You will pay forty thousand U.S. dollars for one-way delivery."

A glimpse of a smile crossed Kay's face. "For the right skipper. What's your name, captain?"

Aris sat silently pondering.

"His name is Aris," John volunteered.

Lilly's face lit up. "He's the one."

Aris eyed the blonde suspiciously. "Which one?"

Quickly Kay intervened. "The one everybody has been telling us about. They all say you are the best skipper for this kind of boat."

Aris smiled, amused at the fake flattery. "Bullshit. No one knows me around here."

Kay's expression drooped. "I mean, that's what the waiter said, and the lady at the marina."

Shifting his stare back to Kay, Aris remained silent, relaxing his hands on the table.

"We will pay forty thousand," Kay replied confidently. "We want to be in safe hands." As if to affirm, she reached out to grasp Aris's open palms in hers.

He gazed deeply into the brunette's eyes, feeling the heat travel from her fingertips straight to every inch of his body.

After several blistering moments, Aris shifted away from the table and climbed onto the rear bench seat. He reached out to tug on the rope holding the back end of the boom, shifting it from side to side.

"The weather is more what you need to be concerned about." Aris shifted his attention to Lilly. "When was the last time you changed the main sheet?"

Lilly's face brightened. "Last night. Fresh and clean. I change my sheets every day."

Unamused, Aris turned to Kay.

Equally puzzled, she answered, "Same as Lilly. But we haven't put sheets on the other cabin beds yet."

Aris again tugged the rope holding the back end of the boom. "This is the main sheet. You two obviously do not have a clue about your boat. Therefore, you are useless to me as crew."

Worriedly, the girls exchanged glances.

"We're fast learners," Kay offered. "Show us once and we'll be as good as any other crew member."

"We can be helpful in many areas," Lilly chimed in. "We know lots of tricks to help you relax… under the sheets."

Aris spun hard towards Kay. "Is she suggesting that you'll be onboard during this passage?"

"Of course," Kay chuckled. "This is our boat."

Aris shook his head. "First, you're inexperienced, which means more danger because you'll need constant babysitting. Second, flowerpot women onboard are trouble! Best you get a flight across the sea and wait for us there." He could see a fire light behind Kay's eyes, so he added, "If we ever actually arrive."

Lilly threw back her head. "I know this trick. You think you'll send us ahead by aeroplane, only you'll never come… because you'll go off somewhere else with our boat. We're not that stupid, you know!"

Aris smiled condescendingly. "I didn't say you were stupid. I said you were a flowerpot."

"Well, my namesake is a beautiful flower." Lilly batted her eyelashes at Aris.

Kay grabbed Lilly by the wrist. "What he means by *flowerpot* is that we're just empty-headed decorations. Right, captain?"

Lilly's expression changed. "That's just mean. I've been called silly before… Just for fun, of course. But never an empty head. I don't like this captain." She turned to Aris, now angry. "We need to look after our boat. We're the boss, not you! Clearly we can't trust you to show up on your own."

John visibly pulled up his courage and stretched out a hand to the suffering blonde. "What Aris meant when he said we might never make it, was that he thinks we'll probably sink and drown before we get there."

Lilly's spirit rallied at John's touch. "You're all in on the trick! We're not just sexy airheads, you know."

"No, ladies. I don't operate that way," Aris stated.

"No way," Kay retorted. "No girls, no deal!"

"Whoa, gutsy lady!" Uri's estimation of the brunette seemed to rise.

"If you're onboard," Aris started to haggle, "the price is double whatever you're offering."

From the corner of his eye, Aris saw the old pontoon skipper following along with every word, now smiling.

Kay's lips tightened into a thin line.

"Do you know anything at all about sailing a boat?" Aris asked.

"No. That's why we're hiring you," Lilly blurted.

Kay threw a wicked glance to silence her.

"So double price of the double. How much is that?" Lilly asked, not reading Kay's signal.

"Eighty thousand dollars!" Uri heralded.

"That's an awful lot of money," Kay lamented. "I'll have to speak to Mother." She pulled out a mobile phone and stepped away to the starboard side.

Kay kept her voice low. Aris strained to make out her portion of the conversation, but John tugged on his arm.

"Her mother? I thought the girls said this was their daddy's boat," John said. "But seriously, why are you pushing for them to say no, Aris? Double the double? Be reasonable!"

"Yeah, even I like the idea now," Uri said. "If you ask me, with such sexy girls, we should do it for free!"

A few moments later, Kay visibly relaxed and switched off her phone. "Mr. Skipper, you are asking too much. We'll pay fifty thousand and no more."

60 The Refusal

John and Uri hooted with delight. But Aris grabbed and tugged them. "Let's go, guys. This job is a no-go."

"Wait!" Kay shouted before they could step off the boat. "I thought we were… negotiating."

Aris hopped out onto the pontoon, motioning for John and Uri to follow.

"Okay, okay!" Kay's voice became panicked. "We'll pay your eighty thousand dollars."

Aris stood stock still, unresponsive. He could see on the small catamaran, the old skipper was practically salivating at the scene.

Puzzled, John and Uri waited on the boat for Aris's decision.

Kay quickly added, "Plus, we'll pay a bonus of twenty thousand more, if the boat is delivered safe and undamaged."

Aris practically snorted and could hear the old skipper do the same.

"The boat delivered in one piece?" Aris fixed his gaze on Kay. "Nothing about the two of you delivered safely? Are your parents not concerned about you?"

"If the boat is delivered safe," she said offhandedly, "it means we'll also be safe. That's why the bonus."

Uri hopped offboard and slapped Aris on the back. "Surely you can't refuse now, buddy. That much money would cover us for a whole year of travelling expenses, with plenty of change!"

John followed suit and closed ranks on Aris. "A hundred thousand dollars? For a few weeks on a pleasure boat with two beautiful girls? Come on! I want to do this badly."

"Shut up, guys." Aris faced Kay. "Even at that price, it's too cheap. Your daddy, mammy, whoever… they know full well that to transfer a sixty-foot cat in a roll-in boat would cost them more than two hundred and fifty thousand dollars. Plus, a hefty insurance premium."

"Who cares?" Uri jumped in. "We'll be getting paid more than what we were expecting—which was zero!"

Aris silenced him with a stern gaze. "You two are not coming, so stay out of it."

"What do you mean?" Uri and John yelled simultaneously. "Of course we're coming," John added.

"Guys," Aris softened. "You will take a flight over and enjoy yourselves for a few weeks in Spain. Then we can meet back up after I bring the boat across the Atlantic."

"If the girls can go, why not us?" Uri asked. "You need strong hands."

"Your Jewish nose just smells the money." Aris clenched and flexed his fists. "Payment is for the skipper only. Crew gets paid whatever I decide."

Uri's eyebrows knitted in a tight scowl.

"I don't care about the money." John's voice was thick. "I know engines and electronics. This boat is full of them—electrical bilge pumps, generators, batteries, inverters. You're going to need someone to help. No offense to the girls, but…"

The old pontoon skipper climbed down from his own rig and stood beside Aris. "Listen to your skipper, boys. I do this crossing every year—in the right season. Even then, it's still dangerous. You all should go get drunk, have some sex, and come back at the beginning of the right season."

"We escaped gangster and firing squads," John defended. "We're not scared of a few waves!"

"You forget," Aris soothed. "I'm the one who got you into all those dangers. You had no choice. But now you do."

John shook his head dismissively. "That's right. You got us into trouble, all by yourself. We need to stick together. We choose to come with you."

Aris's face contorted as he looked back and forth from Uri to John. "Your wives are expecting me to look after you. I can't tell them you died at sea because of me."

"You should listen to the suicidal captain," the old skipper cautioned. "In fact, none of you should go."

"What about the girls, Aris?" John's voice rang rebelliously. "Why are you not telling them to take a plane as well?"

Aris shrugged. "I did warn them, but it's their boat. Not my responsibility."

Kay and Lilly exchanged mute glances as two long-haired men approached. "We heard someone was looking for crew to cross the Atlantic."

Stunned, John and Uri gawked at the two outsiders.

Kay pointed to Aris. "Here. He's the captain."

John whispered under his breath, "They're drifters. Probably druggies. You can't trust them."

Aris brushed off John's comment. "Experienced crew?" he asked the two newcomers.

"We've crossed the Atlantic eleven times—six east-to-wests and five west-to-easts," the taller one informed.

"Sail or power?" Aris quizzed.

"All sail."

Uri crossed his arms and grunted.

"I run a dry boat," Aris advised. "No alcohol or drugs."

"No problem!" both men replied.

"When are we sailing?" the shorter one asked.

"In a couple days, maybe a week."

The taller man grew suspicious. "Which month?"

Climbing back to his small catamaran, the old captain let out a hoot of laughter.

"Mister, nobody crosses the Atlantic this time of the year," the shorter man said.

"I thought you said you were experienced," Aris muttered.

"Exactly," the taller one affirmed. "We lost friends who were crazy enough to try it! Had a couple of narrow misses ourselves, even in the right season." He motioned to his buddy and the two turned to walk away.

Pleased, the old bearded captain called, "Told you no one in their right mind would join you—even with fat pay!"

"We're not refusing!" John was obviously trying to capitalise on the situation.

"Seriously," Uri added. "Those fairies turned you down. You need a crew, including a mechanic," he said pointing to John.

Aris climbed onboard and plopped his rear on the saloon's deck top on the port side, swinging his legs.

John followed suit and sat down next to him. "Let's make a deal, Aris," he said in a soft voice, not girlish at all. "If you find experienced crew… *really* experienced… then I tell you what. Me and Uri will fly over and meet you in Europe."

Aris let his back rest on the deck, one hand behind his head. With his other he reached down to scratch his balls.

Laughing, John said, "Scratch your balls as much as you want. No one else is going to come with you. You'll have no choice but to take us."

"Hey, Captain Suicide," the older skipper shouted. "You should consider yourself lucky. At least you won't die alone!"

Aris lifted his middle finger in reply.

"Up yours too, buddy," the old man called. "Pride and pig-headedness never helped anyone."

Still reclining on the deck, Aris cast his eyes to the sky. "I'm told someone from Belize once made the crossing at this exact time of year… and that he's still alive."

The old man's face turned red. With knots in his voice, he said, "He may be alive on the outside, but he's dead where it counts. All his crew died on that cursed journey."

"Still, he is to be respected." Aris sat up. "He made the crossing and delivered the boat in one piece. He just had the wrong crew. I admire him."

The old captain turned away and hid inside his boat.

Aris angled his torso, staring at the smaller catamaran.

"Was it him?" Uri asked.

Aris nodded sadly. "Screw it all. You have a deal, John. If I don't find anyone experienced, the two of you can come… but you'll have to bear the responsibility for your own necks."

John and Uri exchanged a high-five as Kay approached.

Popping to his feet, Aris shouted, "Announce to the marina staff that you'll pay double the double wages for any experienced crew."

The smile disappeared from John's face. "Bastard!"

All he received in response was a one-finger salute from Aris.

Uri took the bait though. "Just let him try," he counselled John. "Meanwhile you and I can test out the Latin beauties, sunbathe and relax while Aris struggles to find a crew."

"Those girls weren't scared." John's frustration was palpable. "We aren't scared. We came on this trip for an adventure. We want to go, too."

"They're just spoiled rich girls," Uri countered. "They don't realise what's at stake."

Aris hesitantly looked from Uri to John. Then he turned to stare hard at Lilly and finally Kay. "You all want this so badly?"

All four answered with a solid, "Yes!"

Aris exhaled on a long sigh. "Listen. I never once gave up on a route. Only retreated temporarily in the Red Sea, and that was because I lost an engine."

"We won't give up either," Kay reassured.

With a soft, bitter smile, Aris paused. After several moments he pointed his finger at each of them in turn. "You all remember… you asked for this."

For a brief instant, all eyes settled on Aris.

"I don't care who your father or mother is." Aris placed his hands on Lilly's shoulders. "Your ass is mine."

"I like the sound of that!" Lilly wiggled her rear.

Aris turned away. "That means you do exactly as I say. There can be only one captain on this boat! No ifs, ands, or buts!"

"I wouldn't mind some butts." Uri elbowed John and snickered.

"You're the boss, skipper," Kay replied.

Aris made some notes on a piece of paper and passed it to her. "Tell your parents to wire the money to this account. All in advance. Bonus to be paid on delivery. No guarantees… only our best efforts."

"Wise move," the old pontoon skipper shouted. "Money for your soon-to-be widow."

The thought of Gina made Aris's stomach curdle.

61 THE DECISION

Kay placed the call. "Mother, Captain Aris insists on having the eighty thousand dollars in advance, only the bonus on delivery." She read the account number and made some other whispered comments before ending the connection. Turning to Aris, she shared, "Mother has agreed. The money will be in your account within twenty-four hours."

"Call her back," Aris said. "We need cash for supplies both here and in Europe. Ten thousand for here, plus another ten thousand to carry. Not everywhere takes credit cards."

Kay fixed her full attention on Aris, keeping the phone at her side.

Without losing time, he commanded, "Show me where you keep the spare parts for the engines, generators, tools, and repair kits."

Kay looked around, puzzled. "This is not for me to know."

Aris shook his head. "I see you're a daddy's girl. Take my advice and hop that flight overseas."

The girls looked on in silence while Aris continued. "Come on, guys. It's time to learn to be crew. Let's make an inventory of parts and tools, and where they're located."

Following Aris into the saloon, John asked, "Where should we start looking?"

"Pull the seat cushions, open the hatches, and take out everything under the settees. Separate the engine and generator parts from other tools and materials while I will check the batteries."

An hour later, Aris handed a three-page list to Kay. She flipped through it, somewhat mystified.

"Parts, filters, tools, plus food and drink," Aris answered her unspoken question. "You may add any other food or…" he paused before adding, "lady's hygiene supplies."

"But I don't know where to buy all these things," Kay complained.

"Use your brain, girl!" He pointed to the small catamaran. "I'm sure the old skipper will be happy to help you buy everything. Just offer him an incentive."

"What kind of incentive?" Lilly jumped in. "He's too old to…"

Aris snickered. "Don't be misled by the white beard. Old captains can still manage a woman well into their hundredth year."

Lilly's gaze travelled to the old man whose smile was wide, obviously having overheard their conversation.

"Really." She licked her lips. "I can handle that!"

The old skipper shook his head and tipped his cap to Aris. "You have the best crew, all right!"

Rubbing his thumb and pointer finger, Aris said, "Money, Kay. Money is a good incentive to start with. Offer five hundred for his time and expertise." Aris called over to the other boat, "Would that be sufficient, Captain?"

"Five hundred?" Lilly pouted. "For doing the shopping! What about my incentive?"

"Skippers aren't cheap, girl." Aris handed Kay a second list. "We need these engine and hydraulic oils, too. Exactly the ones stated here. The skipper will know where to find them."

Kay held both lists, scanning for something, anything that looked familiar. Reluctantly, she called out to the old skipper, "Captain, would you be able to help us with the shopping?"

With a cunning peek from one girl to the other, the old man asked, "What kind of payment?"

"Next time, keep your mouth shut, Lilly!" Kay scolded.

"It seems your mother can afford to keep her daughters pure," Aris joked. "Offer him a thousand for all the shopping."

Kay's jaw dropped, but to her credit, she didn't shirk the task. Turning to the old skipper, she declared, "No Lilly incentive. Just a thousand dollars to help us obtain what's on Captain Aris's lists."

Nodding, the old skipper said, "Sure, but if it takes more than two days, I want an extra three hundred. Each extra day."

A look of panic crossed Kay's face.

"No…" Aris coached her in a whisper. "That sly old sea dog will take a week to finish. Offer him two hundred as a bonus if he finishes within two days."

As promised, Kay was a quick study. She stiffened her back and shouted, "No! You'll dawdle over it for a month. But I'll pay you a bonus of two hundred if you're done day after tomorrow."

"And what about the little blonde's incentive?" the skipper questioned coyly.

"My sister is not a payment. She was just teasing."

Lilly punched Kay's shoulder. "I *am* curious to see if he can still do it. Maybe I could test him!"

"Shut it," Kay snarled.

Uri winked at John, as if to say, "Game on."

Aris interrupted his buddies' moment of appreciation. "Come on, boys. Let's check external hatches, ropes, sails, anchors, and nets." He stepped forward to the bow, opening the big hatches first. "And Kay, I want the marina electricians and engineers to do a health check on all batteries, cabling switches, and inverters. Once the new navigation electronics are fitted and installed, I reserve the right for final inspection and approval before we embark."

Kay had been nodding along, but at that last statement, she flinched. "Mother organised everything for tomorrow."

But Aris had already jumped from the boat, off on his way into town. Uri and John followed excitedly. "Aris, you're an amazing negotiator," John laughed in a girlish voice. "How did you do that? Even getting paid in advance?"

"Simple supply and demand," Aris replied. "No one else is crazy enough to take the job. If those girls were willing to pay double, they could afford more."

"Who has Jewish blood in him now?" Uri snorted. "Your parts and supplies list is exaggerated, too. It's only a two to three-week journey, but you're outfitting us for a trip around the world."

Aris grunted in disapproval. "Fool! There are no spare parts or stores in the middle of the ocean. One drop of oil, one nut, one fuse, can mean the difference between life and death."

Uri crossed his arms, apparently unconvinced.

"The lack of one can of hydraulic oil is what got me stuck with no rudder in the middle of the Indian Ocean. For want of a single two-cent car fuse, we lost an engine in the Red Sea... battling force-ten winds with gusts of eleven!"

"That's over a hundred kilometres an hour," John marvelled. "No one can sail in that!"

Aris smiled. "More like 120-140 kilometres. We were not sailing, we were motoring. Now do you see why we needed both engines? Last chance to change your mind, boys."

Uri uncrossed his arms, but then crossed them again. "You really are crazy, aren't you?"

"Crazy like a fox, maybe," Aris laughed. "But I negotiated us a hundred-thousand-dollar bounty... when we would have done it for free."

62 ONE LAST CALL

Sitting on the boat's port-side helm, Aris dialled the number by heart. He noticed the old skipper working in the next dock slip. Kay and Lilly busied themselves with the ropes, while Uri and John looked on admiringly.

When his call connected, Aris tuned everything else out and smiled. "I missed the sound of your voice, my son."

"Wh-what? Dad?" Gerry spluttered. "This is a great surprise! How are you doing? Where are you?"

Aris heard the sound of Gerry's office door closing and could picture the hustle and bustle he'd left far behind. He leaned back slightly and let the South American sun warm his face. "Sitting on a boat in Belize. Is Peter there, too?"

"No, he's out meeting with a customer. What kind of boat? Where are you sailing?"

Aris chuckled. Like him, both his boys loved nothing more than to be on the water. "It's a catamaran… similar to the one we used to have. I'm taking it to the Mediterranean on a delivery."

"Huh?" Gerry's voice rang with alarm. "Isn't this the wrong time to cross the Atlantic from there?"

The old skipper looked up at Aris and shook his head knowingly.

"Don't worry," Aris soothed. "I'll follow the winds, catch the Atlantic circle currents, heading north-northeast and climb until we're parallel to northern Europe. Then I'll turn south-southeast. It will give me good wind without having to confront the sea. It will take us a bit longer but will be safer." Gerry's breathing turned heavy enough to hear across the line, so Aris deflected. "How is everyone? The kids? Liza?"

"Not good. Mum is going crazy. She is threatening to commit suicide. She comes back home always drunk. She says she will commit suicide and leave a letter blaming you. You need to come back, Dad."

"Your mum has been threatening to commit suicide and blame me for years now."

"Dad, this is serious. You always said family above all!"

"And I did it. I sacrificed my pleasures for the family. Your mum has become the cancer in my life. You either cut the cancer or it will kill you."

"Think of Liza, Dad. She feels cornered. It's even started affecting her school performance."

"Move Liza. Take her to your house until I return."

Gerry raised his voice. "It's not the same, Dad. Liza needs you, not me!"

Aris could hear a second voice in the background, then Gerry announced, "Peter just arrived. I'm putting you on speaker."

"What's going on?" Aris heard his other son ask, followed by Gerry's voice coaching, "Dad's on the phone. Tell him to come home."

Peter sighed loudly. "Dad? Dad! You gotta come back. Even if you just take a break from your joy adventure for a week or two. The family is disintegrating."

Aris's heart practically melted at this revelation. But every time he thought of Gina, it quickened his resolve. "I told your brother to take Liza home with him. Your mum will never change."

"But she has changed, Dad," Peter volunteered. "She misses you. That's why she gets drunk all the time."

"You're still letting her manipulate you with her lies."

"No, Dad. She confided to me. She needs you back. She wants you—"

Gerry interrupted. "Dad, we can't control mum. We are only her sons. You are the father. It is a father's duty to hold the family together."

"I can't help you this time. I'm committed to sail away tomorrow across the Atlantic. The boat and crew are ready, and I already accepted the payment. I cannot abandon everyone."

Peter's voice rose so loud Aris had to hold the phone away from his ear. "Do you mean to tell me you can't abandon these strangers and their boat, but you can abandon your own family? What's become of you? What about all your sermons—family and love above all?"

"Obviously the element of love is missing, my sons. Your mum is just lying to manipulate you again. Not the first time."

"No, Dad," Peter insisted. "This time she's for real."

Gerry again chimed in. "You're both suicidal. You know it isn't safe to cross the Atlantic eastwards this time of the year."

"You're right, son, but…"

"But what, Dad? Do you have a knowledgeable crew? I mean… I know you know your stuff, but that's still a tough passage this time of year!"

"It does not scare me, Gerry."

"Well, it scares me that you are trying to kill yourself. This is madness."

Aris could hear a muffled exchange at the other end of the line, then Gerry continued, his voice racing. "Why don't I come help you? I can be there on the first flight out."

"No, Gerry," Aris warned. "This is not for you."

"Just wait. Delay your departure just a couple of days. We can talk on the boat."

"I'd love to have you onboard, son," Aris chuckled, "but you have a child of your own now to take care of. Besides, I have John and Uri plus two strong girls."

The line went silent. After a few seconds, Gerry whispered, "So you are having a good time then…"

That gave Aris a little laugh. "The girls are okay, son. It's their boat. They know what they're doing."

"Well… if you're sure you don't need help, but one day. Delay just one day. Let me come to see you, Dad…"

"Even if you come, you will not convince me to change my mind."

The old skipper now threw down his wrench, looked across at Aris and yelled, "Lying to your own son. You don't even have a first mate."

"Who's that?" Gerry asked. "And what does he mean?"

"It's just some frustrated old skipper moaning," Aris redirected skilfully. "Have to go, Gerry. Say hello to everyone. I'll catch up with you once I cross over the Med. Maybe you can join me there."

Aris disconnected before Gerry could ask any more questions that might make Aris doubt himself.

◆ ◇ ◆

Shocked, Gerry pushed a button to disconnect the call. "Dad's never hung up on me before. He really must be in trouble. I know it. I can feel it."

Peter sighed deeply. "Seems we're all in trouble."

◆ ◇ ◆

Aris's gaze fell to the old skipper. "We do have room for one more skipper," he called out. But the man just shook his head and started muttering something about "Crazy Americans."

Aris turned to observe the others who had gathered under the shade of the bimini silently overhearing his call.

Aris slid out of the helm and made his way over. "Let's get the boat ready, guys. We have an energetic ocean to cross."

Lilly was trying unsuccessfully to teach John to tie a bowline knot. Aris marvelled that with all John's mechanical know-how, the art of knot tying had escaped him. Or perhaps it was just the closeness of the curvy woman that had stymied his friend's dexterity.

Aris reached out and guided John's hands deftly through the manoeuvre.

"Where do we tie this other end of the rope?" John asked innocently.

Amused, Aris pointed down at John's trousers. "That, you tie on your penis."

Lilly giggled. "That would be a waste of a good dick!"

***

Aris observed closely as Kay welcomed a team of two onboard to begin installation of the new navigation electronics. "Raymarine," he praised, giving them a thumbs up.

Kay followed Aris wherever he turned, bumping into him and getting in the way in close quarters. "I'll call you if I need you," he said, pushing her away. "Besides, you should be shopping. There are medications on my list. You might have to find a doctor to get prescriptions for some of them."

"Your shopping list keeps expanding," Kay sighed.

Aris gave her a cheeky smile. "We do not set sail until you've gotten us every item on that list."

Kay let out a huff. "But you keep adding—"

Aris interrupted. "Remember! You will do exactly as I say or you can kiss your chance of surviving this ridiculous journey goodbye." With that, Aris jumped off the boat.

Lilly came up behind Kay. "Arrogant asshole."

Aris clearly heard her as he raised his middle finger and continued up the dock.

"That dickhead thinks we believe he's not interested in us. He'll see. We'll teach him some manners…" Lilly was fuming. "And I'll make him cry in bed."

A glimmer of a smile crossed Kay's lips. "They all think they're tough until the girl gets on top of them."

***

Later on, Aris returned but something caught his eye before he could board. He inspected the float of the boat from different angles.

He was still standing perplexed when the old skipper sidled up to him. "I was wondering whether you would spot it."

Aris nodded. "Looks like she drags a bit. We still have to fuel up and fill the water tanks. She'll drag even more."

"Not to mention filling your spare fuel tanks at the stern."

Changing the subject, Aris asked, "How is the shopping going?"

"Had to use all my contacts," the old man answered. "Some parts will be delivered this afternoon, but you'll have everything by tomorrow mid-day."

Summoning Kay, Aris told her, "Get two hundred kilos of small-sized lead, one kilo each."

"Clever move," the old man congratulated Aris. "Have you calculated how much weight it will take at the bows to lift the stern higher and reduce the drag?"

"No time for engineer's calculations," Aris replied. "Just a bit of balancing. Anyway, we're not in a race."

"You are a professional then?" the old skipper assessed.

"No. A pleasure skipper, but I used to own a similar sized cat."

"I don't understand you," the old man said as Kay walked away shaking her head. "You seem like a smart guy. So either you're really crazy, or you have a serious score to settle with yourself."

Aris smiled softly. "Or maybe both."

⸻ ◆ ⸻

Varo watched with binoculars through the car's tinted windows. "So many people frantically working on the boat?"

"Necessary," Victor advised. "Electricians, engineers, and specialists… installing our tracking devices."

Satisfied, Varo lowered the binoculars. "Call that woman detective and Kay and have them meet us here. Don't risk showing your face."

Within the hour, the two women climbed into Varo's car.

Organising the documents on her lap, Varo handed a series of folders over to Kay. "Here is all the boat paperwork, including your power of attorney documentation." She

376

motioned to Victor who pulled an envelope from his jacket pocket. "And here is the balance of the cash, as requested."

Kay frowned. "This skipper is a dictator. I sure hope he's as good as you think he is. That older captain said it's suicidal to cross the Atlantic now. Are you sure we should go?" She paused before adding, "Mother?"

Victor calmly assured, "All skippers are like that. We know Aris is good—that's why we are giving him this job…" Victor's eyes drifted up to meet Varo's. "Despite the outrageous cost."

"But… the other captain is experienced, and he doesn't agree at all," Kay repeated.

The lady detective spoke for the first time. "That old captain is just jealous because we didn't offer him the job. He's good, but too old."

Kay remained unconvinced. "Captain Aris keeps warning us, too. He says Lilly and I should fly over to meet them."

The lady detective shrugged dismissively.

Varo looked to Victor for an opinion.

He also shrugged. "I'm not an expert, but if this Captain Aris is willing to take the job, it must mean it's okay. Or more likely, he's just being dramatic in order to drive up his wages. Remember, he did negotiate double of the double fees."

Kay visibly relaxed. "That he did. A good negotiating tactic, putting the fear into us."

⌑

Back at the boat, a thin-built man with a bloated stomach climbed aboard. He told Lilly, "My name is Fisher. I'm the electronics engineer. I need to inspect all your electricals and generators."

Lilly stared, repulsed by his physique. "Go ahead," she motioned.

First he climbed into the left engine room and positioned two small square devices, one on the engine itself, and another on the generator. Taking readings on his machine, when the light turned green, he nodded in satisfaction and moved to the starboard engine hatch. He repeated the steps on that side of the boat, then passed through the saloon and made his way to the port side hull passage.

Opening two small doors covered in mesh revealed the main electronics system—two inverters, chargers, and all the main switches. Fisher placed one small device on the master inverter charger, then fiddled again with his meter. Smiling, he made his way to the anchor hatch under the mast, where he positioned yet another device, this one twice as large as the others.

Back inside the saloon, Fisher located an electrical outlet and followed a line straight up the wall to the ceiling panel above. Removing this panel, he sorted among the various cables and attached a small circular plate to the one feeding electricity to the plug. He replicated these steps on the other side of the saloon, then carefully replaced both ceiling panels.

Lilly was still parked at the table under the bimini when he returned to the vessel's deck and again consulted his device to see many green lights blazing. "All done. Looks good," Fisher told Lilly and stepped off the boat.

◆ ◇ ◆

From his car, Fisher dialled a number.

"Yes?" Victor's voice answered.

"All done. Two tracking devices fitted on the power cables, activated and ready."

"And what about…" Victor began, "your *other* task?"

"Five units fitted and ready for your orders, sir."

63 Character Growth?

Gina busied herself preparing a meal. Why had Aris reached out to Gerry but not to her?

At that very moment Gina's cell phone rang and she almost decided to ignore it out of spite, but after four rings she pushed the speaker button. "Hello."

A woman's voice came across the line. "Hi, gorgeous. It's half-price party-fever night. What time should we pick you up?"

Gina's voice remained low. "I'm going to fever it at home alone."

"Don't be dull," the other woman replied. "Remember your slogan? Life is for living!"

Gina pushed her knife through the last of the onions and dumped them in the skillet with some garlic. "I don't feel like it tonight. Maybe later. You go have fun."

Shaking her head, she poured olive oil into the pan and turned up the heat before disconnecting the call without even saying goodbye.

◆

That evening, Lilly and Kay welcomed Uri and John and Aris back onboard as the men loaded their personal belongings into the cabins below deck. A bottle of champagne was chilling under the bimini as Aris busied himself at the navigation centre, charting the passage route.

Like a dog trailing its master, John stood behind Aris's shoulder observing. "How do you know what angle to cross the ocean?"

Aris didn't look up from his work. "There are no simple answers in navigation. Everything depends on the prevailing winds and the currents."

Uri popped his head around Aris's other shoulder, then pulled away. "Too sophisticated for me. I'm going to stay focused on my strengths." He turned to gaze at Lilly and Kay in their bikini tops and shorts.

Without losing sight of his work, Aris called to Uri, "The flight option is still available."

When he'd completed the task to his satisfaction, Aris joined everyone under the bimini. "Girls, breakfast at 05.00 exactly. I will take you through safety and emergency procedures, rope and sail handling, and mast climbing. We sail at 07.00."

A look of shock registered on John's face. "We're departing already?" His voice was an octave higher than normal.

"No," Aris soothed. "Tomorrow we go out to shake the boat, for a test, to make sure everything is operating correctly. Then we'll top off the diesel and water tanks. If all is good, we set sail the next morning."

Lilly's eyes were practically bulging out. "No way am I climbing the mast. I'm afraid of heights!"

"Everyone must climb the mast. Even if I have to pull you up with the winch! Meanwhile, practise donning your life jackets and using your harnesses."

"But what about the weather?" Uri asked. "Are these next few weeks good for sailing?"

Aris considered Uri for a moment. "The weather will hold for at least four or five days."

Regaining his composure, John popped the cork on the champagne and began pouring into plastic cups.

"I run a dry boat," Aris reminded everyone. "That means no alcohol and no smoking. So get your pre-sailing drinks done tonight. I'll join you later for a bite to eat."

With that, Aris made his way back to the navigation area. Kay followed and sat beside him. "I'll keep you company. I don't drink anyway."

Aris stared hard at the electronic screen. "Afraid I won't be much company. I need to concentrate on the route planning."

Kay seemed content to just watch. "Don't worry. I won't disturb you. Just here in case you need… something."

Without shifting his sight, Aris gave a nod. He thought about the journey he'd first embarked upon—escape from a home devoid of erotic love, but brightened by the success of his children, even his granddaughter who was probably taking the world by storm in his absence.

He thought of the trials and near-death experiences they'd suffered along the way. John had proved a faithful companion, and even useful at the General's camp. Uri was still a playboy at heart, unworthy of his sweet bride's love and devotion. But just perhaps Uri had been right along. Aris reflected on his series of debacles, falling in and out of love in Mexico and Guatemala. Even now he tried to ignore the heat emanating from Kay's gorgeous body seated beside him.

Finally, he came back to the words she'd just spoken. *"I won't disturb you. Just here in case you need… something."*

Unfortunately, what the five of them needed most was something no love secret could provide.

His stare fixed on Kay, his mind travelled to the Red Sea. The boat he pictured was battered, with its strong stainless pipes bent like candlesticks, the experienced skipper accompanying him and crying out in panic. His younger son Gerry would have grown fearful, his wife Gina with the colour from her face draining to yellow. Yet Aris would not turn back until he heard Gerry's warning, *"Dad, we will not have enough fuel to make it to the Suez."*

Kay's face morphed as Aris silently pondered.

He nodded to himself and whispered his reply to Gerry. "We are turning back."

"Turning back where?" Kay asked. "We haven't left yet."

Aris sighed. "I was wrong. We should not be departing. I will be risking your lives."

"So the old skipper was right!" Kay gasped.

With his lips squeezed tight, Aris nodded his agreement.

Kay looked away but Aris could see her jaw grinding. After a few silent moments she turned her gaze back on Aris. "And what about your quest for that mythical love secret John told us about? You risked your life for that! Will you give up?"

Aris's prevailing silence probed Kay to add, "We all take risks, Aris. It's time for you to decide."

His gaze fixed on Kay, Aris rose to his feet, stern determination in his gestures. "Fuck the love secret. Probably never existed." Then regretful, Aris's tone softened. "Love is a puzzle no one will ever solve. Our ancestors were absolutely right. Love is a lottery!"

Kay took a step closer. "Love is an illusion they poison our minds with."

Aris's jaw ground painfully. "There is only family."

Kay stared as Aris's nostrils bloated, shocked by the sudden wildness of his face.

Reading her surprise, Aris said, "Family is real; family is tangible. Family is not an illusion. Family above all, Kay."

"But you received your full payment. We had an agreement."

"I will refund the money. Just do me a favour. Don't tell John and Uri until tomorrow."

"You are abandoning your friends?"

Two steps away, Aris turned back to see Kay's face slack with shock.

"They are not my friends. Friends are dead weights. Family is more important. Remember, Kay... family above all."

64 Homeward Bound

At the airport, Aris was picked up by his sons, Peter and Gerry. Peter deftly navigated multi-lane traffic with Aris in the passenger seat while Gerry leaned over the centre console from his position in the back, peppering him with questions like when the boys were in grade school "Dad, how was your trip? Was it adventurous? Was it fun? Did you make any friends?"

Aris chuckled and relaxed into the seat, glad for once to not be in charge. "Adventurous would be one way to describe it." He felt his eyelids begin to droop. After so many months of constant adrenaline, Aris could feel the fatigue in his bones. "Nearly got shot."

"Wh-what?" spluttered Peter. "Shot?"

"Twice," Aris confirmed.

Gerry's jaw hung open. Aris heard him gulp for air, then sigh as if he'd had some sort of revelation. "Well, I know you're not a thief… so I'm guessing you must've been having fun with someone else's woman."

"Fun?" Aris laughed. "Yes, I suppose so. But it was more like these women were messing with me. Different cultures have different ways, but then it's hard to understand any women. Men, too, for that matter. Everyone has their own agenda."

Peter signalled a lane change and checked the mirrors before moving to the exit ramp. "Then what happened? Couldn't take your own advice? You always taught us to avoid fights—even if it feels embarrassing."

Pride swelled in Aris's chest. He'd certainly done something right with his sons. "Right off the bat Jim picked a fight with a wrestler… then some Mexican bullied John. There are idiots in every country. But I think the trip really did John some good. He's actually beginning to build up his self-confidence."

"Wow, that's high praise coming from you!" Gerry marvelled. "It sounds like maybe you did make some friends… even though you've always claimed they were nothing but dead weight."

"Hmph," Aris grunted. "They were an absolute pain in my balls, but John is loyal. I'll give him that. Uri is just lucky I didn't string him up by his toenails. He's a spoiled mule, and a philandering chauvinist. His beautiful wife Epi deserves better."

Gerry tapped Peter on the shoulder and made some hand gesture like the two of them had placed a bet, with Gerry coming out victorious.

Aris laughed to himself. "It's like you said many times, Gerry. You don't have to be a perfect match with someone just to socialise. John and Uri were good company. Better than being alone all the time." Not that Aris spent many lonely nights, he mused. "It's business partners who are dead weight," he added with finality.

"And did you discover the love secret?" Peter asked sarcastically.

With a deep sigh, Aris confessed, "I'm not sure about that anymore."

This time it was Peter's turn to gesture to his brother. Apparently, the winning bet had reversed this time.

Gerry lightly slapped Aris on the shoulder. "It's not like you to give up, Dad. What happened?"

Where to begin? Aris closed his eyes and pictured Cali's house in Tampa. "I did discover some clues, and made strong connections." His mind jumped ahead to Drosita's. "Even met an old lady… over a hundred years old… who entrusted me with all that she knew."

Aris found himself daydreaming of the catamaran trip east to Europe that he'd bailed out on, and the quest onward to the Mediterranean in search of the village and the final clues. Was he sure that abandoning John and Uri to their fate wasn't leaving them with a death sentence? A third time? And where would they find another captain?

When Gerry tapped him on the shoulder, Aris sighed and continued. "I hit a dead end in Latin America. The next clue is in Sardinia, in Italy, and I don't even know if the lady is still alive. If I get lucky there, then I still have to find that unnamed village in Greece. I mean, how do you find a village without a name?"

Peter smacked the wheel, then signalled and pulled off into the first parking lot. Dropping the gear shift into park, he turned and faced Aris. "That's why you were ready to embark on a suicidal voyage across the Atlantic?"

Aris gave a sad smile. "Odysseus took the same journey thousands of years before Columbus, in a smaller boat without sophisticated electronic navigation systems. All it requires is a bit of improvisation and guts."

"Uh-huh," Peter nodded. "I can hear it in your voice, Dad. You still have it in mind to go back then. Even if it kills you."

"That's for another time," Aris tried to sound consoling. "I'm back now. Maybe the love secret is a myth anyway." He waved a relaxed hand at his son in the driver's seat, hoping to coax Peter back on the road.

But Gerry wasn't going to let go either. "You're covering up for something. What were these clues you discovered?"

"It's not for your ears, my sons," Aris replied smoothly. "Even these small clues nearly got me and my friends killed."

"That's it then. You found nothing," Peter chuckled. "Still a dreamer!"

"That's exactly how my grandfather described me." Aris found himself smiling at the memory. "You're both probably right. But dreaming doesn't cost a thing!"

From the corner of his vision, Aris could see Gerry waving his point finger. "You don't fool me, Dad. You did find something serious. That's why you haven't given up."

Aris shifted in his seat so he could make eye contact with each of his sons in turn. "For now, boys, I'm back here with you. You and my grandchildren are my focus. Family is more important to me than any love secret. Maybe later, though, if I get the time. Maybe…" His voice trailed off.

Gerry still wouldn't let it rest. "Okay, but you never said who was trying to kill you. Or why."

Aris laughed out loud. "You'd never believe me. Four Mexican brothers—cartel drug traffickers—actually wanted to kill me because I refused to sleep with their sister!"

Peter made a sound like he was choking, but Gerry only laughed. "You're kidding, right? Was the woman that ugly?"

Once more Aris had a vivid memory flash to mind, this time of Katerina in all her voluptuous curves. "No, she was gorgeous… and damn sex hungry. Wouldn't give me even an hour to sleep. But in the end, she just wanted me for the love secret. Otherwise, they would have killed us from day one!"

Gerry was clearly amused. He thumped and jiggled on his seat like a child. "And…? What about the second time you were almost shot?"

Aris fought down the crystal clear image of Celia clad in skin tight leather, holding a riding crop. His pulse hammered, but he kept his words measured. "That girl…" How could he explain to his sons that the wife, correction… *sister-bride*… of the Guatemalan President General had only been hunting for a sperm donor? "She was a sociopathic liar. But deep inside? I think maybe she was just another poor heart longing for true love, and a bit of human touch."

Peter wasn't buying it. "Sounds like you really like her. I suppose you were okay with cheating on Mum?"

Gerry punched his brother on the arm. "It's not like Mum hasn't—"

But Peter punched back.

It seemed to Aris that maybe, despite his best efforts to keep Gina's affairs secret from them, the boys had learned of their mother's tawdry *flirtations*.

Gerry easily dodged the jab. "There's nothing wrong with you enjoying a woman's touch, Dad. It's not like Mum hasn't been depriving you for years."

Peter turned a painful crimson.

Hoping to shield Peter from more embarrassment, Aris decided to shift the subject. Turning to face Gerry he said, "You sound just like Uri, convinced that sex outside of love is man's birthright."

Gerry clapped his hands together like a coach circling up the team. "Man, what an adventure! I wish I'd been there."

Peter coughed to clear his throat. "We've uh, gotten a number of calls from a Miss Chase and her team, asking after your whereabouts and return date. I hate to dig, Pops, but is there something more to this than just a client wanting personalized attention from the CEO?"

An involuntary shudder went through Aris. "Be careful of that woman," he cautioned. "Whoever Varo Chase really is, she has deep connections and dark intentions." He thought back to the chambermaid Rita's words about a remark she overhead the President General make. Had Varo truly engaged the U.S. President and Vice President in an effort to ensure Aris's assassination at the hands of a foreign leader?

Peter's brows furrowed. "I don't understand, Dad. It seemed more like she… well… like she had the hots for you or something."

Aris couldn't help but smile at how uncomfortable this seemed to be for Peter. "Boys, maybe I have some sort of magnet for psychotic women. Can't seem to attract anything else."

Peter's voice rose above Gerry's laughter. "Well, you might be on a quest for a love secret that doesn't even exist, Dad, but I know deep down what you really need is a woman's love. Romantic love. *True love.*"

Aris shook his head. "It's too late for me to find a woman's love, Peter."

"What *did* you find then?" Gerry asked.

Aris gave the question a full moment's thought before answering. "To be honest, I learned a lot about friendship. All my life, I've pushed it away, preferring to be a lone wolf rather than risk being disappointed."

This seemed to satisfy Peter, but it wasn't the full truth.

"I also learned to enjoy a woman's company without falling in love with her," Aris added, then in a softer tone, "and without being married. Uri was a good teacher on that matter, the bastard."

Gerry smiled and practically jumped over the seat to hug him. "I love it! That's a real achievement for a so-called one-woman man. How do you feel about it now?"

Tired. That was the only truthful response, but he'd missed this connection with his sons, with his true family, and could tell they had missed him, too. Now it was his turn. "Enough interrogation about me, guys," Aris said. "Tell me about you and the kids… and Liza. And the team at the office. All the good news first!"

Aris was home. At least for the moment. Family was what truly mattered. As Gerry launched animatedly into the update on every detail of the past several months, Aris remembered his father's grip on his shoulder, and the words that were most resonant in his heart that day. And always.

Family above all else.

BONUS!

As a special gift for you,
download your FREE copy of the novella
Assassin's Love.

Two never-fail assassins! Target and client in the same couple. The devil has drawn his double knives. There will be death! But there will also be love. Who can survive when Eros has drawn his bow and pointed his love arrows?

Claim your free copy at this website:
http://bookhip.com/GZKHQLJ

Enjoyed this novel?

Please consider placing a review!
This will help other readers find great books.

ABOUT THE AUTHOR

CHRIS NEO was born in Cyprus, migrated, and has practised in world-renowned clinics as a hypno-psychoanalyst. His experience in clinical love ailments gives him unique insight into the mysteries of the human heart, soul, and mind. Contrary to popular Freudian doctrine that most if not all psychological ailments derive from sex, his clinical conclusion is that most human psychological ailments derive from love, its lack, or its misconceptions.

A multi-talented individual, Neo has excelled in multiple industries, including tough business environments where competitors went out of business. He recently sold two of his companies and writes for pleasure, drawing inspiration from ancient storytellers like Aristotle to more current masters like Joseph Campbell, Vogler, McKena, McKee, and others.